Father's Secret

By Peter George Markwith

Literary Manager, Janice M. Pieroni – Story Arts Management

Edited by Faviana Olivier and B.J. Elliott

AMAZON.COM

ISBN 978-1520609065

Unified Business Technologies
PRESS

www.UnifiedBizTech.com

Dedicated to the life and memory of

Betty Jean Mawer

July 21, 1932 – October 10, 1988

DISCLAIMER

This is a work of fiction. Every character is fictitious, except movie stars and the following individuals:

- Jacqueline Kennedy Onassis

- John F. Kennedy

- Janet Auchincloss

- Hugh Auchincloss

- Doris Duke

- Lyndon B. Johnson

Every event without exception is fictitious. No resemblance to real persons is intended or should be inferred. When any movie star or the preceding individuals are mentioned, it is not the author's intention to depict their actual characters or lives, and all incidents in the novel, including those concerning such actual persons, business establishments, and locales are imaginary. Any resemblance to any other actual persons, living or dead, business establishments, events, or locales is entirely coincidental.

TABLE OF CONTENTS

PROLOGUE

There's a greenhouse behind the austere looking manor overlooking the rocks of Narragansett Bay. Beneath the leaded glass windowpanes that sparkle in the late autumn sun, George FitzHugh, the mansion's caretaker, flees for his life. It's November 22, 1963. Behind him, a warm but eerie glow—like a thousand swarming fireflies—flickers silently against the ruddy brick foundation of the inner greenhouse wall before receding from view. The torch-like presence, masked by the light of day, disappears as quickly as it came.

Meanwhile, in Dallas, the president and first lady take their fateful ride past the *Texas School Book Depository*. Dressed in that never-to-be-forgotten pink suit, Jackie Kennedy sits next to her husband in the rear of the open-topped limousine. From beneath the pillbox hat that became her fashion trademark, the first lady's face radiates warmth. A wave of her graceful hand and the flash of that forever-famous smile captivates onlookers in an instant—an instant marred with the sound of one bullet then another ripping through the November Texas air...into her husband's throat and skull. Glinting under the lone-star sun, a gun barrel recedes from view into the window of the depository.

At that very moment, George FitzHugh is seized with excruciating chest-pain. His knees buckle, midstride, and the burning in his chest intensifies. But the pain lasts only a moment—as long as it takes for the caretaker's head to meet the unforgiving greenhouse floor.

CHAPTER ONE

Father said he purchased the property in 1964 for "investment purposes." The Newport, Rhode Island papers also reported it as such. But, then again, the papers couldn't report the real story behind Annandale Farm. Nobody could. Now, nearly four decades later, only a few people remain who remember what actually happened at Narragansett Bay that summer of '64. Livingston, our family's then-devoted butler, chauffeur, and cook, is one of them. So is my stepmother, Elly. Only they and a couple of others close to me know the real reason why the forty-room mansion was razed back in 1969.

At times, I have to make a conscious effort to tell myself that it wasn't just part of my childhood imagination. Having passed the mid-point of my own life, it's time for me to tell the story. The only thing that keeps me from completely dismissing that summer as fantasy is the fact that Livingston, my sister Franny, and a few others experienced the mystery with me. My father and my stepmother Elly avoid discussing it to this day. I'm sure they, like others haunted by Annandale Farm, feel certain nobody would believe the truth about the house.

But I need to share the tale because Annandale Farm played such a bizarre role in world history. No more than a handful of folks understand the part the house played in the 1963 assassination...and the supernatural mystery associated with that Newport villa. To this day, the breathtaking prominence on which the mansion once stood remains devoid of construction—a sober and barren reminder as to why no one has ever rebuilt there.

There was something almost magical about passing through the entrance on Ridge Road that marked the beginning of the long, winding drive leading up to the house. I'll never forget the first time I traversed those gates and caught the breathtaking view of Narragansett Bay from across Annandale Farm's broad, manicured lawn. Livingston had driven the family the dusty distance from New

York City to Newport in Father's new Bentley convertible...that is, aside from the brief time we spent making the crossing on the ferry from Jamestown. The Newport Bridge hadn't yet been built, and everyone driving up from New York had to cross by ferry. I can still smell the salt air when I think about that day. I need only close my eyes to see the flotilla of sailboats and yachts cutting across the wake of the ferry as we plowed through the sparkling water towards the docks.

Once Livingston drove the car off the ferry, we all climbed in for the final ride to the house. We sat silently taking in seaport sights as Livingston artfully wove the car through the crowd, making his way towards Thames Street. Riding in our open-topped classic within spitting distance of longshoremen and fishermen made my stepmother, Elly, a bit nervous. I saw her ease up and breathe a sigh of relief once we cleared the docks and picked up speed. It took only a few minutes for us to reach Wellington Avenue and glide past the harbor on our way towards Ocean Drive. Before I knew it, a street sign with the name *Ridge Road* appeared in front of the car. Then, with barely enough time to notice the ivy-covered walls whizzing past the Bentley, Livingston nosed the black convertible through the brick and wrought iron-arched gates and we were there. The gravel crackled loudly under the tires as we drove up the long, graceful drive.

Mr. FitzHugh was there to meet us on that brilliant summer afternoon in June of 1964. He looked a bit of a fright when we first laid eyes on him, waving politely from the front verandah. Had I known then what I know now about Annandale Farm I'd have understood why.

Traditionally, we spent the majority of the year living in our New York City duplex facing Central Park West. Every summer, even for several years after my mother died, Father rented a rambling house on Sea View Avenue in the Wianno section of Cape Cod...that is, until my new stepmother, Eleanor, came into our lives. Although Elly's roots were in Brooklyn, she was a Newport wannabe—a summer social climber aspiring to the glamour and sophistication of the upper-crust scene.

That was the end of quiet coastal summers spent lounging on the sand of quaint and casual Cape Cod. When my eccentric Aunt Julia—Father's sister—caught wind of the fact that Annandale Farm would be going up for sale, she immediately contacted him and my stepmother, Elly. Within hours, the two women conspired against Father and managed to goad him into making an offer on the property. Of course, Father, wanting to make his new bride happy...and unwilling to incur the wrath of my unconventional Aunt Julia, complied. Not one to revel in the trappings of high society, however, Father concocted a plan that involved making a carefully calculated offer on the prestigious waterfront estate. He felt certain his offer would be low enough to neutralize any chances of actually getting the property, yet he felt equally confident it would be sufficient enough to realistically ingratiate himself with Elly and Aunt Julia for having tried.

Despite his carefully masterminded scheme, Father quickly found himself the dumbstruck new owner of a forty-room, pillared mansion on 15 acres of prime real estate overlooking Narragansett Bay.

By appearance, Annandale Farm was a glittering jewel in Newport's crown of stately residences. Completed in 1901 for one General Francis Vinton Greene, the property loomed grand to the yachtsmen and sailors who frequented the sophisticated waters of the bay. The stately house, with its imposing architecture and pillared façade, faced the water from a manicured plateau of lawn. Designed for General Greene by architect and relative, Col. Francis Hoppin, the house commanded a spectacular Northeast view of the bay on property that once comprised part of the vast real estate holdings of colonial land baron, Jahleel Brenton.

The formal flowerbeds and manicured topiary surrounding the mansion amplified its grandeur, while a high stone wall blocking the view of the house and grounds from Ridge Road provided sufficient privacy. With all its overwhelming beauty, even the most discerning eye could never detect the chilling secrets that caused it to change hands so frequently.

Not too long after General Greene took up occupancy, Annandale Farm was traded to Charles Frederick Hoffman in exchange for Mr. Hoffman's property on Newport's less fashionable Yznaga Avenue. The house turned over, time and again, as one society owner after another moved in...then out...promptly putting the property on the market in the process. Had Father and Elly done their homework, I'm convinced they never would have bought the house.

The week we moved in, the *Providence Journal* ran a one-column article with a picture of the estate announcing Father's purchase:

ANNANDALE FARM SOLD; DEED FILED HERE

A. R. Suttons of New York, New Owners, Make No Decision Yet on Use of Property.

That was the headline in 1964. They mentioned Father, Arthur Ridgeway Sutton III; my stepmother, Elly (the former Eleanor Adelaide Hodgewell of Brooklyn, New York); my sister, Frances Millicent Sutton (age 12)...and me—Edward Ridgeway Sutton (age 14).

Funny how sophisticated and proper we all sounded in print. In reality, Father never did completely embrace the life of high society to which he was born...or the stodgy formality suggested by his inherited name. He was the third in our family's line of Arthur Ridgeway Suttons. I always believed he wanted to spare me the empty dullness he experienced as a young boy growing up among society sycophants with their snooty, longwinded names. Anyway, that's the explanation he and Mother always gave me for breaking the chain of family lineage and choosing the name *Edward* for me instead of Arthur Ridgeway Sutton IV. As far as I was concerned, the name *Eddie* suited me just fine.

The article went into some detail about the mansion's architectural characteristics then quickly digressed into a long and boring list of distinguished owners and renowned occupants who had graced its hallowed halls at some point along the way. There was Mrs. Amar Johnson, Annandale's third owner; The Marquis and Marquise de Cuevas—she being the granddaughter of John D. Rockefeller. There were the C.D. Mawers of New York (importers of Spanish olives); the Harold W. Farquars of Pittsburgh (steel); the J.W. Spencers of Providence (shoes); the Norman C. Burkes of Boston (retail); Mr. and Mrs. Milton Pierce…etc. and so forth. Nowhere, however, was there a mention of the reason why the house had changed hands so many times.

Franny felt it, though. I could tell on that very first day. There's something about "special" children that most people don't realize…and Franny *was* special. I never knew about Franny's gift until we moved into Annandale Farm. If it weren't for the fact that I experienced the strange happenings myself, I'd probably have dismissed her peculiar behavior that first day. Children with Down syndrome can become emotionally agitated for no apparent reason. Franny's feelings could run the gamut from loving, unbridled affection to temperamental obstinacy…and anger—all within the same hour. I had thought little of it at first when Franny started crying uncontrollably in the back seat. It began right after we passed through the gates marking the entrance to the property.

"Franny! Franny! Stop that ridiculous crying, will you *please*?" Elly scolded. She reached forward from the back seat and poked Father on the shoulder. "Arthur, can't you do something to make her stop?"

As Elly stared at the back of Father's head imploringly, I studied her. She looked quite striking in her brightly colored, floral silk dress contrasted against the backdrop of the Bentley's red leather upholstery. Her auburn hair shone lustrously in the summer sunlight and fluttered in the flow of air circulated by the open convertible. She had dark green eyes that radiated an alluring dignity. Whenever she smiled, which wasn't often enough, her face lit up the room. In that brief moment, it suddenly struck me why Father had been so attracted to her. He gradually turned his head and spoke softly over his shoulder to me.

"Eddie, son, do me a favor please and give Franny a *Chiclet*, will you?"

"Hmm? Oh...yes, sir." His request caught me off guard. I reached into the pocket of my jacket and pulled out a thin, yellow rectangular cardboard box. It felt light in my hand. Looking through its little cellophane window, I thought the box was empty. I shook it gently then watched one last, bite-sized square of the white, sugar-enameled chewing gum slide into view. Thank GOD, I thought, relieved. To Franny, *Chiclets* chewing gum acted as a universal antidote to just about any problem.

Elly, wincing under the squeal of Franny's wailing, eyed my progress impatiently. No sooner had I worked the lone piece of chewing gum out of the yellow box then she grabbed it from my fingers and pushed it into Franny's mouth. To my astonishment as well as everyone else's, Franny spit the gum out of the open car. She hollered all the more uncontrollably and continued even after Livingston brought the Bentley to a stop in front of the house.

"Really, Arthur, there must be something you can do to stop her," Elly moaned as Franny kicked and screamed more furiously than ever. Father and Elly climbed out of the car along with Livingston. While he made his way back to the trunk, Father and Elly struggled to introduce themselves to Mr. FitzHugh over Franny's din.

"Eddie, why don't you take Franny across the lawn to look at the water," Father suggested to me in quiet desperation. "You can let her run around for a bit and burn off some of that negative energy. There's a good fellow. Elly and I need to talk with Mr. FitzHugh."

I nodded my head in silent acknowledgement, resenting the fact that I was the one who usually got stuck dealing with Franny's outbursts. I paused for a moment to take a closer look at Mr. FitzHugh. He was portly with a rosy complexion and blue eyes—their color amplified by a head of thick white hair. I watched his carelessly knotted, red necktie blow about in the breeze. Looking around nervously, he was unable to mask the discomfort he felt from Franny's tantrum.

With Livingston's help, I managed to pull Franny out of the convertible and plant her feet on the white gravel drive. She purposely let the deadweight of her body strain our grip as she collapsed, melodramatically, on the ground. The stones in the driveway left dirt marks on her bare legs, while her red cotton dress offered little protection from the sharp gravel. Black patent-leather shoes—only moments before smooth and shiny—grew scuffed and dull as she kicked her feet fretfully against the sharp stones.

"You'd best leave her be for the time being, Eddie," Livingston proposed. "I dare say Franny will come out of it in a moment or two."

Feeling annoyed with Franny's behavior, I watched Livingston return to the rear of the car and remove the bags from the trunk. The charcoal-gray blazer he wore coordinated nicely with his pressed pinstriped trousers and chauffeur's cap. Beads of perspiration had formed on his forehead under the cap's visor as he battled with the battery of bags Elly had brought with her.

Although he had recently celebrated his 50th birthday, Livingston lifted the luggage with the strength of someone half his age. I could see his broad shoulders and powerful arms outlined under the tailored fit of his jacket. The wire-framed eyeglasses he wore on the bridge of his nose added an intellectual appearance to his squarely handsome face and athletic build. I hoped I would look half as good when I outgrew my own self-conscious adolescence.

At 14, I stood tall and lanky with long arms and legs accentuated by knobby knees and bony ankles that made me look like I was part giraffe. My saving grace lay in the dark hair and angular good looks my mother said I inherited from her side of the family. Thus, throughout what seemed to me a rather lengthy puberty—aside from the usual teenage bouts with acne and an occasional cold-sore—I managed to maintain a reasonable level of comfort with my overall physical appearance.

"Eddie! Eddie! Come here and look at the lions!" Franny's

voice squealed across the lawn from her point of newly found interest. Only then did I realize that in the brief moments I'd been watching Livingston, that Franny's tantrum had ended. I felt relieved.

A pair of immense, sculpted lions was the focus of Franny's attention. The stone cats were placed prominently at the end of a wide brick walkway that began at the steps of Annandale's pillared verandah and ended at the crest of the grassy plateau where the house stood. A lion crouched on either side of the broad brick walk. They looked like sentinels posted between the house and the wide expanse of lawn that dropped gracefully to the rocky coast of Narragansett Bay.

"Eddie, they're so big and scary looking," Franny said in the nasal, staccato-like voice that typically blurred the enunciation of her words and made communication between those unaccustomed to her peculiar speech difficult. A crop of wind-blown black hair provided contrast to the lily-white flesh-tones of her otherwise lovable face.

"Hey, you're right, Franny." I seized her moment of fascination with the lions to keep her occupied; besides...my own boyish curiosity was starting to kick in.

"Cripes, I've never seen a pair of more awesome looking cats in my entire life!" I marveled. "Hey, howz-about I give you a boost up here and you can climb on this one's back?"

"Ok, Eddie, but make sure you hold onto me. I don't want to fall."

I cupped my hands under Franny's left foot and gave her a leg-up onto one of the great cat's backs. Once safely seated, I held both hands around her waist and then to her surprise released them a few seconds later. She sat proudly still once she discovered her position held secure. I was relieved to see her enjoying herself.

"Hey, Franny, I knew you could do it. Hang on and don't let that big cat run off with you." I remember smiling, hoping to instill some self-confidence in her. She giggled a Franny giggle then quickly became lost in riding her big cat. That was the very moment I first sensed movement on the third floor.

It came from one of the large porthole-like windows flanking either side of the four-columned portico—a grand array of pillars that rose to support the rooftop-level pediment over the front entryway. I noticed that one of the towering columns had a slight list to it, for some less than apparent reason. The flanking porthole windows had a diameter of about five feet and provided architectural symmetry to the mansion's façade. They were trimmed with elaborate rococo molding that contrasted with the otherwise rather austere stucco of the exterior walls.

The motion lasted only a split-second. It appeared as if somebody tilted the glass at just the right angle to catch the sun and send it glinting my way...then moved it back. Franny felt it. I say she felt it because she didn't see it like I did. She was too busy riding her lion. However, the instant the sun flickered off that window, Franny resumed the frantic kicking and screaming that she'd abandoned only minutes before. Luckily, I stood close enough to catch her when she toppled from the back of her beast. Clasping my arms tightly around her waist, I strained to see what...or who might have caused the activity on the third floor. Nothing! A few seconds later, Franny's crying stopped again. I thought of telling Father and Livingston about what I'd seen, but decided there had been enough commotion around our initial arrival already. Besides, I'd been chastised by Elly more than once for having an overactive imagination...and didn't want to suffer the consequences of an embarrassing accusation.

"Eddie! Franny! Come inside and take a look at our new seashore home," Elly shouted as she waved at us from the open front door to the house. A cool summer breeze off the ocean mingled with the scent of summer flowers and floated across the front lawn. I inhaled its fragrance and watched the wind blow the folds of Elly's silk dress into billows of festive color that wrapped around her legs provocatively. Looking back and putting things in contemporary terms, Elly was *hot*. There was no question about it...and my adolescent libido knew it!

9

"C'mon, let's go, Franny. I'll race you through the front door," I challenged. The race directed my 14-year old energy...and hormones in a different direction. We bounded up the brick walkway past Elly, and I skidded to a stop inside the main reception hall a pace or two behind Franny, letting her win.

Even then, at the unworldly age of 14 back in 1964, it was evident to me that Elly had an eye for the finer things in life. I couldn't help but gawk at the elegance of Annandale Farm's interior. Without a stick of furniture in it, the place looked grand. Ornately carved, gilded-age woodwork adorned the reception hall's ceiling, while crème color, wainscoted walls provided a warm contrast to the lustrously dark, parquet flooring. Fluted pillars of the same crème color supported the entry hall's infrastructure and framed the wide, graceful staircase leading to the second floor landing.

Father and Elly bought the place semi-furnished. There were some beautiful old pieces throughout the house that provided us the basics for living during our moving-in period.

"You and Franny can go up and pick out your own bedrooms if you'd care to," Elly offered. "There are seven on the second floor and eight or nine on the third—although you don't want to be on the third floor. Those are the old servants' quarters. You can have any room on the second floor...except the two adjoining rooms to the right of the stairs at the very end of the hallway. That's the master bedroom suite your father and I will be sharing," Elly announced proudly, pointing upward with her slender index finger toward the corner suite of rooms above.

"There are four bathrooms on the second floor, too," she threw in. "Oh, and take a look; some of those bedrooms have a few pieces of furniture in them," she added. "And see which room Livingston might like while you're at it. He's up there, now, putting the bags in our bedroom. We'll move some of the furniture around later...once everybody's decided where they want to be."

"C'mon, Franny," I enthused. The mansion managed to

breathe some life into the normally deadened sense of awareness I had about my surroundings. "Let's go have a look. You can help me pick out my room."

I took the lead, and Franny scrambled up the broad set of thickly carpeted stairs behind me. We could hear the sound of movement coming from the master bedroom suite as we hustled down the wide hallway. The main corridor on the second floor ran the full width of the house from side-to-side and crisscrossed with a spacious, center hall at the top of the stairs. There, French doors led outside to a wrought-iron balcony that overlooked the brick walkway, sculpted lions and breathtaking ocean view, beyond.

A parade of solid mahogany doors leading to bedrooms and bathrooms lined the tastefully wallpapered hallway walls. Franny and I tried each door. From the ample window of one vacant bedroom I could see Father meandering around the flowerbeds with Mr. FitzHugh in the yard. Mr. FitzHugh chattered away excitedly as I watched him gesturing wildly, for some reason, toward the greenhouse situated in the back corner of the property.

When Franny and I finally reached the end of the long main corridor where the hallway took a hard left over the kitchen wing—a service wing extending, perpendicular, to the main structure of the house, we encountered the less elaborate, yet still imposing back staircase with the only access to the third floor. I stood at the foot of the stairs for a while, listening and recollecting the movement I'd seen from the lawn earlier. The only sound now filtered down the hall from the master suite where Livingston shuffled about unpacking Elly's and Father's things. Despite my uneasiness, the temptation to climb the stairs to the third floor and find the room with the porthole window persisted. I put my right foot on the step then paused for a second. Imagination kicked in and I felt myself losing my nerve. The prospect of entering the unknown alone was creepy.

"Franny, c'mon, will-ya? Let's explore the third floor," I suggested, with the hope she'd abandon the room she'd pegged for her own, long enough to accompany me upstairs. I knew Franny would be incapable of any kind of assistance if we encountered some ghoulish apparition, but it eased my fear to at least have someone else at my side. Normally put-off at having her hanging on my shirttails, I was glad to have her around this time.

"Franny...you coming?"

No sooner had I called then Franny bounded enthusiastically out of her new bedroom and skipped down the corridor to join me. I can still recall reaching out and taking her by the hand...then starting up the winding stairway. As we cleared the landing, I could see sun filtering through a small, round window that provided the only source of daylight. I noted a few glass-globed sconces dotting the walls. They appeared barely adequate for nighttime lighting. The thought of climbing that staircase alone after dark made me shiver. I took in the dark wood wainscoting lining the stairwell walls. It melded with the stair risers and snaking, carved balustrade in a kind of overwhelming gloominess. It made me clutch Franny's hand more tightly. Nope, there was no way anyone would ever get me up those stairs by myself once the sun went down.

I breathed a sigh of relief when the glow of sunlight streaming through the landing window illuminated the otherwise windowless third-floor hallway. It also amplified the dusty loneliness greeting us as we crested the top of the stairs. The third-floor thoroughfare ran the full depth of the three-story center section of the house from front-to-back, and no intersecting center hall existed on this story. Unlike the second-floor hall running the full width of the sprawling east and west wings, the third-floor hall running perpendicular to the corridor below, only spanned the central core of the house. A solid bank of austere looking doors lined the length of this windowless passageway. Utilitarian design dominated the décor here, offering no evidence of the opulently appointed floors beneath. I looked at Franny for any kind of reaction. She stood patiently beside me, staring blankly at new territory. No trace of fear or agitation showed on her face.

That's a good sign, I remember thinking as I wiped a thin film of perspiration from my forehead. It made me recall the dampness I'd noticed on Livingston's brow only a short time before.

Walking haltingly, I led the way towards the front of the house, pulling Franny along behind me. We paused halfway down the hallway, stopping in front of a closed door. Bravely I turned the knob and pushed it gently inward. The brass hinges creaked as I nervously waited for the room's interior to come into view.

"That's not so bad, is it?" I said, heaving a relieved sigh at the sight of an empty but brightly-lit room. My adolescent confidence blossomed with the discovery that no demons with missing teeth and twisted faces were poised to leap out at us.

"Okay, Franny. Let's keep going."

I zeroed my eyes onto the doorknob of a corner room at the end of the hallway to my right. I calculated it had to be the room with the porthole window—the window from which I'd detected mysterious movement earlier from the yard. Despite my bolstering courage, I approached the door cautiously, pressing my ear against the wood to listen.

"What are you doing that for, Eddie?" Franny asked loudly.

"Cripes! Be quiet, will ya? I wanted to see…oh, never mind, it doesn't matter anymore."

With my sleuthing totally compromised by Franny's blabbing, I reached down and twisted the doorknob. Throwing the door inward, I prepared for the worst. The only thing greeting us, however, was a room as equally empty as the last. It appeared perfectly square in dimension. The only visible light emanated from the round porthole-shaped window I expected would be there. The afternoon sun shining through the glass made the room bright and warm. I could feel the heat radiating on my skin as I moved closer to the glass. Looking out across the front lawn, Franny and I could see Father and Mr. FitzHugh pacing around the property down by the water. Elly stood at the end of the brick walkway between the two stone lions. She held her hand above her eyes to shield them from the glare while surveying the magnificent view of the bay. I wanted to wave and shout a greeting to Father, so I looked for a window latch. Spotting a tarnished brass hasp on the bottom molding of the window frame, I noticed it was already unlatched. I was surprised to see how easily the window pivoted inward from the bottom on center-placed hinges on either side of the frame. The wind must have blown it open, I thought, recalling the motion I'd seen from the lawn.

Quickly, I pulled the bottom of the window further inward, opening it wide enough to squeeze my lanky body in between the glass and the windowsill. At the time, I had no idea my simple act of whimsy would launch such a commotion. Just as I angled the tilt to about 45 degrees, Franny, who stood directly behind me, let out a wild shriek. The suddenness of her outburst made me blurt out a petrified yell myself that only frightened both of us further and alarmed Elly down below. I spun around quickly to see what had happened.

"Cripes, Franny, you scared the crap out of me. What are you...?" I stopped. The look of paralyzed fear on Franny's face said it all. She stood staring at the open window as though both feet were bolted to the floor.

"What's the matter?" I heard Elly holler up from the walkway below. Her voice drifted in nervously through the open window. I turned to look outside and caught a glimpse of Father and Mr. FitzHugh scurrying across the lawn towards the house. Elly peered up anxiously. She cupped her hands around her mouth to amplify her voice. "Eddie, what's the matter? What's going on up there?"

"I...I...d-don't know," I stammered back. Before I could say anything further, the fear that had held Franny in its frozen grip suddenly released her and she ran, screaming, from the room.

"It's Franny," I called down to Elly, trying to keep my voice calm and steady. "She's all right. Something's scared her though. I don't know what. She's run away. I'm going after her."

I hastily swung the window shut, and after fastening the hasp,

14

dashed out the door. I caught a momentary, backlit view of Franny disappearing down the dingy back stairway. Within seconds I was bounding down the stairs after her, two at a time. The back staircase dumped us out into a service hallway on the first floor near the kitchen. By the time I managed to catch a fleeting glimpse of her, she had already streaked through the kitchen's double-doors, leaving them swinging, noisily, on their hinges. She ran across the tile floor negotiating, rather deftly I thought, the maze of counters and cooking equipment that obstructed her escape route. When I finally caught up with her, she had made her way out the exterior kitchen door and into the bright sunshine of the backyard. No sooner had I grabbed hold of her dress then we collided with Livingston, head on. Reeling with the impact, he dropped the suitcases he'd been carrying into a heap then managed to grab us both in his powerful arms.

"Whoa, hold on here. What's the matter with you two?"

Franny and I stood there struggling to catch our breath.

"Where are both of you running off to in such a God-awful hurry?"

I bent over slightly at the waist and put my hands on my hips to ease my windedness. "Nowhere special, Livingston," I managed breathlessly. "Something spooked Franny upstairs on the third floor and she took off. I was just trying to catch up with her. I've never seen her move that fast before."

I looked at Franny, who'd plopped down on the lush lawn. She sat Indian-style with her legs crossed in front of her, pouting a bit while she twisted a few blades of emerald green grass between stubby fingers. The strange experience left me puzzled. I explained what had happened to Livingston, starting with the movement in the third floor window. He listened intently to me like he always did. I had no sooner finished recounting my story when the screen door to the kitchen clattered open. Father and Elly rushed breathlessly into the backyard followed by a winded and agitated looking Mr. FitzHugh. The door slapped shut with a loud *"bang"* behind them.

15

"Eddie, what the devil is the ruckus about?" Father demanded. "Mr. FitzHugh, Elly and I have been chasing all over the place looking for you." In a gesture of exasperation, he threw his hands up in the air. "Why was Franny screaming like that...and why were you both tearing around the house?," he wanted to know.

I looked at Livingston, momentarily, and debated whether or not I should try to explain to Father and Elly the same string of events I had just divulged to him. I had all but decided to concoct some other story when I heard Franny's muddled voice abruptly break the silence.

"It...it scared me, Daddy. The window scared me," she said plaintively looking down towards the ground. Father stood silently for a few seconds gazing at her. I watched as he glanced in my direction then let his eyes settle on Livingston.

"Apparently Franny saw something upstairs that frightened her, sir," Livingston offered earnestly to Father. "Perhaps you can get her to tell you what it was, Mr. Sutton."

Livingston always addressed Father with respect and formality. To Livingston, Father's social standing warranted it. I decided it must have been part of Livingston's proper training as a butler. Whenever he spoke to Father he always called him "sir" or "Mr. Sutton." Whenever Livingston spoke to me or anyone else about Father in the third person, he invariable referred to him as "the Master."

I watched Father walk over to Franny and crouch down in front of her on the grass. He steadied himself by gently resting his right hand on her shoulder. "Franny, dear," he said quietly. "What did you see upstairs that frightened you?"

Franny pulled a few blades of grass out of the lawn and twisted them fretfully in her fingers. She kept her eyes focused downward. "The window frightened me, Daddy," she simply repeated softly.

"What did she say?" Elly asked looking at Father quizzically. "I swear, I can never understand half of what she says."

I watched Father shoot an annoyed glance in Elly's direction. He repeated what Franny had just said. "She said the window frightened her."

"The window frightened her?" Elly parroted back brashly, scanning the faces around her. "How could a window frighten anybody? I've never heard of such a thing. Why, it's broad daylight...two o'clock in the afternoon. It's not even dark," she persisted. "This sounds an awful lot like the doings of somebody with a wild imagination."

Elly fixed a firm stare on me. Livingston picked up on it and attempted to help me out.

"Eddie says he saw movement up on the third floor a little while ago when he was out in the front yard, Mrs. Sutton. He and Franny went up to take a look. They said they didn't find anything out of the ordinary. Perhaps you could tell everybody what you saw, Eddie," Livingston coached me.

I appreciated his efforts on my behalf, but I wasn't about to knuckle under to Elly's intimidation tactics. Despite the *hots* I had for Elly's good looks, I sometimes found her Brooklyn-bred personality a bit abrasive. Nope, I thought to myself. I'd rather say nothing than defend myself to Elly in front of Father.

"It was nothing," I said dejectedly.

Father glared at me. "Livingston doesn't seem to think so," he shot back. "And I'm sure Franny didn't let out a yell like that just for nothing."

I thought about it some more but decided to hold my ground.

"No, just forget about it. There's nothing to tell," I insisted. "We were just exploring and goofing around. I don't know what made Franny holler like that."

"Very well, young man," Father bristled. "If that's the way you're going to be about it then we may as well put you to work. You can go around to the front and help Livingston carry the rest of the things into the house. Livingston, how many more bags do you have to bring upstairs?"

"Well, there are a few more in addition to these, sir," Livingston replied respectfully, pointing to the suitcases he'd dropped on the ground. "I've only brought up Mrs. Sutton's bags and yours so far."

While Father surveyed the luggage situation and strategized an appropriate bag-toting punishment for me, I caught a glimpse of Mr. FitzHugh muttering under his breath. He shook his head from side to side nervously.

"Oh dear, it's started already! It doesn't usually start right in like this...especially on the first day," he said, easing up the volume of his voice a bit.

Father looked at Mr. FitzHugh guardedly. I knew he wasn't happy about what he'd just heard.

"What do you mean, FitzHugh?" he asked. I could see the trepidation on his face.

Mr. FitzHugh hesitated. I watched him fidget with his tie at the prospect of having to explain further.

"Well...there's no sense in me trying to hide it," he said. "I...I was trying to tell you down by the greenhouse, Mr. Sutton, that odd things happen here. They have for over half a century...and no one's been able to explain any of it. Why, some things would just make your hair stand right up on end. I can tell you that, firsthand, because something I experienced here actually put me in the hospital..." Mr. FitzHugh's voice trailed off as he thought better about saying anything more. I could tell he was reliving that moment—whatever had happened. His gaze drifted downward toward the ground where Franny was sitting. I thought I actually saw a shudder wash over his

18

body. I couldn't tell whether it was fear related to the actual experience...or fear that he'd said something he shouldn't have that made him clam up with such resolve.

"Well...I've said too much already," he announced flatly, mustering an air of determination that made me think it was more the latter. Father sensed it too. He glanced over towards Franny and me.

"Livingston, why don't you take the children into the house to unpack while Elly and I have a chat with Mr. FitzHugh," he suggested. I knew it was more than a suggestion, but protested anyway.

"I wanna stay," I blurted out. "I wanna hear what Mr. FitzHugh has to say about the house. I am 14, you know."

Father paused for a moment, somewhat taken aback by my stubbornness, and I was surprised to hear him say, "All right, son, you can stay...but, Livingston, I do wish you'd take Franny inside."

Livingston responded with the usual dutiful grace he demonstrated whenever Father asked him to do anything. "Yes, sir," he acknowledged without hesitation. "Come along with me, Franny. We'll unpack your things." He extended his powerful hand to Franny, coaxing her to stand. She took hold of it, and with a firm yet gentle grip he pulled her, effortlessly, to her feet. We watched quietly until he led her back into the house through the kitchen door. It slammed closed with a "bang." Father waited a few seconds to ensure they were well out of listening distance then he looked in Elly's direction. Words were unnecessary. I watched a forced smile bloom on Elly's lips. Meekly, she walked over and sat down on the back stoop, folding her hands in her lap. Then, Father put his arm around my shoulder and guided me over to sit down next to her.

"Very well, FitzHugh, we're all ears," Father said, breaking the silence. "Let's have it. We might as well get an idea as to what we're up against here."

Mr. FitzHugh paused, rubbing his chin with the thumb and forefinger of his right hand uneasily. It was more than evident he didn't want to discuss the subject further. I watched him fidget with his tie clasp a bit before giving in.

"This is a strange house," he said wearily. "To tell you the truth, I don't know how much more I'll be able to put up with all the oddball things that go on here." I sensed we were going to learn something, but doubted he'd resurrect the subject of his before-mentioned hospital visit.

"As far back as most folks can remember, there were always peculiar goings-on at Annandale Farm," he went on. "Rumor has it that the nonsense began shortly after General Greene moved into the mansion back in 1901. Simon Merriweather was the general contractor who built the place. 'Lived in town on Hammond Street. 'Constructed some of the other big mansions on Bellevue Avenue and along Ocean Drive, too. His only child—the kid's name was Ollie—hung around on the job site with him a lot. 'Story has it Ollie was a little dim and gave the teachers a hard time. Evidently dropped out of school for a few months here and there; then would go back for a spell when the truant officer put pressure on Simon. Funny...folks never did find out what happened to that kid."

"What do you mean?" I found myself asking as curiosity overcame any previous feelings of inhibition.

"Well, son, all I can tell you is that Ollie disappeared around the same time this old house of yours got built." He gestured with his hand toward the building. "I don't know or recollect a whole lot about Ollie Merriweather myself, but I do know that Ollie's disappearance was one of the biggest mysteries of Newport in its time...and still is to this day."

"How old was Ollie at the time of the disappearance?" I asked intently. To my surprise, Father and Elly seemed to be giving me free reign.

"Don't really know, son. The only one who could probably tell you that is Mabel Keating. Old Mabel used to work next door at Hammersmith Farm—the Auchincloss place. She's Simon

20

Merriweather's sister. Mabel could tell you plenty if she wanted to...only she won't. 'Doesn't ever talk about Ollie Merriweather or her family to anybody. 'All dead now anyway. She's the only one left. Yep, ever since Ollie disappeared back when the house was under construction, Mabel Keating went dumb and hardly spoke to anyone again. To this day she gets real nasty about it too...if anyone dares ask her. Why, rumor has it that even Mrs. Auchincloss next door at Hammersmith Farm got told to mind her own business when she asked Mabel about the story. Mabel was lucky Mrs. Auchincloss didn't fire her on the spot—Mrs. Auchincloss bein' Jacqueline Kennedy's mother and all. No sir-ee, you won't get much of anything out of Mabel Keating...which pretty much means any clue about whatever happened to Ollie Merriweather will stay a mystery forever, once Mabel goes to her reward."

I watched Father grow more impatient with Mr. FitzHugh's attempts to explain away the disturbing welcome we'd just experienced.

"Really, FitzHugh, I don't find this story at all entertaining," he snapped back skeptically. Do you expect us to accept your inference that some ghost or apparition frightened Franny upstairs?"

Mr. FitzHugh shrugged. "I told you before...screwy things have been going on here for years." Whatever hesitation he'd felt about sharing ghostly news seemed to have abated—at least for the time being. In fact, he appeared animated.

"When we were out in the yard earlier, I pointed to the greenhouse and hinted about something that happened to me there," he said looking at Father. "That's where they found me after I had my heart attack...on the very day President Kennedy was assassinated— November 22nd of last year."

Aha, I thought, it looks like we're going to get to the meat of it, after all.

"I actually don't remember much about it...kind of an amnesia thing, which is for the best I guess," Mr. FitzHugh recollected.

"They say nature works that way...you know...blocks out unpleasantness. But, Captain Karl of the Newport Police Department said whatever I saw must have near scared me to death. To this day, I'm still uncertain about exactly what I saw...and what happened."

But I saw Mr. FitzHugh shudder that indeterminate shudder again. He wasn't spilling his guts about the whole story, for sure. At that moment, for some inexplicable reason and to my great disappointment, Father decided to back off and avoid pressing him further. I was just about to pursue the matter more thoroughly, myself, but a glance over in Elly's direction made me let it go. She was sitting, forlornly, on the back stoop wringing her hands. Her beautiful face had a look of overwhelming disappointment. I'd never seen her cry before, but I could tell tears were in the offing. I knew what she was thinking. Dreams of gala balls and elegant dinner parties populated by Newport society were evaporating from her head faster than water from a sizzling skillet. All of a sudden, her composure started slipping away. I could see the tears welling up in her eyes and she began to tremble. Father saw it, too, and quickly shifted gears in an effort to bring the conversation to closure saving Elly from embarrassment.

"All right, all right, FitzHugh," he said soothingly, deliberately steering the focus from Elly by keeping Mr. FitzHugh in the spotlight. "Don't get excited now. November 22nd last year was bad enough for all of us," he sympathized. "I know I'll never forget where I was on the day Oswald assassinated Jack Kennedy. Most of us won't." Father put his hands on his hips and peered, somewhat knowingly, at the mansion's foundation. "Let's not discuss it anymore, shall we? I'm sure we'll all be perfectly fine here at the house. What's past is past...so let's not let it interfere with our future," he offered reassuringly. He turned to look at Elly. His tactic had worked and she'd managed to hold onto her composure.

"Elly, dear, why don't you and Eddie go inside and get unpacked," Father suggested. I'll see Mr. FitzHugh out. I think we've all had enough excitement for our first day." He turned, to look Mr. FitzHugh squarely in the eye.

"Perhaps you could stop around late tomorrow morning, FitzHugh, and we could discuss the arrangements for keeping the grounds."

Mr. FitzHugh nodded and I watched Father put his arm around George FitzHugh's shoulder then guide him away. As the two men disappeared around the corner of the house, I felt an exhilarating rush of energy wash over me. The thought of Mr. FitzHugh's tale and the unexplainable happenings we experienced that day had both my heart and mind racing.

"Okay, Elly, let's go inside like Father said," I suggested trying to hide the growing feelings of mystery and intrigue simmering inside of me. But the intuitive Elly knew exactly what I was thinking. She was as savvy as she was striking...and the sensitivity she'd let slip out that day made me like her all the more. Knowing that she'd second-guessed me seemed to revitalize her prospects of the Newport summer season.

"Now look here, young fellow; just get a handle on that imagination of yours and forget about any haunting business that's swimming around in your head. This is all explainable and I'll be damned if I'm going to let it get in the way of our vacation. I've got parties and luncheons planned...plus I expect to pay a call on Mrs. Auchincloss next door and introduce myself. We'll go find Franny and Livingston then get you all situated in your rooms. This is going to be a *marvelously* interesting summer."

I reveled in the idea of discovering more about Annandale Farm and the mystery surrounding Ollie Merriweather. Elly was certainly right. Without a doubt, this would indeed be a *marvelously* interesting summer!

CHAPTER TWO

The first time I laid eyes on Mabel Keating turned out to be an otherwise dreary and rainy afternoon shopping with Elly at Davenport's grocery store on Broadway. It had been almost a week since we'd first arrived at Annandale Farm and experienced the strange inaugural to the property. Nothing unusual had happened since, and we were all becoming more at ease with our new surroundings. Even Mr. FitzHugh appeared to be more relaxed and mentioned a few times during his daily work routine that the fact that nothing out of the ordinary had further occurred was a very good sign.

Father felt he had the management of the property well in hand and spent a good part of his days fishing off the rocky shoreline, reading on the broad verandah, or playing golf at the Newport Country Club conveniently situated right behind the house. Occasionally, he would place a call to his broker or financial advisors in New York City to review the status of the family trust that funded our comfortable lifestyle.

Elly poured herself into furnishing the house and working the social circuit at the country club. She strategized daily on how she would go about making contact with our high society neighbors. Franny and I divided most of our time outside between fishing, swimming and exploring the grounds. Needless to say, we avoided any further exploration of the house. We occupied our first few evenings playing cards and Scrabble with Livingston, or reading. Father hadn't yet bought a television set, so Livingston took us to the movies at the Strand where we saw Elizabeth Taylor and Richard Burton in *Cleopatra*. It had begun storming by the time we came out of the theater. To say the least, it didn't make us feel particularly at ease returning to Annandale Farm in a barrage of thunder and lightning...and it had been raining ever since.

The inclement weather made for a good shopping day in town, and Elly prevailed upon me to come along with her. Father stayed home to make some business calls while Livingston drove Elly,

Franny, and me into Newport. He parked the car in front of Davenport's then took Franny for ice cream across the street at Cote Pharmacy. Elly and I explored the quaint atmosphere of Davenport's and wandered through its eclectic and delectably stocked aisles. I had just finished pulling a couple of dill pickles out of a wooden, brine-brimmed barrel when I heard Mr. Davenport address an elderly, well dressed lady.

"Well...hello...look who's here," he said with familiarity. "What have you been up to these days dear lady? 'Can't say I've seen you around town for a while. 'Been feeling all right?"

Mr. Davenport was the picture of Norman Rockwell Americana. He wore a knee-length grocer's apron and black elastic armbands on his shirt sleeves. A yellow pencil stuck out from behind his right ear. He was bald except for a fringe of slightly graying hair.

I eavesdropped beside the pickle barrel and pretended to fumble with the tongs in hopes that the ensuing dialogue might further identify the well-heeled woman.

"Hello, Dennis," I heard her reply in a voice that had an air of refined New England breeding about it. "I've been just fine, although a lot of people might hope otherwise...and where I go and what I do isn't anybody's business but my own, I'll thank you to keep in mind," she snipped back at him.

"Yes, ma'am," Mr. Davenport answered looking her directly in the eye. He broke into a smile. She stood there waiting patiently while he plucked the pencil from behind his ear and itemized the few things she'd placed on the counter. It appeared the brief bantering I'd witnessed was part of their regular ritual. She continued unloading groceries on the counter. A flash of brilliance from an enormous diamond solitaire on her left hand couldn't go unnoticed. The ruby colored nail polish on her manicured fingers caught my attention, too, as did her meticulously coiffed white hair. The whole image spoke dignity and elegance. I concluded she must have been quite an attractive woman in her day...and no doubt a very wealthy one.

"So, tell me, Dennis; how are Myra and the two girls doing these days?" I heard her ask Mr. Davenport politely as if the earlier chastisement had never left her lips.

"Oh, just fine. My oldest, Margie, is getting ready to head off to camp for the summer. Myra and the youngest, Amanda, are going to have plenty of time to get better acquainted while Margie's gone. She's such an adventurer and free spirit, that Amanda. I guess she gets it from Myra's side of the family. Lord knows she doesn't get it from me."

The lady at the counter smiled as if she knew better. I watched Mr. Davenport tally up the bill. He stuffed the items sitting in front of him into a paper bag. "Want to sign for these?" he asked politely pushing the pencil and bill-pad across the counter.

"May as well," she sighed, then hastily scribbled her signature.

"I always liked the name *Mabel*," he announced with a wink.

"Well, you know how I feel about it," came the reply.

Mr. Davenport nodded knowingly.

"Come to think of it, I was never crazy about the name *Dennis* either," he responded. "Too bad we can't pick out our names after we've been around for a while, eh?"

"Yes...too bad indeed. Well, goodbye, Dennis," she announced ending their dialogue abruptly. "I'll be in again...before too long," she added, picking up her parcels and heading for the door. The screen door banged shut loudly behind her. I strained to keep her in view as she strode slowly but purposefully past the front window then finally disappeared from my line of sight.

Glancing around the store's interior, I noticed that Elly and I seemed to be the only customers there at the moment. I could hear the squeaky wheels of her grocery cart meandering through the aisles.

Normally on the shy side and always leaning toward the unobtrusive, I defied my own style a bit strolling casually to the check-out counter. The bill pad with the list of items purchased by the lady Mabel sat on top of the counter facing in the opposite direction. I tried to read the hastily scrawled signature upside down and had just about performed the visual acrobatics necessary when Mr. Davenport's bald head popped up, suddenly, from behind the counter.

"Hi, sonny. Those are darn good pickles you've got there," he said noting the transparent pickle bag in my hand. "'Just came in yesterday, as a matter of fact."

I smiled sheepishly.

"Say, I haven't seen you around before," he said cordially. 'You visiting Newport for the first time?"

"Uh, yes…I mean no. Uh…actually, we just moved here a few days ago," I managed to stammer.

"Oh! I saw you pull up and get out of that big black Bentley in front of the store. Say, you wouldn't be the folks that moved into Annandale Farm up on Ridge Road, would you?"

Perfect, I thought. I couldn't have hoped for a better lead-in. Maybe Mr. Davenport would know about some of the infamous legend surrounding our summer digs as well as the mysterious Mabel Keating.

"Yes, I'm Eddie Sutton," I said extending my hand as I'd been brought up to do.

"Well, how do you do, son." He responded, grabbing my hand willingly with a firm and friendly grip. "That your mom back there pushing the shopping cart?" he asked.

"That's Elly. She's my stepmother." I felt funny correcting him. Mine was a generation taught that challenging one's elders was impolite—whether good reason existed or not.

"Ah, your stepmother, eh? Well she looks to be a real nice lady from where I'm standing."

Mr. Davenport slid the bill-pad into his apron pocket. My heart sank as my one chance for confirming whether or not the woman I'd just seen was Mabel Keating disappeared completely. A moment later hope rekindled as Mr. Davenport resurrected the subject of our house.

"Yep, there are lots of interesting stories about Annandale Farm. My wife, Myra, did a lot of housekeeping up there over the years—used to cook and serve meals on special occasions too. In fact, I ought to mention to your stepmother that Myra's available to help out with housework if you folks need her."

Good, I thought. This is going in the right direction. I seized the opportunity to steer the conversation toward the subject of Mabel Keating.

"Mr. FitzHugh, the caretaker up at our house, says that a lady in town named Mabel Keating knows a lot about the history of the place. Do you know her?"

"Do I know her?" Mr. Davenport gave me surprised look. "Why there isn't a merchant in town that doesn't know Mabel Keating. She's been around longer than anybody I know; she's not real friendly though," he tacked on.

"I heard you call that lady at the counter *Mabel*. Was that her by any chance?" I asked rather boldly. Mr. Davenport smiled, seeming to enjoy my questioning.

"Nope! That was *Mabel Pierce*. She's your caretaker's— George FitzHugh's—sister. Her name's Mabel, too, but she hates it. 'Goes by the nickname of *Belle*...has for most of her life. *Belle* Pierce and Mabel Keating go way back. Never could stand each other. They both grew up in town and went through school together. As long as anyone can remember, they've been bitter rivals. Nope, that's not Mabel Keating. I can tell you that for sure."

I watched Mr. Davenport squint as something caught his eye beyond the big, storefront picture window.

"*That's* Mabel *Keating,*" he said, pointing outside to an older woman with blue-tinted hair lumbering down the sidewalk towards Franny and Livingston. Her stout figure swayed each time she leaned, rather heavily, on a brass handled walking stick. Crescent shaped eyeglasses did little to hide a plump and scowling face. It appeared evident that her reputation for being unfriendly preceded her in that several approaching passersby made a conscious effort to avoid her.

We both watched with interest as Mabel Keating approached Livingston and Franny standing on the sidewalk in front of Cote Pharmacy. Franny, preoccupied with consuming the mountain of ice cream piled on her cone, chose the very moment Mabel Keating walked by to dislodge a glob of vanilla-fudge twirl. She managed to collide, head-on, with Mabel Keating, in her effort to rescue it, sending what was left of her ice cream cone to an untimely end atop Mabel's open-toed shoe.

"Uh-oh," Mr. Davenport gasped as I watched the smile evaporate from his face. At that moment, Elly squeaked up unceremoniously behind her overloaded shopping cart, her attention on the pantomime taking place across the street.

"What on earth has Franny gotten into now?" Elly asked clucking her tongue.

The three of us watched Livingston's attempt to intercede on Franny's behalf. The unfriendly scowl on Mabel Keating's face twisted into a rage. She lifted her walking stick and waved it threateningly at Livingston. Shaking her foot in an attempt to free her exposed toes from the gooey grip, she turned her anger towards Franny. Then, all at once, Mabel Keating stopped dead in her tracks. She noticed Franny's Down syndrome features for the first time and stood there in a kind of suspended animation studying the panic-stricken face looking up at her. Franny sobbed from behind a mask of melted ice cream. The woman's animosity disappeared as quickly as it came. The tautness of her mouth eased, softening into a smile. She popped open an enormous handbag, pulled out a pristine-looking linen handkerchief, and began daubing the tears spilling down Franny's face. Mabel wiped the smeared ice cream from Franny's mouth, too, then moments later and with considerable difficulty, bent down to sponge the mound of melting ice cream from her soiled shoe. Using her walking stick for leverage, she stood up then mouthed what looked to be words of reprimand to Livingston. A few moments later, she was back on her way...but not before pausing to gently pat Franny on the top of the head.

"Well, I'll be...!" Mr. Davenport sighed. "In all my days, I never thought I'd see Mabel Keating do something like that. Wait 'til I tell Myra. She'll never believe it." He turned and faced Elly.

"Oh, 'scuse me, ma'am, I'm Dennis Davenport." he said cueing into Elly standing there by the counter. She responded politely by shaking hands while stealing a few parting glances out the window.

"Say, is that your daughter over there?" Mr. Davenport wanted to know.

Elly shook her head. "No...my stepdaughter."

Evidently, Mr. Davenport thought better about commenting further on the ice cream incident involving Franny and changed the subject.

"Oh...well, I understand from young Eddie here that you folks just moved into the old Greene mansion out on Ridge Road." Mr. Davenport smiled. "Welcome to town."

"Why, thank you," Elly responded graciously. "We're very pleased to be here. I've been enjoying myself taking in all the gourmet items that you carry."

"Have to do that, ma'am, to keep the summer folks happy and the trade coming in," Mr. Davenport beamed proudly. "All these big new supermarkets going up everywhere are always undercutting the old established town grocery stores like mine. We offer free delivery service, too, you know. Next time, if you'd rather, you can just call your order in and I'll send Norman Tate, the delivery boy, to the house to drop off your groceries."

"Oh, that would be lovely," she responded genuinely.

"In fact, you can just leave these things here at the counter with me and I'll tally them up. We'll send them along in about an hour as soon as Norman gets back from his last delivery. Will that work for you?"

"Oh yes, perfectly!" Elly answered delighted. "We're making a stop at Arakel Bozyan Antiques up on Bellevue Avenue then heading straight home. An hour should be just fine."

Then, before I could utter another word, Elly had me by the sleeve of my raincoat and we were headed out the door. It all happened so fast, Mr. Davenport didn't even get a chance to ask Elly about having his wife help out with chores at Annandale Farm. To me, having Myra Davenport there would provide another opportunity to shed light on the mystery and intrigue behind the odd happenings we'd already experienced.

When it came to Elly, however, time spent in antique stores hunting down furniture for the house took precedence over everything else—everything, that is, except meeting more of Newport's social elite.

We stood in front of Davenport's as Elly waved at Livingston and Franny across the street, motioning them to return to the car, I wondered if Mr. Davenport's daughter Amanda, and Norman the delivery boy, might also be good resources for finding out more about whatever happened at Annandale Farm. I made up my mind to do some exploring around the house again. Only this time I wasn't about to tackle it with Franny, alone. I decided to wait for Mr. Davenport to call Elly about having his wife, Myra, help out at the house. And who knew what further prospects a connection with Myra Davenport might bring?

In the meantime, it appeared as though Franny had somehow managed to unwittingly create a convenient inroad to Mabel Keating. Who would ever have guessed Franny dumping a glob of ice cream on the foot of the meanest woman in Newport would turn into such a bonus? All things considered, I thought, it had turned out to be a pretty productive day!

CHAPTER THREE

Every time Aunt Julia visited, the household went into an uproar. She was Father's twin sister, and possessed a vivacious yet controlling personality. As Father put it, "Julia isn't always right...but she's never wrong!" During the years Mother was alive, she would often comment that she could "never get used to having a flamboyant, self-aggrandized society psychic like Julia lurking about in the family." I'm sure that was part of the reason Elly seemed nervous that first day Aunt Julia arrived at Annandale Farm. The indisputable fact that Aunt Julia had an uncanny, sixth-sense was enough to make just about anybody uncomfortable—or at least put them on their guard. She was so gifted, in fact, that the New York City Police Department had called her in on more than one occasion to help them crack otherwise unsolvable cases with her intuitive powers.

I was sitting by the open, second floor window of my bedroom that summer of '64 when Aunt Julia drove through the gates. I had been peering through an old but powerful telescope Father had bought me years before. It provided considerable entertainment for me on otherwise uneventful days. I used it frequently for sighting watercraft in the bay and getting an up-close look at the impressive parade of military vessels that cruised past our house. Occasionally, I would zero-in on a passing yacht or pleasure craft, and was sometimes fortunate enough to catch a glimpse of some nautical erotica taking place onboard—the unsuspecting participants in the throes of their seagoing passions, unaware they were satisfying the raging libido of an adolescent. I also took equal satisfaction in spying on neighbors—or at least the few whose estates I could see from our property. The Auchincloss estate was one of them.

But that particular day, I abandoned my telescope and libido-driven search for seaworthy sex when the massive tires from Aunt Julia's Duesenberg crunched across the gravel drive and her gigantic car coasted to a halt under the portico. Nobody else we, or for that matter anybody, knew drove an enormous, 1934 robins'- egg blue Duesenberg Dual Cowl Phaeton convertible. Exhaust racing through four right-hand mounted, gleaming chrome manifold-pipes made the air pulsate. Protruding gracefully from beneath the endless expanse of hood, the silvery pipes added an air of muscular dignity to the sleek lines of this classic American beauty. My adolescent hormones raged with excitement listening to the "whomm-whomm-whomm" of the idling engine—a 320 horsepower, supercharged straight-eight. Framed with elegant, chrome grillwork and capped by a lissome hood ornament, the silken power plant propelling this majestic giant far exceeded the measure of any rivals of its day.

A few minutes later the motor stopped and the reverberations died quietly away. I saw Livingston courteously open the driver's door bidding Aunt Julia a cordial hello. Quickly and dutifully he made for the rear of the car to unload the mountain of luggage piled into the compartmentalized back seat, and rack-mounted steamer trunk suspended over the back bumper. I couldn't help but wonder what fashion concoctions Aunt Julia's luggage contained. She was known as much for her extravagant and eccentric taste in clothing as she was for her penchant for exotic automobiles.

I watched Father make his way over to the Duesenberg with Elly following behind. He extended a steadying hand to his sister as she stepped out from behind the huge steering wheel and onto the running board. Aunt Julia's pristine Duesenberg SJ Phaeton, purchased new by my grandparents in 1934 for $15,000, had passed to her when an unfortunate automobile accident involving the Duesenberg claimed both their lives in 1944. Fully restored after the wreck and now meticulously preserved, the classic "Model SJ" designed in Pasadena by the Walter M. Murphy Co. looked as good today as when it first left Fred Duesenberg's Indiana factory 30 years earlier.

"Hello, Julia," Father said warmly, greeting his sister with a kiss on the cheek. "Elly and I have been looking forward to this little visit of yours for some time now. My, don't you look quite Isadora Duncan-ish in your flowing scarf!" He kidded her, flashing that famous Sutton smile—an attractive physical trait given to Father's side of the family that had somehow managed to skip by me in the gene pool. A mirror image of it beamed back at him from his twin sister's face.

Aunt Julia wore an ankle length, white linen shift accentuating the height of her tall but well-conditioned figure. An enormous agate medallion suspended on a thick, gold chain clung to her bust-line, and large gold earrings—identical, but smaller versions of the medallion—hung from her earlobes. The fringe from the endlessly long, floral-print silk scarf that Father had kidded her about dusted the tops of her shoes. The scarf had been streaming from Aunt Julia's neck when the high-profile motorcar roared up the driveway.

Even from the distance of my bedroom, I could hear the clink and jingle of Aunt Julia's gold charm bracelets resonating with the melodramatic movements of her arms and hands. They were as much her trademark as the Duesenberg and the diamonds worn on nearly every finger. The collection of gems sparkled in the sunlight, complimenting her pink-painted, two inch-long fingernails. The sophisticated sweep of her dyed, platinum-blonde hair was held in place by a headband matching the colors of her fashionable scarf.

"Arthur, darling," I heard her coo dramatically to Father through a pair of pink-painted lips. Parting in that ever-captivating Sutton smile, they revealed a perfect set of dazzling white teeth. She threw her arms around his shoulders and hugged him. As twins, they shared a great commonality in feature, form, and manner. I noted the striking similarities in their faces and tall, dignified carriages. They shared the same graceful movements when they walked. Curiously, however, Father did not seem to possess the psychic talents that had been granted to Aunt Julia.

"Arthur, it's been so long since we've all been together," Aunt Julia mused as a pout crept over her regal looking face. "Why...we haven't really spent any time together at all since you and Elly got married." She stopped abruptly then turned to greet Elly standing quietly in the driveway next to Father.

"Eleanor, it's so good to see you again, dear." I watched Aunt Julia embrace Elly politely then continue her dialogue with Father scarcely missing a beat.

"Arthur, this is such a beautiful place. I'm so glad you and Eleanor took my advice about making an offer on it."

I nearly missed seeing Aunt Julia subtly tip her head in Father's direction and wink at him discreetly.

"Why it reminds me of Mimsy and Chip Parkhurst's place in Palm Beach...considerably larger though, I dare say."

I watched Father roll his eyes and shoot a telling glance in Elly's direction just before they all disappeared from view beneath the back portico. I could hear Aunt Julia's voice monopolizing the conversation as it trailed off into an indistinguishable drone.

Out by the car, I let Livingston entertain me for a few more minutes by watching him scurry around the Duesenberg with a look of total exasperation on his face. He flipped the rear windshield-cowl covering the compartmentalized back seat forward, and unloaded an imposing pile of expensive-looking leather suitcases, lining them up neatly next to the car's running board. Picking up four matching leather Pullman bags—one under each arm and the others in his strong hands—he reeled a bit under their weight. For a moment it appeared as though even Livingston, for all his strength, would fold under the load. But he didn't; within a matter of moments he staggered away under the back portico disappearing, fully laden, from view.

Oh well, I thought to myself. Today looked like a good day for resuming my investigation. I would leave the adults to entertain themselves while I headed off for further exploration of the house and grounds.

Myra Davenport had made an appearance at the house the day before, helping Livingston clean and make up a guestroom in anticipation of Aunt Julia's arrival. She had brought her daughter Amanda along with her to help with the dusting. Myra hadn't proved bashful and wasted no time following up on her husband's suggestion that she ring up Elly to make it known she was available to help out with housework. I was glad she did. The part-time employment agreement with Myra Davenport had netted me a newly found resource and friend. Amanda Davenport and I seemed to hit it off quite well. She had her father's friendly and disarming personality that made talking to her easy. The adventurous streak, to which I remembered hearing Mr. Davenport allude in his earlier conversation with Belle Pierce, was clearly evident. I had become so taken with Amanda's curious nature that I lost sight of my objective to interrogate her mother when we first met. A further distraction came in the form of Norman Tate—Mr. Davenport's delivery boy. Norman had been to Annandale Farm several times already delivering Elly's groceries. Amanda had introduced me to Norman during the course of a delivery stop at the house. It didn't take long for the three of us to start hashing over the strange doings my family experienced on the day of our initial arrival. My own excitement had been fueled by the fact that Norman and Amanda knew the local lore of Annandale Farm, which including its rumored hauntings...and a legend of hidden gold somewhere on the property.

With that intrigue in mind, I arranged for Norman and Amanda to meet me at the main gate up on Ridge Road at four o'clock that afternoon. Norman lived on Brewer Street, about half way between our house and Davenport's Grocery Store. Although Norman had his driver's license, he had difficulty getting access to the family car, so he planned to bike over to the house after work.

Amanda and the Davenports lived a few blocks away from Norman on Holland Street. Amanda's time was mostly her own, once the daily chores at home were finished. She agreed to bike over and join us at four o'clock too.

Once the luggage sideshow put on by Livingston ended, I decided to make my way down to the living room to greet Aunt Julia. When I got there she embraced me in a suffocating hug. Somehow, I managed to endure her usual barrage of interrogating questions such as: Did I like it at Annandale Farm? How were my grades? Where did I want to go to college? Had I made any friends yet?

Her tedious probing plus the self-absorbed monologue that

followed drove me to utter distraction. During the course of this inquisition, I managed to present an attentive appearance by fantasizing about what Amanda, Norman and I might find in our upcoming search of the house and grounds. Finally, a pleading glance in Father's direction at just the right moment—a moment that must have reminded him of a time when he, too, had been held hostage by Aunt Julia's incessant rambling—managed to win me a nod of approval signaling the "okay" to leave. The moment it came, I politely fled then scurried across the back lawn to the prearranged meeting place with Amanda and Norman by the main gate.

When I arrived, Amanda was already there. She sat straddling the branch of an old apple tree growing just inside the entrance to the property. Her pink Schwinn bicycle had been propped against its tree-trunk below her dangling feet. I noticed she had braided her red hair into pigtails tied neatly at the ends with light blue bows, and an ample smattering of freckles peppered her pretty face. The denim coveralls she wore looked to be about a size too large, and partially masked a gray T-shirt with a store logo and the word "Davenport's" splashed across the front. From her vantage point in the apple tree, she could see beyond the tall brick wall bordering Annandale Farm's perimeter. I watched her wave an enthusiastic hello to Norman Tate as he pedaled up on his bike from Ridge Road. A lit cigarette dangled from the corner of his mouth.

"Ooooooh, Normy, don't you look cool," Amanda taunted as Norman pushed open the heavy wrought iron gate just enough to squeeze his lanky frame and bicycle through. Smiling broadly, he pulled the gate closed behind him. The wrought iron clattered like a jail cell door when he latched it. Positioning his bike against the tree next to Amanda's, he blew a puff of cigarette smoke up towards her. Annoyed, she jumped down from the branch, scolding him as she landed.

"You shouldn't be smoking, Norman. If my father ever caught you smoking at the store, he'd really let you have it...besides, it's bad for you."

"Ah, you're just being a prude," he jibed back at her. "Someday you'll think differently about smoking." His smile broadened as he watched Amanda grow more aggravated.

Norman's face always had an expression of pleasant inquisitiveness. He had a high, furrowed brow and determined lantern jaw. A slightly soiled Red Sox baseball cap worn cockeyed hid a good portion of his tousled brown hair. Like Amanda, he also sported a "Davenports" T-shirt but wore it tucked into a pair of well-worn blue jeans. A flashlight with a chrome clip on the end dangled noticeably from one of his belt loops. From all counts, Norman looked ready and willing to hunker down and do some serious exploring. He plucked his cigarette from the corner of his mouth and ground it out in the grass with his foot.

"There; satisfied?" he challenged Amanda.

She breathed a sigh of relief through a subtle victory-smile.

"C'mon, will ya?" I said eager to get underway. I motioned towards the house. "Let's get going. Norman, I don't care if you smoke…just don't let anyone in my family catch you. It wouldn't be good."

Because Norman and Amanda weren't from the same side of the tracks as Father and Aunt Julia, I didn't want to give them a reason for interfering with my newly formed friendships. I had always managed to make friends easily, in the past, and enjoyed the company of both guys and girls. However, I had discovered, all too dishearteningly, that the majority of relationships I formed with kids of my own social standing didn't last very long. Once they found out about Franny, and word traveled back to their parents that I had a Down syndrome sister, it didn't take very long for relationships to unravel. Part of me resented Franny for it, but another part of me instinctively knew that I was better off. The world we lived in was populated with society hypocrites, so the fact that Franny's condition insulated me from their myopic point of view became a blessing I'd count among many in my latter years.

But that summer of '64, while the three of us strolled across the freshly mown lawn towards the house, the cooling sea breeze felt refreshing in the afternoon sunshine pounding down on us. I thought back on my earlier decision to wear a pair of faded red Bermuda shorts and a white pocket T-shirt. I was glad that I did, even though Aunt Julia made it a point to comment on my overly casual appearance, wrinkling her nose in disdain.

"Okay, where should we start looking?" Norman asked, snapping me into the excitement of the moment. We all got caught up in it.

"What about the basement?" Amanda threw out. She pointed towards the kitchen screen door. It made for easy access to the intimidating back staircase and what had to be a nerve-racking descent to unimaginable subterranean horrors. I cringed inwardly at the idea of going down there, but gave no sign to indicate Amanda's suggestion actually left me with a sinking feeling in the pit of my stomach.

"That's okay with me," I lied, but at the same time heard myself saying, "...or how 'bout the greenhouse?"

"Greenhouse? Cellar? There's always the attic too," Norman added, forcing his voice two octaves lower into a demonic, half-crazed cackle.

"Stop it," Amanda ordered. "I say we head for the cellar. That's got to be the scariest place of all...but the only way you'd get me down there is on a bright sunny day like today."

"What do you say, Sutton?" Norman asked, his voice returning to normal while throwing the decision into my court. "Whadd'll it be?"

I thought for a moment then fibbed boldly, "The basement's fine with me." I even threw in a shrug to punctuate my feigned nonchalance. I refused to be shown up as a coward—especially by a girl.

"Okay, then, let's go for it," Amanda yelled, setting her legs in motion and making a beeline for the kitchen door in the distance. Not to be outdone, Norman and I took off in hot pursuit. A few minutes later, we were inside scrambling down the service hallway towards the dismal back staircase. We stopped at the top of the cellar stairs, peering into the eerie darkness below. I flipped on the light switch, and the wall sconces dotting the walls of the staircase flickered to life. Their feeble light cast a dim, underworld glow on the basement stairwell beneath.

"Who's going first?" Amanda wanted to know.

Silence.

"All right, it's my house...I'll go first," I volunteered. I couldn't believe the words were coming out of my mouth. I must be crazy, I thought, taking the first step and easing my way cautiously down the winding stairs. Amanda and Norman followed a few paces behind. At the bottom of the stairs we were met by a large, solid steel door. A sturdy looking lock occupied a space above an equally substantial looking doorknob. We paused for a moment, exchanging anxious glances. I could feel the tension building at the prospect of going further. Timidly, I placed a hand on the doorknob. As quickly as I put it there, I pulled it away.

"Aw, come on. Don't be such a scaredy-cat," Norman goaded. Then, in a flash, he grabbed the knob and quickly pushed against the heavy door with his lanky frame. It gave way under his weight, swinging open on creaking hinges. Total blackness stared back at us. Norman unceremoniously removed his flashlight from its place on his waist and shined the concentrated beam inside.

"Quick, there must be a light switch nearby," Amanda enthused, groping along the wall next to the doorjamb. "Click!" The darkness vanished as she flipped the switch.

Our eyes adjusted to the gloom of the cavernous, windowless basement and the room came into focus. It was pretty evident that the basement hadn't always been windowless. The outline of arched casement frames now plugged solidly with mortared cinderblock could be made out at regular, eye-level intervals along the walls. I counted twenty all together. We mustered our courage and stepped carefully forward. Norman was the first to spot something on the far wall of the cellar.

"Look, over there. It's another doorway. See?" Amanda and I could see it, too—a heavy, wood-paneled door fixed dead-center on a concrete dividing-wall cordoning off a large section of the basement.

"Pfssssst! Plunk!"

"YEOW!" Amanda yelped and clutched at my arm as the nearby hot-water heater spluttered to life. Norman and I nearly jumped out of our skins.

"Jeez, why did you do that? It's only the hot-water heater," Norman chided. "See?" He gestured, annoyed, toward the southerly corner of the cellar where an ancient-looking, cylindrical water heater now hissed away dutifully at its job.

"Sorry, this place gives me the creeps," Amanda snapped back. "I'm curious to find out more about this big ol' house of Eddie's, but I can't wait to get out of here!"

My feelings exactly, I thought at the mention of my name...but found myself saying differently.

"Aw, c'mon; don't be chicken. We only just got here," is what came out of my mouth.

I must be nuts, I remember thinking. Yet, a further examination of the huge basement revealed nothing but expansive emptiness. Our collective curiosity wouldn't allow us to leave without first determining what was behind that heavy wooden door Norman spotted, so we pushed on. Approaching the door cautiously, we stopped a few feet away—as though it possessed intentions and we were assessing them. The door had a sturdy looking lock on it with a heavy, brass-handled latch. I deferred the honors of trying to open it to Norman, which he did tentatively. Gripping the door handle, he pressed on the latch with his thumb then gingerly gave the door a pull to see if it was locked. It wasn't. Feeble light from the dimly illuminated basement crept slowly into this newly discovered room as Norman inched open the door.

"Well, I'll be," he cooed sweeping the beam of his flashlight along the damp gray walls. "This must be an old wine cellar."

There was no question it was the wine cellar. Row after row of slanted, notched-lipped shelves covered the walls from top to bottom. The room felt penetratingly damp and cold for some reason; much damper and colder than the rest of the basement. I could smell the faint odor of wine that must have spilled from broken bottles onto the floor. A round, grate-covered drain occupied the middle of the floor.

"Okay, I've had enough," I heard myself surrendering. "What do you say we get out of here and head elsewhere?"

Norman paused for a moment then shrugged casually. "Sure, I don't care. There're lots more places to look. Where next...the attic?"

When he shrugged his shoulders, the motion of his body altered the path of the flashlight beam slightly. A bright, flat shiny object barely visible under the lowest shelf on the back wall of the wine cellar caught the light briefly and bounced it back at us.

"Hey wait a second. What's that?" I asked moving toward the source of the reflection. As I got closer, the angled, bottom shelf only a few inches above the concrete floor blocked my view of the spot where the object lay. I had to get down on my hands and knees on the dirty floor then fish around under the shelf to find it.

Ah, there it was. I sensed the touch of cold metal against my fingertips and pulled the treasure out into the light. I held it between my thumb and index finger in plain view for everybody to see.

"It's a key," Amanda announced. I saw the sparkle of curiosity in her eyes as she moved closer to get a better look at it. The brass finish twinkled under the dim light. I turned it over and over several times in my fingers. Norman moved in to examine the find, too.

"Hmm, I wonder what it's for?" He said what we were all thinking. "It's real unusual looking too. I've never seen one like it."

The key was elaborate. With one sweeping motion, Norman plucked it out of my fingers then strode out into the main part of the cellar where the light was better. Amanda and I watched through the open wine cellar door as he held it up under one of the naked light bulbs glaring brashly from its utilitarian socket.

"Try it in the wine cellar door," I suggested.

Norman walked over to the heavy wine cellar door and tried to insert the key into the lock, first one way and then another. It didn't work.

"Try the basement door," I offered next.

Amanda and I followed Norman to the sturdy, steel basement door and watched him fumble trying to insert the key. It didn't fit that door either.

"Why do you suppose a key like this would be lying underneath a shelf in this old deserted wine cellar?, Amanda asked. "Don't you think that's odd?"

"Cripes, I don't know," I said with a shrug. "Maybe somebody reached into their pocket for a handkerchief or something ages ago and it fell out onto the floor. If you couldn't see where it landed, it would be real hard to find without a flashlight—'specially hidden from view under that bottom shelf like that. The lighting in the wine cellar is really bad. The only reason I spotted it in the first place was 'cause Norman accidentally shined his flashlight on it from across the room. Even if you were standing right on top of it you couldn't see it under that bottom shelf."

44

"Well, let's see if it fits any other locks around the house," Amanda said and added, "but later. Right now, I've had enough of this creepy cellar. I didn't know there weren't any windows down here. Why do you s'pose they've been all been cemented up?" She looked around at the blocked up windows. I thought I saw her shudder.

"Beats me," I answered, glancing over at Norman.

"Hey, don't look at me; I'm no expert. I'm just the local delivery boy," he said. "But Amanda's right. What do you say we get out of here and head someplace where there's some daylight? This place gives me the creeps too."

We put out the lights and hastily vacated the basement. A minute or two later we were outside contemplating our next maneuver. We huddled together on the kitchen door-stoop like crows on a wire looking out across the rear lawn. Norman flipped the newly found key into the air, nonchalantly, at various intervals and caught it deftly with his right hand each time it came back down. He tossed it once again and I saw the look of surprise on his face when the key vanished.

"My, now what's this for?" The unexpected sound of Aunt Julia's voice directly behind me made the three of us jump. Craning our necks, we turned around and stared up at her imposing figure.

"Aunt Julia, I...I didn't hear you," I stammered.

"Of course you didn't. That's because I didn't want you to," she said with a trace of a grin. "If I'd wanted you to hear me you would have." I watched her hold up the key she'd snatched out of mid-air, and examine it in the afternoon sunlight.

"Well, aren't you going to introduce me to your friends, Eddie?" she prodded, simultaneously turning the key over and over, contemplating its use.

"Oh...sorry." I jumped to my feet. Norman and Amanda did the same. "This is Amanda Davenport and this is Norman Tate," I offered awkwardly. "Uh...Amanda...Norman, this is my Aunt Julia Sutton."

"How do, ma'am," Norman mumbled, extending his hand and sheepishly looking downward. Aunt Julia shook it. I could tell by the look on her face that Norman's lack of poise was noted.

"Hello ma'am," Amanda said politely. She curtsied slightly, looking Aunt Julia firmly in the eye. Contrary to Norman, the well-executed greeting scored big points.

"Well, how do you *do*?" Aunt Julia flashed her dazzling smile then unexpectedly sat down on the back stoop, smoothing the line of her dress in the process. "Why don't the three of you sit here next to me and tell me what you've been up to...and what you think this key is for. It's a very unusual design, isn't it?"

She gestured for us to join her by patting the concrete stoop with her hand, as if it were a fluffy seat cushion. Feeling obligated, I sat down beside her. Amanda sat down next to me, and Norman haltingly lowered himself onto the stoop next to Amanda. I could smell the perfume Aunt Julia always wore—an overpowering scent of lilacs. I never liked it.

"We don't know what the key is for," I said flatly. "We found it in the basement a few minutes ago while we were exploring. It doesn't fit any of the locks down there."

Aunt Julia's eyes narrowed. "In the basement you say. That's interesting. Well, you won't mind if I hang onto this then will you? I'll give it to your father and see if he knows what it might be for." We watched as she slipped the key into the pocket of her summer shift. Then, without missing a beat she asked, "So, what did you find in the basement while you were down there—anything interesting?"

"Nothing except that key," Amanda said shifting her glance in the direction of Aunt Julia's pocket. "It's eerie," she added. "All the windows are filled in with concrete. There isn't any outside light coming in at all."

"Where did you find the key?" Aunt Julia asked, dismissing Amanda's observations.

Norman's face lit up. "In the old wine cellar, ma'am," he responded quickly. "Luckily I had my flashlight." Norman pointed proudly to the flashlight dangling from its clip on his belt, the bashfulness demonstrated a few minutes earlier fading. "Eddie spotted it under the bottom shelf in the wine cellar. Kind of interesting it should be there, don't ya think?"

Aunt Julia reached into her pocket and brought the key back out into the late afternoon light.

"Hmm, yes...interesting indeed," she said. 'Odd that it should be lying about in such an old deserted place."

"That's what we thought," Amanda chimed in. "Pretty mysterious, wouldn't you say?"

"Yes, yes, *mysterious* is a better word for it," Aunt Julia agreed then tucked the key back into her pocket. Then with the same suddenness with which she'd opted to invite us to join her on the stoop, she stood up and turned to look at the foundation. Her eyes scanned the mansion's perimeter, studying the neatly blocked up windows. All at once she shuddered.

"Ooh, I've just felt a shiver," she announced, not trying to hide it. Shielding her eyes with her right hand to block the sun, she scanned the ground in a straight line from the basement foundation out across the lawn...and over the wall to the adjoining property of Hammersmith Farm. A few seconds later she breathed a quizzical sigh then turned to face us.

"Well, I dare say you've been quite busy," she affirmed aloud. "You're sure there isn't anything else you saw while you were down in that old crypt of a cellar?," she asked with interest.

I thought about the brief time we'd spent together in the basement and what we'd seen—which didn't amount to much. "No, ma'am, nothing that I can think of," I answered respectfully.

"Just that noisy, sputtering old hot water heater," Amanda added with a shrug.

"Yeah, that was about it," Norman said, throwing in his two cents. "The place was creepy. We couldn't wait to get out of there."

A nod from Aunt Julia signaled satisfaction. I realized she'd been interrogating us…and more than that, I recognized for the first time, that she had her own agenda. All at once, she turned her head in the direction of the old greenhouse looking solitary and isolated in the afternoon shadows on the lush back lawn. Then, in the brief moment it took for us to shift our gaze in that direction and pause to take a momentary glance, Aunt Julia was gone—vanished with the same stealth-like suddenness with which she'd appeared.

Today, as a middle-aged adult recalling her cagey behavior, I've come to realize the relationship I had with my Aunt was approaching an interesting juncture at that time. Often enchanted by the hypnotically psychic charms she possessed, I had begun to understand that Aunt Julia actually had a greater, more self-serving use for her "gifts." I had caught a glimpse beyond the threshold of childish amusement into an adult world of willful and possibly dangerous intention that day.

"Look, I think I've had enough exploring for one afternoon," Norman said through a yawn. "It's getting late and I've got to go to work tomorrow."

"I've had enough too," Amanda echoed, apparently taking in the changing colors of the late afternoon sky. It's going to be dark soon and I don't want to be stuck poking around in some scary, out of the way place when the sun is going down."

I couldn't have been more relieved to hear both of my friends proclaim that they wanted to call it a day. I, too, had experienced enough exploring for one afternoon. And Aunt Julia's behavior had taken me off guard. I needed some time to contemplate what might be behind it.

"All right. Why don't we tackle the attic next...but on another day?" I suggested, purposely seasoning my voice with enthusiasm—enough to ensure my own plans wouldn't get derailed.

"OK, see you soon, Eddie," Amanda said with a smile and a friendly wave as she headed across the lawn towards her bicycle.

"Yeah, see ya, Sutton," Norman said, following her lead.

I stood there in the receding warmth of the late afternoon sun and watched my two new friends amble across the lawn. The flare of a match followed by a puff of smoke signaled that Norman couldn't wait for a cigarette. Amanda launched into a reprimand, and I heard their argumentative banter fade to a hum as they picked up their bikes and walked them towards the wrought iron gates at the foot of the drive. The muffled clatter of the steel latch and creak of the heavy hinges signaled their departure. The freckle-faced redhead and her lanky companion mounted their bicycles, and pedaled out of view.

Well, I thought to myself, exhaling a sigh—a sigh mixed with equal portions of satisfaction and relief—tomorrow is another day!

CHAPTER FOUR

The early morning hours following the previous day's basement exploration started with nothing out of the ordinary. I rose early—around seven o'clock—slipped on some sneakers then headed downstairs in my PJs to eat breakfast with Livingston in the kitchen. Always up and ready before the rest of the family, Livingston had prepared a morning meal of crisp bacon plus his famous scrambled eggs and warm, buttered English muffins. Somehow, eating at the large round oak table in front of the open window surrounded by the friendly informality of the kitchen made the food taste extra good. The aroma of salt air provided added seasoning.

Father, Franny and Elly were nowhere to be seen that morning. Neither was Aunt Julia. Livingston made no mention of them so I figured they were all still sleeping. Although I thought nothing of it at the time, in retrospect, it was unusual for Father to be in bed at that hour. His normal morning routine during this particular summer had been one of rising at dawn and walking to the main gate to pick up the daily paper at the foot of the driveway. It would be no surprise to see him sitting on the front verandah every morning well before seven. Typically, he would be fully dressed with paper and coffee cup in hand grumbling about how "the idiot of a paper boy" had again managed to toss the newspaper into the hydrangea bushes lining the drive beyond the gate.

By the time I had finished my breakfast, I heard the huge grandfather clock in the front reception hall chime. It was one of Elly's newly acquired trophies. Given the early hour, it appeared that I had the distinctly unusual advantage of singly owning what I considered to be the better part of the day. I decided to take advantage of the opportunity and putter around the yard before dressing. It wasn't often in our tumultuous household—especially with Franny and Aunt Julia around—that one had the satisfaction of communing silently with nature on so brilliant a summer morning. In fact, I thought, it would probably only be a short time before Aunt Julia would rise to vaporize the tranquility of the morning by bellowing a greeting to me across the lawn from her bedroom window.

As I stepped out onto the verandah, the enticing scent of sea air mingled with the fragrance of roses from the garden stimulating my senses and quickly obliterating any earlier thoughts of Aunt Julia. Walking around the perimeter of the house, I marveled at the beauty of the geometric flowerbeds so painstakingly maintained by Mr. FitzHugh. A lush carpet of freshly mown grass provided additional aroma and colorful contrast. Bursting rose blossoms in a palette of white, pink, yellow and red merged with the flawless blue of the morning sky to create a spectacular array of color. Nature's canvas was enhanced even further by the backdrop of Narragansett Bay. I watched the gulls circling overhead and followed their movements as they drifted and glided on a swirl of soft ocean air. Observing one of the big white birds landing on the roof of the greenhouse, it suddenly occurred to me that there was no sign of Mr. FitzHugh. Normally he was bustling over the grounds, tilling the flowerbeds and pulling weeds well before seven. The big, spoke-wheeled garden cart he used brimming with tools and bags of fertilizer or peat moss could always be spotted somewhere on the property. And the greenhouse door would typically be propped open to allow him easy access. Interestingly, today, there was no sign of either Mr. FitzHugh...or his garden cart. The door to the greenhouse, however, flopped gently to and fro as intermittent gusts of morning breeze teased it.

I walked slowly towards the corner of the property where the large, turn-of-the-century structure stood. The closer I came to the imposing leaded-glass building with its ornate Victorian architecture, the more my overly active imagination kicked into high gear. The recollection of Mr. FitzHugh's story about being scared nearly to death there on the day of JFK's assassination suddenly materialized in my head. Approaching the greenhouse, I could hear the creak of rusty door-hinges with each sweep of the windblown door. The eerie sound triggered my overly active imagination and I immediately envisioned the ghoulish face of some demon lunging at me as I crossed the threshold.

51

With deliberate caution, I paused for a moment outside. Beyond the swinging door, ample light spilled in through the glassed-roof panes illuminating successive rows of flower seedlings on waist high tables. A broad aisle ran between the tables starting at the front door, and continued straight back to the rear of the greenhouse. Side-aisles branched off at different junctures along the way. The entire view was broken up by what looked to be tallish hemlock bushes in green plastic pots reaching skyward at random points along the aisles. Water pipes fitted with sprinkler heads hung from the overhead roof supports for irrigation purposes.

The bright sunshine streaming through the leaded glass did wonders in dissolving my imagined fears. Feeling more at ease, I reached out my hand and steadied the swinging greenhouse door as it swung by one more time. I looked down at the ground and saw a lone, medium-sized rock lying near the doorjamb. Mr. FitzHugh always used it to prop the door open. Picking it up with both hands, I pushed the wooden screen door back with the weight of my body and wedged the rock solidly against its bottom. Stepping across the threshold and inside, my conjured-up imaginings dissipated.

So this is Mr. FitzHugh's hang-out, I remember thinking. The abundance of flowering plants grabbed my attention as I moved slowly up the main aisle scrutinizing the array. In the rear of the greenhouse, a large, cast-iron wood stove mounted on a concrete slab dominated one corner. No doubt it provided heat on chilly days when the natural light of the sun failed to make its scheduled appearance.

The care and effort that Mr. FitzHugh put into nurturing his family of seedlings seemed evident. Had I not become so mesmerized by the bounty of his hard labor, I might have paid closer attention to where I was walking. Nearing the third aisle that branched off to the left, a section of the greenhouse stocked with Jersey tomatoes on heavily-laden vines attracted my attention. I instinctively headed for the ruby color, but rounding the corner of the aisle where they stood, an object protruding into the pathway caught my left foot. I stumbled, losing my balance and tumbled, spread-eagled, onto the graveled floor. Instinctively, I put my hands out in front of me to break the impact, and found myself wincing as sharp-edged gravel dug deeply into the palms of my hands. My immediate reaction was to look around to see if anyone had witnessed my clumsiness. The stinging pain in my hands persisted and I propped myself up on my elbows, straining to see what caused my fall. There, directly adjacent to my own foot, I spotted the toe of a black rubber boot. Further examination revealed there was actually a foot in it.

At this point of horrifying realization, my eyes focused on a blood-soaked face lying only inches from my own. Its own lifeless eyes stared back at me from what had to have been an obviously brutal death. The stiffened corpse lay parallel to me on the floor beneath a table containing flats of red and white striped petunias. At first glance, the victim's hair looked to be a reddish brown. However, I quickly realized, to my added horror, that blood from a deep gash in the top of the victim's head had actually saturated a healthy cropping of what originally appeared to be white hair. The matted, congealed mass shone rich auburn. Only then did it dawn on me that the lifeless body lying next to me was Mr. FitzHugh. My eyes bulged.

I tried to yell, but couldn't utter a sound. My tongue and throat felt dry and constricted. Only a small, barely audible squeak eked out through my trembling lips. Then mercifully, I mustered all of my petrified strength and managed to force sound up through my diaphragm. A loud, meaningless "Arrrrrrgggggggghhhhh!" was all that came out. Then, it seemed as if by magic, I suddenly overcame the paralyzing fear holding me. I scrambled to my feet, propelling myself into the yard shouting as I went. Seconds later, Livingston appeared from around the corner of the house bounding toward me in full stride. I saw Aunt Julia throw open her bedroom window and peer at me from across the lawn through what looked to be a confused veil of morning drowsiness. Moments afterward, Father and Elly staggered out into the morning sunlight in their bathrobes and pajamas, their sleep-sensitized eyes squinting under the sun.

Curiously, Father wore a pink, fur-trimmed satin robe that belonged to Elly. I watched him hastily strip it off and throw it across the arms of a rocker on the verandah. I gathered he must have grabbed it by mistake in his half-wakened stupor.

"Eddie, Eddie, what in God's name is the matter?" Father hollered as he and Elly broke into a gait and hustled towards the greenhouse. Livingston got to me first. He clasped my shoulders with his strong hands. "What's wrong, Eddie?" he said in that soothing and reassuring voice of his that always put me at ease.

"In there...in there," I stammered, gasping for breath and pointing to the open greenhouse door. "It's Mr. FitzHugh."

Livingston disappeared cautiously through the greenhouse door as Father and Elly reached my side.

"In there," I panted again. "It's Mr. FitzHugh. Cripes, I think he's dead."

Father's eyes widened. Elly gasped. "What? Eddie, if this is your imagination at work again...," Elly started to say.

"It's nobody's imagination," Livingston shouted, cutting her off from inside the greenhouse door. "It's FitzHugh all right...and he's quite dead. 'Been dead for some time I'd say by the look of things."

Father put his arm around my trembling shoulder. "Eddie, son, are you okay?," he asked compassionately, drawing me to his side. "Come back into the house with Elly and me, son, while I call the police."

He turned and called to Livingston. "Livingston, you'd better stay out here by the greenhouse until the police arrive." Livingston nodded and waved a silent acknowledgement.

Heading back in the direction of the house, I saw Aunt Julia appear through the front door tying the sash of a long, oriental print bathrobe around her waist. She looked confused.

"Why whatever...?" was all she managed to mutter before Father impatiently cut her off.

"It's FitzHugh," he said curtly. "Eddie found him in the greenhouse."

"Is he all right?" Aunt Julia inquired.

"Afraid not," Father snapped. "I've got to call the police."

Within less than five minutes after Father's phone call, a squad car roared up the driveway with lights flashing and sirens wailing. A second police cruiser and an ambulance followed. Captain Karl stepped out onto the gravel drive as Father, Elly, Aunt Julia and I walked down the verandah steps. A few seconds later, five policemen and four ambulance attendants were scurrying towards Livingston who waved them on from the greenhouse.

"Stay here with Elly and Julia," Father ordered as he hurried after the cortege.

The three of us stood on the driveway in silence watching the rescuers gallop across the dew-covered grass toward Livingston.

"Where's Franny?" I asked. It occurred to me that none of us had seen her during the excitement. Elly looked at me blankly.

"I don't know," she answered. "I suppose she's still in bed."

"I doubt even the wail of these sirens would awaken her," Aunt Julia added. "That child sleeps like a rock."

Nodding and knowing they were probably right, I hesitated. "I'm going up to see—just to make sure she's okay," I decided anyway.

"Fine, suit yourself. Only you'd better come right back down," Elly cautioned—the warning issued more from a position of control than concern, I sensed. Heading off without bothering to reply, I scurried through the front door then up to the second floor, taking the stairs two at time. When I reached the closed door to Franny's bedroom, I stopped outside to listen quietly for a few seconds. There was no indication of any activity. Quietly, I turned the doorknob

55

pushing the door open a bit. Peering into the shade-drawn darkness, I could see Franny's form on the bed. She was breathing the sounds of a deep, comfortable sleep.

Good, I thought. At least she's well and accounted for. I started to leave, pulling the door closed all but about an inch when something on the floor in front of her bed caught my eye. It looked like some empty boxes of *Chiclets* with their contents strewn around on the rug. I inched the door back open to get a better look. Morning sunlight seeping in around the edges of the window shades provided visibility. I moved in closer. They were *Chiclets* all right—only they weren't scattered around. My stomach dipped at the sight. Carefully arranged at the foot of her bed were what looked to be the contents of three packages of the white, candy-coated chewing gum. The fact that Franny hadn't eaten them was odd enough itself. I'd never known a full box of *Chiclets* to survive in her presence for more than a few minutes. What was more extraordinary was that they formed the letters of a name: *Ollie*. I instantly thought of Mr. FitzHugh's reference to Ollie Merriweather—the builder's kid who went missing years ago. Mr. FitzHugh had mentioned Ollie the very first day we'd met him at Annandale Farm.

I stood there transfixed. What amazed me most was the fact that Franny had arranged the gum the way she did...because she didn't know how to spell! At this early stage of her mentally challenged life, she hadn't yet mastered the craft.

Glancing in her direction, I saw no sign she was stirring. I knelt down and picked up the *chiclets*, one-by-one, then deposited them in a pile on top of Franny's dresser. I could have simply left them there I suppose, but for some strange reason something told me to remove the evidence. Slipping slowly out the door, I pulled it closed behind me and headed back downstairs.

Later, as I stood near the verandah next to Father, Elly, Aunt Julia and Livingston, we watched in a semi-hypnotic state as the retreating foray of flashing red lights faded from view beyond the gates. The ambulance carrying Mr. FitzHugh's body trailed the tiny motorcade.

Before his departure, in the process of launching an investigation, Captain Karl had interrogated me quite thoroughly. Throughout his questioning, he was considerate of both my age and the circumstances. He demonstrated equal consideration when dealing with Father, Elly, Livingston and Aunt Julia. He wanted to know a number of things: Had we heard or seen anything out of the ordinary that morning or the previous day? How long had we known Mr. FitzHugh? Had Mr. FitzHugh ever said anything to indicate someone might be holding a grudge against him? Did we know about Mr. FitzHugh's heart attack in the greenhouse nearly a year earlier— on the day of JFK's assassination? And lastly, did we know about the dubious reputation surrounding the house and property in general?

Father got annoyed at Captain Karl's innuendo around the house and property. He also wasn't too thrilled to hear reference made to Mr. FitzHugh's near-death experience again...especially since he had made it a point to downplay its occurrence on the afternoon of our initial arrival. In fact, Father had returned immediately following his goodbye to Mr. FitzHugh that day to tell Elly and me we should keep quiet and say nothing about any of the "ridiculous nonsense" Mr. FitzHugh had dredged up.

Needless to say, Father did well at controlling himself when Captain Karl raised the issues about the house—a response for which I was quite grateful since I had already unwittingly tampered with the murder weapon. Had I been more observant, I would have noticed that the rock I wedged against the greenhouse door had blood and scalp fragments on it when I picked it up and used it as a doorstop. Captain Karl wasted no time identifying it as the murder weapon. The fact that I had handled it didn't make him very happy. I imagined, for a moment, that the thought crossed his mind whether I might have had reason to kill Mr. FitzHugh. But looking back, the notion only gave evidence to how active an adolescent imagination I actually possessed. Captain Karl never did ask any questions indicating I was a suspect.

The scream of sirens that day, gradually faded away to a

whisper and became inaudible. Soon, I found myself pondering the mysterious *Chiclet* chewing gum message spelling out the name *Ollie* on Franny's bedroom floor. I couldn't help thinking there was something in it connected to Mr. FitzHugh's death. But I said nothing to anyone. Who could have possibly put the message there? The only people around when Mr. FitzHugh first made mention of Ollie Merriweather were Father, Elly and me. I certainly hadn't done it; and the thought of Elly or Father going through such an exercise—especially after Father made it a point to avoid even discussing the subject of ghosts and hauntings—seemed ridiculous. Had one of them said something to Livingston? Even if they had, suspecting that Livingston would stoop to such a tactic appeared equally ludicrous. It had to be somebody else—but who?

"I suggest we all take a deep breath and get dressed," Father announced to us all, now that the excitement had died down. "There's been more than enough commotion here for one day!"

So with that, we all climbed the front steps leading up to the verandah. I decided to take a shower, get dressed, then talk to Franny about the message I'd found at the foot of her bed. Maybe she'd seen something that would give me a clue as to how it got there.

Once through the front door, I headed up the grand staircase to my bedroom. Father, Elly, and Aunt Julia followed, and Livingston went straight to the kitchen. During the ascent to my room, I heard Elly whispering nervously to Father about having the locks changed on the doors...and perhaps looking into a security system. Aunt Julia seemed unusually quiet. In fact, I didn't hear her utter a single word.

"I'll look in on Franny again," I volunteered.

"That would be good, son," Father acknowledged.

Within 15 minutes, I had showered and dressed then hurried down the hall to Franny's room. After a quick rap on the door with my knuckles, the familiar sound of Franny's nasally staccato voice bade me enter. Still wearing her nightgown, she sat on the floor in front of her bed playing with some dolls. Her jaw twitched away as she worked on a wad of *Chiclets*. There was no doubt in my mind that the gum she was chewing came from the stock used to spell out the name *Ollie*. Other pieces of gum were scattered, haphazardly, around her on the floor. The squashed remains of some of the empty boxes poked out from underneath her backside as if they were trying to wiggle out and escape.

"Franny, where did you get that gum you're chewing?" I asked.

"Aunt Julia gave it to me," she answered.

"When?"

"When she came."

"You mean the day she got here?"

"Yes."

"Have you been playing with them?." I wanted to know.

"I've been eating them," she admitted innocently.

"Yes, I know you've been eating them...but were you making designs with them on the floor, too?"

"Uh huh." There was no hint of uncertainty in her reply.

But how could Franny know how to spell? The mystery persisted. Franny said that Aunt Julia had given her the *Chiclets*—on the day of her arrival at Annandale Farm.

Hmmm, I thought to myself. No way! If Franny had *Chiclets* in her possession, regardless of the quantity, there was no way they'd last more than a few hours—let alone a period of days. She had to have gotten them more recently.

"Franny, I want you to think for a minute. Where did you get those *Chiclets*? I know you didn't get them from Aunt Julia on the day she arrived."

Franny looked me blankly in the eye. "Yes, I did," she insisted. "Aunt Julia gave them to me and said they're mine...even though she took them back afterwards. She said I'd have to come to her and ask her for some whenever I wanted them."

"Aha," I said nodding my head. "I see. Did you ask her for them this morning?"

"No, I didn't."

"Well then how did you get them?"

"I went to her room late last night to ask her—only she wasn't there. Her room was empty, but I went in anyway and took them." Another innocent confession.

"I see," is all I said.

That solved part of the mystery—the *Chiclet* part—how they came to be in the house. But how they came to be in Franny's bedroom spelling out the word *Ollie* on the floor at the foot of her bed still remained a question. So did Aunt Julia's whereabouts around the time it happened. Where was she, if she wasn't in her room, when Franny pilfered the *Chiclets*? And could Aunt Julia have known about Ollie Merriweather? But then again, Aunt Julia did have a gift of the psychic. It appeared as if I had a lot more detective work on my hands than I'd imagined...and I knew I hadn't imagined anything that had taken place that day.

CHAPTER FIVE

The town buzzed with talk of Mr. FitzHugh's murder while the newspapers provided some intrusive coverage of the crime. Pictures of Mr. FitzHugh, Annandale Farm, and the now infamous greenhouse loomed at readers from the front pages of the *Providence Journal*. Some write-ups either alluded to, or recounted the story of, Mr. FitzHugh's near-death the year before in the same place.

"To date," the papers said, "no suspects have been identified...but the motive behind the killing appears to be robbery."

Mr. FitzHugh's wallet had been taken, as well as a ring and the wristwatch he always wore. Adding to the melodrama, Mr. FitzHugh's sister, Belle Pierce, suffered a stroke shortly after being notified of her brother's murder. When I heard the news, I couldn't help remembering the elderly, refined lady I'd observed in Davenport's grocery store a short time ago, and how she differed so in style and appearance from her down-to-earth brother.

Father and Elly grew increasingly irritated at the clusters of reporters and gawkers gathering daily on Ridge Road for a peek through the main gate at the crime scene. Livingston fastened *No Trespassing* signs onto the wrought-iron grille-work and secured the gate-handles with a heavy-duty padlock. For a period of several days, whenever we drove through the gates, flashbulbs would pop and onlookers would point rudely at the Bentley and its occupants. We kept the top up and the windows tightly closed until we were well out of range of the commotion.

The gruesome discovery I'd made presented another challenge for me. I had trouble getting to sleep at night. The distorted, bloodied image of Mr. FitzHugh's face haunted me whenever I closed my eyes. Father, Elly, and Aunt Julia considerately avoided conversation about the matter, while Franny, understandably, was oblivious to the entire event. The only person who provided any solace was Livingston—the lone household member in whom I felt genuinely comfortable confiding my innermost feelings. But it had been that way ever since my mother's death.

As the days following the murder ticked by, I noticed a shift in my feelings. Curiosity began getting the better of me. It may have been the growing mystery around Mr. FitzHugh's death that rekindled my interest in finding out more about Annandale Farm, but in any case, I found myself making plans one day to meet Amanda and Norman at the Newport Historical Society to do some investigative research. On that particular morning, Livingston drove Elly, Franny and me into town for another round of shopping, while Father and Aunt Julia went fishing off Annandale Farm's jetty. They had thought themselves clever using the promise of ice cream at Cote Pharmacy to goad Franny and me into tagging along, but I already had my own agenda. I made it a point to tell Elly that I wanted to be dropped off at Washington Square to see what the coming attractions were at the Strand...and to just walk around downtown on my own for a while. It all came off without a hitch, with Livingston dropping me off on Touro Street in front of the Strand Theater. I agreed to meet Elly and Livingston at Cote's in an hour and a half's time. Livingston, who knew where I was actually headed, winked at me as I waved goodbye from the curb.

When I arrived at the Historical Society, Amanda and Norman were already sitting on the front steps waiting for me. The Historical Society occupied an old brick, Federal Colonial building on Touro Street only a little way up from the Strand. Perched on a hill between Touro Synagogue and the First Church of Christ Scientist, it looked rather austere. I climbed up the steps to greet my friends. Following a brief caucus, Amanda timidly opened the front door a bit and the three of us squeezed through the narrow space...as if doing so would somehow minimize our being noticed. A prim looking, middle-aged woman peered at us over the frames of half-reading glasses from the solitary quiet of a cluttered desk near the foyer.

"You children want anything particular?," she wanted to know.

"We'd like to see what information you've got on Annandale Farm," I answered bravely.

She sat there looking at us in silence for a moment or two as if she hadn't heard a word I'd said.

"Oh, Annandale Farm," she finally twittered, irritated. "I suppose you kids are all stirred up about that murder over there. Well, just about anything and everything you'd ever want to know about Annandale Farm is upstairs." She pointed to a sharply angled mahogany staircase near the foyer, going up to the second floor.

"Just make sure you're careful about how you handle those old books and documents," she ordered in a drill-sergeant-like tone.

"Yes, ma'am," I mumbled back respectfully as the three of us shuffled towards the staircase. The old risers creaked under foot as we climbed the stairs leading to a large, open research room lined with rows of floor-to-ceiling bookcases. Windows running lengthwise in the back of the room let in plenty of light. The bookshelves stood perpendicular to the windows, and in the foreground there were four large reading tables available for spreading out materials.

The three of us stood there feeling a bit intimidated by overstuffed shelves crammed with books and volumes of historical documentation. It was Amanda who spotted three enormous, black scrapbooks sitting on the tabletop nearest to us. A worn but readable white label pasted on the front of one of them read: *Historic Mansions of Newport*. There was a clatter of sliding chairs as Norman, Amanda and I quickly settled down to plough through the books. We each grabbed one. The volume I picked up had a label that read: *Mansions of Ocean Drive*.

When I opened the frayed fabric cover, the first thing I saw was an aerial picture of our house and the accompanying headlines of an October 1963 article in the *Fall River Herald News*. The article read:

"SUMMER WHITE HOUSE RENT REPORTED $2000.00-a-MONTH: NEWPORT, (UPI)—President and Mrs. Kennedy's rented

Newport estate, Annandale Farm, will be used next July and August as the summer White House. Senator Claiborne Pell, D-R.I., said the Kennedy's own home at Hyannisport would be occupied during the summer by the President's brother-in-law and sister, Mr. and Mrs. Sargent Shriver. The leased property here is on Ridge Road, a part of Ocean Drive, and adjoins Hammersmith Farm, the estate of Mrs. Kennedy's mother and stepfather, Mr. and Mrs. Hugh D. Auchincloss."

I would have read further except for the fact that we hadn't noticed the presence of another attendant sitting quietly at a desk in the back of the upstairs research room. The creak of old floorboards broke my concentration and announced her whereabouts. I looked up to see a plump, elderly woman hobbling towards us on a cane. With a number of lumbering strides, she reached the end of our table then stood there scowling down at us, her brass handled walking stick planted firmly on the floor by her right foot. I recognized the blue tinted hair and the crescent-shaped glasses on the bridge of her nose. It was none other than the infamous Mabel *Keating*.

I forced myself to smile and managed to squeak out a polite "Hello." Norman and Amanda, who were caught up with the scrapbooks they were reading, looked up just in time to see Mabel respond with a half-hearted grunt. Amanda stifled a gasp and Norman froze. I saw his eyes open wide in a petrified stare that clearly said: What's *she* doing here?

"What are you kids looking for?," Mabel grumbled at us then kept on talking. "I was going to put those books away *again*, but Lord knows every time I do somebody else comes wandering in asking to see them. I'm only here two Thursdays a month, and right now the way things are going, I'm beginning to think that's two Thursdays too often."

Her eyes widened when a photograph of Annandale Farm suddenly caught her eye, and she quickly realized what we were doing there.

"Say, that's a *bad* place," she warned. "I'd stay away from there if I were you."

I hesitated for a moment, wondering if I should tell her who I was and decided to take the plunge.

"I live there," I said.

She looked at me incredulously.

Gambling on the friendly goodbye Franny had elicited from her on the day of the ill-fated vanilla fudge twirl incident, I introduced myself. "My name is Eddie Sutton," I said. "These are my friends Amanda Davenport and Norman Tate."

Mabel didn't respond. Amanda and Norman squirmed in their seats.

"My sister Franny is the one who dropped ice cream on your foot in front of Cote Pharmacy a while ago."

"Glory be!" she snorted in recognition. "That little girl's your sister?" I watched Mabel's face transform a bit as she made the connection. It morphed, first, to a look of surprise bordering on delight then fear mixed with anger. "That child shouldn't be in that house...and for that matter, neither should you," she fumed. "Why, that evil old mansion should have been torn down years ago." I could see the grip of her meaty hand tighten on the handle of her walking stick as she spoke. "Simon should never have built it in the first place. That's when all the trouble began," she carried on. The knuckles on her hand started turning white as she squeezed the walking stick handle all the more tightly. "Don't think I haven't thought about putting a torch to that place myself. The only thing that stops me is the fact that they'd lock me away somewhere for sure if I did."

Out of the corner of my eye, I could see Amanda pivot the scrapbook she was reading so Mabel could get a look at it. By now, I wasn't sure if we'd all be better off just getting up and leaving...but before I could figure out the answer, Amanda made a bold move. "Does this have anything to do with what you're talking about?" she asked bravely. The page of the scrapbook in front of her was opened to a newspaper article dated August 25th 1940. Its headline glared up at us: *"LOCAL TRADESMAN DIES IN FREAK ACCIDENT AT ANNANDALE FARM—OSWALD KEATING ELECTROCUTED"*

Mabel stood frozen, staring at the words in front of her while we sat for what felt like hours. Her chin trembled slightly and it looked like her eyes might be filling up.

"That happened over 20 years ago and I remember it as if it were yesterday," she said in a near-whisper, breaking the awkward silence.

Amanda was gaining confidence about sharing what she'd learned from the yellow-edged news clipping. "It says here that Oswald Keating's only surviving relative was his wife, Mabel," Amanda added boldly, parroting aloud what she'd read in the newspaper text.

Heaving a resigned sigh, Mabel reached for a nearby chair and dragged it up next to us at the table. Slowly, with what appeared to be considerable pain, she eased herself into its seat, leaning on her walking stick to ease the effort. All at once, it seemed like the impenetrable barrier of icy hostility behind which she'd hidden for decades suddenly began to melt. She scanned the room making certain we were still alone then leaned in closely towards us, speaking in a whisper.

"You kids don't know the half of what's gone on at that house," Mabel said in a secretive voice. "Oswald Keating was my husband all right. And to this day nobody can convince me that what happened to him at Annandale Farm was any accident."

She glanced around the room suspiciously a second time before continuing. "My Oswald happened to be one of the best electricians of his day—that's why my brother Simon always used him whenever he built a new house here in Newport. Oswald did all the electrical work at Annandale Farm. He knew every fuse and wire in that place inside-out." She punctuated her statement by rapping her walking stick firmly on the floor.

"He went up there that day to do some work for Milton Pierce, one of the owners of the house...only poor Oswald never came back."

Looking closely into the vibrant green of Mabel's eyes, I saw what looked to be a film of tears glimmer ever so faintly. And the more she spoke about her late husband, the more those eyes flickered with a youthful glint—a sparkle belying the crow's-feet and deeply etched lines that spoke her true years. In that instant, it seemed like the *real* Mabel Keating lived behind a mask—one that could be shed when the moment was right to reveal a youthful masquerader untouched by the passage of time and distortions of anger.

As quickly as it came, however, the glow vanished—replaced by the bitter mask of resentment and contempt more familiar to the few she encountered in the course of her reclusive existence.

"I think my Oswald stumbled onto something when he was up there and saw more than he should have," Mabel said acidly, once again punctuating her comment with a rap of her cane. "Somebody just plain did him in. That's what I think."

She paused for a moment's reflection then launched into an angry tirade about Milton Pierce and his wife, fueled by rekindled memories. "I never did trust that Milton Pierce," she said contemptuously. "He was a real shady sort—one of those New York city-slicker types. And that gold-digging wife of his, why she..."

Norman had been sitting quietly fanning through the pages of the scrapbook in front of him when he interrupted without thinking. "Why would someone do him in? What could your husband have possibly seen at Annandale Farm that would make somebody want to kill him?," he blurted out innocently.

Mabel's eyes bulged making it obvious she was more than annoyed at Norman's intrusion. She wasn't used to being interrupted by anyone, let alone an inquisitive teenager; plus the questions Norman unthinkingly posed hit close to home. She turned and made a visual sweep of the room to confirm, yet again, that nobody had been eavesdropping then narrowed her eyes down on us through the crescent-shaped lenses of her glasses. It was something that told us our conversation was over and that we'd clearly crossed a line we shouldn't have.

"That's enough. I've told you kids too damn much already," she blustered, rapping her walking stick on the floor. She locked her piercing green eyes on mine. "Just heed what I'm telling you, son," she warned. "Be on your guard day and night at that house—especially as far as that sister of yours is concerned." Then she paused, momentarily, perhaps having thoughts that she might be frightening us. "Lord knows I'm not trying to scare you," she said, the sharpness in her voice waning. "Just trust me when I tell you there's more going on at that house than meets the eye...but God knows you've probably figured that out by now," she said, her eyes flickering at this sudden realization.

The banjo clock on the adjacent wall suddenly struck noon.

"Cripes, I'm due to meet Elly at Cote Pharmacy," I blurted out realizing the lateness of the hour. "C'mon, we've gotta go. 'Bye, Mrs. Keating...and thanks!" I said meaning it.

Mabel sat in her chair, watching the three of us scramble to our feet—the racket of chair legs on well worn floorboards announcing our movement. As we bolted for the stairs, all I could think about was the lecture I'd no doubt get from Elly if I arrived too late.

"Mind what I told you," Mabel hollered after us. "And make sure you don't tell a soul what I said...!" Her voice trailed off into silence. I caught a final glimpse of her as I glanced back over my shoulder while we pounded down the stairs. Back out on the front steps, I bade a hurried goodbye to Norman and Amanda then scurried across town to meet Elly and Livingston. On my way, I reflected on the findings we'd made that day and puzzled over the connection they might have to Mr. FitzHugh's death. Whatever else happened, I was determined I wouldn't let my imagination and the emotional ranting of an embittered and lonely widow like Mabel Keating distort the truth.

Little did I know, that day, how ineffably true Mabel Keating's warning would turn out to be.

CHAPTER SIX

After leaving the Newport Historical Society, I arrived at Cote Pharmacy ten minutes late. Luckily, Elly didn't seem too upset. She, Livingston and Franny were already seated at the counter waiting for me. As usual, Elly looked beautiful. She could wear a rag and make it look like a designer gown. I felt a twinge of jealousy watching the counterman at Cotes eye her shapely figure as he whipped up a vanilla frappe from the other side of the counter.

Before I had gotten there, I'd already made up my mind to tell Elly the simple truth about my morning—or at least a slightly abbreviated version of it...the worst offense being an omission of my morning encounter with Mabel Keating. Over lunch, I shared that I had walked through Washington Square after checking out coming attractions at the Strand—something that had taken about five seconds in my hurry by the theater. Then, I said in further adjusted truth, that I had meandered my way up Touro Street towards the Historical Society where I ran into Amanda and Norman. Curious to know more about our old house, I explained, we poked our heads inside the Society's door on a whim, and one thing led to another. Before we knew it, we were engrossed with a bunch of old books about the Newport mansions and Annandale Farm. We had simply lost track of time.

Not only did Elly accept my fictionally enhanced explanation for being tardy without question...she couldn't have been more pleased. The idea that my friends and I would engage in something constructively educational on our own without being asked delighted her—especially if it involved some of Newport's Gilded-age mansions. My story earned an approving wink from Livingston.

"So what did you learn?," Elly asked enthusiastically biting off a mouthful of her egg salad sandwich.

"Well, did you know our house was rented to President Kennedy and Mrs. Kennedy to use as the summer White House?" I answered with a major leading question.

She stopped chewing, put her sandwich back on her plate and sat there staring blankly at the soda fountain in front of her for a few seconds.

"Yes...yes, I did," she finally answered, regaining her voice and in the process exchanging a brief glance with Livingston. He didn't even blink.

"That's one of the reasons I'm eager to meet Mrs. Auchincloss next door," Elly enthused a bit overdramatically, I thought. "She's Jackie Kennedy's mother, you know. The mutual connection with Annandale Farm makes for a bit of a social entrée...although the unpleasant circumstances leading up to our getting the house does make things a bit awkward," she added. "You know; had President Kennedy not been assassinated..."

"Oh, I see. Nobody's ever mentioned the connection with the President before." I said, somewhat surprised by my own bravado at having asked the question so pointedly, and even more surprised by Elly's direct, albeit what I felt to be, semi-contrived response. Her evasiveness made me feel less guilty about my own truth-bending. I decided to say nothing and see if awkwardness spawned by silence might work in my favor. It did.

"No...no...we didn't want to play that angle up," she continued, feeling obliged to fill the void. "We thought it best to keep that aspect quiet...that is your Aunt Julia did. When the house first came on the market, Julia was afraid that notoriety associated with the Kennedys and their choice of the property as a summer retreat might drive the price up—you know—increase the number of people bidding on the estate." She paused a moment, reflectively. "Astonishingly, though, it didn't," she added with what looked to be genuine surprise.

I was just about to ask why, when Elly looked at her watch.

"Well, it's getting late. I want to make one extra stop before we head for home. I've got a little something in mind that ought to tie in nicely with your visit to the Historical Society, Eddie. Livingston, you know where we're going," she said to him, making an obvious effort to change the subject and quickly move on.

Livingston nodded. "Yes, ma'am," he answered respectfully. "I suggest we hurry along if we're going to cover the ground you'd like to before dinner." He gave no hint of complicity in either the withholding of information about Annandale Farm's past, or the "one extra stop" Elly had planned for us that afternoon. We gulped down what was left of our sandwiches and ordered ice cream cones on the way out. I saw Livingston's eyes widen a bit when Franny asked for vanilla-fudge-twirl. While Elly settled the bill at the counter, I quickly grabbed six boxes of *Chiclets* out of the candy display in front of the nearby cash register and paid for them. A few minutes later, we were driving along Bellevue Avenue and I had a sinking feeling in the pit of my stomach about where we might be headed.

Bellevue Avenue enjoys a notable history in that it serves as home to the majority of Gilded-age mansions that helped put Newport, Rhode Island on the map. Marble House, Rosecliff, Belcourt Castle, and Beechwood, to name a few, all occupy prestigious places along this opulent avenue where American royalty the likes of the Vanderbilts and Astors built summer "cottages" emulating the grand chateaux and palaces of Europe.

Just as I feared, that "one extra stop" Elly insisted on making happened to be at The Breakers—Newport's most renowned, seventy-room summer cottage. Not until Livingston turned onto Ruggles Avenue and headed towards Ochre Point were my fears realized.

The Breakers, like many of these once privately owned estates, had been opened to the public by the Preservation Society of Newport County. During the course of our 1964 summer, Elly made full use of the mansion's accessibility for gleaning new ideas on decorating our own house. On this particular afternoon, she had no qualms about dragging Franny and me along with her while she made notes about the mansion's décor on a clipboard. Much to my surprise, even Livingston opted to tour The Breakers. I listened half-heartedly as he read aloud tidbits pertaining to the mansion's history from a brochure.

"In 1895, Cornelius Vanderbilt II commissioned architect Richard Morris Hunt to build this Italian Renaissance-style house situated on a 13 acre site overlooking a rock-strewn section of Atlantic coast. It was here, from the crashing waves and pounding surf breaking over the boulders, that this magnificent, cliff-side house derived its name," Livingston expounded.

My mind wandered as he read and Elly took notes. Franny held Livingston's hand and was surprisingly tolerant the entire time we were there. I'd given her a box of Chiclets to keep her occupied. We drifted through this gilded museum that, in comparison, made Annandale Farm look like a modest guesthouse. I kept thinking about Mabel Keating and the find we'd made that morning at the Newport Historical Society. We would have to go back there again. Now that we knew Mabel volunteered there two Thursdays a month we could time our next visit to coincide with one of her duty days. Mabel knew far more than the history records told. What mysterious events of long ago could be so powerful that their lingering aftereffects still posed a threat more than sixty years later?

With Mr. FitzHugh's murder fresh on my mind, I wondered how his death and other past events related to the strange happenings we encountered on that first day of our arrival: Mr. FitzHugh's warnings about the house being haunted; the flash of bright light from the third floor room with the porthole window, and Franny's strange behavior...especially in that third floor room.

What made Franny shriek when I opened the window? My back had been towards her at the time. Perhaps I hadn't noticed something with my back turned, I thought. The more I hashed it over in my head, the more it made sense to go back to that room and to take Franny with me...as much as I didn't want to. Whenever we did, we'd have to go before sunset...not for any other reason than my own fears about going in the dark.

It seemed like we were at The Breakers long enough to qualify as residents. Franny had polished off two boxes of Chiclets, and Elly's clipboard was overflowing with notes when we finally left. By the time Livingston steered the Bentley through the front gates at Annandale Farm, the sun had slipped considerably lower in the afternoon sky. We had driven home along Ocean Drive following the jagged coastline that continued beyond the end of Bellevue Avenue. Fortunately, the gawkers and photographers had already called it a day, no doubt seeking solace in the local restaurants or bars in town. I hoped the excitement surrounding Mr. FitzHugh's death was finally starting to die down.

Once he'd parked the car and carried in Elly's parcels, Livingston fixed dinner and served Father, Elly and Aunt Julia cocktails on the verandah. While they were occupied, I managed to round up Franny and drag her along with me to the gloomy back staircase leading up to the third floor. She balked initially at going up, but relented when I bribed her with another box of the *Chiclets* I'd picked up at Cote Pharmacy. It wasn't long before the two of us stood on the second floor landing looking up the stairs. Plenty of daylight still shone through the small window on the landing, but even so, I flipped on the wall switch, illuminating the feeble sconces dotting the stairwell walls. Grabbing Franny by the hand, the two of us began the remainder of our ascent.

At the top of the stairs, the angle of the late afternoon sun etched spooky, elongated shadows across the walls and floors, and the floorboards creaked under our feet—things I didn't remember from the first time we made the climb. I could feel my heartbeat picking up while we shuffled slowly and deliberately down the long hallway towards the door at the end of the corridor. I paused to glance at Franny. She had a look of peaceful contentment on her face, her mouth stuffed to the brim with chewing gum. All seemed well. When we reached our destination, I hesitated for a bit before working up enough nerve to reach, timidly, for the doorknob. A twist, a quick push of the door, and we were in. This time, no sunlight streamed through the porthole window. Instead, we stood in the purple-hued quiet of the late afternoon. I studied Franny's face closely. No reaction. Inching our way towards the circular window, I haltingly reached for the hasp and unlatched it. My eyes never left Franny's face as I did. She was looking directly at the window, but showed no reaction. Slowly, I began pivoting it outward from the bottom in small, purposeful increments about an inch at a time. Still nothing. A little more. No reaction. More. Nothing. Once more…

That did it. Franny's face twisted into a mask of terror. She shrieked. I looked at the window noting nothing unusual then quickly scanned every inch of the empty room. From where I stood, I couldn't see anything that would frighten her.

"Franny, what's the matter? What are you scared of?," I asked.

In a flash, she turned and bolted for the door.

"What's the matter, Franny? There's nothing there."

I pulled out a box of *Chiclets* again and waved it at her. No good. She kept yelling and tried to get around me. As fast as my fingers could move, I opened the cardboard box and shook a piece of gum out into the palm of my hand. I popped it into Franny's mouth and it worked like a sedative. All at once, she stopped struggling. Gingerly, I reached behind her and closed the door. She leaned her back against it. Chewing voraciously, she grabbed the box of *Chiclets* then slid slowly to the floor where she sat, Indian-style—legs crossed in front of her.

Seizing the moment, I quickly positioned myself where Franny had been standing and examined the angled window. I even crouched down so my head was at the same level as Franny's when she had screamed. Nothing unusual; only a reflected view in the windowpanes of the concrete steps and the pillared portico gracing the mansion's oceanfront entranceway below.

"Cripes, Franny, I don't get it. What's the…"

I stopped abruptly and watched Franny shake the remaining

contents of the *Chiclets* box out onto the floor. A second later, her hands were moving deftly—arranging the enameled-white pieces of chewing gum into letters.

She crafted an "O" first. A few seconds later, she constructed a "D." Part of what looked like an "S" emerged next, but she'd run out of gum. I yanked another box from my pocket and hastily shook the contents out onto the floor. Concentrating intently, she finished the "S."

"O-D-S." What did "*ODS*" mean?

Pausing for a moment she studied what she'd written. Then using the stubby thumb and index finger of her right hand, she picked up two of the *Chiclets* from the "D" and stuffed them into her mouth. She brushed away the remaining *Chiclets* that formed the letter "D" and with some other nearby pieces, recreated the letter "S" next to the "O." It wasn't long before the completed name shone back at me from the floor in white-enameled lettering:

Oswald.

CHAPTER SEVEN

I puzzled for days afterwards about the names Franny had spelled out in Chiclets on two separate occasions—first, "Ollie" on her bedroom floor the day of Mr. FitzHugh's murder, and now the name "Oswald" written on the floor of the increasingly bizarre room with the big porthole window. There had been some doubt in my mind, given that Franny couldn't spell—and I hadn't witnessed her in action the first time—that Franny could have crafted the name "Ollie" in Chiclets on the floor of her bedroom that day. But this time, I was there. I saw her spell out the name "Oswald" with my own eyes in that third floor room. There were more pieces to the puzzle, too. Since Franny couldn't spell, it meant some other force had to be directing her—a realization that pretty much confirmed the supernatural existed...and that something, or someone, living in a different dimension was trying to communicate with us.

On a level of lesser significance, but equal on a scale of enigmatic measure, was the mystery of who Ollie and Oswald actually were—although I had a pretty good idea—and exactly what it was this supernatural entity was trying to tell us about them. When it came to filling in the missing pieces of the former puzzle, two candidates presented themselves, both of them weighing in, equally, in the realm of plausibility. One possibility was that the more recent message Franny had channeled pertained to Lee Harvey Oswald, and I'd received a clue intended to send me down a path leading towards the discovery of who was actually responsible for JFK's 1963 assassination—Lee Harvey Oswald himself, or perhaps some band of conspirators; a concept that more and more people were starting to believe.

Another option was that the Oswald in question was none other than Mabel Keating's late husband, tradesman Oswald Keating, electrocuted in the basement of our house back in 1940. Perhaps the clue Franny spelled out in chewing gum was intended to launch us into discovering some hard realities behind Oswald Keating's death that had never come out before.

Then there was the matter of confirming who "Ollie" might be, and how "Ollie" fit into what was fast becoming a multi-dimensional puzzle. Mr. FitzHugh told us about how Ollie Merriweather had disappeared at the time Annandale Farm was built back in 1900. I felt reasonably sure there was a good chance the "Ollie" whose name Franny spelled out was one and the same. And the clincher was that no matter how anyone tried to fit the pieces together, the events unfolding at Annandale Farm were akin more to an episode of Rod Serling's *Twilight Zone* than a summer vacation.

As memorable as these initial happenings still are to this day, the actual day that Father decided to buy a new television set for Annandale Farm tipped the scales forever towards the third dimension in the multi-dimensional puzzle department. This wasn't because of any regularly scheduled programs we watched on the twenty-one inch, color *Zenith* console that showed up at the door one sparkling summer day. Rather, it was the assortment of *unscheduled* broadcasts we started receiving on that TV set that rewove the fabric of everyone's lives...forever.

Father bought the TV because the movies playing at the Strand weren't particularly up to his standards. Any film that didn't star Doris Day, Rock Hudson or Jimmy Stewart automatically failed to meet Father's definition of a quality movie. And if Father didn't approve of a movie, then it was a "no-see" for everybody—especially for Franny and me. I consider myself lucky to have gotten to see *Cleopatra* at all that summer. The only reason we actually got away with it was because Father somehow had the mistaken notion the movie was a documentary on Egypt. Livingston knew otherwise, but took us to see it anyway. He later caught a bit of flack from Father, once it came out that Liz Taylor—someone Father considered to be "an overpaid, oversexed home wrecking minx"—had the starring role.

One evening during dinner, I had started reeling off a list of coming attractions I wanted to see at the Strand. Not unexpectedly, Father vetoed virtually every candidate I put forward as, "not within the realm of acceptable viewing for a 14 year-old boy."

Back then, the movie subjects I had chosen were greatly influenced by the persona of Jayne Mansfield, whom I had the incredible good fortune of bumping into one summer afternoon on Thames Street. Having arrived for the Newport Jazz Festival, Jayne had walked the streets of town dressed in the shortest shorts and the tightest blouse I'd ever imagined possible. Seeing her curvaceous wonders outlined in skin-tight cotton stimulated my adolescent libido considerably, thus shifting any previous motion picture interests in cowboys and Indians or cops and robbers—to sex. Needless to say, after getting a firsthand look at this Hollywood bombshell live and in person, I became an instant fan of any picture promising even the slightest glimpse of Jayne Mansfield's ample endowments.

"Arthur, every one of those movies can't fall into the 'no-see' category, Elly challenged Father on the matter. "The children have to have *some* form of entertainment during the summer...and buying a TV will at least eliminate some of the otherwise inappropriate entertainment you'd rather they didn't see."

It was to Elly's credit that Father finally opted to yield to this logic and invest in a television-set. Looking back, if she hadn't pushed him on the TV matter, there's a good chance the story you're reading now might never have unfolded the way it did...or even at all. In any case, buying a TV served as the means in Elly's mind, and eventually Father's, of effectually dismissing any pubescent pleadings on my part to go see the likes of Jayne Mansfield, or any other inappropriate starlet, on the silver screen. Of course, a television-set back in 1964 required the installation of a roof antenna—that is, if one intended to get decent reception. To that end, Newport Electric erected a beauty, attaching it with steel strapping to one of the mansion's four graceful chimneys. Father deemed it to be quite an eyesore but, having already made the commitment to all of us, "bit his tongue" and let the architectural blemish slide.

Newport Electric ran the antenna wire down along the outside of the house and into the drawing room where Father liked to sit in the evening after dinner. The wire ran through the interior studs and connected to a convenient receptacle mounted neatly on the wall.

Two contact screws became the connection-point of the TV to the powerful antenna. The only step required to complete the installation of our new state-of-the-art *Zenith* was to attach a six-foot length of antenna wire running from the back of the television set, to the wall receptacle—something that Newport Electric was going to come back the next morning to do. Somehow, they had run out of antenna cable, but just after they'd left, Livingston found a couple of three foot sections of discarded scrap wire in the trash. We were impatient to get the TV working, and the operation of splicing the two pieces of scrap wire together to form the one needed six-foot section seemed easy enough to do. Franny and I were appointed to execute the delicate process. Franny held the wire, and I—carefully guided by Livingston's precise, supervisory eye—made the connections.

I can only assume some supernatural force floating in the air that night, perhaps related to sporadic bursts of heat lightning, enabled what happened. Father and Elly had taken Aunt Julia to dinner at the Newport Country Club as part of a gala fund-raiser for the Ida Lewis Yacht Club. Franny and I had eaten a leisurely dinner with Livingston in the kitchen then adjourned sometime after dessert to perform the delicate operation of hooking up the new television set to the wall receptacle.

I remember the evening air hung with humidity as twilight eventually settled in over the estate. The water in the bay had become quite placid, and intermittent flashes of heat lightning illuminated the few boaters that were still bobbing about in the harbor.

Following Livingston's instructions carefully, I stripped the insulation off the ends of the two pieces of scrap antenna wire to bare the metal threads that would carry the signal from the large roof-antenna to the set. Using a screwdriver, I attached the ends of one three-foot wire section to the wall receptacle. Taking the other piece of scrap wire, I attached the bared ends to the television-set contacts.

"Here, Franny," I instructed, "hold the ends of these two loose wires while we get some electrical tape to insulate the connection in the middle."

With that, I handed the bared ends of each three-foot section to Franny who was sitting on the floor nearby. Moments beforehand, Livingston had turned on the *Zenith* so he could monitor the quality of the picture as I hooked up the cable. Nothing but fuzzy snow whirled around, irritatingly, on the picture tube. By handing the exposed ends of the separate cables to Franny, I inadvertently made her the means of completing the circuit. Across the room, an oval, gilt-framed mirror hung on the wall in front of the television. From the location where I stood, I could see the reflection of the TV screen in the silvered glass. That's when the startling phenomena began. Both Livingston and I failed to notice it at first—a cluster of what looked to be tiny insects gathering around the television set. Quickly we realized they weren't insects. They had a translucent glow. Then, they began to homogenize into a cloud-like formation that hovered eerily around the TV.

All the while, Franny sat on the floor, Indian-style, eyes cast downward with a vacant look in them. The picture tube reflected in the mirror across the room, however, looked anything but vacant. The moment Franny grasped the ends of the exposed wire in her stubby little fingers, the picture-tube on the TV set had flickered to life. The irritating snow had already dissipated, replaced by a series of images flooding the screen in rapid-fire succession. One after another of broadcast-quality scenes reeled by with remarkable clarity. But the frenetic pace at which the pictures appeared and disappeared on the screen made them difficult to comprehend. All the while, this strange, luminescent cloud hovered over the top of the television cabinet. From the speakers, a pulsating, rhythmic beat began in short, staccato-like bursts—like someone trying to speak, but only able to articulate portions of every word: "wha–no–top–can–ook–der–nam–sip ."

Livingston and I, wide-eyed at the unfolding broadcast, had difficulty identifying any of the audible muddle or confused imagery streaming from the TV screen and speakers. I caught a glimpse of one scene that seemed, unmistakably, to be Annandale Farm—but with some remarkable differences. The house looked to be in a state of horrendous disrepair. The same neglect seemed to grip the lawn and flowerbeds. In the background, near a section of the wall bordering the yard on Ridge Road, I could make out the Victorian-style greenhouse. Next to it, where today a mighty oak towered nearly the full height of the three story house, I saw what clearly looked to be the same oak tree—but its height was only a fraction of its present day stature. The same applied to a number of other trees and shrubs on the property. What we were observing appeared to be a picture from Annandale's *past*. A similar image streaked by, and for an instant I could have sworn I saw a car that looked like Aunt Julia's trademark Duesenberg parked in the driveway. But these images whizzed by with such speed that Livingston and I couldn't keep up. A picture would flash up on the screen for no more than half a second then disappear as another took its place. Some of the pictures were of people— people we couldn't recognize. A few looked like they were dressed in clothes from the 1940s, while others seemed to be wearing turn-of-the-century attire.

We were whisked to what looked like a construction site with mounds of earth piled around and what appeared to be, by 1960s standards, antique tractors and excavating equipment standing idly by. Another shot took us inside a cave or cavern. But just as some of them began to repeat, the screen suddenly reverted to snow while, simultaneously, the luminescent vapor cloud began to dissipate.

Livingston and I looked over at Franny. She had dropped the wires and had gotten up on her knees. She seemed a bit groggy. I watched her yawn and rub her eyes.

"Franny, pick up the wires again," I encouraged her. "Pick up the wires and hold the ends in your hands."

She moved slowly, pausing to stretch, then reached down to pick up the bare ends of the antenna wires again. There were a few quick visual flickers. The vapor cloud fluttered a bit and then there was nothing. The cloud vanished and the television screen reverted to snow. I turned and looked at Livingston. He didn't say a word. Whatever the unexplainable conditions were that enabled Franny to become some kind of paranormal energy receiver, they had gone. What power caused an innocent, life-challenged girl like Franny to suddenly become a conduit to visions transmitted from some other dimension?

From that point forward, I became determined to solve the mystery behind Mr. FitzHugh's death and discover the secrets of Annandale Farm's past while, simultaneously, uncovering what—or who—had invaded Franny's psyche.

She seemed exhausted after her encounter with the *Zenith* that night. Livingston took her upstairs and tucked her into bed. I waited for him to come back downstairs, and we fiddled around making the final connection of the TV to the aerial...without Franny filling the gap as a go-between this time. During the process, we kept mulling over what had happened and finally agreed it would be better not to say anything about it to Father or anyone for the time being. When we finally managed to successfully connect the TV to the wall receptacle the way we'd originally intended, the colossal aerial up on the roof *and* the *Zenith* worked perfectly. To Livingston's delight and mine, we finished just in time to catch a local broadcast of *The Beverly Hillbillies* followed by *Green Acres*—two of what are to this day my favorite reruns.

Later that night, when Father, Elly, and Aunt Julia returned from the Newport Country Club around ten-thirty, Livingston and I greeted them in the front foyer. I could tell immediately that Aunt Julia sensed something had happened. I watched her start to remove her hat—some crazy concoction of stuffed birds and flowers—then saw her stop dead in her tracks. Holding the hat by its brim, she inhaled deeply then tried to suppress the startled look on her face—an involuntary widening of the eyes and pursing of the lips that momentarily gave her feelings away. Try as she did, she couldn't hide it. I knew she knew something paranormal had gone down.

"Well, how did you and Livingston make out in the television department?," Father asked casually, unaware of Aunt Julia's reaction. He seemed to be in an affable mood having, no doubt, partaken of a fine dinner and some equally fine wine at the country club.

"Great, sir," I replied. "Everything works swell. Livingston and I just watched a couple of the *best* shows," I answered truthfully, exchanging a knowing glance with Livingston. Aunt Julia looked at me warily.

"Well, where's Franny?," she wanted to know. "Off to bed, I suppose?" She eyed the drawing room discreetly then glanced upstairs towards Franny's room. Something told me to play things cautiously.

"Yeah, Franny was really tired tonight," I said. "Too much TV, I guess." Livingston and I exchanged another look.

"Too much TV isn't good for anybody," Aunt Julia said tersely. "In fact, I think it could be very harmful in certain situations."

I saw Elly exchange a startled look with Father.

"Really, Julia," Elly spoke up bravely, surprising all of us. "I do wish you wouldn't imply anything negative about the TV. Arthur and I only recently decided that a TV in the house would be better than having the children watch some of the movies scheduled to run at the Strand."

Father stood there quietly and didn't move a muscle. Aunt Julia looked his way for a moment, as if expecting him to back her up. When he didn't, she conceded to Elly without challenge. I watched her finish hanging her hat on the coat rack then fuss a bit uncomfortably with her platinum-dyed hair.

'Way to go, Elly, I thought. Now you're cookin'! Already won over by her pretty face and sexy figure, my overall opinion of her jumped even higher with the polite, but precisely targeted stake-in-the-ground she planted at Aunt Julia's feet.

"Well then, I guess I'll go in and see what's playing on our new television," Father announced proudly, motioning towards the drawing room. "Care to join me, Elly?" he asked, offering her his arm. She nodded, and with a confident smile wrapped her arm in his. "Julia, how about you?" he added.

"No thank you, Arthur," she declined politely. "I'm feeling rather tired tonight. If you and Elly don't mind, I think I'll be going off to bed."

"Suit yourself," Father said without protest. "Actually, that sounds like a pretty good idea for some other people too. How about it, Eddie?" He looked directly at me, gesturing with an extended thumb towards the stairs.

"Come on, Eddie, I'm turning in, myself," Livingston said. "What do you say we both hit the hay?"

I decided to call it a night without a struggle. Had we not experienced the peculiar happenings with the TV earlier, I probably would have put up more of a fuss and lobbied to watch the *Late Show*.

"Yes, all right," I heard myself say. "I'm feeling kind of tired too. Good night. See you tomorrow."

As Livingston and I climbed the stairs behind Aunt Julia, I could smell the heavy odor of her lilac-scented perfume. It made my nose itch like it always did. When we reached the second floor, she turned and nodded an aloof goodnight then headed for her bedroom. We watched her slip through the doorway and heard the latch click behind her. I spoke to Livingston in whispers as we continued down the hall.

"Livingston, Aunt Julia acted strange when she came home tonight, don't you think? I'll bet those psychic powers of hers have been picking up vibes, too. What do you s'pose she sensed? It must have been that weird stuff we saw on the TV."

Livingston paused. "I don't know, son," he said softly. "I know what you mean, though. Somehow she knew something had gone on here tonight—and Lord knows it certainly did. But then again, maybe we're reading too much into things. Personally, I think we're better off to just let the dust settle a bit. There's been an awful lot of excitement in this house lately. Why don't we get a good night's sleep and see how we feel about it in the morning?"

What Livingston said sounded pretty good to me. I felt too worn out to do anything else but go to bed anyway. I hugged him and we said our goodnights in the hallway. When I opened the door to my room, the air drifting in through the open window seemed less humid. I changed into my summer pajamas then washed up for bed and brushed my teeth. Climbing between the sheets, I thought of Franny and the strange encounter. I wondered how she was doing. Although confident she must be sleeping like a baby, my conscience got the better of me and I decided to check on her. I had just cracked my bedroom door open about a half an inch when I saw Aunt Julia poke her head out of her own bedroom and scan the hall in the opposite direction. Carefully, I narrowed the opening of the door to a mere fraction and watched. A few seconds later she looked my way then ducked out of her bedroom carrying a flashlight. She had changed her clothes, but wasn't wearing a robe and pajamas. Instead, she had on a black summer jacket, black slacks, and a pair of black sneakers. I continued watching, unobserved, as she hurried down the hall towards the back stairs.

Where would she be going dressed like that...and with a flashlight? I wondered. At that moment I decided Franny must be okay, and opted to check up on Aunt Julia instead. I hastily grabbed a *Pen-light* flashlight from off of my nightstand. Then, as soon as Aunt Julia disappeared down the back stairs, I slipped quietly out of my room, following her at a safe distance. An adrenaline rush had replaced the feelings of weariness I felt before. I couldn't believe the good fortune of my timing at having spotted Aunt Julia heading out on a mysterious night prowl. Everything seemed exciting until I reached the back staircase not too many paces behind her. That's when I realized she hadn't switched on the stairwell wall-sconces. Some light radiated up feebly from the first floor where Father and Elly were still watching television, but the darkened stairwell filled me with a sense of foreboding. I wanted to switch on the lights. I remembered the vow I made to myself on that first day of our arrival—no one would ever catch me going down those back stairs alone after dark...let alone without any lights. Somehow, however, my sense of purpose won out and I found myself creeping ever so slowly down the back stairs to the service corridor on the first floor.

Peering into the inky-blackness that marked the way to the cellar, I could see a faint glow of light emanating from the tip of Aunt Julia's flashlight as she made her way further to the basement. I suppressed a panicky gulp as the thought of going down there whipped up my imagination. I hesitated and nearly turned back, but instead found myself inching my way downward. I hugged the outer wall of the stairwell hoping to minimize hitting spots in the steps that might creak. Perhaps I would have been better off if I had turned back. But fate found its way that night, and as soon as the sound of the creaking basement door subsided, I sneaked down the stairs in pursuit. I could barely see as I got to the bottom, but felt uncomfortable switching on my flashlight for fear Aunt Julia might spot its narrow, concentrated beam.

I groped for the cold steel of the door then finding it, pressed my ear against its surface, listening for any sound that might give a clue as to Aunt Julia's whereabouts. Beyond the steel door, I heard the creak of corroded hinges—the sound of another door opening then closing. It was followed by the click of a latch. I knew it had to be the wine cellar door. The earlier excursion I'd made with Norman and Amanda had confirmed that no other door existed. I took a deep breath and eased open the heavy steel portal to the basement. The hinges creaked a bit, but my giraffe-like physique allowed me to slip through a narrow opening without making too much noise. The room was pitch-black. I strained my eyes looking for any sign of light from beneath the wine-cellar door. Nothing. Enveloped in the eerie darkness of that damp, cavernous cellar, I felt myself starting to panic.

Driven purely by fear, I fumbled for my *Pen-light*, and flipped it on as quickly as I could. Shining the narrow beam in every direction I searched for signs of Aunt Julia. Still nothing. I guided the light in the direction of the wooden wine-cellar door, cautiously working my way towards it. My heart pounded at the prospect of confronting Aunt Julia. What would I say to her? What excuse would I use for having followed her—and what might she say...or do to me? I reached the wine-cellar door and put my hand, half-heartedly, on the latch. I could feel my pulse pumping in the veins on the side of my neck. The image of Mr. FitzHugh's blood-soaked skull crept in and further fueled my fear. I teetered on the brink of beating a retreat to the safety of my room. It was at that very moment that the antique hot-water heater in the far corner of the basement chose to sputter to life. The sudden *"whoosh"* of the nearby igniter scared me so, that I tripped over my own feet. The flashlight slipped from my hand, and I tumbled towards the floor. Instinctively, I reached outward and felt my hand graze the nearby door handle. I grabbed onto it. Doing so broke the momentum of my fall and, at the same time, released the door latch. The wine-cellar door sprung open. Reaching down quickly to retrieve the fallen light, I aimed the beam inside the wine cellar. Expecting to see Aunt Julia dressed in full night-stalker regalia, it came as a shock when my trusty *Pen-light* revealed nothing but empty rows of wine shelves. Shining the light in every conceivable crevice revealed no trace of Aunt Julia—or anything, for that matter.

For an instant I panicked. The idea that she had somehow eluded my earlier sweep of the cellar popped into my head. At any moment she would creep up from behind and slam the wine-cellar door behind me. Then, having somehow obtained a key, she would lock me in this tomb-like cell for all eternity. I turned to bolt from the room at the prospect, but stopped in my tracks. Mingled with the scent of damp cellar air, another odor—one familiar and potent—teased my nostrils. It was the fragrance of lilacs.

"Cripes, PU!" I found myself muttering aloud in the solitude of the deserted basement. Reflexively, I held my nose. I knew by the scent that Aunt Julia had been there. I had gotten to the basement only seconds after she had. I heard the wine cellar door creak open, and then close. Had she dashed in and then out so quickly that I hadn't realized it? No, it wasn't physically possible. I stepped back out through the wine cellar and made a careful sweep of the basement again. I hadn't heard the creak of the basement door hinges. She couldn't have slipped out. Was she hiding in the basement darkness somewhere that I hadn't seen? The thought that she might be...and that *I'd* become the prey refueled my sense of panic.

I noticed that next to the wine-cellar door, there was a light-switch tucked into a small recess beside the doorjamb. Because of its unobtrusive location, I hadn't seen it the first time we'd explored. I flipped it on. Nothing happened. I flipped it on and off a couple of times. Still nothing. Suddenly, more confident than fearful, I shined my flashlight across the room toward the wall-switch next to the main basement door. I strode over and flipped on the lights. Not a soul in sight. I walked the entire perimeter of the cellar and found nothing. If Aunt Julia had gone into the basement—which she definitely had—that meant, somehow, she had to be coming out. The fact that she wasn't there had to mean that some kind of secret passageway existed. The logical place had to be the wine cellar.

That night, I spent the better part of an hour searching for some kind of secret passage. I felt along the empty wine shelves and the walls. I searched along the doorjamb. I poked, prodded, and pulled every conceivable spot I could see. I couldn't find *anything*. Finally, exhausted and frustrated, I decided to wait Aunt Julia out. I closed the wine cellar door and walked over to the main light-switch by the basement door. I switched on my *Pen-light* then turned out the lights. Shining its powerful, narrow beam on the hot-water heater, I walked to the far corner of the windowless basement and crouched down behind the hissing dinosaur. Thinking back, I must have waited for a good two hours. And as exhausted as I felt, I never closed my eyes once. Adrenalin kept me alert. Finally, overwhelmed with frustration, I left. Climbing the deserted back stairs, I could see all the lights were out on the first floor. Father and Elly had probably gone to bed long ago. Ascending the stairs to the second floor, I headed wearily towards my room. I could see there were no lights on anywhere in the house—anywhere, that is, except for one. As I made my way down the long, darkened corridor, I could see a sliver of light shining brightly from beneath one of the heavy mahogany doors. Moving shadows visible through the threshold indicated activity inside. As I got closer, I could hear the jingle of charm bracelets and an all-too familiar voice humming away from within. The potent scent of lilac perfume drifted through the heavy wooden door. It was Aunt Julia's room…and she was back.

CHAPTER EIGHT

The day finally arrived that Elly had been anticipating. We'd been invited for brunch next door at Hammersmith Farm with Mr. and Mrs. Auchincloss. I found out about it the morning following my night of searching for Aunt Julia in the cellar. Worn out from my fruitless sleuthing, I slept until lunchtime that day. I had just finished dressing and was coming down the stairs when Elly burst through the front door brimming with excitement. She had gone to do some shopping and had the good fortune of running into Janet Auchincloss at Blaine Jewelers on Thames Street. A conversation with the former first lady's mother ensued while the two women admired a 15-carat, postage stamp-sized emerald ring in the display-case. When the salesclerk greeted Mrs. Auchincloss by name, Elly wasted no time introducing herself as the new owner of Annandale Farm. According to Elly, one thing led to another and before she knew it, Mrs. Auchincloss had invited us all over for brunch on the coming Sunday.

I could have cared less. My sole interest centered on figuring out what Aunt Julia had been up to the night before, and where she went. Also, I was trying to piece together all the disjointed fragments of mystery hurled at me since our arrival. To Elly, it was a monumental victory.

When the Sunday of social reckoning arrived, Father, Elly, Aunt Julia and I dressed for the occasion. We had already attended morning services on Touro Street, thereby establishing the tone of our attire. Elly must have changed her clothes five times that morning in anticipation of brunch at the Auchincloss estate. She finally settled on some elegantly demure outfit she'd bought locally, while Aunt Julia donned one of her no-doubt exorbitantly priced, but less exotic-than-usual outfits. I was surprised to see her looking quite the picture of the refined country gentlewoman.

Father and I stayed dressed in the new navy, brass-buttoned blazers with coordinating slacks, and bright summer neckties we'd worn to church. Franny, however, was excluded from this event.

Although Mrs. Auchincloss made it a point to include *all* of us, Elly prevailed on Father to keep Franny at home with Livingston. There were plenty of times when I was glad not to have Franny around...but this wasn't one of them. As fond as I was growing of Elly, there sometimes developed a point of contention between us when it came to including Franny in certain family activities. Looking back, all I can do is blame it on the mentality of the era—a period of time when prominent families took great pains to hide their human misfortunes. In any case, Elly won this round and Franny stayed home with Livingston.

Arriving at Hammersmith Farm, I was impressed by the graceful informality of the place. Rising on a bluff of land overlooking Narragansett Bay, the property was bordered on the East by Fort Adams—an historic military base and fortification built in the early 1800s—and on the West by Annandale Farm. Interestingly, as I would find out later that day, our Newport neighborhood—if one could call it that—had been home to the summer activities of yet another President. During the summer seasons of 1957, 1958 and 1960, President Dwight Eisenhower and his White House staff took up residency at nearby Fort Adams.

Hammersmith Farm's mansion house dated back to 1887, although an earlier manor house on the property had been erected in 1641. Serving as the childhood home of Jackie Kennedy from the time she was twelve, her stepfather's 97 acre estate was a mixture of Newport elegance and country living. Driving through its main gate on Harrison Avenue, we'd all noticed a herd of Black Angus steers grazing comfortably in a nearby pasture. The mansion, still standing to this day, is a large shingled Victorian that sprawls across acres of beautifully landscaped grounds. From the tranquil back terrace overlooking the bay, I could see our house plainly, with the "God-damned eyesore of an antenna" sticking up on the roof, as Father always referred to the new TV aerial.

Back in 1953, Hammersmith Farm had also been the site of Jackie Kennedy's wedding to then Senator John (Jack) F. Kennedy. It was during the summers of 1962 and 1963 that Hugh Auchincloss had offered Hammersmith's use to President and Mrs. Kennedy as the summer White House. For all its historical significance, the house had a comfortable and homey feel. Elly loved the décor, and spent a good portion of the time we were there taking mental notes. The rooms were airy, light, and elegant. Father was more taken with the recently redesigned gardens by Washington landscape architect Boris Timshenko. The only thing that seemed to capture Aunt Julia's attention was the view of our house from the Auchinclosses' terrace. The entire time we were there, she kept looking across the wide expanse of lawn separating our house from Hammersmith Farm.

For me, the visit was a colossal bore, and I couldn't have cared less about being there...except for one thing. It happened after we'd finished eating, and the conversation took a turn towards the late president's use of Hammersmith Farm as the summer White House. We were seated out on the terrace chatting when I decided to bring up one of the facts I'd discovered during our initial visit to the Newport Historical Society with Mabel Keating.

"I came across some old newspaper clippings that said our house would have been the summer White House if the President hadn't been assassinated," I stated flatly. Elly, Father and Aunt Julia looked stunned.

Mrs. Auchincloss hesitated, then in her own unique style, rose to the occasion.

"Why yes, Eddie, that's true. The Secret Service didn't like the location of Hammersmith Farm for security reasons. They thought it was too visible from the road."

"Quite right," Mr. Auchincloss added. "They thought Jack would be too easy a target staying here. Pretty ironic, isn't it...given the way things turned out and all. Who'd have thought it? Well anyway, that's why Jack and Jackie decided to rent Annandale Farm. It offered all the amenities of a presidential retreat—including a secure location. That brick wall running behind the property on Ridge Road offered both security and seclusion."

"Yes, it seemed perfect," Mrs. Auchincloss said. "So when the previous owner of your house signed the lease with Jack, along with an option to buy by The Department of the Interior, we were all delighted. As an added security measure, the Army Corps of Engineers drew up plans to construct an access tunnel between Hammersmith Farm and your house. It would have run right under the very patio we're sitting on here and connected to the basement under the west wing of your place."

That was the moment Aunt Julia dropped her drink. The Waterford crystal old-fashioned glass crashed to the terrace floor and shattered into a million pieces. She leapt to her feet.

"Oh, I'm so sorry, she blurted. "How clumsy of me...I'm so embarrassed. Please forgive me."

Not having much of an option, Janet Auchincloss responded graciously. "Oh, think nothing of it," she said. "It was an accident, of course."

Mrs. Auchincloss rang for a maid who dutifully swept away the remains of Aunt Julia's drink and, in the blink of an eye, efficiently handed her an identical replacement. At that point, the conversation would have gone in a different direction, if I hadn't persisted.

"Well what happened after President Kennedy's assassination?" I asked bluntly.

"Eddie!" Aunt Julia gasped, her voice tinged with reprimand. "Don't you think that's enough?" I saw her look at Father who appeared kind of edgy, himself.

"No...no that's perfectly all right," Mr. Auchincloss countered before anyone else could respond. "That's a very logical question, young man," he said looking me square in the eye. "It's actually kind of a sad story though. The previous owners of your house lived there for quite a while. In fact, up until they bought the place, it seemed like everyone moved in and out of that house faster than a jackrabbit. Of course, you know the old rumors that circulate about it—the mysterious hauntings, the cache of hidden gold and all. Every bit of it a lot of nonsense, if you ask me. Of course, they did have that incident over there the day Jack was killed in Dallas. The caretaker was found near-dead on the property. I can't remember his name."

"George FitzHugh?" I offered.

"Yes...yes, that's right. George FitzHugh. And now you've had that nasty business with old FitzHugh turning up murdered in your greenhouse—an awful thing!"

Mr. Auchincloss paused for a moment to think.

"Now, getting back to the question you asked, son, from everything I've heard, the previous owners had run out of money and had really let the place go. Lord knows if it hadn't been for Jack and Jackie leasing the place, I think they'd have had to file for bankruptcy. It turned out to be a wonderful deal for the owners. The whole estate looked like a dilapidated ruin until just before you bought it. The Federal Government had come in and renovated the place from top to bottom—inside and out. That was part of the deal. Of course, once Jack was assassinated and the deal fell through, they couldn't very well undo it all, now could they? The only thing that hadn't been started was the construction of that tunnel. Of course, that got scrapped, too. That's why the house eventually came up for sale. When the lease got cancelled, the folks who lived there couldn't afford to keep it anymore."

While Mr. Auchincloss had been telling his story, I kept a close watch on Aunt Julia. It seemed she got more and more uncomfortable with each new piece of information shared. I wondered why. She kept looking across the lawn in the direction of our house. The talk about the tunnel seemed to upset her most. It was all quite an interesting revelation, I thought.

"Well that's all very interesting," Father chimed in. "I have to admit that when they renovated the house they didn't fix everything, though. One of the four pillars on the front portico has a slight list to it. 'Bothers me to no end; looks to be some kind of a problem with the concrete footing."

"I expect they would have taken care of a major structural repair like that when they dug the tunnel," Mr. Auchincloss suggested, adding to the dialogue. "Of course that never happened...and...well everyone knows the rest."

"Yes...well, I suppose you're right," Father conceded politely. "We really ought to change the subject anyway, don't you think?"

"Just one more question," I pleaded.

"EDDIE!" Aunt Julia scolded. Father raised an eyebrow. Elly sat there, noticeably uncomfortable.

"No, no, that's all right," Mr. Auchincloss said again defending me. "Let the boy ask his questions."

With all the confidence I could muster, I blurted it out.

"Who *was* the previous owner?"

As I asked the question, I looked at Father, Aunt Julia and Elly. All three of them looked nervous.

"Why, let me think for a minute," Mr. Auchincloss said scratching his head. His eyes shifted in Mrs. Auchincloss's direction. "I've got a great memory for dates and numbers," he said. "But when it comes to names, I'm not so good. The fellow died toward the end of the War as I remember...a heavy drinker and gambler. Left the wife without much of anything except that big wreck of a house. Luckily she had her brother—FitzHugh—to help her with the house and grounds. What was the husband's name again, Janet?"

Mrs. Auchincloss sighed, obviously impatient with Mr. Auchincloss's lapse of memory. Perhaps it was a point of ongoing irritation, I thought.

"Don't you remember?," she bristled. "His name was Milton; Milton Pierce."

"Oh, that's right. Milton Pierce…and what was the wife's name again?"

"Good heavens, dear, can't you remember anything?," Mrs. Auchincloss chided. "Her name was Belle…Belle *Pierce*."

CHAPTER NINE

I had spent most of my time following the brunch at Hammersmith Farm cautiously snooping around our basement for clues as to Aunt Julia's earlier, late-night disappearing act...but without success. I did manage to get a private moment later with Father in his bedroom, and asked him if he knew anything about the history of our house or about Milton and Belle Pierce, the previous owners. He said he really didn't.

"To tell you the truth, Eddie," he said honestly. "I never paid any attention to the details when I bought this place." Then he paused, as if there were something further he had to say.

"Whatever you do," he suddenly whispered, "don't ever tell Elly or your Aunt Julia what I'm about to share with you. OK?"

Startled and eager to hear what he had to say, I nodded my head in agreement.

"First of all, it came as a real shock when Elly and your Aunt Julia told me that the offer I'd made on this property had been accepted. I never dreamt in a million years that the owners would accept the lowball bid I put in. Once they did, though, I just turned everything over to the lawyers to handle. Your Aunt Julia and Elly handled all the rest. Finding out all that background information from Mr. and Mrs. Auchincloss at brunch...especially that business about the summer White House, the tunnel, the hidden gold and everything...was as much of a surprise to me as it was to you. I had no idea about any of that—let alone the identities of the previous owners and the screwy history around this place."

"Oh...I see," was all I could manage to say. I accepted Father's word without hesitation, but still wondered why Elly knew about the summer White House details, and Father didn't. I had been raised not to challenge the statements of my elders—especially my parents, so I decided not to pursue the subject. Besides, I loved Father and had no reason to doubt his integrity. Strangely, though, it looked as if he was hedging around saying something further to me—as if he'd omitted something important from what he'd just said, and now thought better of withholding it. Any chance of his rectifying the situation ended quickly, however, when the bedroom door swung open abruptly and Elly swept in carrying a vase of freshly cut roses from the garden.

"There. Now aren't these lovely? It's just what this room needed," Elly said, exuding delight as she set the vase on a nearby table then fiddled with the stems, putting the final touches on her arrangement. Seeing Father's demeanor change with Elly's entrance, I decided to excuse myself and avoid any possibility of ending up in a compromising situation.

"Well, I guess I'll catch up with Franny and see what she's up to," I lied as I made for the door. I saw Father flash me a don't-forget-what-I-told-you look on my way out.

The comment he'd made, and his request that I keep the information he'd shared secret, puzzled me. I found myself struggling to reconcile all the fragmented and mysterious bits of information I'd obtained thus far. After pondering things for a while, I came to an interesting conclusion. I made up my mind to try and repeat the paranormal event Livingston and I experienced with Franny on the day the new *Zenith* had arrived.

Several days later, the opportunity presented itself.

For every summer for as long as I can remember before my mother died, Livingston would drive Father, Mother, Franny and me into Boston for an outdoor performance of the *Boston Pops* on the Charles River Esplanade. First, Livingston would drop us off at Haymarket where we'd climb the rough, wooden stairs to the rustic, second floor dining room of Durgin Park and partake of a scrumptious, prime-rib dinner. Afterwards, having topped off the meal with fresh strawberry shortcake and whipped cream, we'd squeeze back into the car for the short ride over to the Hatch Memorial band shell on the

Charles River Esplanade. Once there, Father and Mother would set up folding aluminum chairs at the head of a red and white checkered blanket they'd brought. Crammed in amongst thousands of enthusiastic Bostonians, Franny and I would lie on our backs and look up at the stars. I'd point to each one in tempo with the music—as if the stars were notes floating on some musical measure of sky, while the sound and rhythm of Arthur Fiedler conducting The Boston Pops lilted in the background. To this day, it's a memory I cherish. So does Livingston.

That summer, Father had made plans for all of us, including Elly and Aunt Julia, to attend an upcoming Boston Pops performance on the Esplanade. The thought of going made me feel nostalgic, but with Mother gone, I somehow knew it would never be the same. Even though Father insisted that he'd made the plans for both Franny's and my benefit, I respectfully and vigorously declined. On top of holding the sacredness of our Boston Pops rituals near and dear, I was bothered by the fact that Elly felt so uneasy about taking Franny out to dinner in restaurants and public places. It reinforced my decision not to go. And as much as Elly was becoming a member of the family, there were still certain things or events involving my late mother and me that I preferred to keep reverent. This happened to be one of them.

With that in mind, I volunteered to stay home with Franny. Doing so would also allow Livingston the opportunity to better enjoy the outdoor performance, not having to worry about Franny and me. He could sit inside our parked car along Storrow Drive, with the top down savoring the music.

Surprisingly, Father accepted my proposal with a minimum of protest. He seemed to understand how I felt and respected my feelings. Not only did he support my decision, but knowing I'd be home alone with Franny, he had Livingston drive to Davenport's Grocery Store to pick up a favorite eat-at-home meal for both Franny and me—*Swanson* TV dinners. Then, as a further gesture of good will, Father encouraged me to invite Norman and Amanda over for supper, too, so they could enjoy an evening of TV with me.

Everything worked out great all around. Mr. Davenport let Norman take the delivery truck. Norman drove Amanda over to our house, and when everyone left for Boston the real fun began. First, we had the perfect opportunity to look for the secret passage in the wine cellar, which I felt certain had to be there. Franny helped, and we spent a good two hours searching the spooky basement for the slightest evidence of it. Finding nothing, and time becoming a factor, we abandoned our basement search and concentrated on hooking up Franny to the *Zenith* for round two of paranormal TV viewing.

The logistics for staging the supernatural event couldn't have worked out better. By sheer luck, even the weather cooperated. The air that night hung thick with humidity and the mercury in the thermometer held steady at an uncomfortable 90 degrees. Heat lightning flashed across the bay in the distance. I made sure the time of evening and the TV channel selection matched those of the initial event.

When I gave the signal, Norman and Amanda pulled the *Zenith* away from the wall and disconnected the antenna wire from the wall receptacle. They left one end attached to the television. I attached one end of a shorter, four-foot lead with bared wire ends— an accessory I'd bought earlier—to the wall receptacle. I handed the other end to Franny who grabbed it securely with her left hand. I turned on the television and slipped the bare end of the wire running from the TV into Franny's right hand. A lot of snow fluttered around on the tube. This went on for a while. In boredom, Amanda, Norman, and I strolled out on the verandah to catch the awesome sight of a brilliantly illuminated aircraft carrier gliding by. While the three of us watched, Norman pulled out a pack of *Winstons* and brazenly lit up a cigarette...much to Amanda's displeasure. Purposely annoying her further, he offered both of us a drag. Feeling bold and wanting to be cool, I ignored both Amanda's and my own earlier warning to Norman about smoking and accepted; besides, there were no adults around to worry about. It was the first time I'd ever tried a cigarette. I pushed the paper shaft into my mouth and inhaled deeply. Moments later, I found myself coughing and gagging in reaction to the vile tasting fumes. What was so great about this, I wondered? Norman roared with laughter. Amanda bristled with disgust. Never again, I vowed as I snuffed out the butt and we buried the incriminating evidence in the shrubs by the verandah.

When we finally went back inside, things were beginning to happen. Norman and Amanda were stunned speechless. The strange luminescent vapor cloud that had formed during the first encounter hung around the television set once again. Franny had begun "receiving" and the images were rolling in. With her head bowed low and eyes looking blankly at the floor, pictures flickered across the tube in rapid-fire succession. The three of us struggled to make sense of what we saw. Once again, the audio coming over the television speaker pulsed at us in indistinguishable and irregular bursts of sound.

"Hey, I recognize that place," Norman said as a picture flashed by then disappeared in a few nanoseconds. "That was an aerial view of your house and Hammersmith Farm. Did you see the wall running behind the house on Ridge Road...and the open pasture in between your house and the Auchincloss place?"

Another picture flew by the screen.

"Hey, I recognize that one too," Norman yelled. "It's the same aerial view—only this time Hammersmith Farm is there...and your house isn't. Did you see all that stuff piled around that huge ditch? That was excavating equipment. It looked like a picture of when they must have been digging the foundation for your house."

I had to admit, Norman seemed to be doing a better job than Amanda and me of recognizing landmark photos. Then, I swore I saw Aunt Julia's Duesenberg parked in the drive. Amanda thought she saw a shadow of familiarity on some of the faces flashing by on the screen, but she couldn't quite place them. The more we struggled to comprehend the barrage of pictures—images of people, places and things we couldn't identify—the more the three of us became increasingly frustrated. If only we could slow the pace...and stabilize the sound.

We were just about to call it quits when a thunderstorm

rolling in from across the bay started to affect the reception—for the better. As lightning flashed in the distance, I could make out a curtain of torrential rain moving slowly over the water towards the house. High winds were beginning to kick up, and the once distant rumble of thunder grew into a menacing growl—a precursor to the jarring booms soon to engulf us. I looked at Franny sitting quietly and blankly next to the television cabinet. She seemed no worse for the wear, given the duration of the session so far. I decided it would be okay to continue.

At this point, the pictures we were watching began to stabilize into a more homogenous flow. Following a noticeable and significant discharge of lightning into the bay, what were previously unrelated frame-by-frame snapshots whizzing by in confused disorder gradually transformed into a free-flowing video of synchronized activity. The audio improved slightly too, in that we could now make out an occasional name mentioned, and parts of sentences or phrases.

Norman, Amanda, and I sat in front of the picture tube as a fuzzy image formed on the screen then clarified. At the same time, the mystical vapor floating above the television took on a more distinguishable shape. Slowly, it manifested until it resembled the form of a featureless face. There was the shape of a head and neck. Ears and a brow—a nose and eye-sockets evolved. I don't know how or why, but for some reason, we could sense it posed no threat. I can't explain why the three of us felt that way to this day. We just did. And while we sat agape watching vapor and shape compose, the image never took on enough definition to present a clue as to who the animated specter might be...or might have been.

Back on the television screen, a tall rather burly looking workman materialized wearing a blue uniform—work pants, a jacket, and a cap. He held a long, rectangular toolbox in his right hand. Closer examination revealed the words *KEATING ELECTRIC* splashed across the broad shoulders of his jacket. When he turned to face us, a cluster of keys dangled from the belt loop of his trousers. We were awestruck. The scene panned back—almost deliberately—revealing a black truck, probably from the 1930s or 40's, with the same name written in gold letters on its side. In the background, a large white house dominated the scene. It was the mansion house at Annandale Farm—our house. Could this be Oswald Keating, we wondered? Just as I thought it, Norman said it. "Hey, I'll bet that guy is Oswald Keating." Then Amanda piped in. "I saw his face in one of those other pictures that flashed by us before."

We watched intently as this man we'd decided was Oswald Keating climbed the steps to the front door and pushed the doorbell button. During the course of the paranormal broadcast, we could pick up clearly stated fragments of audio. We heard the bell ring then the front door creak opened. The lady standing in the threshold bore a striking resemblance to the woman I'd seen the first day I visited Davenport's grocery store. But she looked considerably younger. The broad-shouldered blouse and platform shoes she wore, combined with a dramatic flip to her blonde hair, affirmed a 1940's period. The three of us had seen enough old movies to know that much.

"Do you know who that is?" Amanda probed.

"Sure do." I said. I saw Norman's eyes widen with surprise. The three of us looked at each other as I blurted out the name.

"Belle Pierce."

Seeing a much younger Belle Pierce made me recollect our brunch-time discussion at Hammersmith Farm. With the information Mr. and Mrs. Auchincloss provided, it helped me figure out that the period in which this scene was unfolding must have been around the time Belle Pierce came into her own by marrying wealthy financier and gambler Milton Pierce.

And I further remembered that the day the three of us had visited the Historical Society, Mabel Keating had said her husband, Oswald, was electrocuted while he was doing work for Milton Pierce at Annandale Farm. The more the paranormal TV show played out, the more I saw that things were connected.

I made it a point to keep my eye on Franny during all of this—

making sure she wasn't unhappy or going into some kind of psychic overload. She seemed fine. She'd taken her usual Indian-style position on the floor next to the TV with her legs crossed in front of her. She flashed me a flicker of a smile when she realized I was watching her.

Meanwhile, the mysterious vapor-face continued to hover inertly above the *Zenith* while the past-driven play, courtesy of Franny's fingertips and psychic sensitivities, unfolded in front of us. I switched my imagination into high gear to piece together the jigsaw puzzle of events bombarding us. From what we saw and heard on television that night, it was evident that Oswald Keating had been called to the mansion to do electrical work some summer in the 1940's, and while he was there he connected with Belle Pierce. We watched Belle begin prodding Oswald for clues about hidden gold. She kept dropping comments and leading questions in an effort to find out what, if anything, he knew about where this gold might be hidden.

Through our psychic TV channel, Amanda, Norman and I watched Belle follow Oswald down the backstairs to the basement— the same gloomy staircase I'd followed Aunt Julia down only a few days ago. Oswald plopped down his toolbox and pulled out some tools. Belle Pierce bantered with him casually while he began working on the main fuse box. On more than one occasion, references were clearly made to "*gold*" and "*murder,*" as well as the names *Oswald, Mabel, and Ollie*. What Amanda, Norman and I didn't know is that we would actually witness Oswald Keating's electrocution that night.

Pausing to monitor the gale inching its way closer from across the bay, I realized we might actually have to pull the plug on our TV viewing if the storm got too intense. Making this decision difficult, however, was the storm's continued influence on the reception. The more the atmosphere became charged with energy from the intensifying electrical activity, the *better* both the sound and picture seemed to be. Outside, I could see and hear huge raindrops beginning to plop on the wrap-around verandah and splatter on the broad brick walkway. The life-sized, sculpted lions standing guard on either side of the walk took on a ghostly appearance under the blitz of flashing lightning. All through the growing maelstrom, Franny sat calmly and blankly next to the *Zenith*.

"KABLAM!" A violent thunderclap made the three of us jump. At that very moment, the video and audio stabilized to regular broadcast quality. It was as if we were watching an episode of *The Outer Limits*. Whatever force was governing the supernatural scenes playing out, it provided a chilling glimpse into the long-obstructed past. Belle Pierce conversed with Oswald Keating—the husband of her arch-rival. Their voices came across the TV speaker in an exaggerated and eerily hollow tremolo.

"Oswald, we've known each other for a long time now," Belle said. "Didn't Simon Merriweather ever mention anything to you about gold or hidden treasure here at Annandale Farm? I know you and he were always close."

Oswald had a long screwdriver and was removing the large, rectangular faceplate covering what turned out to be the main fuse-box.

"You've asked me that before and I've always told you the same thing," Oswald responded disinterestedly. "Simon got more and more peculiar towards the end. I didn't put much credence on the things he said."

"Well what exactly did he say?"

"Oh, I don't know; a lot of gibberish." Oswald paused reflectively for a few seconds lowering his screwdriver to his side.

"He did mention his concern about leaving Ollie behind."

It was then, in her zeal to find out more, that Belle seemed to make the mistake of saying something she shouldn't have.

"I never could stand that kid. Ollie was hiding something from me that day..."

Belle caught herself in mid-sentence, realizing she'd said too much. Oswald turned and looked at her long and hard.

"Ollie? What do you mean Ollie was hiding something from you *that day*?" Oswald said somber-faced. "You were with Ollie *that day*—the day Ollie disappeared? You never mentioned it during the investigation."

Belle quickly turned and headed for the stairs. "Well, I guess I'd better not keep you from your work, Oswald," she sputtered. We'll talk more about this later."

"KABLAM!" Another huge shock of thunder riding a brilliant bolt of lightning suddenly shifted the scene. The screen went momentarily blank then switched to a shot of Oswald working diligently on the fuse-box. There in the shadows of the cellar was the blurred outline of a figure moving towards another box on the wall with a protruding lever. It was the switch for the power-main which Oswald had carefully placed in the *off* position.

All the while, Oswald continued working conscientiously. He gripped the screwdriver tightly with both hands, apparently struggling with an overly tightened screw that wouldn't yield. The harder he concentrated, and the tighter he gripped the screwdriver, the closer we saw this other figure coming toward the power-main. Although the picture had been clear moments before, for some reason it lost clarity, leaving the figure little more than an animated blob.

Enthralled by what was happening, I took a split second to break away and look at Norman and Amanda squirming with the realization of what was about to take place. I knew what was happening, too. Our three voices mingled in crescendo: "Look out, Oswald. Let go of the screwdriver. Look out behind you!"

But the voices of the living fell on death-deafened ears. Our only role in this drama spun from yesteryear would be that of observer—and certainly not savior. The strange, vapor-formed head held steady over the television as we screamed out our warning. Much to our horror, we watched the fuse-box on the TV screen erupt into a shower of sparks. Oswald Keating's entire body convulsed violently with the flow of electrical current coursing through him. A cloud of acrid-looking smoke rose from blackening arms while the hair on the top of his head smoldered. He twitched and shook spasmodically.

"*MY GOD, MABEL, NO!*" were the only words we could make out between the screams. "My God, *Mabel*, no!" A few seconds later, gravity and the deadweight of Oswald's own body separated him from the electrical current that incinerated his life.

The three of us sat there on the floor, captivated in kind of a horrified voyeurism while the thunder overhead collided in deafening swells. Lightning arced across the sky. Then, all at once, the vapor-image hovering over the *Zenith* evaporated as if frightened away by some malignant force. At that same moment, my hand touched something wet on the floor. At first I wasn't aware of it. But as my senses heightened to the presence of something foreign in the room, I began to clue in. Afraid to take a look, I moved my hand a bit and felt something hard. I mustered up enough courage to turn and see what it was. It was a black rubber boot, and the shadow of what appeared to be a tall, ghoulish-looking figure looming over me shrouded in black wearing an ankle-length rain slicker. Rainwater dripped steadily and methodically off the hem of the slicker onto my wrist and hand.

In that instant, a flash of lightning illuminated the sight, inducing me to let out a loud, involuntary yell. Franny dropped the antenna wire immediately, sending the reception of the *Zenith* whirling into oblivion. The picture disintegrated into an ocean of meaningless snow and she burst into a gale of frightened tears. I heard Amanda and Norman gasp. There, amidst a growing puddle of rainwater stood the intimidating figure of Aunt Julia.

She untied the hood of her poncho-like raingear, and sliding it back away from her face, shook out her mane of platinum-blonde hair.

"Just what are you kids up to?" she asked in an outwardly casual but inwardly hostile tone. I knew she knew what we'd been doing—just like she'd sensed that something had happened earlier with Franny and the TV. In fact, I felt certain that she'd returned for that very reason.

"Yeah, what are you kids doing?" I heard Father call out casually from the front vestibule. The reassuring sound of his voice as we recovered from the surprise of Aunt Julia's stealth-like arrival put me somewhat at ease.

"We came home because your Aunt Julia felt uneasy," he hollered up the hall. "You know how she is about sensing things."

I could hear Father along with Elly and Livingston fumbling in the foyer, pulling off wet raingear. A few seconds later, Father padded into the drawing room in his stocking feet. Elly and Livingston were a few paces behind. By now, Franny had stopped crying and we had gotten over our initial shock. Amanda, Norman, and I squirmed a bit in front of the snow-screened *Zenith*. Protruding from the wall at a noticeably cockeyed angle, it was the center of everybody's attention. The disconnected antenna wires lay limp on the floor where Franny had dropped them. I knew I'd have to think fast—and I knew Livingston realized exactly what we'd been up to. I counted on his discretion. Norman and Amanda stood there mutely while I spun a rather believable yarn.

"We were watching TV and this big thunderstorm blew up from across the bay," I began. "Things were pretty scary out there, and I remembered that the instructions that came with the TV said we should disconnect the antenna during a bad thunderstorm…so that's what we did," I lied. Norman followed my lead and reached down to pick up the screwdriver lying nearby. He ceremoniously held it up in full view for everyone to see. We held our collective breath.

"Well that certainly was quick and responsible thinking," Elly interjected, breaking the ice. "Don't you think so, Arthur?" She looked at Father. He nodded in agreement. I exchanged a discreet and momentary glance with Livingston that told me he'd back me up.

"I'm glad to see everything's all right then," Aunt Julia offered somewhat believably. "I had this nagging premonition that something might be wrong, and I suggested to your father and Elly that we return." She gestured dramatically as she spoke. The charms on her gold bracelets jingled and danced with each move she made.

"I'm happy to see that everything's under control too, Eddie," Father said. We were only a few minutes away from curtain time at the Esplanade when the announcement came telling us the concert had been cancelled due to the weather. Rather than hang around, we just headed for home. Funny how things work out sometimes, but it seemed like the right thing to do—particularly given the way Aunt Julia felt."

Aunt Julia smiled a knowing smile and looked directly at Franny. Drained, Franny had fallen into a deep sleep right in the middle of the drawing room floor. It had taken no more than a few seconds. I felt a shiver wash over me fueled by a strong feeling of trepidation—a biological warning telling me that Franny was in some sort of danger.

"Well, Norman," Elly said looking him square in the eye. "It seems as if the rain has let up for the time being. Perhaps it's a good time for you and Amanda to make a dash for home?" She looked at Amanda, too, giving her the same cue then glanced over at Franny sleeping soundly on the floor. "Maybe it would be a good idea for all of us to get to bed," she suggested.

Father agreed.

"Come on, Amanda," Norman said willingly. "Grab your stuff and let's get going. I don't want to get caught in another one of those cloud-bursts on the way home if we can help it."

In a matter of seconds, Norman and Amanda politely said their thank-yous and goodbyes then headed out the door. I could hear the sound of the delivery truck rattling down the driveway as they drove out the front gate onto Ridge Road. It made me wonder why I hadn't heard the Bentley pull up earlier. I suppose it had to do with the noise from the storm and the fact that we were engrossed in our TV watching. Just how much did Aunt Julia or anyone else see? I wondered.

"Well, I think it's time we called it a night," Father yawned. "Today has been a pretty busy day. I don't think there's anything left here that can't wait until tomorrow, do you?"

As I ambled toward the stairs with a groggy Franny in tow, I looked back and caught a parting glimpse of Aunt Julia twirling the bare ends of the antenna leads between her thumb and index finger. She had an expression on her face that told me she saw and knew more than she'd let on.

Yes, Father was right. There certainly wasn't anything left that couldn't wait until tomorrow. And tomorrow was bound to be one heck of a day!

CHAPTER TEN

I slept late the following morning. Most of the night I lay awake in bed, tossing and turning while I played the television show we'd seen over and over in my mind. A couple of times I got up and cracked the door open to peer down the hall towards Aunt Julia's room. Both times I could see shadows moving within the thin band of light from beneath her closed door. At some point in the wee hours of the night I dozed off.

When I finally came downstairs around ten-thirty the next morning, I strolled into the drawing room. Livingston was moving around dusting some of the bric-a-brac that Elly had been accumulating. Through the open windows, I could see the sun shining brightly over Narragansett Bay. The air drifting into the room smelled fresh and clear—purified by the previous night's storm and the tangy salt of the sea. I took a moment to look around ensuring that Livingston and I were completely alone.

"Morning, Livingston," I said.

"Morning, Eddie. Sleep well?"

"Well, not really. I tossed and turned most of the night. How about you?"

"Slept like a baby...but I can understand why you were awake. You were all caught up in that experiment you three kids were dabbling in, weren't you?"

"Yeah, I s'pose so," I agreed. "You know how much...CRIPES, what happened to the television set?" At that moment I realized the *Zenith* no longer occupied its familiar space on the wall. In its place sat a marble topped chest of drawers.

"Well, you've slept in this morning, and a lot's happened while you were counting sheep. First, Newport Electric came and picked up the television a little after nine. Then Arakel Bozyan Antiques delivered this new chest of drawers shortly afterwards. Your stepmother bought it the other day when I drove her into town."

Dumbfounded, I sputtered my next question.

"Wh-wh-why did they t-take the television away?"

"From what the service man said, they got a call first thing this morning. The Master apparently asked that they come over right away and pick it up. He said the Master wasn't pleased with the way the television had been performing. Apparently, the master's trying to make up his mind whether to replace it or just get his money back."

"WHAT?" I blurted. "That doesn't make any sense. Why would he think that?"

"I don't know, Eddie, but I did overhear your Aunt Julia tell the Master that the antenna connection appeared to be faulty.

I was thunderstruck.

"Look, never mind about the television set," Livingston said calmingly. "It's probably just as well the blasted thing is gone for now. What went on with that, I'll never know...and I'm beginning to think it's the way things should be." He placed a strong hand on my shoulder and smiled.

"Eddie, how would you like to take a ride in your Aunt Julia's Duesenberg with me? She made an appointment this morning over at Cummings Motor to have the accelerator looked at. Apparently it's been sticking a bit and she's nervous about driving it."

Although I was disturbed about the missing television set, hearing Livingston's latest offer went a long way toward easing the sinking feeling in the pit of my stomach. I'd always lusted after Aunt Julia's Duesenberg, and in my mind the only thing better than driving it had to be riding in it. I jumped at Livingston's suggestion, and although the idea didn't lessen my concern over the recent series of events, it did provide a temporary diversion.

I gobbled down a bowl of Cheerios along with a couple of pieces of toast and before too long we were on our way. During breakfast, Livingston had told me that Father and Elly had driven Franny and Aunt Julia in the Bentley to Easton's Beach for the better part of the day. It came as no surprise to me, since the rocky water's edge in front of our house didn't prove very conducive to swimming or sun-worshipping. Even though we all enjoyed its privacy, Elly and Aunt Julia complained regularly about the uncomfortably stony surface and the beach's lack of bathing-friendliness. Easton's on the other hand— also known as First Beach—held a greater attraction for bathing. Its flat, sandy shoreline made access to the water relatively painless. The unobstructed environment also posed less of a challenge to Franny who had always been somewhat unsteady on her feet. According to Aunt Julia, lack of privacy seemed to be its only drawback.

Realizing I'd be able to spend a day relatively free of family scrutiny and involvement, I happily accompanied Livingston out to the garage. He pulled his chauffeur's cap out of his back pocket and donned it, while I opened the arched, double-doors protecting the Duesenberg from the elements. I couldn't help but marvel at the car's elegant girth. Imagination kicked in as I visualized myself sitting behind the wheel, driving the automotive masterpiece. I conjured up pictures of myself cruising through town under the ogling eyes of all the young girls and to the envy of all the jocks. I even fabricated a scenario involving Jayne Mansfield and put her in the passenger seat next to me. Eventually, plowing my way through a blizzard of imaginary and erotic automotive encounters, I managed to secure the garage doors then climb into the Duesy next to Livingston. Watching him artfully manipulating the complicated combination of levers, switches, and pedals needed to start and drive the 320 horsepower motorcar, I forgot all about Jayne Mansfield. Both the air and my ears hummed with the sound of supercharged exhaust pumping through the chrome manifold pipes of Aunt Julia's car. Livingston pushed both feet down, respectively, on the clutch and brake-pedal then carefully eased the floor-mounted shift-lever into gear. Moments later, we were rolling out of the garage and through the front gate onto Ridge Road.

Sea air filled my nostrils as we flew along Wellington Avenue past familiar sights like the Ida Lewis Yacht Club. Heads turned as Aunt Julia's dazzling blue behemoth cut a course through the streets, leaving a wake of captivated summer admirers craning for a look at her heart-pounding piece of automotive machinery.

Livingston whipped the enormous steering wheel about and pumped the clutch and brake pedals with no small amount of effort. The Duesenberg's lack of power-assisted steering coupled with manual, hydraulic brakes presented quite a challenge to the driver when it came to operating the car. I could see Livingston's powerful arms flexing under the stretch of his jacket sleeves with each pull on the wheel as he, simultaneously, manipulated the pedals and gearshift lever. Noticing the degree of effort, coordination, and dexterity it took for a muscular man like Livingston to maneuver the Duesenberg, I became increasingly aware of just how strong Aunt Julia must be beneath her layers of feminine finery. This realization fueled my apprehension as I recalled the night I followed her to the basement. What unexpected physical odds might I have encountered had I actually been forced into a firsthand confrontation with my eccentric aunt?

"WHOA!" Livingston's sudden yell startled me as the car careened at a breakneck clip into the parking lot at Cummings Motor. I hung on tightly to the side of my seat and the Duesy swerved dangerously. Livingston's hands and feet danced over the pedals and levers in a reflexive blur. To my amazement, the Duesenberg hurtled towards a row of brand new sedans parked directly in front of us then finally screeched to a halt, missing the parked cars by inches.

"Damn! Eddie, are you all right?" Livingston swore as he swiped off his cap and wiped a bead of perspiration from his forehead with his sleeve.

"Your Aunt Julia wasn't kidding when she said that accelerator pedal got stuck. I thought for sure we were going to collide head-on into that row of new cars before I could stop this thing." He gestured towards the lineup of shiny new sedans parked neatly side-

114

by-side in front of us.

"Yeah, I'm okay, Livingston," I said. I had barely gotten out the words when a salesman came bristling out of the showroom towards us.

"Hey, what's the matter with you?" he yelled at Livingston. "Don't you know better than to come flying in here like that? You could have wrecked that row of brand new cars with that monster."

"Sorry, good man," Livingston apologized politely. "We're here because I was told the accelerator pedal's been sticking...and it certainly does. Wouldn't you know there wasn't a single problem with it on the way down...until just the moment we pulled in. Thank God I was able to stop in time."

The salesman saw the frightened look on both our faces and changed his tune.

"OK, Buddy," he said apologetically. "I didn't realize. The service department is right over there." He pointed Livingston in the direction of a large overhead garage door.

"Before you try to start that thing up and move it again, I suggest you go in and talk to the service manager. You'd better let him take care of it."

"Right," Livingston affirmed. "You wait here, Eddie. I'll be right back".

I watched Livingston disappear into the service department then come out five minutes later. He climbed back into the car and gingerly maneuvered the Duesenberg into an open service bay, directed by the hand motions of the service manager who made a noticeable effort to stand clear of the car. It took less than an hour before the sticky accelerator pedal was fixed and we were on our way.

The Newport Historical Society was our next destination. I'd talked Livingston into taking me there while we waited at Cummings

Motor. Along the way, we stopped at the Cote Pharmacy lunch counter for a quick bite, and when we finally arrived at the Historical Society, it happened to be a day when Mabel Keating wasn't on duty. Although I would have liked to have chatted with her, I thought perhaps the fact that she wasn't there worked out for the best. It didn't take long to find an article about a 1944 visit my late grandparents made to Annandale Farm...with Father and Aunt Julia. The write-up was in the society pages:

STEAMSHIP HEIR ARTHUR RIDGEWAY "RIDGE" SUTTON AND WIFE REUNITE WITH FAMILY IN NEWPORT.

The article, as well as another we found, went on to describe in detail the reconnection of my now late grandmother Sutton with her long estranged brother...*Milton Pierce.*

My eyes met Livingston's, and I saw an equally astonished look on his face as we read the social announcement.

"Cripes, Livingston, did you know about this? Did you know that *Milton Pierce* was my grandmother Sutton's *brother*? That means old *Belle Pierce* is...my great aunt."

I could see by the look in Livingston's eyes as he digested the news, that he didn't know.

"No, Eddie. It's as much of a surprise to me as I'm sure it is to you. I'm trying to think back now and remember some conversations I might have overheard between the Master and your mother that would put this into context."

"Livingston, you weren't with us when my grandparents were alive, were you?"

"No, I wasn't. I didn't come to work for the family until 1946—two years after your grandparents were killed in an automobile accident...some years before you were born. But I do remember something. I remember being about my business one Sunday afternoon many years back when I overheard the Master and your mother talking about an uncle—an estranged uncle. His name was Uncle *Milton*. They talked about how the Master's mother—your grandmother Sutton—hadn't spoken to her brother...this Uncle Milton, for decades. As I recall, Milton Pierce was your grandmother's *older* brother. Well anyway...this Uncle Milton had a terrible reputation for drinking and gambling. Your grandmother Sutton had written him off completely when he failed to show up for her wedding to your grandfather.

I recall them saying that Milton had been asked to give your grandmother away on her wedding day—but instead he spent the time in an orgy of drinking and gambling. He never showed up for the ceremony or the reception. Your grandmother was devastated, of course, and had to walk down the aisle alone. Both of your grandmother's parents were deceased at the time. She never forgave her brother...or saw him again, as I recollect. At least that's what I remember. This newspaper article here means there must have been some meeting or reconciliation though, seeing as your grandparents came to see Milton Pierce at Annandale Farm."

"Livingston, do you know what this means?" I reasoned. "It means that Father, Aunt Julia and maybe even Elly are hiding something they don't want discovered about the house. I think they've known all along that there's some dark, mysterious secret that has to be kept quiet. It means that Belle Pierce knows about it too. And Mr. FitzHugh...he must have known. That's why he was murdered. But what could it be...and how could anything be so important that somebody would kill over it?"

I sat quietly, staring into Livingston's eyes searching for an answer.

"Eddie, I don't know, but it's a sure bet somebody—or some*thing*—is trying to tell us about it. We both caught a glimpse of that on the television set. Your Aunt Julia knows too. That's why she talked the Master into having the TV removed. We'd best be *very* careful about this...*very careful* indeed."

Sitting there with Livingston, I recollected the night I followed Aunt Julia to the basement.

"Livingston, remember that night—the first night we set up the TV and saw those crazy images?"

Livingston nodded.

"Well, after you went to bed that night, I happened to peek outside my door and saw Aunt Julia duck out of her room all dressed in black."

"Hmm, where did she go?"

"She went to the basement. She slipped down the back stairs with a flashlight and went to the cellar. I followed her. I'm sure she didn't see me. But when I got down there, she simply disappeared. There wasn't a sign of her...except the smell of that stinky lilac perfume she wears. She went into the *wine cellar* and just vanished."

"What did you do?"

"I hid behind the hot-water heater and waited for her to come out—only she never did. I hid for about two hours. Then, when I finally gave up and went back to my room I passed by her bedroom door again. I could see her shadow moving around under the door. Somehow she managed to get back without my seeing her."

"Very puzzling, Eddie. Very puzzling indeed. Only for now, I suggest we keep today's discoveries to ourselves. That other business with the television has got me baffled as well. But I think it's best not to say anything about any of this right now until we get a chance to talk to Belle Pierce. As your great aunt, she no doubt holds an important clue to all this mystery."

"But Livingston, Belle Pierce is in the hospital with a stroke. 'Member? It happened only a few hours after she found out about Mr. FitzHugh's murder."

"Yes, yes, I remember...but who's to say we can't go pay a little visit to her in the hospital. I'll drive you over there."

"Now?"

"Why not? There's no time like the present. The rest of the family won't be back until late this afternoon. They're at Easton's Beach. Remember?"

I thought about Livingston's suggestion carefully.

"Livingston, s'pose somebody sees us...or the Duesenberg parked over at the hospital? S'pose Belle Pierce calls the house and tells Father or Aunt Julia we've been snooping around asking a lot of questions. I saw Belle Pierce in Davenport's grocery store once. She didn't seem real friendly."

"Well, that's up to you; only I don't think we're going to get to the bottom of what's going on any other way. Look, if it makes you feel any better, I'll drop you off then take the car back into town and kill some time window-shopping. I'll give you a certain amount of leeway—say about an hour—then come back and pick you up. Besides, I think you've got a lot better chance of getting something out of her alone than with me tagging along. 'Might be intimidating, if you know what I mean. I think an old, frail woman like that would be a lot more comfortable sharing stories with her friendly, 14 year-old great-nephew than with some 50-something stranger dressed in a chauffeur's uniform."

I thought about it then conceded. Quickly, we returned the yellowed newspapers and politely said our goodbyes. On our way to the hospital, we stopped at a pay phone where Livingston called patient information to check on Belle Pierce's condition and ability to receive visitors. The attendant said that Belle's condition appeared stable and that visitors were allowed. After giving Livingston the room number, the operator also confirmed that no visitors were there at the moment.

Making one more stop along the way to pick up a bouquet of

119

flowers, we finally coasted to a side entrance of the Newport Hospital around two-thirty that afternoon. I hopped out and wasting no time, Livingston sped away with a promise to be back in an hour. We agreed that if I wasn't waiting when he came back, he would circle the block every five minutes until I came out.

Once inside, I purposely avoided going to the main reception desk to check in, and it took a little doing for me to find my way through the corridors to Belle Pierce's room. I pasted on a friendly smile and kept my floral bouquet highly visible along the way in an effort to legitimize my presence. Both props did their job and eventually I found myself standing outside Belle Pierce's hospital room. Next to the doorframe I noticed a plaque with slots for two names. Only one slot had a name stuck in it. The room looked to be a semiprivate with Belle its only occupant. Peering through the open door, I could see a pair of feet sticking out from under the covers of the bed nearest the window. A partitioning curtain blocked my view of Belle Pierce's head. The freshly made-up bed closest to the door was empty with no sign of anyone in residence.

Haltingly, I entered and made my way across the room. I could hear the sound of life-support equipment laboring away dutifully in the background. Peeking around the room-dividing curtain, I saw a spider's web of tubes, hoses, and cords running between Belle's body and various medical devices. She lay flat on her back with her eyes closed and mouth gaping open. A plastic oxygen tube had been inserted into her nostrils. I recognized Belle's face from that first and only encounter with her in Davenport's grocery store soon after we'd moved in. I could also see the resemblance she bore to the beautiful and vivacious face of the woman in Franny's TV broadcast. Now, she looked a far cry from the dignified lady I initially saw in Davenport's, or the younger manifestation broadcast through Franny's psychic video. Her once neatly coiffed hair lay collapsed around her forehead in stringy ringlets. A lack of makeup accentuated the age spots and deeply creased wrinkles in her face.

Moving closer to the bed, my toe accidentally caught on the base of the rolling meal tray causing some items resting on it to rattle.

Nothing appeared to be wrong with Belle's hearing. Her eyes popped opened and she seemed alert. The left side of her face drooped. Her right hand suddenly grasped the bed-rail and she pulled herself upright a bit. She couldn't seem to move the left side of her body at all.

"Who's there?" she asked cautiously. Her words were noticeably slurred from the stroke.

I held up the bouquet of flowers in my hand and forced a smile onto my face.

"'Scuse me, ma'am. My name's Eddie Sutton," I volunteered softly, "I...I thought I'd just stop around and see how you were doing."

"Who?" she snapped.

"I...I live over on Ridge Road...at Annandale Farm...in your old house," I said.

"GREAT SCOTT! Annandale Farm? What on earth are you doing here?" she blustered.

"Well...ah...er...I'm hoping you might explain—or at least help me figure out—some of the weird stuff that's been happening at the house." I paused for a moment trying to decide if I should bring up the subject of her brother's death. "And I'm really sorry about what happened to your brother," I found myself saying sympathetically.

I watched her eyes rivet on mine.

"Damn fool!" She muttered. "I told that idiot brother of mine..." Her voice stopped mid-sentence as she contemplated why I was really there.

"So you came to see a dying old woman, did you?" She eyed me up and down cautiously for about a half minute. Apparently deciding I posed no real threat, she continued, albeit with some difficulty.

"Well, my boy, take a good look. This is what years of trying to be something you're not gets you. Not a very pretty sight, is it? Don't end up like me," she warned, wagging the long and ancient index finger of her right hand in my face. The once lustrous, red nail polish looked chipped around the tips of her fingernails. Also, the brilliant flash of her big diamond was noticeably absent. I could see a thin, light colored mark on her ring finger where the band of the enormous solitaire had been. A moment later, she softened a bit and reached feebly for the floral bouquet I held out to her.

"My, aren't you sweet to bring this...for a total stranger, no less. 'Dare say, I can't remember when the last time was anybody brought me flowers."

I found myself feeling sorry for her as a feeble smile found its way onto her lips. I pulled a nearby chair over to the side of the bed and sat down. The chair legs grated noisily on the hard, linoleum floor.

"Mrs. Pierce—like I was saying—a lot of weird stuff has been going on at Annandale Farm. Your brother's murder is one of them. I'm kinda hoping you can explain a few things to me."

She looked into my eyes intently.

"The less you know about that house, the better off you'll be, son. That house has brought nothing but hardship and misery to anyone who's owned it. I ought to know. I lived there longer than anybody else ever could."

She paused for a moment to painfully change her position. Reaching over, I helped her adjust the covers under her chin. She seemed appreciative. I thought for a moment about what I would say next then made up my mind.

"Mrs. Pierce...or can I call you...Aunt *Belle*?," I said, taking a leap.

Her eyes gave her away. I knew she knew.

"My, my, my...Aunt Belle, is it? Well yes, I suppose it is. So you figured it out. Yes, son, I'm your great Aunt Belle all right. HA! *Great* Aunt! Pretty funny, wouldn't you say?" she snorted. Only my name really isn't Belle...it's Mabel. *Belle* is a nickname. Never did like the name Mabel...ever since I met that hulk of a cow, Mabel Keating. But Mabel Keating was only a girl when we first met...or maybe I should say a heifer," Belle added caustically with relish and a chuckle.

I didn't let on that I already knew what she was telling me.

"Why has everything been such a mystery?," I asked timidly.

She paused again. I could see her thinking. The sound of labored breathing combined with the beeps and clicks of the life-support machinery were all I could hear. A nurse poked her head in the door, momentarily, and saw we were visiting. She smiled and quickly left, afraid of intruding.

"Look here," Belle slurred. I could sense anxiety in her voice. "I'm going to tell you something that probably only two other people on earth know right now...and whatever you do, son, don't you dare tell another *soul* what I'm about to tell you. Do you understand? Absolutely N-O-B-O-D-Y," she said, spelling out the word.

I nodded my head.

"*Swear* to me you'll not tell another soul."

"I swear," I promised

Belle grasped the bed-rail next to her tightly and pulled herself closer to my ear.

"I know where the gold is hidden at Annandale Farm," she whispered. Relaxing her grip, she settled back. "Can you believe *that*? I've lived in that accursed house for decades and we only figured out where the gold was hidden last year. But by then it was too late. I'd already signed that confounded lease with President Kennedy and his wife. *Blast*, if only I'd found out sooner."

123

She grimaced in pain, wheezing to catch her breath.

"You said *we*," I reminded her.

"Yes, I did say *we*...only right now, to my knowledge, there aren't too many of *we* left alive—and this member of *we* won't be alive much longer," she said pointing to herself.

Perspiration was forming on Belle's brow. I snatched a couple of tissues out of the box on the night table and daubed her forehead dry.

"Thank you, son," she said appreciatively.

"Who are the others?" I asked eagerly.

"You mean who *were* the others?" she corrected me. "My brother, George, was one of them. He's paid for knowing with his life. Now there are just two of us plus that other evil-minded devil who know...but the devil will be coming for me soon. That's why I've got to tell you."

Belle wheezed and coughed some more then pulled herself closer.

"It's why the President was assassinated, you know...because of the gold," she whispered.

I gasped.

"Yes, yes, that's right," she went on. "If the Army Corps of Engineers had put that tunnel in between the two houses, they would have run smack into the gold vein. It's worth billions and billions of dollars, you know. Simon Merriweather knew that too."

So *that* was it. That explained why Aunt Julia dropped her glass that day at the Auchincloss estate at the mention of the tunnel. That explained why she kept looking out across the lawn towards our house. Was she the "devil" Belle Pierce mentioned? And who was the other person she alluded to? I fired off a barrage of questions: Aunt Belle, where's the gold vein hidden? How do I get to it? It's through the wine cellar, isn't it? The key we found—that has something to do with the gold, too, doesn't it? ...And who's the other person you're talking about?"

At that moment, Belle grabbed my arm, squeezing tightly. "Shhhh, that devil's coming for me. Listen, do you hear that?"

I thought for an instant that Belle might have dementia. Then I held my breath and listened. I could hear the sounds of life-support equipment clicking and beeping methodically in the background. Then I heard it. A new but familiar sound that broke the rhythm of the machinery—that unmistakable jingle that always accompanied the melodramatic movements. And the voice; suddenly I could hear that deep, booming voice reverberating down the hall from the nurses' station. My eyes widened with panic, I jumped to my feet and pushed the chair back against the wall then hustled to the door to peek out into the corridor. There, standing in front of the nurses' station at the far end of the hall stood a sight that made my heart leap with fright.

Aunt Julia.

"Cripes, what'll I do?" I muttered under my breath.

"Quick, son, get into the bathroom and close the door behind you," Belle ordered. "If that devil's here for the reason I think, it won't take very long," she slurred. "Before you go, though, put that metal bedpan over there on the table within my reach," she said. "Now you listen for the sound of this thing hitting the floor. When you hear it, crack the bathroom door a bit to make sure the coast is clear—then run as quick as you can. That bedpan hasn't been emptied since this morning, so it'll cause quite a distraction when it hits the floor—and make quite a mess for that matter too," Belle chuckled. "Now remember what I told you, son. Don't you say a word to anybody about what you've heard today."

"I'll be back another time," I said. "I've got a million more questions I have to ask."

"It doesn't matter. That's all you're going to get from me. There isn't going to be another time...I can feel it. Now, be a good boy and do as I've told you and you'll be all right. Get into the bathroom and close the door...and here, you'd better take these flowers too." She poked the bouquet of posies at me haltingly. I could tell she wanted to keep them, but knew she couldn't.

I grabbed them and made a dash for the bathroom. I could hear the familiar jingle of Aunt Julia's charm bracelets growing closer from down the hall as I ducked into the bathroom. The door was located conveniently adjacent to the exit. Just as I pulled it closed, I heard Aunt Julia rattle into the room. I pressed my ear to the door in an effort to hear as much as I could. Listening through the closed door proved difficult. The life-support equipment chugging noisily away in the background didn't help either, nor did Belle's slurred speech. I could make out what sounded like an exchange of greetings between the two women, and I heard chair legs scraping across the hard linoleum as Aunt Julia pulled one over towards the bed. I could only catch a word or two each time one of them spoke. I clearly heard the words *gold* and *murder*. I longed to be able to open the door so I could hear better. A few seconds later I heard the unmistakable clatter of Belle Pierce's bedpan crashing to the floor. Aunt Julia shrieked! Simultaneously, the sound of chair-legs scraping noisily against the floor and Aunt Julia's bellowing voice filled the air. I cracked the door opened just enough to peer out and got a clear glimpse of Aunt Julia's back.

"Here, at least do one thing for me and push that damn call button, will you," I heard Belle say as she held firmly with her good hand to Aunt Julia's wrist to keep her in position. I didn't waste a second. While Belle artfully kept Aunt Julia's back towards me, I made a mad dash through the door. Briskly, I made my way down the hall in the opposite direction of the nurses' station. To my relief, I spotted an exit sign over the door to a stairwell and quickly beat a retreat down the stairs. Within minutes, I found myself walking towards the main lobby, flowers still in hand, and heading for the safety of the outdoors—that is until I caught a glimpse of the Bentley parked out front. Through the glass doors I could only see the back of the car. The convertible top was up, and through the narrow rear window I couldn't quite tell if anyone was in it.

Obviously Aunt Julia's day at Easton's Beach had come to a close. Was anybody in the car? I wondered. Not willing to risk it, I looped around the hallway in the opposite direction in search of another way out. I checked the clock on the wall as I hurried by. Exactly fifty-five minutes had elapsed. If I didn't get out to the street in the next few minutes and intercept him, Livingston would begin making the first of his five-minute interval drive-bys with the Duesenberg...right in front of the Bentley. The sight of the all too familiar Duesenberg with Livingston behind the wheel would certainly raise questions from anyone waiting in the Bentley.

I found an employee entrance where I could easily slip out and make my way towards the street, unseen. To my horror, however, just as I pressed the push-bar and flung the door open wide into the sunshine, I caught a glimpse of Livingston in the Duesenberg rounding the corner. He was on course for a direct encounter with the Bentley. My only chance of interception lay in my ability to outflank the Duesenberg by sprinting towards it. Fortunately, my giraffe-like build afforded me a pair of long, powerful legs that served in good stead when it came to running. As an accomplished member of the Track and Field Team at school, I was well prepared for the task. Without hesitating, I made a mad sprint, waving my yellow floral bouquet furiously at Livingston as I went. Luckily he spotted me and slowed the car to a stop before rounding the point in the road that would have put him in full view of the Bentley. I yanked open the front passenger door and jumped in, hollering hasty instructions to Livingston about turning the car around. We did a quick about face and soon were heading back to the house. On the way, I filled Livingston in on what Belle Pierce had told me—but at the same time took special precaution to heed her warning about how much I shared. Not telling Livingston about the hidden gold or assassination plot against JFK proved difficult, but I did as she said. Livingston puzzled about why Aunt Julia had shown up at the hospital. I felt certain I knew why, but didn't dare say.

Later, as we pulled the garage doors closed behind the Duesenberg then headed across the drive to the front verandah, I thought about all the unanswered questions I still had for Belle Pierce. Foremost in my mind were questions about JFK's assassination...and that *key* we found in the wine cellar. The key had to be part of the mystery too. So did Oswald Keating's electrocution.

Hurrying up the front steps and into the house, I tried to figure out the best way to get back to the hospital for another visit with Belle Pierce. Maybe Livingston could drop me there tomorrow, I thought.

CHAPTER ELEVEN

The hours following my afternoon with Belle Pierce at Newport Hospital proved terribly frustrating. Adding to the trauma of nearly running into Aunt Julia, I wondered if Father and Elly had been there, too, waiting in the parked Bentley with Franny. I hardly said a word to anybody at supper that evening. I went to bed early and tossed and turned all night long. I felt as if I were becoming paranoid...but somehow sensed my fears were justified. For the first time ever, I locked my bedroom door and slept with the window latched too. As an added precaution, I balanced a tambourine on the inside doorknob with the idea that its fall would alert me to any would-be intruders. Ever since the night of the big thunderstorm, I had experienced increased feelings of anxiety and a terrible sense of foreboding.

When I came downstairs the next morning, Father sat on the verandah reading the morning paper with a cup of coffee at his side. Still consumed with unanswered questions from my brief encounter with Belle, my mind raced as I half-heartedly headed out to say good morning to him. I stood there silently at first. His face was hidden behind the newspaper he was reading.

"Morning, Eddie," I heard him say from back of his paper. He made no effort to lower the newspaper and make eye contact.

"Morning, sir," was all I could muster.

"How'd you sleep, son...okay?"

"Fine, sir," I heard myself saying. Did you have a good time at Easton's Beach yesterday? I never did ask you about it last night."

"Yes, Eddie, we did; quite a lovely day, as a matter of fact."

Father kept speaking to me from behind his newspaper.

"I understand you went with Livingston to take care of getting Aunt Julia's Duesenberg repaired. Did you and he have a nice day?"

129

At the moment Father asked his question the shock hit me. For the first time, I noticed the headline staring at me from his open paper facing me. In bold black letters it read:

"MABEL 'BELLE' FITZHUGH PIERCE — LIFELONG NEWPORT RESIDENT SUCCUMBS FROM NATURAL CAUSES."

I felt my guts churn as Father finally lowered his newspaper and looked me in the eye.

"Eddie, did you hear me? I asked you a question. Did you and Livingston have a nice day yesterday?"

"Huh? Oh...ah, yes. Livingston and I had a very nice day. Ah...excuse me, Father. I just remembered I left something up in my room. I'm going to run upstairs and get it."

With that, I dashed in the house and flew up the stairs to my room. Once there, I locked the bedroom door behind me then flopped across the bed. My stomach was in knots. I couldn't believe what I'd just read. Belle Pierce was dead. I had just seen her. The paper said from natural causes. Could it be just a coincidence? But Belle Pierce had been afraid for her life. No, it couldn't be coincidental. Was Aunt Julia capable of killing? Did my flamboyant society aunt have the makings of a murderess? Perhaps it was she who had killed George FitzHugh. I had to find out more—so much more. Now that Belle Pierce was dead, I'd lost a critical link to the past. I needed to know more about the gold vein and its connection to President Kennedy's assassination. I had to know more about Aunt Julia too. I decided there was only one person left who could provide a meaningful link from events of the present to events of the past: *Mabel Keating*.

Having taken a few minutes to regain my composure and being careful not to attract attention, I unlocked the door and went out into the hall to look for Livingston. I found him changing the bed linens in Franny's room. Quietly and deliberately I walked in then closed the door behind me. Livingston paused from his chores.

"Livingston, have you seen the morning paper?" I asked.

I could tell by the blank look on his face that he hadn't.

"It's Belle Pierce," I said. "Cripes, she's *dead!*"

Livingston blanched. "You're kidding?," he winced.

"No, it's in the paper this morning. The headline says it's from natural causes."

Livingston pursed his lips and exhaled a soft whistle.

"Right now we don't have anyone else to talk to except Mabel Keating. She's s'posed to be on duty at the Historical Society this Thursday. I'm gonna go in and see her again."

"What about Amanda Davenport's mother?" Livingston suggested. "Myra Davenport told me once—when she helped me out with some of the cleaning—that she worked for Belle Pierce at Annandale Farm. Myra said it started before she and Dennis Davenport were engaged to be married. As I recollect, she mentioned she started working here around the time the War ended. That would make it 1944 or '45. Who knows? Maybe Myra Davenport even helped out the weekend your grandparents stayed here."

"Livingston, you're a genius! If you can get me into town, I'll get Norman Tate to drive me back in the delivery truck. That way I can take my time meeting with Amanda's mom...if I'm lucky."

Suddenly the realization hit me.

"Livingston?

"Yes, Eddie."

"Livingston, if Myra Davenport *had* been here during that time wouldn't she have already put the pieces together and mentioned it? I mean, wouldn't she have added up two and two and recognized Aunt Julia by now...and the Sutton name? And wouldn't Aunt Julia *surely* have recognized *her*?

He thought about it for a few seconds then nodded.

"Well, people do change you know, Eddie. It's been 20 years already. Perhaps they both looked quite differently then...and as far as names go, *Sutton* is certainly not uncommon."

Something else to ask Myra Davenport about, I noted.

"Okay," Livingston said. "I'll take you. I'm driving your stepmother into town as soon as I'm done with Franny's room. Just do me a favor, will you, and clear it with the Master or her? I don't want to get caught in the middle of anything."

"Deal," I blurted throwing my arms around his waist. I hugged him as hard as I could. He hugged me back and I reveled in it. Not more than forty-five minutes later I found myself waving good-bye to Elly and Livingston in front of The American Café on Thames Street where they'd dropped me. I told Elly and Father that I'd be grabbing lunch there alone then window-shopping and meeting up with Amanda and Norman for a late afternoon matinee at the Strand. Father made it clear the TV wasn't coming back anytime soon, and reluctantly agreed to let me go to the movies—despite the fact that none of his favorite actors were playing.

I made my way across town and over towards Amanda Davenport's house on Holland Street. The Davenports lived in a modest but comfortable two-story, white, frame Victorian with Williamsburg-blue shutters and a matching front door. When I arrived, Amanda was outside snipping off the dead buds from a row of petunias that bordered a whitewashed picket fence surrounding the front yard. She smiled broadly when I strode up. The freckles on her face had grown more noticeable from prolonged exposure to the summer Newport sun. She looked really cute.

"Hi, Eddie," she beamed. "What are you doing here?"

"I came to see your mom, if she's home."

Amanda's face dropped a bit with disappointment.

132

"Gee, I was hoping…," she started to say, but never finished. Then she quickly changed the subject to her mother.

"Sure, Mom's home; she's in the kitchen baking some bread. Come on, I'll take you inside. Isn't it weird about old Belle Pierce dying like that so soon after her brother?" Amanda clucked. "My mom couldn't believe it. She did say that she wasn't surprised though. 'Probably the shock of it all, she said. I know Mom did work for Belle Pierce for a good many years. I'll bet there are *lots* of things she could tell you about what went on at Annandale Farm in the old days. She never shares any of it with me though—not even when I ask her. Let's go in. Maybe she'll talk to you about it."

With that, Amanda grabbed me by the hand and led me into the kitchen. Myra Davenport stood over the kitchen table kneading a batch of freshly mixed bread dough in a yellow, white-rimmed *Pyrex* mixing bowl. She wore a full-length apron to protect her summer cotton dress spattered with flowers. Graying red hair was pinned up away from her face—a pretty face that glowed with friendly warmth. She beamed me a welcoming smile.

"Well, hello, Eddie," she said. I could tell she was surprised to see me even though she tried not to show it. "To what do we owe this honor?" she asked, her smile widening.

"Eddie wants to ask you some questions about Belle Pierce," Amanda blurted out.

I saw the smile vanish from Myra's face.

"Hmm, Belle Pierce, you say. Quite a shame, wasn't it, about her passing on? So sudden…but then again not really, I guess." Myra rubbed her hands together briskly, brushing the bread dough off her fingers. Then she washed her hands under the running water of the kitchen faucet wiping them dry on the end of her long, white apron. Pulling a kitchen chair out from under the table, she sat down and motioned to Amanda and me to do the same.

"What do you want to know, Eddie?" she asked as I eased

myself into a cane-seated kitchen chair.

I hesitated for a minute, wondering if I was making a mistake by talking to Myra. Would she tell Father I'd been to see her? I wondered. Or worse, would she tell him what I came to see her about? Too late now to back out, I thought. Oh well, here goes.

I began telling Myra about the discovery of my grandparents' visit to Annandale Farm back in the summer of 1944. Myra listened intently. Once I'd finished my story, she sighed deeply and folded her hands on the table in front of her.

"Oh yes, I remember that weekend," she said with a waver in her voice. "I remember that weekend as if it were yesterday. I'd only been working for Milton and Belle Pierce for a short time when your grandparents came to visit at Annandale Farm. Dennis and I were just getting started back then. He had dreams of opening up his own store, but the war was just ending and money was tight. I welcomed the chance to pick up some extra cash cooking and cleaning for Belle Pierce on occasion at Annandale Farm."

She paused for a moment to reflect.

"Back then I went by my maiden name of Dellacorte," Mrya went on. "People used to call me *Della* for short. It was kind of a nickname. I dropped it after I married Dennis and switched to using my given name of Myra."

I tapped the nearby table leg with my index finger as I listened to Myra's story. Perhaps that helped explain why no one ever made mention of having met Myra Davenport years earlier at Annandale Farm. Twenty years was a long time, as Livingston had said. People do change—and in Myra's case her name changed too. Nobody had ever met a "Myra" before. It had been a woman named "Della" who served dinner and did the housework back in 1944.

"You know, Eddie," Myra said with intensity coloring her voice. "There's only one reason I'm going to tell you what I'm about to tell you."

134

She looked over at Amanda and then squarely back at me.

"But it's important you don't tell Amanda's father," she cautioned. "He doesn't put any stock in the supernatural. In fact, he gets mad at me when I even bring up the subject.

The supernatural, I thought. This is getting interesting. I nodded in agreement. So did Amanda.

"When Amanda told me about that ghostly encounter you kids had with Franny and that television set I just couldn't believe it. You see, I had a similar experience when your grandparents came to Annandale Farm back in 1944."

I saw Amanda's eyes widen and felt mine do the same.

"When Amanda told me about some of the images you saw on that TV, I felt a shiver go up and down my spine," Myra said. "I've never told this story to a soul—and especially not to Dennis. Unless you were there, you wouldn't have believed it."

Amanda and I sat there, captivated, as Myra recounted the story of my grandparents' war-era visit to Newport back in June of 1944.

"I remember that big car your grandparents drove coasted up the driveway at Annandale Farm sometime in the mid-afternoon. It was a beautiful afternoon—June 7th to be exact. I remember the date so well because the Allies had just invaded the beaches of Normandy the day before. The news wires were all a-buzz; in fact, Milton Pierce had been sitting on the front verandah listening to news reports on that old crystal radio set of his when your grandparents arrived. The radio had a long wire and a funny looking ear-piece he used to wear."

Myra's description of Milton Pierce left no doubt about his penchant for drink. She said he sat bundled up that day in a blanket on a wicker chaise lounge nursing gin and tonics. His ruddy complexion evidenced the characteristics of a man given to a long developed habit of excess. A large, heavily veined nose dominated his face. Wisps of fine, white hair twirled lightly about in the afternoon breeze, and a pair of deeply set, bloodshot eyes aided in making him look well beyond his then sixty-five years.

Myra said that as my grandparents' car came to a halt in front of the verandah, the screen door had opened and Belle Pierce stepped out into the breeze. She wore a silk summer dress evidently looking very much the lady of the manor. Waving and smiling to her arriving guests, Myra said that Belle made a snide-comment to Milton saying that the house and grounds had grown worn and tired—much like him.

Apparently the house did indeed look tired back in 1944—and for the nearly two decades following. Even though George FitzHugh dedicated a goodly portion of his time towards upkeep, it wasn't enough. The once dramatic rose gardens had diminished to a collection of densely infested weed islands—each populated by only a few sparsely blooming rosebushes. The golf course-green lawn had burned to a crisp from the summer sun, and its once fairway-like appearance now resembled a crabgrass laden patchwork quilt. In addition, the mansion had fallen into disrepair. Although the white stucco exterior had held up well against the corrosive salt air and intense summer heat, the wood trim had not. Paint peeled in wide sheets from the woodwork of the verandah and most of the window frames, leaving exposed, wound-like markings marring the finish. Also, one of the four giant pillars on the towering front portico had developed a considerable list—the result of severe settling of the underlying concrete footing. Completing this picture of architectural blight, the once graceful greenhouse lay in a shambles with many of its leaded glass panes shattered or cracked.

All in all, back in 1944, Annandale Farm could be likened to the dilapidated and time-encrusted wedding cake eternally preserved by Charles Dickens' eccentric Miss Havisham in *Great Expectations*.

Myra alluded to the legend of hidden gold on the property as she spoke.

"Most people simply dismissed the gold lore," she recollected, "but Belle Pierce seemed obsessed with the idea that the story could be true. That...and a lot more...became evident the day your grandparents arrived."

Myra said that stepping out of the gleaming Duesenberg, my grandparents were a striking contrast to the dismal picture of eroding decay. Myra also said that Aunt Julia—only nineteen years of age at the time—had accompanied my grandparents on that trip to Newport.

With Myra's making reference to Aunt Julia, I decided to ask her if she had ever approached Aunt Julia about their encounter some 20 years earlier.

"No," she said, "to tell you the truth, I've avoided bringing up the subject. Personally, I don't think your aunt recognized me after all these years—or even remembers that I was actually there at the house. Back then, Belle Pierce and everyone else who knew me called me *Della*. I was about 25 pounds lighter then too, and had my hair different—long to my shoulders and dyed blonde." Amanda and I smiled as Myra pinched the sides of her noticeable midriff.

"There were a lot of strange things that went on at Annandale Farm around that time that I'd just as soon forget about," Myra said. "Some of it is just plain scary. I probably should have spoken up about it back then, but I was afraid—afraid of Belle Pierce in that she'd tell everyone I was crazy and I'd lose my job. But now that Belle is dead, I guess it doesn't really matter anymore."

Myra turned and looked directly at me. "Still, I think it's best that you don't let on to your father or Aunt Julia that I was around back then—some things are best just left alone."

I was relieved to hear her say it and nodded my head in vigorous agreement.

Myra recounted that while my grandparents conversed with Belle and Milton Pierce on the verandah, Aunt Julia wandered about the grounds exploring the estate. It was when Aunt Julia drew near to the base of the front portico that Myra said she reacted to something. Apparently that ended, however, when George FitzHugh suddenly appeared. He had been working in the greenhouse. After introducing himself to Aunt Julia, George walked her back to the verandah.

Myra said that Belle went through the usual hostess niceties. She introduced George to my grandparents then offered everyone a cool drink and something to eat. While Myra served the drinks and hors d'oeuvres, an interesting conversation ensued.

Apparently, Aunt Julia's psychic gift became a major topic of discussion that interested Belle Pierce to no end. My grandmother Sutton had shared that day that Aunt Julia had been having deep, trance-like spells or blackouts. During these trances, Aunt Julia could do some remarkable things. When appropriately questioned, for example, she could determine the location of long lost or missing articles. Also, the deep secrets of deceased friends and relatives were miraculously uncloaked and later verified by people who intimately knew them. In some cases, these people were the victims of an intimate family atrocity or a crime which they'd never revealed. It was all quite astonishing.

Belle Pierce must have seen Aunt Julia's gift as an opportunity for finding the long elusive treasure she'd sought for decades—a means of locating the missing pieces of the puzzle that would lead her to the gold. However it happened, a séance wound up being scheduled for later that evening.

"Milton Pierce, on the other hand, was apparently more of a skeptic," Myra told us. "He opted to sit alone out on the verandah listening to the war news on his antique crystal radio set.

'Fine, have it your way, Milton,' Belle had said dismissively. 'Listen to that fool radio of yours. The rest of us will go ahead without you.'

It was nearly 9:30 PM that night when Myra finally cleared the remains of dessert and coffee from the dining room table. Belle and the troop of prospective séancers headed for Annandale's drawing room. There they took their places around a pedestal-based game table. Aunt Julia sat next to Belle, who in turn sat next to George FitzHugh. My grandfather and grandmother Sutton completed the circle. That's when Milton Pierce changed his mind and decided to join in. He'd been heading out to the verandah with radio set in hand, but suddenly became intrigued by the sight of the séance. The ice cubes from a freshly poured gin and tonic clinked in the glass tumbler he carried as he made his way towards the table. In his right ear, the radio ear-piece hummed with the latest war news. Myra had just switched out the lights when Milton had his sudden change of heart and barged in.

"'Hmmm, maybe I'll sit in for a few minutes to see how this séance thing goes,'" Myra told us he said. He plunked himself down between your grandparents, sliding his drink onto the table. Then he fine-tuned the radio receiver to bring in the latest war news. A full moon hovered dramatically over Narragansett Bay, bathing the room in soft but eerie light.

'Milton, put a coaster under your glass before you ruin the table, will you?' Belle scolded. Obediently, Milton snatched a coaster from a stack on the table placing it under his perspiring glass.

'And turn off that fool radio,' Belle snapped.

Milton nodded, but apparently never complied. Everyone placed their hands, palms down and flat, around the rim of the table. Each person touched the tips of his or her own two thumbs together. Next they touched the outstretched pinky of each hand with the pinky of the person on either side.

'Perfect,' Aunt Julia said approvingly. 'Now, it's very important that nobody breaks the chain of physical contact. And it's also important that we concentrate on the same thing. In this case, it's *gold* or some kind of treasure we're looking for...so it would be good if that's what everybody thought about.'

Myra said that Milton sat hunched over the table rather uncomfortably and seemed very preoccupied. The annoying drone of an announcer's voice rasped from the crystal radio's ear-piece. Milton kept it held securely in place by a wire bracket stretched across the top of his head. He wasn't tuned into the dialogue going on around him.

'Milton!' Belle snapped. 'Did you hear what Julia told you about not breaking the chain of hands?'

Milton looked up distractedly. 'I heard…I heard.' he mumbled in a deep, gravelly voice.

'Think about gold and treasure…and don't break the connection of hands,' Belle repeated—which Milton promptly did just long enough to drain his glass of gin and tonic. Ignoring the coaster easily within reach, a distracted Milton set his empty cocktail glass directly on the tabletop while Aunt Julia went on with her instructions.

'Now it's better if nobody speaks during the séance. Silence is best, but that said, a word spoken here or there won't actually interfere with making a connection to the other side. It can distort the connection, however—make it erratic or unclear. Now, it'll take a few minutes before I slip into a trance. Mother, you know what to do," Aunt Julia said, looking at my grandmother.

'Is there somebody in particular Julia should try to make contact with on the other side?' my Grandmother Sutton wanted to know. 'Someone passed on who might have known something about where this gold or treasure might be hidden?'

No one spoke up.

"The moonlight shining into the room from across the water illuminated everyone's faces," Myra recalled. "I could see everything, because I was standing in the background—in a kind of nook where the fireplace met the wall—you know; so I could tend to anyone's needs on a moment's notice, should anybody want anything. Belle always liked her servants to be both attentive and innocuous. To her, I was just another piece of furniture in the room…but I could see it all. I could see Belle and her brother exchanging glances. Everyone just sat in silence for a good minute or more until Belle finally spoke up."

"'Simon Merriweather is the person to look for,' Belle volunteered. 'He's the one who built this house…and if anyone has an idea where that treasure might be hidden, Simon's most likely the one.'"

Myra said that Aunt Julia repeated Simon's name quietly, over and over. 'Simon Merriweather…Simon Merriweather…Simon Merriweather.' They watched attentively as Aunt Julia closed her eyes and began breathing slowly and deeply. Her head bobbed from side-to-side; then in long circular motion as if she were exercising her neck.

Inhale…exhale…inhale…exhale. Head back; head to the side; forward…then backward…round and around.

It took about five minutes for Aunt Julia to go into a full trance. When she finally did, she slumped forward in her chair—her forehead hovering inches above the tabletop in front of her. Strands of platinum hair danced on the polished tabletop as she swayed gently to and fro. The only sound to be heard was the muffled and increasingly irritating drone of Milton Pierce's radio set pulsating from his ear-piece.

Then something even more unusual happened, Myra shared with us. A barely distinguishable swarm of what first appeared to be gnats began to materialize around Milton Pierce's head. At first, Myra said she thought they were insects. Then she noticed their odd, translucent-like form.

"These things certainly weren't bugs," Myra insisted.

As they vibrated, the tiny particles compacted more tightly and eventually homogenized into an opaque cloud. The mist drifted eerily around Milton's head, hovering in close proximity to his ear-piece. The swarm lingered as if held there by some magnetic-like force. Myra said she watched from her place, standing in the drawing-room against the wall, while Aunt Julia's mouth began opening and closing, indiscriminately, but without emitting a sound.

Apparently Milton Pierce broke the silence first.

'Wha...what the hell...?' he sputtered, his head tilting in an effort to listen to his resonating ear-piece more clearly. The familiar voice of the announcer had changed to a new and barely distinguishable monotone. Suddenly, the ear-piece dislodged from his ear, landing with a "thunk" on the table in front of him. It came to rest against his empty cocktail glass. The vapor-like halo surrounding Milton's head migrated to the tabletop along with the earpiece.

The tumbler sitting on the table contained nothing but a few ice cubes, but began acting like a small amplifier. A nasal voice with a staccato timbre began vibrating through the crystal cocktail glass. Amplified by the hardwood of the tabletop, a word could be picked out here and there through the static then the words became clearer. At that point, Milton actually draped his earpiece on the edge of the glass.

"Needless to say, it was *very* spooky," Myra said. "First, the word *Ollie* came. Then came a bit of static and it sounded like the voice said *Oswald* and then *the key.* There was more static, then the word *Simon* came next followed by *murder*.

We all heard *gold* and *murder* repeated two or three more times as plain as day," Myra insisted. "And let me tell you, the word *murder* really caught everyone's attention." Myra swore an oath, holding up her right hand as though on the witness stand. "After that, there was nothing but silence—then out of nowhere this God-awful, mournful cry and the word *cellar.* Then to everyone's surprise—and more to one person's than any other—we all heard the name *Mabel* clear as a bell, followed by the word *murder.*"

All the while, Amanda and I sat there listening, it was evident that Myra was reliving the moment. Her hands trembled, although we pretended not to notice, and her eyes grew wide with a borderline look of terror.

"I'll never forget that haunting, tormented voice...and that eerie energy-halo swirling around Milton's cocktail glass and ear-piece," Myra recollected. "And while all this was happening, your Aunt Julia had begun writhing about in her chair—as if she were having an epileptic fit or something. She twitched and gyrated in a kind of weird synchronization with that odd voice coming from Milton Pierce's radio. Each time the voice on the crystal set spoke, your Aunt Julia twitched about more spasmodically."

Myra paused to collect herself for a moment. She wiped the palms of her perspiring hands on her apron and got up to get a glass of water from the tap. Amanda and I just sat there without saying a word. After taking a few sips, she was back telling her story again.

"I watched your aunt mouthing words with no sound coming out of her lips. Then all at once she blurted it right out: 'Who are you?,' she demanded. Why, it startled me so that the hair on the back of my neck stood right up on end."

Myra reached behind her, stroking the back of her neck with her right hand. Clearly, she was experiencing the same reaction.

"'Are you someone who died in this house?' Your aunt asked next. There was silence then the voice on the radio crackled across the wire in a short burst."

"'*The key!*' it said almost pleading-like...hauntingly. Then there was silence again."

"'Are you someone who died in this house?' your aunt repeated."

"'*The key!*' the voice echoed back."

"'Where did you die?' your Aunt asked."

"'*The cellar!*' The voice wailed sorrowfully."

"'Are you someone known to us? Why isn't your spirit at rest? Where did you die?' There was nothing. Then..."

"'*This house,*' the spirit said woefully. '*Mabel knows! Gold!*

Oswald holds the key!'"

"Well with that, we all saw Belle Pierce let go a shudder that could be seen and felt clear across the room. Watching her reaction made my skin crawl," Myra remembered. "And then Belle suddenly lunged across the table, sweeping the radio, ear-piece, and crystal tumbler onto the floor with a single thrust. The glass shattered. Milton just sat there gazing at his busted radio and the broken glass glimmering at him in the moonlight. Belle just flopped backward into her chair—drained of energy, I suppose."

"'BELLE! Why on earth did you do that? Are you nuts or something?' Milton hollered at her."

"Then right at that moment, your Aunt came out of the trance. And as God is my witness, I felt certain that Belle Pierce recognized that those clues broadcast across her husband's radio set were about her. It was all muddled with static and muffled by old technology, but the voice crying out was audible to everyone in that room."

Myra told Amanda and me that from that point forward, Belle moved quickly and brought the séance to a close. Soon afterward, my grandfather apparently announced they were turning in for the night. They were going back to New York City in the morning after a stop on Bellevue Avenue to visit Doris Duke at Rough Point—her Newport estate, so a good night's sleep was in order.

It was at this juncture of telling her story that Myra told me something I never knew. She said my grandparents were fast friends with Doris Duke and they socialized regularly. Doris Duke's estate was situated on a brow overlooking the ocean. The mansion was erected on ground where Bellevue Avenue and Ocean Drive meet. Built on a spectacular rock-strewn section of Atlantic coastline, the house was constructed during the years of 1887–1889 by Frederick Vanderbilt, the brother of Cornelius Vanderbilt. The stone mansion and manicured grounds were subsequently purchased and extensively remodeled during the years of 1922–1924 by tobacco tycoon James

Duke. Upon his death in 1925 my grandmother's good friend, Doris—James Duke's only daughter—became the sole beneficiary of a vast fortune that included, among other things, the Newport house and his expansive tobacco holdings.

Myra told Amanda and me that after the séance, she escorted my grandparents and Aunt Julia to their rooms, making certain they were comfortable.

Now, some 20 years later, here I was sitting around the Davenport's kitchen table, listening to the story as if it had happened yesterday. I asked Myra if she could share anything about the moments leading up to my grandparents' departure.

"I'm afraid not," she answered apologetically. "That's all I know. After I said goodnight to your grandparents, I went back down to the kitchen and finished cleaning up. Then I went home. Belle Pierce told me she wouldn't need me the next day since your family was leaving. It wasn't but a few weeks later that I found out your grandparents had died in an automobile accident; such a terrible tragedy. They were lovely people!"

Amanda piped in with her two cents.

"Why don't you ask your father about the visit your aunt and your grandparents paid to Annandale Farm back then?," she posed.

I thought about it for a minute.

"No, I don't think I should ask," I said. "It wouldn't be smart. I'm feeling kind of alone at the moment."

Myra's face looked sympathetic, but all at once, it seemed like the right time to leave. Perhaps, I thought, my upcoming meeting Thursday with Mabel Keating at the Newport Historical Society would shed more light on this dilemma I was trying to solve...and the direction in which I needed to go.

"Well, I guess I'd better get going now," I heard myself say.

"It's getting late and I told my family I'd be getting a ride home from Norman Tate. Do you know if Norman's over at the store?" I asked my two friends, revealing the obvious lack of planning behind my visit. Luckily, Myra nodded her head in the affirmative.

"Yes, he should be there—unless he's out making a delivery. I can give you a ride home, Eddie, if you like."

I thought about Myra's offer and decided against it.

"Thanks, Mrs. Davenport, but I think I'd better stick with my original idea, if you don't mind? It's not that long of a walk over to the store from here."

"All right, if you think that's the best thing. Only please don't say anything to Dennis about our conversation if you see him. Can I count on you, Eddie?"

"Sure!" I said. "You have my word."

With that I thanked Myra and left. I was only about a block away from Davenport's when Norman whirled around the corner in the delivery truck, screeching to a halt at the curb.

"Hey, where 'you going, Sutton," he inquired with a smile through the open driver's window. Taking a final drag on the cigarette he was smoking, he flicked the butt into the gutter. Instinctively, I stepped down off the curb and squashed out the glowing embers with the heel of my shoe.

"To look for you," I said poking my face in the open window. The smell of cigarettes lingered in the cab. Definitely not for me, I thought, remembering my one and only attempt at smoking. "I need a ride home when you're done. Can you give me one?"

"Sure! I just made my last delivery. Hop in."

In a flash I ran around to the passenger side and jumped into the front seat beside Norman. Seconds later, we were rattling down

Thames Street towards Annandale Farm. The smell of cigarettes quickly vanished in the fresh air. On the way home, I shared with Norman my concerns resulting from the last and only hospital visit I'd paid to Belle Pierce and how Aunt Julia had shown up there only hours before Mabel died.

"Hey, wait a minute," Norman said. "That all happened yesterday—around three o'clock, you said? Well, I can tell you one thing for certain, your Aunt Julia couldn't have been at the hospital around three o'clock."

"What do you mean?" I asked. "Why do you say that?"

"Because I saw her at Easton's Beach at three o'clock."

"WHAT? How can that be? You've got to be wrong."

"Believe me, I know your Aunt Julia. I saw her walking up and down the beach—she must have walked by the place I was sitting about five or six times. She had on one of those big floppy hats that matched this yellow, kind-a beach sarong she'd wrapped herself up in. That walk of hers is unmistakable. She didn't see me though. I was lying on my stomach on a beach-blanket and wearing sunglasses. I was there with my cousin, Vinnie. It was my day off, and Vinnie came over from Providence to spend the day."

I mulled over in my mind what Norman had just shared. There was no doubt that I had seen and heard Aunt Julia at the hospital yesterday at the same time. Her presence and the sound of her voice were unmistakable. So were those obnoxious charm bracelets.

"Cripes, Norman, think about the time. Are you absolutely *sure* you saw my aunt around three o'clock yesterday? Could you have been wrong?"

"Nope! No way! I saw her at three o'clock all right. I know because I had just looked at my watch. I'd promised my mother that Vinnie and I would be home by four-thirty, and we were watching the time pretty closely."

"Did you see Father and Elly there too—with Franny?"

"To tell you the truth, the beach was pretty packed. I didn't see them around, but I have to admit I didn't make it a point to look either. By the time Vinnie and I left a little after four, I didn't see a trace of your aunt—or anyone else I knew for that matter. Like I said, I wasn't really going out of my way to look though."

The thought of what Norman shared seemed incomprehensible. How could Aunt Julia have been in *two* places at once? I sat quietly for the rest of the ride home pondering the enormity of the implications. Were Father and Aunt Julia conspiring together in some kind of charade—or were Father and Aunt Julia working independently? Did one—or both of them—murder or conspire to murder Belle Pierce...and probably George FitzHugh too? And how did the death of Oswald Keating fit into all of this—as well as the disappearance of Ollie Merriweather? What about Elly...and Franny? I wondered. How much did they know about what went on that day—or other days for that matter? My mind raced. I didn't dare talk to Elly about any of it. But I could certainly approach Franny...as long as I did so in such a way as to minimize the risk of anyone else finding out. I thought about the 1944 séance Myra Davenport shared; and the newspaper articles revealing that my grandparents and Aunt Julia had been to Annandale Farm decades prior to our own arrival. But most of all I thought about Belle Pierce's last words to me about the gold...and JFK's assassination.

A few minutes later, as the dilapidated delivery truck rattled through the front gate of Annandale Farm, I saw the house looming up at me larger and more forebodingly than I'd ever felt before. It seemed as if the giant structure now suddenly possessed a power all its own—a power so penetrating and diabolical that it permeated the minds and souls of anyone occupying its haunted domain.

Was it the house and all the mystery enshrouding it that caused me to inwardly quake with this sudden realization...or was it the idea that Father and his sister were waiting for me there? Waiting within its lore-laden walls to implement some heinous plan that would ultimately satisfy their demented lusts...and perhaps cost Franny and me our lives. I knew, now, this wasn't my overactive imagination playing tricks on me. This was real.

As I stood on the front steps of the verandah watching Norman wave goodbye, I wondered what new, nerve-wracking trauma awaited me. The only thing that kept me from turning tail and racing up the driveway was the fact that Franny—innocent Franny—needed me. The thought of her facing life-threatening danger alone made me feel petty and guilt-ridden over past resentments—resentments stirred by the annoying intrusions her condition could bring into my own life.

The fact that Livingston could be counted on comforted me. With these thoughts in mind, I put one foot in front of the other and made my way up the stairs to the verandah. Through the open windows, I could hear the clatter of dishes coming from the dining room as Livingston laid out the table for supper.

It was going to be a very long night, I thought to myself—longer than any I'd ever experienced during the course of my 14-year life.

CHAPTER TWELVE

During dinner and all through the rest of the evening, I kept a very low profile and spent most of it intentionally silent. I figured the less I said, the better my chances were of not accidentally spilling the beans about what I knew—or thought. I imagined Aunt Julia sensed this because she went out of her way to try to stimulate conversation. As much as part of me wanted to respond—solely in the interest of minimizing suspicion—I rigorously applied the rule of letting "discretion be the better part of valor" and kept my mouth shut. This went on throughout dinner and during the time spent afterwards, sitting on the verandah with Father, Elly, Aunt Julia and Franny watching the sunset.

I had resolved to quiz Franny about her visit to Easton's Beach during the course of putting her to bed and waited patiently for the moment when Father would announce bedtime. A little after nine o'clock, Livingston came out on the verandah to inquire as to anyone's needs. At that point, Father made his pronouncement and declared it to be a few minutes past Franny's bedtime. Glad that the time had finally come, I decided to take advantage of the situation by announcing my own intention of turning in for the night.

"I'll help Livingston take Franny up to bed," I volunteered. "I'm feeling pretty tired myself."

"You must be, son," Father chimed in. "You've scarcely said a word all evening. Is everything all right?"

"Yes, sir. I'm just feeling kinda rundown," I lied. "I'll help Livingston tuck Franny in for the night and get a good night's sleep myself while I'm at it."

"Eddie," Aunt Julia interjected. "Maybe you ought to take a couple of aspirin before you go to bed. I've got some in my handbag."

"Aspirin? Do you think that's really necessary?" Elly

interjected with a concerned look. "He didn't say his head hurt or anything. He just said that he felt overly tired tonight. I don't think we really need to give him anything, do we?"

I welcomed Elly's intervention as she shot an insistent look at Aunt Julia then Father.

An alarm bell had instantly gone off in my head. Don't take the aspirin, it rang out at me. In fact, this internal alarm bell triggered a whole wave of new thoughts about poison and what fate Father or Aunt Julia—or both of them for that matter—might have in store for me if they suspected I knew too much.

"No thanks. I'll be fine," I heard myself say. "I just need a good night's sleep. C'mon, Franny. Let's go up to bed."

I took one of Franny's hands, and Livingston took the other. I could feel Father's and Aunt Julia's eyes following every movement as the three of us abandoned the verandah for bed then disappeared through the front door. I looked over my shoulder as we ascended the stairs to ensure nobody followed. Once we got to Franny's room, I quickly closed the door then herded Franny and Livingston towards the edge of the bed. There we sat in silence for a few minutes while I collected my thoughts and determined the best way to broach the subject of Franny's visit to Easton's Beach. I had told Livingston during a private moment before supper about Norman's sighting of Aunt Julia there.

"Hey, Franny, did you have a good time at Easton's Beach with Elly, Father and Aunt Julia?" I probed.

Franny sat mutely on the bed twirling the ends of her hair between her thumb and index finger.

"Uh huh," she mumbled.

"What did you do?" I asked.

Twirl; twirl; twirl.

"I don't remember."

"You don't remember? Whadda ya mean you don't remember?" I smiled at her calmly. "You were there, weren't you?"

"Uh huh...but I don't remember."

"Franny, why don't you remember?" I was growing impatient.

"I was asleep."

I looked at Livingston, exchanging glances of curiosity.

"What do you mean you were asleep?" I asked. "Why were you sleeping?"

"I guess I felt tired...so I went to sleep. I took a nap."

Franny smiled. She liked keeping us guessing. I looked at Livingston again.

"Franny, did anybody give you anything to swallow—pills or somethin' like that?" I pursued.

"I don't know. I don't think so."

"Well, when did you wake up from your nap?"

"I don't know...after I got home, I think."

"You didn't wake up from your nap 'til after you got home? That's interesting!" I said to Livingston.

"Franny, why don't you go into your bathroom and wash up for bed, dear," Livingston suggested. She hopped off the bed and trundled into the bathroom adjoining her room. We waited until we could hear water running to resume our conversation.

"Livingston, I can't figure it out," I whispered. "Aunt Julia couldn't have been in *two* places at the same time. One of them had

152

to be a double. Trouble is, the only witness to what went on at Easton's Beach happens to be a 12 year-old kid with Down syndrome...who was asleep the whole time. Kind of a problem, don't you think?"

"Yes, it certainly is...in more ways than one. Eddie, why would someone go to all the trouble of impersonating your aunt anyway?"

I pondered Livingston's question. I didn't really have a watertight answer.

"Cripes, I don't know—for an alibi maybe—to cover up killing Belle Pierce."

"It doesn't work, Eddie. Think about it. First of all, the paper said that Belle Pierce died of natural causes, so there isn't any hint of a murder to even cover up—at least that we know of. And secondly, you said your Aunt Julia arrived at the hospital with the same flurry of commotion that typically accompanies her wherever she goes. If somebody wanted to commit murder, they certainly wouldn't make their presence at the scene of the crime so obvious."

What Livingston said made sense. He paused. "Hmm, unless, of course, that somebody was impersonating someone they wanted blamed for the murder."

That sounded good to me.

"Livingston, that's got to be it. I'm willing to bet money that Belle Pierce *didn't* die of natural causes...and her killer was impersonating Aunt Julia—just in case they didn't pull it off. The only thing the double didn't count on was Norman Tate spotting the real Aunt Julia at Easton's Beach."

"Hmm, did he spot the real one at Easton's Beach?" Livingston challenged. "What makes you so sure of that? Which was the imposter?"

I didn't have to think long about that one.

153

"This is what really scares me, Livingston. I think it's Father."

Livingston looked stunned. He shook his head in disbelief.

"I *hardly* think so. I could never believe that. Eddie, I really think your imagination is going too far this time."

"Livingston, I'm really scared," I pleaded feeling desperate. "I don't know what else to think. When I went to talk to Myra Davenport earlier today she told me all about the visit my grandparents made to Annandale Farm back in 1944. You were right. She *was* there at the house. They held some crazy séance the night before my grandparents left."

I felt the tears starting to well up in my eyes. I loved Father, and the last thing I wanted to believe was that he could be a murderer. Livingston responded compassionately.

"Eddie, I agree with you. I don't know who else could pull it off, either. But why would the Master want to kill Belle Pierce?"

By now tears were running down my cheeks and dropping onto the front of my shirt.

"I think it's 'cause of something that happened back in 1944," I sniffled—"when Aunt Julia visited Belle Pierce and her husband Milton at Annandale Farm. I think it has to do with the hidden gold. I think that gold is behind *everything* that's been happening at Annandale Farm." I paused for a moment to wipe my nose with my sleeve.

"Somehow the gold is connected to other deaths at the house, too," I insisted. "—Oswald Keating's and Mr. FitzHugh's. It all started with Ollie Merriweather's disappearance back in 1900. In some way, the tunnel that was s'posed to connect Hammersmith Farm with our house figures into it all. And I have to tell you something else."

I hesitated, pondering the warning Belle Pierce had given me about sharing her secret. Livingston looked at me in anticipation until I finally just blurted it out. "Belle Pierce told me not to tell anyone, but I have to tell you. She said that she found the gold and that there was a plot to assassinate President Kennedy. She said that Aunt Julia was in on it. So is some other person, but she didn't say who. Now Belle Pierce is dead. Oh, Livingston, what are we going to do?"

I couldn't go on. I had to stop to wipe the flow of tears running down my face with my hands. I felt Livingston put his powerful arm around my shoulder and give me a comforting squeeze. I could tell, although he found it hard to believe, the news I'd just shared about the Kennedy assassination shocked him enough to make him think about it.

We could still hear Franny pottering around in the bathroom brushing her teeth. She took a long time to accomplish most tasks, and often held up the works when we were trying to get somewhere. I was glad her doodling gave us an added moment of privacy.

"Eddie, this is a pretty big nut for a 14 year-old boy and two of his young cronies to try and crack on their own," Livingston offered as I worked at regaining my composure. "I'm here to help you, but maybe we should call Captain Karl and ask for his intervention. If you're right—especially about this Kennedy plot—then these are dangerous waters we've entered. If the Master is involved along with your Aunt Julia, then your stepmother could be part of it too. This could be *very* dangerous. We could be jeopardizing the safety of Norman Tate and Amanda Davenport as well—and possibly Amanda's parents. What do you say we go to Captain Karl?"

I hadn't thought about it before, but calling Captain Karl didn't feel right to me for some reason.

"Cripes, Livingston, who would *ever* believe all of this?" I found myself saying in protest. "Captain Karl would start posing questions to Father, Aunt Julia and Elly. It could all backfire on us. I think we have to try to piece this together on our own. We don't have any other choice. And it's too late to turn back. We can't just ignore it or pretend nothing's happened. We have to go forward."

I paused for a moment to think about who besides Mable Pierce might be able to help solve the growing list of mysteries facing us. There was only one person I could come up with.

"There is someone who could help us put the puzzle pieces together," I said. "I'm sure everything began with Ollie Merriweather's disappearance back in 1900. Ollie must've known something or stumbled on something—something to do with the gold. Mabel Keating's the only one alive now with any idea of what could've happened to Ollie Merriweather. Tomorrow is Thursday and Mabel will be helping out at the Historical Society. I'm gonna ask you to drive me over there so I can talk to her, Livingston. You've gotta help me. You're the only one left I can trust or count on. Will ya...please?"

Livingston smiled a loving, paternal-like smile.

"Of course I'll help you, son. You know I will. Do you think I'd leave you to deal with this all on your own?" Then, before I knew it, he was talking about my late mother.

"God bless your sainted mother. Just before she died, she asked me to look after you and your sister and protect you. I swore to her I would. That's a promise I'll not break. She was a lovely woman, your mother—an angel come to earth. If you think I'm going to leave you to fight dragons on your own, you're mistaken, my boy. I'm with you all the way, son."

For a moment, I thought I saw tears in Livingston's eyes. I knew he loved me and meant every word he said. I knew he'd cared about my mother, too...but I'd never heard him speak with such emotion about her before. Then, in an instant, the moment was broken. The bathroom door creaked open and Franny pranced out in her poodle-plastered summer pajamas ready for bed.

"I'm ready to go to Lilly White's party," she announced with a grin.

"OK, Franny," I said. "In you go."

I watched Livingston whack her playfully on the backside as she bounced into bed.

"Goodnight, Princess," he told her. "Sleep tight and don't let the bedbugs bite." Then he leaned over and gently kissed Franny goodnight. It was as if his recollection and mention of my late mother had stimulated some kind of paternalistic feeling within him. Then, he flipped off the light and in a flash became his more composed, gentlemanly self again.

Stepping out in the hall and pulling the door closed behind us, we headed towards my room. When we reached my door, I opened it and turned on the light.

"Will you be alright, Eddie?" Livingston asked.

"I'm okay now," I said, and I really felt that way.

"You'd better lock your door—just to be safe."

"I have been for a while now," I confessed with a sheepish smile. I reached towards Livingston and wrapped my lanky arms around him, giving him a hug. He hugged me back. I felt safe and protected in his powerful hold.

"Goodnight, son," he said. "I'm not far away. If something frightens you, just come and get me—or give me a yell if you have to. I'll be there."

"Thanks, Livingston. G'night."

I closed and locked my door, leaving the key securely in the keyhole. Then I did a complete check of my closet, the bathroom, and under the bed. I checked the windows to make sure they were securely latched too. Convinced that all was secure, I balanced the tambourine—my makeshift security system—on the doorknob for good measure. Outside the wind was starting to whip up and I could see flashes of lightning in the distance as I got ready for bed. A storm was in the making for sure.

When I finally put out my light and climbed between the sheets, I lay awake for quite a while watching and listening to the storm grow closer. Eventually, I relaxed my grip on the baseball bat I now kept under the covers next to me in bed. The crash of the approaching thunder and the sound of rain pelting the window reminded me of the two television encounters I had with Franny and the paranormal. From my position in bed, I could see the light shining under the door from the hallway.

Suddenly it went out. I looked at my clock. The luminous hands indicated ten o'clock. A moment later, I thought I heard the floor creak just outside my door. I tightened my grip on the baseball bat. I lay there frozen—afraid to make a sound. About five minutes must have elapsed during the course of which I was surrounded by the boom of crashing thunder and the sound of driving rain pounding more incessantly on the bedroom window. Flashes of lightning provided intermittent glimpses of my surroundings. Then, to my horror, the thing I most feared happened. With the aid of a well-timed lightning flash, I saw the doorknob on my bedroom door slowly starting to turn. A second later, the tambourine balanced on the knob slipped onto the floor with a jangle. I bolted to my knees in bed and raised the wooden bat over my head, poised to strike.

"Who's there?" I managed to say in a wimpy sounding voice.

The only response I heard was the sound of footsteps retreating down the hall. I was frantic. I wanted to call for Livingston, but fear paralyzed every part of me.

Compounding my terror, I heard another sound—a rapping at my bedroom window. I whipped around in my bed holding my baseball bat in a striking position. A sudden flash of lightning illuminated the view beyond the window and I saw the source.

I breathed a sigh of relief, put down my bat, and walked over to the window where the loosened television antenna wire was rapping against the windowpane. The wind had pulled a couple of the guides from their anchor points, leaving the wire slack and twisting in the wind. Relieved, I started heading back towards my bed. That's when the idea struck me. I had seen an eleven-inch, portable television set in the window of Newport Electric during one of my walking excursions in town. I had more than enough money saved to meet the $109.00 price tag, and could easily smuggle it up to my room. The set would be easy to hide too. I could stuff it in the back of my closet behind the pile of clothes and junk that seemed to grow larger each day. Once I had the TV in my room, it would be a simple process to splice a lead into the antenna wire outside my window and create a private viewing chamber. At some discreetly timed moment— a time when Father, Elly, and Aunt Julia were out—I could resume our paranormal television sleuthing with Franny. Of course, luck would have to be in the cards to guarantee the right kind of atmospheric conditions. But, it wouldn't be that easy. Even if the stars came into alignment, weather-wise and otherwise, and I managed to pull the event off, none of us could really pull together any kind of message from the sights and people whizzing across the screen.

Then another idea hit me. I could speak to Mabel Keating and see if she'd agree to a television séance in my bedroom. It seemed like a real long shot, but I knew I had to try. Norman and Amanda would certainly be willing to drive Mabel over to the house in *Davenport's* delivery truck, even on short notice.

I lay awake the entire night mulling over my plan in my head. It distracted me from thinking about the earlier attempted break-in to my room.

The following morning I rose and dressed before 6:00 AM. I ate breakfast in the kitchen with Livingston, telling him through a mouthful of scrambled eggs about my harrowing experience with the would-be intruder the previous night. He didn't like it. I also unveiled the plan I'd concocted for splicing into the TV antenna and recruiting Mabel Keating for a séance in my room. Livingston didn't like that either, but over the course of breakfast, came around enough to agree that he wouldn't try to stop me.

After breakfast, I spent the next hour or so fishing off the rocks in front of the house. From my vantage point I could see Father, Elly and Aunt Julia sipping morning coffee on the verandah. Franny played with some dolls on the brick walkway leading up to the house. She sat, Indian-style, between the two sculptured lions standing guard at the beginning of the front walk. Only a few minutes had gone by when I first noticed the shimmer of light dancing on the rocks around my feet. Initially, I didn't pay any attention, assuming it was the result of sunlight reflecting off the water. Then I realized it wasn't coming from the direction of the water. It came from the opposite direction— the direction of the house.

I turned abruptly and the light caught my eyes, temporarily blinding me. Raising my right hand above my forehead to block the glare, I peered across the lawn. There it was again—just like that first day we'd arrived at Annandale Farm. The round, porthole window on the third floor had been angled to catch the light of the morning sun and send it glinting my way. Someone—or some *thing* in that third floor room was trying to get my attention. Then, I heard Franny crying and screaming. She lay face down on the brick walk kicking her feet furiously—reacting the same way she did that first day we arrived. I saw Father rise from his chair on the verandah and hurry towards her.

While all this played out, I got the idea of hurrying up to the third floor to see what I might find. I reeled in my fishing line then ran across the lawn towards Franny. By the time I reached her, Father was already there comforting her with his arm around her shoulder. I stood on the grass looking at them both. The crying had stopped. A quick glimpse in the direction of the house told me the porthole window was closed.

Father eyed me from the slight distance between us, but seemed occupied with comforting Franny. Everything seemed so strange, surreal and overwhelming. I thought about the frightening night before in my room. There was also Mr. FitzHugh's grizzly murder and Belle Pierce's sudden death. And why had Father been wearing Elly's pink satin robe the morning I'd stumbled on Mr. FitzHugh's body? Was there any truth behind the secret Belle Pierce shared about hidden gold and the Kennedy assassination? Aunt Julia's behavior was increasingly mysterious and bizarre, while Franny's crazy clues spelled out in *Chiclets* added to the ever-thickening mix of psychic muddle. On top of it all, Myra Davenport's story of the 1944 séance and the fact that Belle Pierce was actually Father's aunt by marriage only added to the riddle surrounding Ollie Merriweather's 1900 disappearance and the recent sideshows on the *Zenith*.

I looked at Father with his arm around my sister and suddenly realized he was a stranger. Yet oddly, I felt no animosity towards him, nor was there any sense of danger in his immediate presence. I saw nothing but good intention in his eyes as he interacted with Franny. Without saying a word, I skirted my way around the two of them and hurried off towards the back of the house. I sensed Elly and Aunt Julia watching my every move from the verandah.

The screen door snapped closed behind me as I hustled into the kitchen and caught up with Livingston. He had just slipped on his jacket. I told him what had happened.

"Yes, I heard Franny screaming outside. It's stopped now. Is everything all right?"

"Yeah, everything's fine now, Livingston, but there's somethin' really strange going on in that third floor room with the porthole window. There's somebody...or some *thing* up there tryin' to signal me."

I wanted to get upstairs as fast as I could, and having Livingston go with me seemed like a really good idea. He wouldn't have anything to do with it, though.

"Now listen, Eddie. I agree there are a lot of peculiar and alarming things happening here, but I'm not going to encourage your pursuits or do anything that might jeopardize your safety...or Franny's for that matter."

"Please, Livingston, just go upstairs with me for a minute," I begged, "before it's too late. It might be already," I heard myself conceding.

"Yes, well let's just say you're right about it being too late already and leave it at that, shall we?" His tone that told me he wouldn't budge an inch. I knew better than to push it any further.

"Okay," I relented. "But don't forget you said you'd drive me into town to meet with Norman and Amanda," I reminded him. My eyes flickered as I switched to my alternate plan.

I had called Norman and Amanda around eight o'clock that morning, and after describing my previous night's adventure, got them to agree to meet me at the Historical Society. I'd asked Livingston over breakfast if he'd drive me into town to meet them and he'd said he would.

He picked up his chauffeur's cap, donned his jacket and snatched a shopping list off the kitchen counter without saying another word. I smiled smugly inside and took care not to let it show. Propping my fishing rod in the corner by the back door, we headed outside to the verandah to tell Father, Elly and Aunt Julia we were going out. The three of them were sitting in rocking chairs along with Franny who'd simmered down and seemingly settled into rocking away a good part of what was left of the day. I was surprised to see them all there. I'd have thought, for sure, that Aunt Julia would have sensed something with her paranormal radar and tried to interfere.

"Alright, have a good time, son," was all that Father had to say when Livingston told him we were going into town.

"Oh, and Livingston, pick me up a *New York Times*, will you?, Aunt Julia requested. "I'd like to see what's going on back in the City."

I knew, even though everything seemed like it was back to normal, that an undercurrent had crept into our collective behavior amongst the growing melodrama, and we would never be the same. There was no going back to the way our family had been—or at least how I'd thought we'd been—and it was the price I'd have to pay for valuing the pursuit of truth over family loyalty.

When Livingston dropped me off in front of the Historical Society, Norman and Amanda were both waiting on the front steps. I filled them in on the latest morning's happenings, my plan for buying another television and my intent to conscript Mabel Keating for another TV séance. Nodding their approval, we went inside. Mabel sat behind the reception desk, looking up over the top of her crescent shaped glasses as we trundled into view.

"Well, look who's here," she sputtered, suppressing what looked to be the slightest trace of a smile.

"Mrs. Keating, we…we need to talk to you," I stammered. "We…we need your help real bad."

"Yeah, *real* bad," Amanda echoed. "Please, Mrs. Keating, you've gotta help us," she pleaded.

"Hold on there you kids. What's all the ruckus about anyway? Don't tell me it's trouble up at that evil old house?"

Mabel peered at us. She pushed herself away from the reception desk, grabbing her walking stick as she rose. Lowering her voice to a whisper, she looked around to make sure nobody else was in view.

"You kids come with me," she said. "We'll go upstairs; nobody's up there yet."

We nodded then headed up the stairs with Mabel painfully pulling up the rear. She motioned us to a corner table.

"Now sit down and tell me what this is all about…and take your time doing it. I don't want to miss anything." I thought it was interesting how the tough façade that had originally intimidated us no longer seemed there. I spewed out my story about Aunt Julia's visit to the hospital followed by Belle Pierce's demise—and Norman's simultaneous sighting of Aunt Julia at Easton's Beach. I confessed about how scared I'd been the previous night—how somebody tried to come into my room after dark. Amanda talked about the mysterious key we'd found in the basement, which reminded me of the night I trailed Aunt Julia to the wine cellar where she had disappeared...only to surface mysteriously later in her room.

I rambled on about the encounter we had on the day we arrived at the house—the third floor porthole window that spooked Franny. I told Mabel how Franny spelled out the names *Oswald* and *Ollie* with *Chiclets*—even though Franny couldn't spell. I brought her up to date about the day we had cocktails at the Auchincloss estate — and Aunt Julia's reaction to the mention of the once-planned tunnel between our house and Hammersmith Farm. I went on about what Livingston and I had found in the old newspaper articles—about discovering that Belle Pierce was really my great aunt...and how Father, Aunt Julia, and Elly had never let on.

I thought better of it, then wound up spilling the details of Myra Davenport's encounter with Aunt Julia in the 1944 séance and the mysterious happenings with Milton Pierce's old crystal radio, including the mention of the gold and Ollie Merriweather. Amanda reiterated her mother's mentioning how Belle Pierce had reacted so oddly upon hearing her own name mentioned—the name *Mabel* coming across on the crystal radio set through some ghostly medium.

Mabel Keating listened with piqued interest. At points she nodded as if we were validating things she already knew or suspected. At other times she nearly jumped out of her chair with shock. This was particularly evident when I shared the bizarre experiences that Livingston, Norman, Amanda and I had with Franny and the *Zenith*...and how we witnessed the televised murder of her husband, Oswald. I told Mabel how Father had the TV removed afterwards, at Aunt Julia's prompting.

Mabel gasped when we told her about Oswald's electrocution, and how *Ollie's* name kept coming up time and again. It created a perfect lead-in for sharing my plan to hold a séance in my room so we could find out more about Ollie's disappearance...via my soon-to-be-acquired portable TV.

164

"Mrs. Keating, I have an idea for finding out more about all of this stuff—and maybe solving your husband's and Mr. FitzHugh's murder at the same time...but we need your help," I said. I waited for her reaction.

"Go on," she responded, nodding her head.

"This may sound crazy, but I believe the disappearance of your nephew, Ollie, is the clue to *all* the weird stuff that's gone on at Annandale Farm. If we can find out what happened to Ollie, I think we can find out how all the pieces of these other mysteries fit together. Please, we need you to tell us everything you can about him—and then we need to try to contact him through my sister Franny on the TV. I know this all sounds crazy, but I can't think of any other way. Will you help us?"

The three of us waited quietly, letting the barrage of information we'd heaped on Mabel soak in. Her right hand trembled as she clutched the brass handle of her walking stick while the fingers of her left toyed with a gold chain she wore around her neck. None of us had ever really noticed the chain before. She rolled it gently between her thumb and index finger without saying a word. Her care-creased face looked sad—almost defeated. From the corner of one of her sparkling green eyes I noticed a teardrop forming. Gradually, it crested her lower eyelid and splashed on the tabletop in front of her.

I exchanged uncertain glances with Amanda and Norman, wondering if I'd gone too far. Then, gently, Mabel tugged on the gold chain around her neck and carefully pulled out an oval-shaped, gold locket from beneath her blouse. She caressed its lustrous surface gently with her fingertips. Looking at the locket, it was easy to see it was old...and probably quite valuable. The top and edges were hand-engraved with a beautiful floral design. It was quite thick, and a meticulously crafted catch on the edge revealed that it opened like a book. We held our breath with anticipation as she gently manipulated the catch with her fingers and opened it. When she spread the halves apart, it revealed a third, hinged section in the middle. The two outer halves each held very old pictures—each fitted and framed very neatly inside. Two additional pictures were framed, back-to-back, within the center section. The pictures on each of the two outer halves were men. One of them looked exactly like the man we'd seen electrocuted during the television séance. We knew it had to be Mabel's husband, Oswald. The other man looked quite distinguished with a handlebar mustache and dark, wavy hair. He wore a suit and tie that appeared to be turn-of-the-century fashion. We couldn't see the pictures in the center section—at least very clearly.

"You see these pictures," Mabel said, her voice wavering. She held the locket up for us to get a better view.

"These are the people who were close to me. This one's my husband, Oswald." A hint of a smile blossomed on her lips as she spoke his name. Then, she pointed to the other man.

"This handsome fellow—this fellow was my brother, Simon Merriweather. Her voice broke slightly when she spoke his name.

"Simon made a fine husband and father—if ever there was such a man. I cared for him as much as I cared for Oswald."

We looked on, captivated, while she opened up her memory to us. She flipped the hinged, center section of the locket like the page of a book. It revealed a period picture of a lovely woman.

"This picture you see here, children, is Simon's wife, Felicity— Felicity Marston. A fine family, the Marstons—just the kind of family you'd expect a man like my brother to marry into."

We watched as she tapped the photo lightly with the tip of her index finger for a few seconds before flipping over the center section of the locket, again, revealing one last photograph—a photograph we'd all anticipated but never expected. Leaning across the table to get a closer look, I lost my balance and nearly fell out of my seat.

"This," she said with a wavering voice and solemn look in her eye, "...this is Ollie Merriweather, My brother's one and only child."

Catching a glimpse of Norman and Amanda's faces, I saw their jaws drop and their eyes pop...just as mine must have. As the picture staring back at us came into view, it seemed hard to believe at first. Gently, and only after getting a nod of permission from Mabel, I reached out my hand and cupped it beneath the locket, raising the antique photograph closer.

"Mrs. Keating?" I asked compassionately. "What was Ollie's full name?"

Mabel stared down at the picture, seemingly oblivious to anything else. She spoke the words gently and with a feeling of deep reverence in her voice:

"*Olivia...Olivia Marston Merriweather.*" She said. "Simon always liked to call her *Ollie*. She was 12 years old when she disappeared back in 1900.

I studied the photograph. Ollie's hair was cut in a pageboy. It framed her impish looking face and highlighted its features much in the same way Franny's hair did. In fact, the thing that was most astonishing was that Ollie Merriweather's haircut wasn't the only thing similar to Franny. Ollie shared the same physical attributes of all children like Franny. Ollie Merriweather was a Down syndrome child.

Making the revelation all the more remarkable, Ollie not only bore a close resemblance to Franny—she looked *exactly* like Franny. To the unfamiliar eye, they could easily have been twins.

"My God," Amanda blurted. "She looks *exactly* like your sister."

"*Unbelievable,*" Norman sputtered. "They're dead-ringers."

Mabel sighed. "Now you know why I was so taken with your sister when I first laid eyes on her," she said. "The only difference is that my Ollie had green eyes—like mine. Otherwise, there's no disputing Ollie is a dead-ringer for your sister," Mabel whispered. "That's why I'm so concerned for her safety. There are strange powers and evil deeds a-plenty at that old house of yours. The sooner you and she get away from that place, the better off you'll both be."

"Cripes, but how can we do that?" I lamented. "There's no way Franny and I can just pick up and leave. There's nowhere else to go. And even if we did, Father wouldn't let us. Neither would Aunt Julia or Elly. We know too much—Franny and me." But as I said it, I knew that we knew too little to prove anything, too. Father's, Aunt Julia's and Elly's obsessive interest in the house was winning out. And our own wellbeing had become subverted by it."

"It's that damned, confounded gold," Mabel concluded, adding emphasis to her statement by rapping the tip of her walking stick on the floor. "That gold's behind all the evil doings at Annandale Farm. Lord knows, the old saying that *'the love of money is the root of all evil'* sums it up. Greed! Yep, that's what's behind it all—pure greed. And I'll tell you kids one thing..."

Mabel paused to look around the room, making sure that nobody had come in.

"The reason Ollie disappeared is directly related to that damn gold, Simon knew it. In fact, he told me as much, himself, after Ollie vanished."

Amanda let out a delicate gasp.

"What did he say?" she asked.

Mabel looked around again. Her hands trembled as she took the locket and slowly closed it. The latch clicked into place with a snap and she leaned closer towards us.

"Now I've never breathed a word of this to another living soul," she whispered. "In fact, the more I think about it, the more I think I shouldn't say a word about it now..."

She paused for a moment reflecting on her latter statement then, obviously dismissing it, went on.

"Simon said that he and Ollie had discovered a massive gold vein at the house. They discovered it one night by accident after everybody else working at the site had gone home. There! I've said it," Mabel proclaimed, tucking the locket into her blouse with an air of finality and what sounded like a sigh of relief at having finally shared her long held secret.

Amanda, Norman, and I looked at each other.

"For sure, that's why Aunt Julia dropped her glass at the Auchinclosses'," I blurted out. "She dropped it when Mr. Auchincloss mentioned a proposed tunnel between the two houses. Aunt Julia must've discovered the location of the gold. That's what she was doing the night I followed her to the basement and she disappeared. Where d'ya think it is, Mrs. Keating?"

Mabel stared at me quizzically. "Damned if I know," she grunted. "Simon never did say. He swore me to secrecy and made me promise I'd never mention it to anyone. Never did say where it was. 'Said he'd show me in due course, but never did…then he up and died, real sudden, of a heart attack. Ever since then, I've kept that secret, but I never did know where the damn gold was hidden."

"Then it's not just a legend?" Amanda said—her eyes filled with wonder.

"Oh, there's gold there all right," Mabel answered back. "And there are people who'd do anything to get their hands on it. Why, that gold-digging Belle Pierce…she was one of them; her brother George, too. They were in cahoots to find it."

A determined look—a look seasoned with just a hint of satisfaction crept across Mabel's face.

"HA! They never did though—or if they did, they found out too late to do anything about it," she said, rapping her walking stick firmly on the floor in front of her again.

"What do you mean they found out too late?," Norman asked.

Mabel's face became contemplative. "Well, I'd venture that if Eddie's Aunt Julia, father and stepmother know where the gold is, Belle Pierce and her brother must have known too. That's why George and Belle were both killed."

"But we don't know if somebody actually did murder Belle Pierce," I challenged, finding myself unexpectedly taking a stance more akin to Livingston's.

Mabel frowned. "I don't believe it. It's too coincidental." Then her face blossomed into a broad smile.

"Glory be! That's it. I'm right. They must have discovered the location of the gold," she said with conviction, slapping the palm of her meaty hand on the tabletop for added emphasis. "Only it must have been *after* Belle Pierce signed that lease and option to buy on Annandale Farm with President Kennedy. HA!," she half-laughed. "It's pretty funny when you think about it; Belle Pierce and her brother George spending decades searching for that gold and never finding it. Then, when their own money finally runs out, they're forced to lease Annandale Farm to President Kennedy with an option to buy...and somehow manage to stumble on the gold vein *afterwards*."

"Are you sure?" I asked, knowing it most probably had to have unfolded that way.

"Well it all makes sense," Mabel answered. "Think about it. All that gold just sitting there right under their noses—and they couldn't do a damned thing about it. Now that's pretty ironic, don't you think?" Mabel's face lit up then suddenly the glee vanished.

"Dear God, it couldn't be possible, though, could it?" she gasped, her demeanor shifting dramatically.

"What?" Norman asked.

"The assassination." Mabel spoke the words softly. Her face blanched.

"You mean President Kennedy's." Norman said flatly.

"Yes...yes...President Kennedy's. Dear God in heaven, they couldn't have gone that far could they?"

"Ya mean...ya think the gold discovery was really behind President Kennedy's assassination, too?" I stammered in disbelief.

"TOO? Who else thinks so?" Mabel blurted with a start.

I gasped an inner gasp at my faux pas in nearly revealing what Belle Pierce had told me and how I'd been instructed not to share it with anyone...ever!

"Uh...uh, I mean *besides*...you know...in addition," I lied.

"Oh...I see. Well yes, that's exactly what I'm thinking," Mabel affirmed.

I watched the color drain from Norman and Amanda's faces.

Mabel continued. "Think about it. The Federal Government had an option to buy that house. And the Army Corps of Engineers had drawn up plans to excavate a connecting tunnel between it and Hammersmith Farm. The tunnel, no doubt, would have run smack into the gold vein. If that happened, everything would have been lost. Old Belle Pierce and her brother could never have gotten their greedy hands on it. The gold would have become the property of the Federal Government."

"But that would mean most certainly that Father, Aunt Julia and Elly were in on it too," I despaired. "NO! NO, that couldn't be possible. That's *pa-postrus!*" I argued, naively mispronouncing the word.

"Shhhhhh," Amanda scolded. "Be quiet. Keep your voice down. You're making too much noise."

We looked around. Fortunately nobody was to be seen.

"It may not be as impossible or preposterous as it seems, my boy," Mabel chided. I could see the lights going on in her head as she unveiled what she believed to be the plot.

"They had too much to lose—that conniving Belle Pierce and her stupid brother. They would have spent decades searching for that gold for nothing. Your father, stepmother and Aunt Julia—if they knew about it—had a great deal to lose, too. My guess is that your Aunt Julia found out about the gold during that 1944 séance you learned about from Myra Davenport. I can only imagine what other information that psychic aunt of yours might have discovered that night," Mabel concluded.

My lower lip trembled. It all seemed incomprehensible to me—that Father, Elly and Aunt Julia could be part of a conspiracy to assassinate JFK. Not only was it incomprehensible. It was, indeed *pa-postrus*...or was it?

"Cripes, it just can't be true," I objected adamantly. "It can't be."

"Well there's only one way to find out, son," Mabel warned. "You're going to have to put on that TV séance you've been talking about—you and your sister. It's the only way we can know for sure now."

Norman, Amanda, and I stared at each other in silence. One at a time, knowing that the séance was the only way, we nodded our heads in agreement.

Mabel *was* right. The only way any of us could revisit the past was through the TV with Franny. I prayed that Mabel would be wrong, though, about Father and my family. But deep inside—deep within my heart of hearts—I feared that she wasn't.

How could we pull off this séance?, I wondered. Trying to pull it off in secret seemed overwhelming. But we did have an ace in the hole we hadn't had before—an ace whose mind and connections were sharper than the razor-edged rocks lining the coast of Newport: Mabel Keating.

CHAPTER THIRTEEN

The day finally arrived. The four of us sat silently as the dilapidated delivery truck rattled across Thames Street on the dusky drive towards Annandale Farm. Livingston had dropped me at Amanda's earlier on the premise she and I were going to Cote Pharmacy for an ice cream. The sun had nearly slipped below the horizon line, and the torch-like glow radiating from its fiery retreat painted the sky in a canvas of dazzling color. Through the open window of the truck, the humid summer air rushed in against us. Way off in the distance—in a northeasterly direction from across the bay—I could see dark, ominous storm clouds mustering their forces. It seemed as though the weather conditions would be perfect for Franny's TV séance—that is, if everything evolved according to plan. The four of us were crammed in the front seat. Norman had the wheel, and Mabel Keating was pressed against the passenger-side door, her meaty right arm draped out the window, engulfing the opening. Amanda and I were squashed between Mabel's ample girth and Norman. I stole a glance in Mabel's direction. A look of cool detachment was on her face, those steely green eyes looking beyond the end of the road and the present moment—into some world or dimension outside human boundaries. The creak of the truck's sagging springs and the rattle of its worn out chassis were the only sounds that kept me grounded in the present. Without their jarring clatter, I might have been drawn into Mabel's moment. And from there, it would have been a short distance into the wanderings of my own imagination with my focus lost on the tasks at hand. There were a lot of them. We had planned and patiently waited for this opportunity. A number of things had to happen if the séance was going to be successful, and so far the synchronization of these events had miraculously fallen into place.

First, we needed the right weather conditions. The last two séances proved that a heat-laden, electrically charged atmosphere saturated with high humidity made for the best results. The more intense the lightning and the higher the humidity, the better the audio/visual quality of the psychic images broadcast over the television would be. So far, the weather conditions predicted for this evening, now beginning to manifest, were ideal.

Second, we needed a TV set. To that end, I tasked Livingston with stopping at Newport Electric to purchase the eleven-inch portable television I'd seen advertised in the storefront window. I ponied up the cash and Livingston handled the execution. He smuggled the TV up to my bedroom where we kept it neatly hidden in my clothes closet. We could pull it out of hiding on a moment's notice and splice the set into the huge, rooftop antenna up on the chimney.

Third, and probably the *most* difficult, was getting Father, Elly, and Aunt Julia out of the house for a prolonged period of time. To accomplish this, Mabel had come up with a brilliant idea. It involved enlisting the aid of Mrs. Auchincloss next door.

The relationship between Mabel and Mrs. Auchincloss was an interesting one that went back years. Despite their differences, they had long maintained an association of mutual respect. Janet Auchincloss thrived on gossip and had been trying to pry information about Ollie Merriweather's disappearance out of Mabel for decades without success. Having once been employed in service to Hugh and Janet Auchincloss, Mabel decided she would leverage her former employer's curiosity and their past relationship to ask for a personal favor. The favor consisted of Mrs. Auchincloss—at Mabel's weather-induced bidding—spontaneously inviting Father, Elly, and Aunt Julia to dinner at Hammersmith Farm. The dinner invitation would be timed to coincide with an appropriate atmospheric forecast. If conditions appeared favorable for a séance, Mabel would call Mrs. Auchincloss who agreed to spring into action and launch a last minute invitation. The price for this favor would be Mabel sharing with Mrs. Auchincloss whatever findings came out of the séance about Ollie Merriweather.

"Of course, I won't really tell her anything important," Mabel told us, "Just enough to give her something to talk about with her society friends." And there was no question that Elly would drop everything at the slightest opportunity of furthering her relationship with the Auchinclosses.

Now, a week later—inspired by a Coast Guard warning of severe summer weather and Mabel Keating's plan—Father, Elly and Aunt Julia sat as dinner guests of Janet and Hugh Auchincloss at neighboring Hammersmith Farm. The final obstacle to launching a TV séance at Annandale Farm had been eliminated. The three of them had driven to Hammersmith in the Duesenberg. On cue of their departure, Livingston called the Davenport's to sound the all clear to Norman, Amanda and me. We'd been waiting there in anticipation of his call. Next we rang Mabel Keating to say that we were on our way to pick her up. By the time the delivery truck clattered through the front gate, it was a little after 9:00 PM. Norman brought the truck to a halt under the front portico as a rumble of thunder announced the growing presence of the approaching storm from across the bay. Mabel opened the truck door and slid off the tattered seat onto the driveway with a grunt. We climbed out behind her as she steadied her ample frame, planting her walking stick firmly in the gravel. She stood for a moment looking up over the roof of the truck towards the looming house her late brother built. Grabbing her by the elbow to help her across the drive, I could feel a shudder course through her body. She turned and looked at me. Without saying a word, she inched her way across the loose gravel surface and made her way up the front steps. Livingston, with Franny by his side, held the front door open as I escorted her in. She nodded politely to Livingston then stopped in front of Franny just long enough to say hello and pat her on the right cheek with the palm of her hand. Norman and Amanda trailed behind.

Our ragtag procession paused in the front foyer as Mabel stopped to scan the surroundings. She rotated slowly in a full circle taking in the details of the architecture. Meanwhile, upstairs, Livingston had already hooked up the portable television in my bedroom by splicing an antenna lead into the master cable running outside my window. The enormous antenna strapped to the chimney above now had a direct line to my room. Livingston had bared the ends of the newly spliced lead and attached another, shorter lead directly to the portable *Zenith* sitting on the dresser. In addition, for Franny's protection, he incorporated a fuse into the connection outside my window. Should lightning happen to strike the antenna during the course of our séance, the fuse would blow, preventing any harm to Franny. The only thing needed to complete the circuit was Franny herself.

As we all ascended the stairs to the second floor, I let Mabel set the pace. She paused at intervals along the way to catch her breath while simultaneously examining the surroundings. I could tell they stimulated memories from the past—from decades gone by. If only I had a way to tap into her consciousness and see what they were. An occasional burst of lightning followed by a rumble of rapidly approaching thunder intensified the suspense.

After what seemed like a considerable amount of time, our procession finally arrived at my room. With a push, the door creaked opened and we filed in. Livingston had set a straight-backed chair next to the dresser for Franny—in between the spliced antenna lead and the shorter lead attached to the television set. As an added precaution, we focused the telescope I used for stargazing and the sighting of seaside sex, in the direction of Hammersmith Farm. Much to our good fortune, the Auchincloss property was one of only a few estates to be seen from the vantage-point of my bedroom window. In fact, the view across the vast expanse of lawn to Hammersmith Farm was completely unobstructed. With telescopic aid, not only could a misguided astronomer see the house and grounds...but also the activity taking place behind the windows and French-doors off the back terrace. There, in plain view, we could easily monitor the presence and movement of Father, Elly and Aunt Julia as they sipped cocktails on the sprawling patio and consumed a gourmet dinner in the elegantly appointed dining room.

While Amanda manned the telescope keeping an eye on my family, Livingston and I ushered Franny to the television.

"You okay, Franny?" I asked.

"I'm fine, Eddie," she mumbled.

"You don't mind doing this again?

"I don't mind," she answered. The timbre of her singsong voice assured me she was okay with it.

With that, I flipped on the TV set. Livingston gently poked the bare ends of an antenna lead into each of Franny's pudgy hands. Grasping the wires tightly, she sat staring blankly at the wall across the room while Mabel eased her broad beam onto the foot of my bed. It creaked painfully under her weight but guaranteed she had a straight-on view of the television screen.

By now, oversized raindrops had started to plop on the windowsill and splatter against the glass. The thunder that had been rumbling threateningly in the distance pounded percussively close by. Lightning arced over the bay. Bolts of electricity forked out menacingly across the sky sending electrified, skeletal fingers clawing in every direction. The five of us stood there watching snow flicker on the TV screen while Franny sat motionless in her chair. The air hung thick with sticky moisture clinging to everything it touched. In less time than I expected, the gnat-like cloud began forming around the portable Zenith. Everyone's eyes, including mine, widened at its sight. I thought Mabel's eyes would pop right out of her head. The snow on the small screen began to diminish and the first signs of a clear image began to materialize. This time there was no successive parade of still shots whizzing by in rapid succession. Instead, as the cloud evolved into the recognizable shape of a human head, a kind of psychic soap opera began to unfold. First, the drawing room of Annandale Farm appeared. Surprisingly, it didn't look too different on-screen from the way it did today. There were some different furnishings and drapes, but otherwise it looked very much the same. A number of figures could be seen around the room.

"Glory be, that's Myra Davenport," Mabel blurted out. "People called her *Della* back then." Mabel raised the crescent-lensed glasses dangling from a gold-link chain around her neck and adjusted them on her face. It was easy to tell by the resemblance to Amanda that we were looking at a much younger Myra Davenport.

"Land sakes…look there. There's that gold-digging Belle Pierce," Mabel hissed. "She was a conniver, that one…and there…that's her husband, Milton—old lush! By God, I can't believe it; it's as if time stood still. 'Has to be back in the 1940's from the look of things—the clothes; and the age of them all. They look twenty years younger. Would you look at that hairstyle on Belle Pierce? Why, she looks like Joan Crawford."

"Who's that, Mrs. Keating?" Amanda asked pointing to a tall, dignified older man standing next to an attractive, well dressed woman. I knew before Mabel said anything.

"Those are my grandparents," I answered for her. "That's my grandfather Sutton and my grandmother."

Just then, Mabel gasped.

"And look there, would you? That's George FitzHugh standing next to the mantelpiece. I can't believe it's him. He looks about thirty pounds lighter."

Indeed it was Mr. FitzHugh—a much younger George FitzHugh. More intriguing, however, was the figure standing nearby in the drawing-room door. Young, and in her late teens or early twenties, my Aunt Julia was easily recognizable. I exchanged a knowing glance with Livingston. His eyes were fixed on the TV screen as well as the faceless, three-dimensional figure. The phantom seemed to glower at us from psychic cyberspace.

"Land sakes," Mabel piped in. "Why, from the way everybody's dressed and the way things look in that drawing room, I'd say it's the summer of '44." She paused for a moment, to study the décor then snapped her fingers with sudden realization.

"How can you be so sure of the exact date?," I found myself asking rather bluntly.

"The only reason I'm sure," Mabel said looking me square in the eye, "is because your Aunt Julia is there, and because Belle Pierce was all abuzz about your grandparents coming up from New York City to pay a visit. They only came once, though—at least as far as I know. There's one other thing that pinpoints the date, exactly, for me," Mabel persisted, her expression turning serious. "That night was the fourth anniversary of the day my Oswald died at Annandale Farm," she shared, her eyes widening at the recollection. I knew better than to challenge her.

So we were looking at June 7th 1944 on the *Zenith*—the night of that first, radio-powered séance described so clearly to me by Myra Davenport. And from the look of things, it appeared the séance had just ended and my grandparents were saying goodnight before retiring to their room. The psychically transmitted audio allowed clarity enough for us to make out that folks were retiring for the evening. Myra Davenport—a.k.a. *Della*—led the way, and soon everybody disappeared from view going up the stairs.

After they were gone, we watched Belle Pierce move in closely next to her brother, while Belle's husband Milton fidgeted sulkily with the remains of what looked to be a smashed crystal radio set on the table. Apparently bewildered by the events of the evening that had just taken place, Milton's face looked gaunt and tired.

"Milton, you seem weary," we heard Belle say in a patronizing, dismissive tone. "Perhaps you might be better off going up to bed now, too, dear." Donning a forced smile, Belle motioned towards the stairs. Milton took her cue, and with some grumbling that bordered on theatrics, picked up the remains of his crystal radio set and exited the room. He could be heard dragging his feet up the stairs. The coast was now clear for a conversation between Belle and her brother. Little could Belle have known that two decades later, her exact words would be replayed via supernatural video.

"Well, George, who do you suppose that was talking on Milton's radio?," Belle asked, annoyance as much as awe present in her voice.

A young and significantly lighter-weight George FitzHugh paused before answering. Then, lowering his head, he said, "We both know who that was, don't we Sis?" He raised his face to meet his sister's. "Ollie Merriweather had an unmistakable voice, as I remember," George said, his voice piqued with suspicion. "There's no mistaking it."

Belle feigned innocence.

"Why, whatever do you mean, George? Ollie Merriweather? You've *got* to be kidding. Everyone knows Ollie Merriweather disappeared years ago..." Belle's voice suddenly trailed off. A lifetime of sibling insight had won out and she quickly realized her brother knew when she was lying. She responded by pulling a chair away from the table and plopping down into it.

"Look, George, let's be frank," she said, resigned. "You know as well as I do that we've been chasing gold at the end of Annandale Farm's faded rainbow for decades...without much success. The money I've saved up over the years is just about gone...and Milton's money isn't much more than an alcoholic memory."

I looked away from this unfolding drama, momentarily, to get a read on Mabel Keating. She sat glued to the television screen as though watching an Emmy-winning soap opera. The others in the room were equally riveted. Only Franny sat in her chair oblivious to it all; head bowed, staring blankly at the tops of her shoes as the gift she possessed—its psychic force reaching backward through time, uprooting the past from ether-like soil of yesteryear—allowed us a glimpse of eternity through a portal opened by God for mortal viewing. How ironic, I thought, to be blessed with such a gift and remain oblivious to the power it held.

I turned back to the TV, its broadcast and drama unfolding, accepting the enigma at face value. Through our lens of telepathic

181

viewing, I watched Belle Pierce share her innermost secrets and expose the shackles of greed that had bound her for decades to Annandale Farm until finally liberated by death not long ago at Newport Hospital.

"George, that pittance of mine, plus what little you've scraped together over the years is all that's keeping this foundering boat of ours afloat," Belle said, gesturing with a symbolic sweep of her hand around the room. I noticed a flash of brilliance from what looked to be the big diamond I'd seen on her hand that first day at Davenport's Grocery Store. I wondered where it was now.

"At the moment," she said mustering as much poise as the circumstances would allow, "I wouldn't say things look all too encouraging, would you?"

She stared at her brother penetratingly. He nodded in somber agreement.

"Tell, me, Sis," George said dryly, "you know what happened to Ollie Merriweather, don't you?"

Belle hesitated. She seemed to be collecting her thoughts— perhaps contemplating the séance that took place only a short time before and how much everyone else could have pieced together. I looked again at Mabel Keating. She was fixated on the answers to secrets about her family locked up for over half a century.

"Yes, George, I *do* know what happened to Ollie Merriweather," Belle finally volunteered, having shed all inhibition.

With that, I saw Mabel Keating rise slowly to her feet, her steely green eyes locked on the television screen. Beads of perspiration glistened at the base of her hairline. I noted for the first time that she was sweating profusely. The thumb and index finger of her left hand rhythmically twirled the gold chain holding her locket around her neck.

"But before we get into what happened to Ollie

Merriweather, George, we need to worry about who else realizes that *I know* what happened to Ollie or—perhaps more importantly—*who else* has the means to find out."

At this point Mabel Keating exploded. "Why, that no good conniving tramp!" She ranted. "I've known all along that Belle Pierce had something to do with my Ollie's disappearance; that cheap floozy! Society harlot!"

Mabel's eyes glared. Meanwhile, outside my bedroom window, the thunder crashed mercilessly. Rain pounding against the windowpanes had turned to hail and a blitz of fiery lightning clawed at the sky. Just above the television set, an interesting dynamic also began to occur. For the first time, we noticed the faceless form hovering over the TV began to refine its features. The signs of a female countenance began emerging from the psychic clay. A nose, mouth, hair, ears, eyes.

The *eyes* are what caused the hair on the back of my neck to stand up on end. They bore all the signs of Down syndrome eyes. They were emerald green. I knew they were the eyes of Ollie Merriweather. I kept my gaze fixed on the forming specter, while trying not to miss anything happening on the *Zenith*. Back on screen, George and his sister continued what was fast evolving into a clash of sibling rivalry.

"Tell me, Sis, exactly who are you worried about?," George asked, his voice awash with consternation. "Why, I'll bet you're afraid that psychic Sutton girl is going to find out what happened to Ollie Merriweather; and maybe even worse, *who* was responsible...not to mention she might find out the location of that damned gold you've had us hunting for all these years."

Belle smiled a wry smile.

"Yes, George. You couldn't be more right. That's *exactly* what I'm worrying about," Belle said, her voice seasoned with sarcasm. "You can be so intuitive at times. Julia Sutton is definitely onto something. It doesn't take much to figure that out."

"She may not be the only one onto something," George countered. "What about Milton?"

"Milton! You can't be serious. Why, that *lush* of a husband of mine is too preoccupied dissipating what's left of his miserable life with booze to be onto anything that doesn't have a 90-proof label attached to it. He's so saturated that he'll have no memory whatsoever of tonight's happenings. And even if he did, he'd most likely think he dreamt it."

Belle smiled slyly again. "Hmm, maybe a bottle strategically placed on Milton's nightstand? You know…just to be sure…?"

"You're going too far, too fast, Sis. You can count me *out* if that's the direction you're heading. I won't be a party to sending someone to their ruin."

"Oh, all right then. Have it your way," Belle conceded, greatly annoyed. But what about Della? You know…Myra Dellecourt?"

We all looked at Amanda. Hearing her mother's maiden name, she abandoned her lookout post at the telescope in favor of what was happening on the television. It got her full attention. So did the haunting likeness of Ollie Merriweather. The ectoplasmic form simply hovered at a height of about eight to ten inches above the portable *Zenith*, its green-hued eyes staring blankly into space—the same blank look that Franny had in her eyes while she sat quietly in my room holding the antenna leads so we could all witness history in the remaking.

"Good heavens! *Della*!" George said. "She's the last person I'd worry about. She's planning to marry that grocery clerk—Dennis Davenport. They're hard pressed for money right now, she tells me. I suspect Myra will be happy just to keep her job. Why would you worry about her stirring anything up?"

"Point well taken, I suppose," Belle conceded. "But, just to be safe, I'll let her know discretion is expected…and we'll settle for nothing less."

"Hmmph!" Amanda muttered at hearing her mother's integrity compromised. She turned to resume her position at the telescope as lookout, this time ignoring the floating specter over the TV—so close she could have touched it as she walked by.

"Now those Suttons—they're a very different matter," Belle maintained. "They're smart, wealthy and sophisticated. In short, they know too much and they can't be bought or intimidated...though, now that I think about it, it doesn't really much matter. Any information we glean from the séance or otherwise that helps pinpoint the gold's whereabouts is a risk worth taking."

I thought about what I heard Belle Pierce saying. She was actually right for other reasons, too. The reality of finding hidden gold at Annandale Farm had fallen by the wayside of anyone's imagination long before the time of the War. Public consensus was that if ever there were truth in the overrated legend, the gold would have been discovered decades ago. In 1944, a broken-down Newport mansion occupied by a bunch of human relics didn't hold much promise for hitting the jackpot—legendary or otherwise. Plus, my grandparents had plenty of money of their own at that time. Belle Pierce owned the estate and any finds of value made on the property had to be hers. Belle Pierce was worrying needlessly.

On the *Zenith*, George rubbed his chin with his thumb and index finger and repeated exactly what I was thinking.

"Sis, I think you're worrying needlessly about anyone trying to worm their way in on the gold legend. The Suttons have too much money to worry about that. It isn't even on their radar screen. But tell me...," George said, his voice taking on a more serious tone. "Ollie just didn't disappear...did she?"

With that, the hovering specter over the *Zenith* suddenly became reenergized. The ectoplasmic neutrons, as I call them, started vibrating up and down and in and out at an accelerated rate, reacting to George FitzHugh's remark. The green eyes suddenly appeared more alert. George pressed his point.

"Ollie just didn't simply disappear, did she?" he repeated.

The ectoplasmic neurons accelerated even more. The wraith's countenance grew angry. Its mouth opened and closed as if trying to communicate, but no sound came out.

Belle finally gave in, heaving a sigh of resignation. "No, Ollie didn't just simply disappear," she said, sounding relieved at having spoken the truth, but not completely.

The specter's features quickly morphed from anger to what looked like excited anticipation.

"Ollie died, didn't she, Sis?" George said with a tone of finality that all but confirmed what we'd suspected all along.

The ghost of Ollie Merriweather, alive with netherworld energy as it hovered above the *Zenith* began a slow, rhythmic motion—nodding "yes," wanting us to know that the truth was near and the time had arrived for its telling. On the TV, Belle Pierce locked her eyes on her brother's.

"She died a terrible death," Belle said, emotion edging into her voice for the first time. She looked away, breaking eye contact with her brother.

"Ollie knew about the gold...didn't she?," George persisted.

Belle began fidgeting nervously, staring down at her hands. "Yes...yes, she knew about the gold," she conceded reluctantly. "That's how I found out about it."

"Did you kill her, Sis?," George asked bluntly. He waited for his sister's reply.

Belle sat silently for a seemingly long time and didn't reply. The paranormal life form above the television stopped its rhythmic swing and hovered in place.

186

Meanwhile, like the rest of us, Mabel Keating sat glued to the TV. Perspiration streamed down her face. Her expression seemed to border on rage one moment, and fright the next. Above the television set, the psychic hologram of Ollie Merriweather sparkled with clarity. For the very first time, in front of our astonished eyes, the trace of a smile suddenly blossomed on its lips. The moment didn't last long.

"KABLAM!" An explosion of thunder directly overhead roared out from the night, preceded for only a nanosecond by an accompanying lightning strike. We all but jumped out of our skins. The picture on the TV screen evaporated instantly. So did the ghostly countenance of Ollie Merriweather. Sparks exploded down the antenna wire stopping at the fuse juncture Livingston had inserted in the circuitry. I thanked God that instant for the insight He'd provided Livingston...and for Franny's protection.

"Glory be!" Mabel shrieked. Outside, we heard the sickening clatter of metal growing louder. I turned to look just as the huge antenna streaked past my bedroom window in its smoldering descent to the ground. The steel strapping once holding it securely in place on the chimney, trailed like a metallic kite tail. The mass of twisted wreckage plummeted to its unfortunate end, disintegrating on impact.

Amanda threw open the window as Livingston and I scrambled for a closer look. We peered over the sill to take in the destroyed remains on the lawn below. Affirming our conduit to the world beyond was completely obliterated, I shifted my gaze upward toward the sky. The hail had turned back into light rain and I could see the storm moving in a Southwesterly direction away from us. The bad weather was abating. Stealing a glance across the lawn in the direction of Hammersmith Farm, I caught the glow of headlights gliding down the drive from behind the trees and shrubs. A car was leaving the estate.

"Quick, Amanda, look through the telescope and tell me who you see," I hollered. Amanda leapt to it.

"I see Mrs. Auchincloss, I think; and Mr. Auchincloss, too.

There's a maid and butler standing next to them. They're all looking out the French doors and across the terrace in our direction."

"Do you see Father and Aunt Julia? Do you see Elly?" I wanted to know.

"No, I don't...wait a minute. I do see your Aunt Julia. She's outside on the terrace under the awning. It's dark on the patio so it's hard to see. I think I see your stepmother too."

"What about Father? Can you see him anywhere?"

Amanda swiveled the telescope on its tripod scanning the area.

"I can't see him. He could be there in the shadows or somewhere else in the house...but I don't know. I can't see that well. A big tree is down and leaning against their house. It looks like it's taken down the telephone lines with it.

"Cripes, we've gotta act fast," I said issuing orders. "They must've seen that lightning bolt strike the antenna from across the lawn. I saw headlights moving down the driveway. It's probably Father on his way home to see what's happened. We've gotta get Mrs. Keating out of here before he gets back." It was as if I could see the future playing out like a movie in my mind as clearly as the past had been presented only seconds before.

"Livingston, can you get rid of the television and the wires?," I asked. The wave of organization I felt surprised me as much as it did the others. "Father'll see the delivery truck when he pulls in through the gate, but that's OK," I reasoned. "I'll just tell him that Norman stopped by for a visit after they all left."

But there was still the matter of Mabel Keating.

"Amanda, can you help Mrs. Keating down the back stairs and help smuggle her into the back of the delivery truck?," I asked setting our evacuation in motion. "You'd better stay with her and keep out of sight. Norman and I can keep Father busy while you do it."

With that, everybody sprang into action like a troupe of practiced actors. Amanda and Mabel made their way hurriedly towards the back stairs. Livingston gathered up the remnants of the smoldering indoor antenna wiring from my room along with the portable TV while Norman and I bounded down the front staircase towards the foyer. I grabbed a Parcheesi board-game from the drawing room as a prop, and quickly set it up on a card table just as the headlights from the Duesenberg gleamed through the front gate. Norman and I hurried out onto the verandah to meet Father. I saw Father eyeing the delivery truck as he pulled in and stepped out of the car.

"Is everybody all right here?" he urgently wanted to know. "We saw lightning strike the house. A big tree came down and took out the phone lines at the Auchincloss estate. We couldn't call you." Father noticed Norman.

"Norman, what about you? Are you okay?"

"A little scared, Mr. Sutton, but other than that, I'm okay. Amanda and I came by to visit Eddie just before the storm blew in. We were playing a game of Parcheesi when this big bolt of lightning struck the TV antenna," Norman fibbed, doing a good job of twisting the truth.

Father looked at me suspiciously. Fortunately, Livingston chose that moment to emerge onto the verandah with Franny.

"What's happened over here, Livingston?" Father hollered to him from the driveway.

"As near as I can tell, sir, it appears the television antenna took a direct hit. Everybody is all right though," Livingston hollered back.

"Well, we'd better have a look around to see the extent of the damage, now that the storm's abated," Father decided.

189

I got nervous. So did Livingston. What if Father ran into Amanda and Mabel making their dash for the delivery truck while he poked around outside for damage? I hoped Amanda and Mabel were being discreet...and speedy. The best thing Norman and I could do was to try and keep Father occupied in the area by the destroyed antenna until the other séance fugitives were in the clear. Fortunately, the antenna's remains had come to rest in a location a good distance away from the parked delivery truck. The only obstacle remaining lay in the fact that the back door Amanda and Mabel would be using could be seen from the location of the antenna. Livingston realized this too.

"I'll get Franny off to bed," he said. "I'll be back in a few minutes." With that, he ducked back inside pulling Franny along with him. I imagined he'd intercept Amanda and Mabel before they came out the back door. Given Mabel's difficulty walking, let alone negotiating stairs, I estimated Livingston had plenty of time. Norman, Father and I headed towards the side of the house where the lightning had struck. We were nearly home-free when Father threw us a curve.

"I'm going inside to get a flashlight," he announced unexpectedly. "I'll be right back."

I watched, horrified, as Father turned and headed directly for the back door. Then, at that very instant, I saw the back door slowly opening. So did Norman...and so did Father. I breathed a sigh of relief when Livingston reemerged. There was no sign of Mabel or Amanda. I didn't know if they'd made a dash for the truck through the front door or were hiding somewhere in the background.

"I'll be right back. I just want to grab a flashlight," Father said to Livingston, hurrying towards him.

"There's one in the kitchen, sir—in the pantry next to the refrigerator," Livingston volunteered as Father approached. Livingston politely held the door open, but not before quickly slipping his arm back inside the doorjamb. I knew it was a signal to somebody inside. I could tell by the expression on Livingston's face that Mabel and Amanda were still there. Seconds later, Father was inside. Livingston strolled across the lawn to where Norman and I were standing.

"I signaled them to duck down the back stairway to the cellar," he told me in a low voice. "I expect they'll have the sense to hide out in the basement until we give them word that the coast is clear. I sent Franny up to her room to get ready for bed on her own."

It took Father a couple of minutes to return with a flashlight. We meandered around in the garden where the antenna had landed. Father shined the light up towards the roof, examining the house for signs of damage. He and Livingston perused the rest of the mansion's perimeter and concluded the house was okay.

"Everything looks fine from here," Father said satisfied. "I'm going to head back to the Auchinclosses' and pick up your Aunt Julia and Elly. We should be back in just a little bit."

"Okay Father," I said. Father turned and spoke to Livingston.

"Livingston, by the way—that damn accelerator pedal is sticking again," he complained. "I almost ran off the road on my way over here. You'd best get it looked at again."

"Yes, sir," Livingston said, surprised.

With that, Father hopped into the Duesenberg and drove off. As soon as the taillights disappeared from beyond the front gate, Norman, Livingston and I made a beeline for the back door and the cellar. The sound of our footfall echoed on the stairwell as we tramped down the steps. Reaching the heavy, steel door, I helped Livingston push it open. It creaked eerily on its hinges. Light spilled out into the stairwell from the cellar. The naked light bulbs glaring back at us from the basement ceiling amplified the starkness of the windowless expanse. There wasn't a sign of Mabel Keating or Amanda anywhere, and in the corner the antiquated hot water heater sputtered away dutifully at its job.

"They must have gone back upstairs," Norman suggested. We were just about to dash back in that direction when Livingston noticed the wine cellar door ajar. Pulling it open part way, he peered inside around the edge of the doorjamb then yanked it all the way open revealing the wine cellar's emptiness. He spotted the unobtrusive light switch tucked against the doorjamb and flipped it a few times but nothing happened. It didn't surprise me.

"It doesn't work," I said. "I tried it the night I followed Aunt Julia down here. The bulb is dead."

"Well there's nobody here anyway," he shrugged.

We turned to head out. That's when I noticed a footprint in the dust on one of the empty wine shelves. It caught my eye below the dangling, inoperative light bulb. The footprint was small and freshly made—by a sneaker. Amanda wore sneakers. I looked up at the bulb.

"Livingston, will you reach up and yank on that light fixture please?," I said speaking my mind.

Livingston reached up, then lightly tugged on the fixture. Nothing happened. He tugged on it again, but harder this time.

"Creeeeeeeek!" To our astonishment, the broad set of vacant wine shelves lining the back wall of the wine cellar started to move. The hiss of hydraulic pistons and the whir of electric motors were an accompaniment to the mechanical choreography unfolding. In a slow, methodical sweep, the wide expanse of shelving slid backwards about a foot then began descending into the floor. Behind it, a vestibule equal to the full width of the wine cellar—a width Livingston estimated to be approximately 24 feet and about eight feet in depth— came into view. Standing in the vestibule wearing expressions of amazement, equaled only by our own, were Amanda and Mabel Keating. Amanda smiled and waved coyly from behind the retreating shelves. Within seconds the shelving disappeared neatly and completely into a recess in the floor. The top of the shelves formed a flush and seamless bridge across the recess. Clearly, the unit had been engineered to operate fully loaded with wine bottles too.

"Look what we've found," Amanda effused. With that, Mabel rapped the brass handle of her walking stick against an enormous, vault-like door located behind them.

"Clang, clang, clang," the sound reverberated. A row of bell shaped, steel-shaded ceiling lights illuminated the vestibule area.

"Well, I'll be...!" Livingston muttered, his jaw dropping.

"This lever here operates the shelves," Amanda demonstrated. "See?"

With both freckled hands she squeezed a pair of tarnished, brass handgrips crowning a steel lever protruding from the floor. Throwing her full weight against the lever, she ratcheted it about twenty degrees. The hydraulic dynamics hissed and whirred again as the shelves started rising from the floor. She ratcheted the lever back again and the shelves descended. Norman whistled with amazement then swore.

"Oops! Sorry," he said noticing the look of disapproval fired in his direction by Mabel...who swore with great regularity herself.

"How did you find out about this?" Norman asked Amanda.

"Mrs. Keating told me to climb up on the shelves and tighten the light bulb in its socket. I lost my balance and grabbed onto the light fixture. We didn't know it controlled the mechanical shelves. The weight of my body pulling on the fixture activated it."

"That's right," Mabel nodded.

"Look over here," Amanda bubbled. "See? There's a lock on this door. I'll bet the brass key we found fits this lock."

Amanda pointed to the sturdy lock while Norman, Livingston and I walked across the threshold created by the top of the wine-shelves for a closer look. Examining the lock, one could only conclude Amanda had to be correct.

"The child's right," Mabel affirmed. Again she thrust the tip of her cane purposefully on the ground emphasizing her conviction.

"What do you suppose is behind that door?" Livingston said, verbalizing what we were all thinking.

"Now, you know as well as the rest of us that this has to be the way into the area where Simon kept the gold," Mabel chided. She paused for a moment admiring the sophisticated engineering of the mechanical shelves and sturdy, bank-like vault door.

"Leave it to my brother, Simon, to come up with security like this to protect his interests," she marveled. "This setup has been here for decades. Only Simon could have engineered something like this," she said full of pride.

"But how are we going to get our hands on that key?" Amanda anguished. "Your Aunt snatched it away from Norman only a short time after you found it. She told us she was going to give the key to your father."

"Yeah, I know. That lock is pretty heavy duty looking too," I said. "It's not a lock we're going to be able to pick. Whatever we're going to do, though, we've got to work fast. Father will be back soon with Elly and Aunt Julia. I don't know if Aunt Julia ever did give Father that key. I never asked him...and I'm certainly not going to now."

The more I thought about it, though, the more I tended to doubt that Aunt Julia had given the key to Father. She had to have taken it with her the night I followed her to the cellar. There must be *another* way out of that area behind the locked vault door, I reasoned...but where? It was the only explanation as to how she got back up to her room without my seeing her that evening.

"Right now I think the thing to do is to button up this place and worry about getting the key later," Livingston suggested. "We'll have to go about finding the key carefully," he warned. "We need to get a hold of it without anyone realizing, then go about getting a duplicate made. It's the only way to get in here and open that door undetected."

"You're right," Mabel seconded. "That's the only way we're ever going to find out what's behind the blasted door. Now you two have got to be *real* careful," she warned. "People have been killed already because they knew that gold was here—and my Ollie was one of them."

I could see the faint trace of tears in her glittering green eyes at the mention of Ollie's name.

"Eddie, you and I can work together on this one," Livingston suggested. I felt relieved and cared for hearing him say it...especially given the betrayal I'd found within my own family.

"Come on, we'd better get out of here," Mabel barked. "It's too dangerous to stay any longer."

With that, we quickly moved back across the threshold into the wine cellar.

"Okay, now let's hope a tug on this light fixture is going to put everything back the way it was," Livingston said.

He yanked forcefully on the dangling light fixture. We held our collective breath.

"Hissssssss! Whirrrrrr!" The syncopated sound of the precision machinery accompanied the smooth ascent of the wine-shelves back to their original position. We watched the entire wall unit glide neatly over the last few inches of its automated journey then slide seamlessly closed with an audible "click."

"Shhh, We'd better hurry. C'mon," I whispered.

With a great deal of effort and considerable help from Livingston and me, Mabel Keating made her way up the basement stairs to the first floor landing. Breathlessly, she continued out the back door under the escort of Norman and Amanda. Livingston and I hustled to the front of the house to run interference for them just in case Father, Aunt Julia and Elly had arrived. Fortunately, they hadn't, but the wind was now blowing from the direction of Hammersmith Farm and I recognized the pulsating purr of the Duesenberg making its way down the drive at the Auchincloss estate. I could also hear Aunt Julia bellowing goodbye to her host and hostess as they drove off.

On the lawn, Livingston and I could make out three forms moving slowly but purposefully towards the delivery truck parked in the driveway. All would have been fine if it weren't for the fact that Mabel Keating lost her footing on the irregularity of turf.

"She's down," I heard Amanda yell.

Livingston sprang into action. Before I could take a step, he bounded across the lawn like a deer. It would be only a matter of a minute or two before the Duesenberg pulled through the front gate.

"Norman, start up the truck and turn it around so it's facing the front gate," Livingston commanded. "Put the headlights on high beam so they're shining directly at it. Amanda, you open up the back doors of the truck and jump in...only both of you *hurry!*"

As I stood on the front verandah nervously clenching and unclenching my fists, I saw Norman start the truck and swing it around to face the main gate. The headlights bathed the entrance and surrounding brick wall with light. Not too far in the distance, I could hear the motor of the Duesenberg getting closer. Its fine-tuned rumble spilled over the top of the wall along Ridge Road and drifted my way with the wind. I thought for sure we were doomed to discovery...until I saw Livingston suddenly bend down and scoop up Mabel's enormous girth with one adrenaline fueled swoop of his mighty arms.

"LAND SAKES!" I heard Mabel cry.

Just as the headlights from the Duesenberg flashed through the front gate in a roar of supercharged exhaust, Livingston deposited Mabel in the back of the truck with a thud. I could hear it even from where I stood. The back of the rickety truck took a noticeable dip as its antique springs sagged under the weight of Mabel's overloaded carriage. I could hear her grunting and cursing as Amanda tugged desperately on her arms in an effort to help her sit up in the windowless rear of the panel truck.

Illuminated by the blinding headlights facing them, I could see Father, Elly and Aunt Julia shading their eyes and squinting to overcome the annoying glare. The Duesenberg faltered momentarily at the gate as Father eased up on the gas in an effort to see better. It bought Livingston just enough time to slam the rear double-doors of the truck and pound his fist on the steel skin signaling Norman to pull away. I could still see Amanda and Mabel floundering around in the back of the truck as Livingston shut the doors. With a sputter and a cough, the decaying truck sprang to life and lurched towards the main gate. Norman cut the high beams and slowed just enough to smile and wave a friendly goodbye to my aggravated family.

"'Night," he yelled out the open cab window as the truck clunked past the Duesenberg and sputtered off into the summer night.

"Well of all the nerve!" I heard Aunt Julia complain as the Duesenberg crunched to a halt on the gravel drive. "The audacity— blinding us with his headlights like that. The next time I see him I think I'll give that boy a piece of my mind."

"Good evening, Miss Sutton." Livingston interrupted, greeting Aunt Julia then Father and Elly. I could see him discreetly rubbing the small of his back with his right hand as he approached us.

"Norman's just a typical teenage boy," he said sympathetically. "Boys that age aren't always tuned into everything they should be mindful about," he offered in Norman's defense.

I was pleased at the tactful manner in which Livingston defused the incident and put Aunt Julia very politely in her place.

"Was there a problem with Norman's truck?" Father asked Livingston. I could see Father assessing the situation as he wondered why Livingston had been standing behind it when they pulled into the drive.

"I think there's always something the matter with that old wreck of a truck, sir," Livingston said with a smile. "Norman had a bit of a problem getting it going. I had to put my back into it, so to speak, to get him out of the driveway. The next time I talk to Dennis Davenport I'm going to suggest it might be time for him to invest in a new one. I'm getting too old to be pushing dead weight like that around." Livingston rubbed his back again. He and I exchanged an inwardly knowing smile.

"Had to push 'er, eh?" Father offered with an unsuspecting wink. "I had an old car like that myself once," he reminisced. "Had to park her facing downhill whenever possible so I could get a rolling start." Father smiled remembering the time. Livingston and I knew we were home free.

"Livingston, do you mind putting the Duesenberg in the garage?" Aunt Julia interrupted. "I'm really feeling a bit tired from all the excitement tonight." She massaged her forehead and the nape of her neck. "And I've got an absolutely *splitting* headache. It must be all that damn heat and humidity. I can't wait to take off these clothes and go to bed."

Aunt Julia paused momentarily, looking towards the house. I watched her nostrils flare ever so slightly as she glanced up at the sky.

"The clouds seem to be breaking," she observed. "That hail was just awful." Reaching a long graceful arm towards the Duesenberg, she danced her two-inch fingernails over the expansive hood and caressed the lustrous paint with the palm of her hand.

"Thank goodness we left the car under the porte cochère at the Auchinclosses'," she said. "I'd hate to think what that barrage of hailstones would have done to this lovely finish—"

"By the way, Livingston," Father chimed in, distracting us from Aunt Julia's romantic interlude with her car. "I'd appreciate it if you'd take the Duesenberg into the shop again tomorrow first thing. That sticky accelerator is dangerous. I don't understand it; we just had the problem fixed and it's back again. Hang onto the keys after you put the car away and take care of it for us, will you?," Father said, gesturing toward the dashboard.

I peered discreetly into the passenger compartment to steal a look at the key ring protruding from the ignition. It was Aunt Julia's. I could tell by the engraved, silver name tag hanging from the ring.

"Yes, sir," Livingston replied.

"How's Franny, son?," Father inquired, directing his attention toward me. "That lightning strike didn't frighten her too badly did it?"

Franny! How was Franny? Gosh, darned if I knew, I thought. Hopefully, she had put herself to bed. We hadn't checked on her since Livingston sent her up to her room.

"Oh, she's fine, sir, I'm sure," Livingston ad-libbed. "She went up to bed a little while ago. Eddie, why don't you peek in on her while I put the car away? I'll be up as soon as I've finished."

"Sounds good," I said following his lead. "See you in a bit." I bade a hasty goodnight to everyone and headed straight for Franny's room. Livingston caught up with me there about 10 minutes later. Luckily, Franny had been obedient and had gotten herself ready for bed on her own. Oftentimes she'd lose focus on what she'd been told to do, but this time, she'd not only gotten herself ready for bed, she lay sound asleep snoring blissfully between the sheets. I could only guess that the energy drain from the séance had completely worn her out.

"Where are Father and Elly?" I asked Livingston quietly.

"They've headed off to bed themselves," he whispered back. "Now, take a look at this and tell me if the key you found in the wine cellar is on it."

He jiggled Aunt Julia's key ring in my face.

"Here it is," I said singling out the unusual brass key and grasping it between my thumb and index finger. "I'd recognize it anywhere. It's pretty distinct—a lot heavier and longer than most keys. Plus it has this unusual scrollwork on it," I pointed out by twisting the key so Livingston could see the deeply engraved handwork that set this particular key apart from any other.

"Good," Livingston said, all the more relieved. "Now we've got to act fast and get a duplicate made first thing tomorrow morning. I'll stop at Coris-Tine Locksmiths on Spring Street before I take the car in to be fixed and get a couple of back-up keys made just as a precaution. We won't get another chance like this, so we'd better make the best of it."

I nodded. Sitting silently, side-by-side, on the end of Franny's bed, we enjoyed a bit of calm following the evening's storm. The sound of Franny's peaceful snoring cut through the silence at regular intervals. We continued conversing in whispers. I don't know if we did so for Franny's benefit or more to ensure our own privacy.

"Livingston, tomorrow night you and I are going down to the basement to find out what's behind that vault door."

"While the Master and his sister are home...and your stepmother, too? I don't know if I like that," he protested. "What if something goes wrong? Suppose they hear us or spot us? Then what? Your aunt has that uncanny sixth sense about her. She knows an awful lot about what's going on without necessarily being close to the action. In fact, I thought for a minute out in the driveway she might have sensed something had transpired tonight—something more than just the lightning strike."

"Maybe you're right. We'd better not take the chance. Got any other ideas?"

Livingston thought carefully.

"The evening after tomorrow I'm driving the Master, your stepmother and aunt to the Newport Country Club for dinner. They'll be there for hours. Since it's only a short distance away, that will allow plenty of time for driving back home, checking out the gold vault, and getting back at a reasonable hour to pick them up. Why don't you see if Norman can pick up Mabel Keating and Amanda? We're supposed to be leaving for the Club around seven, so tell Norman to call from the nearest pay phone about that time to make sure we're actually gone. I wouldn't want him charging into the driveway before we've left."

"Okay. That's a good idea. Meantime, I'd sure love to know the answer to that question."

"Ah...you mean if Belle Pierce actually did kill Ollie Merriweather?"

"Yeah."

"I know what you mean. I've been wondering the same thing—that is in between all the commotion." Livingston reached behind him and rubbed the small of his back again.

"I don't think I want to pick up Mabel Keating again anytime real soon," he said snorting out a chuckle. "She has to weigh a good two hundred and fifty pounds or more."

The informality of Livingston's behavior made me smile broadly. "I know," I said. "You deserve an Olympic gold medal. Frankly, I didn't know how we were going to get out of that one. Cripes, you're amazing!," I said meaning it.

"Well, I'll sleep tonight, that's for sure," Livingston sighed.

We were just about to turn in when Franny mumbled in her sleep. I would have ignored it except I heard her say, "*Ollie*."

"Shhh, listen, Livingston, Franny said something about *Ollie*. There...she said it again. Did you hear it?"

Livingston nodded. "Could you understand her?" he asked.

"I think so."

"It's Ollie...it's Ollie, don't you see? Look through the porthole, because that's where I'll be."

"There, she said it a second time; it's a riddle," I deduced. I figured the porthole had to be the third floor window—the same window that made Franny scream with fright on more than one occasion.

I repeated Franny's riddle.

"It's Ollie...it's Ollie, don't you see? Look through the porthole, because that's where I'll be."

"It's too late now, Livingston...and besides, everybody's home. But, tomorrow sometime we're going up to the third floor—after you get back from the locksmith and getting the Duesenberg fixed. We'll go up to that porthole room in the early afternoon—you, Franny and me...when it's still daylight. Once and for all, we're going to find out 'zactly what it is that Franny sees in that window."

"Okay, Eddie. Although right now, son, I've had just about all the excitement a guy my age can take. I'm going to bed. Good night, son."

I felt the urge to throw my gangly, adolescent arms around him and hug him for all his worth...and did exactly that. A second or two later, I felt his powerful arms surround my shoulders in a caring embrace.

"It'll be all right, Eddie," he told me. We both looked at Franny snoring peacefully in her bed. "It'll be all right for both of you," he reassured me. "I won't let anything happen to either one of you. I made that promise to your mother years ago."

If only I could count on Father like I counted on Livingston, I thought. How unnatural it felt to be afraid of one's father.

"Goodnight now, son," Livingston whispered as he opened the door to Franny's room and stepped into the hallway—but not before scouting that the coast was clear.

"Try to get a good night's sleep," he counseled me. "We've got quite an intense few days ahead of us."

"Goodnight, Livingston," I whispered back. "Thanks for being there for us."

I slipped into the hallway after him and pulled the door to Franny's room closed then headed to my own room. A few minutes later I lay in my bed behind a securely locked door watching lunar light spill through my window. All traces of the storm had vanished leaving the moon partially veiled by a layer of hauntingly translucent clouds. Suspended over the ocean, its Halloween-like aura fueled my imagination—but not enough to keep the weariness of an event-filled day from overtaking me. In a matter of minutes I drifted off, entertaining visions of ghouls and gold while the tambourine sentinel hanging from my doorknob kept its silent vigil.

CHAPTER FOURTEEN

The next morning, I woke around seven and ate a hearty breakfast with Livingston. We chatted in low whispers about what we might discover behind the locked vault door. The series of unearthly video encounters didn't go without discussion either. Livingston wasted no time cleaning the dirty dishes after laying out the dining room table with the usual continental breakfast for Father, Elly and Aunt Julia. Shortly thereafter, the baritone purr of the Duesenberg drifting down the driveway announced Livingston's departure for Cummings Motor and the locksmith shop. He took Franny along with him for the ride.

I decided to spend the time they would be gone up in my room peering through my telescope. Over at Hammersmith Farm, I could see several workmen already tackling the tree toppled the night before by the storm. Geysers of sawdust spewed into the air as chainsaws hacked though the fallen tree. The buzz of the saws hummed in my ears from across the lawn. Mrs. Auchincloss stood on the sidelines watching the men work. Through my telescope I could see her lips move as she gave an occasional order to the workers. It reminded me of an old Charlie Chaplin movie—lips moving with no sound to be heard.

Down by the water's edge of our own property I could see Father, Elly and Aunt Julia dressed in bathing suits and carrying aluminum folding chairs in preparation for some time at the beach. Having consumed their continental breakfast, they were navigating the rocks towards the spot they typically occupied for sunbathing. A renegade breaker broke unexpectedly nearby, soaking them all in chilly sea-spray. I found myself laughing out loud at the sight of Aunt Julia recoiling in horror while flying surf drenched her fashionable bathing regalia. A rogue wave collapsed her wide-brimmed sun hat like a wilted petunia around her head.

204

Once they settled down though, I grew bored and turned my attention to the bay. The thought of ogling some scantily clad debutantes tanning their curvaceous bodies on the deck of a cruising sailboat or motor-launch offered greater appeal—far greater than mundanely observing my family sunbathing or tree surgery at the Auchincloss estate.

To my delight, I spotted an open bow-rider about twenty-four feet in length anchored a few hundred yards off shore. I could see three muscular men naked from the waist up sipping beer and lounging on the seats. There were an equal number of voluptuous looking female companions with them in bikinis. They all seemed to be enjoying themselves. Apparently they felt the early hour and isolated anchor point afforded them ample privacy, because a moment later they decided to take an early morning dip—a skinny-dip. I watched bug-eyed as the men, one-by-one shed their bell-bottom trousers then plunged, hairy and naked, off the side of the boat into the water. To my disappointment, the girls were more modest. They slipped into the bay from the stern of the boat then deposited their bikinis on the rear swim-platform. I found myself straining to telescopically devour as much of the erotic water sport as I possibly could. Needless to say, the event provided a brief but sorely welcome respite from the fear-driven anxiety I'd grown accustomed to feeling.

I lost track of time during this eye-candy interlude then much to my surprise, Livingston suddenly appeared at my bedroom door with a duplicate set of keys sealed in a plain, manila envelope. A glance at the clock on my night table revealed I'd been actively engaged in telescopic voyeurism for nearly two hours. I quickly shifted my attention to the business at hand.

"Cripes, you got them," I said, bounding to my feet.

"Yes, I got them—and through no easy means, I dare say. The key required a special blank that wasn't in stock. I had to wait while the fellow over at the locksmith's shop called around to try and locate some. The style is *very* old, evidently. He finally found two blanks at a shop several towns away. I had to drive over and wait to have them made up. Needless to say, I never did get that sticky accelerator pedal fixed on the Duesenberg. If he mentions it, I'll just have to tell the Master they were too busy at Cummings Motor. Hopefully I can get it done sometime over the next few days."

"Okay, at least you got the keys, I said. Where's Franny, by the way? Is she down...? Oh, there she is."

I hadn't noticed Franny standing quietly in the hall behind Livingston.

"Let me just take a look through the telescope to see if everyone else is still at the beach sunbathing," I added. "If the coast is clear, we can go upstairs to the room with the porthole window to see what we can find out."

I realigned my sites with the beach-front below and made a quick scan of the rocks where Father, Elly, and Aunt Julia had been sitting. There they were.

"It looks like Father's fallen asleep with a newspaper over his face," I observed. "Elly and Aunt Julia are slathered with suntan oil and stretched out on their aluminum chairs. It looks like they're dozing too."

· "I'd say we've got some time before they start to come to and head back up to the house for lunch," Livingston estimated. "We'd better get going if we're going to do this."

With that, the three of us headed down the hall to the back stairs and hustled up to the third floor. The door to the room with the porthole creaked spookily as Livingston pushed it open. It smelled musty and had a different feel than the other times I'd been in there. This time it felt clammy. The bright sunlight streaming in the round-paned window from the front seemed ineffective in improving the atmosphere.

I had brought an ample supply of *Chiclets* with me—about a

dozen boxes—and quickly scattered the contents of four of them onto the floor… just to be prepared. Peering out the circular window, I could see Father, Elly and Aunt Julia still in beach-front slumber. With caution, I reached to release the window hasp. It was already unlatched. Somebody or some *thing* had preceded us.

"Livingston, why don't you sit down with Franny on the floor while I tilt this window at various angles. Maybe you can get a glimpse of whatever it is that keeps frightening her."

Livingston grasped Franny's left hand and the two of them sank slowly to the floor in the middle of the room. Franny wasted no time picking up a fist full of *Chiclets* and stuffing them into her mouth.

"Cripes, Franny, not so many. We may need those."

"Sorry, Eddie," she mumbled.

"Now look at the window here and tell me what you see," I said pointing to the window.

She gasped. "Eddie, I don't like looking into that window. It scares me."

I could barely make out her words slurred by the wad of *Chiclets* crammed in her mouth.

"Why, Franny? Whadda ya see?"

"I don't like it, Eddie. It scares me."

"Franny, whadda you see?"

"What do you see, Franny?" Livingston repeated.

I began angling the window at differing degrees. Livingston kept his eyes focused on the window, craning his neck in different directions as I pivoted the windowpane. His eyes never left the glass. If they had he would have noticed the words Franny had started to spell out on the floor with *Chiclets*. Her pudgy fingers danced deftly as she

207

created letters out of gum.

"*Windo*" and "*seller*" materialized first. Although misspelled, I felt confident their author meant *window* and *cellar*.

"Livingston, you're missing the show," I said gaining his attention.

"What? Oh...oh my, so I am."

And at that moment things got normal—at least for the porthole room.

Franny shrieked and leapt to her feet. Whatever she saw in that window had come back again. Livingston pulled Franny close to him, muffling a scream in his clothing. His embrace helped console her.

"Shhh, shhh, be quiet, Franny," Livingston comforted. Franny stopped. I checked the beach with a quick glance to make sure nobody heard. Father, Elly and Aunt Julia hadn't moved.

"Franny, it's all right," Livingston assured. "Eddie and I are here with you."

"What is it she sees, Livingston? It has to be something reflected in the glass."

Livingston strained to take a closer look.

"All I can see is the base of the pillar supporting the front portico—you know, the one that's always been leaning—the one that drives the Master crazy."

"Can you see anything else?"

"Nope! Not a thing."

I stole a look at Franny peering out from beneath Livingston's powerful arm. The sleeve of his jacket enveloped her small, delicate

208

frame as he held her protectively at his side. Her jaw gyrated furiously on the gum she was chewing. I thought of the riddle Franny had recited in her sleep the previous night:

It's Ollie...it's Ollie, don't you see? Look through the porthole, because that's where I'll be.

Could it be what Franny saw wasn't a reflection? If I hadn't looked *through* the window at that very instant, I'd have missed it— the specter forming from beyond the glass. The semi-transparent image glowing faintly, manifested as it rose from the footing of the listing pillar. Tiny particles—paranormal atoms that clung to each other through some supernatural law of nature—melded to form a startling apparition.

"Cripes, Livingston, do you see it?" My voice had a noticeable tremolo.

"See what?"

"That figure...that th-thing!"

Livingston released Franny from his embrace and moved closer. I was standing in front of the porthole window. He didn't have to answer. I could tell by the look on his face that he could see it. The materialization of a figure, the likes of a young girl, evolved before us. Its naked and gnome-like body, although semi-transparent, had a pallid quality of color about it I would liken to the flesh tone of a cadaver. There were terrible gashes in the torso—a long row of large puncture wounds perforating the front of the body. One's imagination might allow that the badly wounded specter had been caught in the gripping jaws of some oversized, devouring beast. The sight of this astonishing apparition floating in broad daylight just outside the window made my heart pound. I fought the urge to flee, and had Livingston not been standing close by my side, I think I might have. But then for the first time I caught a good view of the phantom's face when it opened its eyes. They were a soft shade of emerald green and provided the only color visible throughout.

Contrasted against the deathly pallor of its skin-tone, the eyes were radiant. And the face...Livingston and I both knew that face. That's when all feelings of fear left me. No wonder Franny had reacted the way she did during the previous times we'd visited the porthole room. Who wouldn't be spooked at seeing a ghostly vision with a face that mirrored your own? This was the same green-eyed phantom that hovered over the television set in my room. This was Franny's look-alike—the ghost of Ollie Merriweather.

Why hadn't I seen it the previous two times Franny and I had visited the porthole room? Was I too consumed with trying to see a reflection of something in the glass? Or did Franny's psychic gift allow her to see and experience things that the other ninety-nine percent of us couldn't? Perhaps my own level of extrasensory awareness had to be heightened prior to telepathic events before my senses could perceive the metaphysical presence.

What about Franny? Livingston and I had been completely distracted. What was she doing? I tore my eyes away from the vision just long enough to steal a view of her busy hands constructing words from the pile of *Chiclets* I'd dumped on the floor. *OSWALD* had been spelled out neatly. So had the word *MURDER*. There might have been more words and letters had Franny not eaten them. She didn't seem frightened anymore either.

We would have made further progress if Father, Elly, and Aunt Julia hadn't chosen that particular moment to end their sunbathing and return to the house for lunch.

"They're on their way back," Livingston announced pointing to the trio by the water's edge. "I hope they haven't spotted us. We'd better get out."

I looked out towards the water beyond the ghost of Ollie Merriweather suspended in front of me. I could see Father and Elly packing up their things. Aunt Julia already had her towel and folded lawn chair stuffed under her arm as she navigated her way over the rocks toward the direction of the house. I watched her pause at one point to sniff the air while she looked in the mansion's direction. I backed away cautiously from the window.

"You're right, Livingston, I hope they haven't spotted us."

Taking care to keep out of sight, Livingston fastened the hasp on the window. A few seconds later we were scrambling around on the floor collecting Franny and her scattered *Chiclets*. Then, as we bolted for the door, I turned for a last look at Ollie, but she wasn't there. I halted in my tracks but Livingston kept on going. He hustled out into the hall dragging Franny by the hand. I could hear the two of them scurrying down the deserted corridor.

"Come on, Eddie," he yelled back over his shoulder, "we haven't got much time."

"Come on, Eddie," Franny parroted back in her nasally staccato voice.

I paused long enough to walk a few paces towards the window, hoping I might spot Ollie once more. I saw Aunt Julia instead. She had reached the edge of the lawn and was making good time. I was about to give up and go when a flicker of movement on the portico steps below caught my eye. I watched, captivated, as the specter of Ollie Merriweather decomposed into a formless vapor-cloud and vanished into the pillar footing beneath me—sucked into its base like dust into a *Hoover*. Midway across the lawn I could see Aunt Julia. She'd stopped dead in her tracks and was staring up at the porthole window. I turned and bolted out the door, sprinting past Livingston and Franny on my way down the back staircase.

"To the kitchen," I yelled to them as I raced by. The kitchen door banged against the hallway wall from the force of my entrance then creaked methodically to a stop on its spring-loaded hinges. Yanking a carton of milk from the fridge with one hand, I grabbed three glasses out of the cupboard with the other. I all but flung them onto the kitchen table then pulled a tin of Livingston's Tollhouse cookies out of the pantry. By the time Livingston and Franny arrived, I'd poured the milk and tossed some napkins onto the table. We'd no sooner slid into our seats when the kitchen door creaked open and Aunt Julia popped her head in. We waved nonchalantly as she stood there eyeing us. Her wilted sun hat drooped around her ears. When she finally left, Livingston and I went through a ritual of swearing Franny to secrecy—an exercise she loved. It consisted of all three of us stacking our hands, alternately—palms down one on top of the other—chanting the words: Keep a secret, save a life. Tell what happened—pay the price!

Then we'd lower our sandwich of hands to about knee level and swoop them upward high above our heads before making a break. Franny loved it. Curiously, the exercise always proved very effective in securing her confidentiality—not that there would be any retribution from Livingston or me if she had slipped up. Somehow, she always managed to sense the right level of discretion in spite of her severe disability.

Later that night, the dinner conversation focused on the investigation into Mr. FitzHugh's murder and the lack of progress the police seemed to be making on the case. Elly seemed particularly outspoken.

"I don't understand why Captain Karl hasn't been able to identify any suspects," she complained. "The police have certainly had enough time by now to gather clues and round up the culprit." Elly picked up her water goblet and washed down a piece of Parker House roll. I kept a close watch on Aunt Julia anticipating her reaction to Elly's remark.

"I'm sure that whoever murdered George FitzHugh has long since left the area," Aunt Julia retorted. "In fact, I can sense it. In the past, whenever I've assisted the New York City Police Department in solving a crime, I've always been able to sense with my psychic sonar if the perpetrator was still nearby. And right now I'm not getting any blips around George FitzHugh's killer...which makes me feel safe in saying the culprit no doubt fled."

As I sat with fork in hand pushing peas around on my plate, I could only wonder if Aunt Julia was telling the truth or lying to cover up her own part in the crime. One couldn't really tell for sure. Aunt Julia droned on about her heightened sensory perception. I tuned her out and turned my attention towards Father. Seeing him at the table so handsomely dignified made it all the harder as I pondered the involvement he might have had in Mr. FitzHugh's death too. At that moment, apart from Franny, Livingston and me, the only other person in the family about whose innocence I felt reasonably certain was Elly.

Watching her from across the table, I couldn't help admiring her beauty. In fact, for a moment, I forgot the sticky situation at hand and mentally left the scene. In my fantasy, I was looking through my telescope once again at that boat in the bay—the one that bobbed around with its crew of naked passengers reveling in their lusts, their sculpted bronzed bodies flashing under the sun and water as they performed every kind of erotic exploit imaginable. For an instant I envisioned Elly as part of it all. But then as I crossed the threshold between eroticism and decency, the idea suddenly cheapened, leaving me battling my own guilt.

"...Eddie! Eddie!" I heard Father say. "Aunt Julia is talking to you."

"What? Oh, 'scuse me...I wasn't paying attention."

"We know you weren't paying attention," Father scolded.

"I'm sorry. Excuse me. You were saying, Aunt Julia?"

"What I was saying, Eddie, was that I really wish you wouldn't socialize quite as much with that grocery boy...what's his name again?"

"You mean Norman Tate." Elly said.

"Yes, Norman Tate. He really is an irritating sort of fellow—shining the headlights in our eyes last night, for example. Besides, he's hardly our sort. He's a delivery boy and I doubt you'd find other children from respectable families socializing with the delivery boy."

I looked at Father. He sat there quietly chewing his food. I hoped he would defend the friendship I'd formed with Norman. He didn't. Other than Livingston—Norman and Amanda were my only allies. Was it now Father's and Aunt Julia's strategy to start picking them off one-by-one? Perhaps Aunt Julia knew more than we suspected about our trip to the third floor a few hours ago—or, worse, saw Livingston dump Mabel into the back of the truck the night before. I was just mustering the nerve to challenge Aunt Julia when Elly spoke up in Norman's and my behalf.

"Don't you think you're being rather harsh, Julia? I think Norman's rather a nice young man...although I think he smokes. I've noticed the smell of cigarette smoke on his clothing when he comes to the house. He's always very polite when he comes to drop off groceries, though, and he *is* prompt. Oh, I know that old delivery truck is annoying, too...but that's not his fault. Dennis Davenport is the one responsible for that. Arthur, don't you agree?"

Father just sat there. I saw him exchange a glance with his sister. The jig was up on Norman's smoking. I knew that wouldn't help matters.

"Arthur!" Elly said firmly. "Did you hear what I said about Norman?" Father hesitated, but spoke up.

"Yes...yes, I agree."

Aunt Julia looked annoyed—the look of someone recognizing a league against her.

Good old Elly, I thought.

"Well then, that's settled," Elly proclaimed ending the discussion about Norman.

I beamed with the inner glow of victory. We'd even gotten around the issue of Norman's smoking without a hitch.

"So, Eddie, just what were you and Franny doing up in that

third floor bedroom this afternoon?," Elly asked out of blue, sending me reeling. My inner glow went coal black. I felt my guts churn. So much for victory!

"Your Aunt Julia went up there this afternoon and found two *Chiclets* on the floor behind the door." Elly presented two pieces of the sugarcoated gum in her upturned palm. I gulped.

"I must have dropped them up there, ma'am," Livingston interjected politely. He had just swept into the room carrying a mountainous Black Forest cake.

"The children and I were up there this afternoon scouting out a new place to do some stargazing. That large, porthole shaped window looked like the perfect place to locate Eddie's telescope—only it turns out that center pivoting hinge gets in the way."

I exhaled a sigh of relief. Livingston to the rescue.

"The *Chiclets* were in the pocket of my jacket, ma'am," Livingston added. "I gave them to Franny to keep her occupied. A few of them must have dropped in the process."

"Very well," Elly replied. She looked nervously at Father.

"It's just that we don't want the children to get hurt exploring where they shouldn't," she said looking back in Livingston's direction. He nodded warily.

Now this was a shocker—a 180-degree turn-around by Elly. I never would have guessed it. But that's how things were going lately—nothing for certain. So much for my thinking Elly was above suspicion.

After supper, we played a game of Parcheesi while listening to the radio. The prospect of ever watching television again had long vanished with the untimely and melodramatic end that befell the monstrous roof antenna. The space probe, *Ranger 7*, had just landed on the moon and we were listening to the radio announcer describe some of the pictures everyone else was watching on television. Add to the evening's earlier confrontation by Elly our afternoon encounter with Ollie Merriweather's ghost, and it made for quite a night. Thus, when it came time for me to head up to bed, I went with a good deal of consternation. As I lay there in my room with my tambourine strategically in place, I knew, full well, my meager security precaution would be ineffective against intruders from the spirit world.

Regardless of this realization, however, I felt surprisingly unthreatened by the apparition we'd seen. Although cloaked in ghastly pallor and covered with ugly, ulcerated puncture wounds, the memory that haunted me most vividly was the specter's gentle but anguished face—its sorrowful green eyes reaching out to me as if beckoning to be put to rest. Undisturbed amidst the otherwise jarring testimony of my immediate surroundings, I fell into a deep and restful sleep that found me awake the next morning, refreshed and exhilarated.

The day was bathed in sunshine. I couldn't wait for the hour to arrive when Father, Elly, and Aunt Julia would climb into the car and drive to the Newport Country Club for dinner—a short hop, considering the club's Harrison Avenue address was actually within walking distance from our house. Not wanting to arouse further suspicion from anybody, both Livingston and I made it a point to spend most of the day fishing and swimming in full view off the rocks by the house. Franny joined us. Livingston planted an oversized beach umbrella on a spit of sand in between some rocks and we slathered up with suntan lotion. We ate a picnic lunch on the front lawn and kept cool by sipping ice-cold lemonade from a giant thermos and taking periodic dips in the bay. Aunt Julia disappeared for most of the day, driving off early in the Duesenberg to get her hair done and do some shopping. Father and Elly read for a good part of the day on the verandah and went inside for a few hours after lunch to take a nap. The whole time they were gone, however, I couldn't help but feel they were watching us from inside.

By the time we decided to call it quits around five o'clock, we had reeled in quite a catch. The fish were really biting that day and even Franny had managed to land more than a fair share of the two dozen or so flounder and bluefish we'd hauled in. Around 5:30 PM, Aunt Julia roared through the gate in the Duesenberg; her freshly coiffed hair wrapped in a long, flowing scarf that trailed out behind her in the breeze. Later, she made it a point to let Livingston know she was *not* happy with the fact the accelerator pedal still stuck and expressed her "disappointment" at his not having followed through with the repairs.

Undaunted, Livingston apologized profusely offering the explanation that the service department at Cummings Motor had been overbooked that day and he had to make an appointment for the following Monday. Aunt Julia seemed to buy it, although it didn't lessen her level of irritation.

The moment of their departure for the club finally arrived a little before 7:00 PM. Livingston pulled the Bentley out of the garage and parked it next to the Duesenberg adjacent to the portico. He was preparing to put the Duesenberg back into the garage when Aunt Julia, Father, and Elly came out dressed for dinner. Father looked quite grand in his white dinner jacket and cummerbund. Elly wore a strapless, white satin Chanel evening gown that accentuated her marvelous figure. I knew that's what it was because she couldn't stop talking about it. I noticed Livingston's eyes light up at the sight of her. I, too, have to admit that Aunt Julia looked quite elegant. She had on a long evening gown made of pink chiffon that opened at the neck. Diamonds dazzled in the fading daylight from a necklace draping her collarbone.

"Never mind putting that away now, Livingston," Aunt Julia countered as he started climbing into her car. "The weather forecast calls for clear skies for the next few days. Besides, I'm famished. I'd just as soon get to the club as soon as possible. You can put the Duesenberg away later."

"Yes ma'am," Livingston obeyed. He hopped out of the Duesenberg and walked back over to the Bentley. Holding the door open courteously, he helped the ladies into the back seat. Father climbed in taking his place next to him in the front. In less than a minute, they were crunching down the gravel drive and heading out the front gate. I stood excitedly on the verandah with Franny, watching them leave. With my right hand shoved in the pocket of my pants, I ran my fingers over the brass key that would momentarily unlock the secret of Annandale Farm's gold.

Then I heard the telephone jangle, and sprang to answer it. It was Norman calling from a pay phone as planned to see if the coast was clear. Five minutes later the old delivery truck rattled through the front gate and stopped next to the Duesenberg. Amanda and Norman hopped out onto the drive then helped Mabel out of the front seat.

It was impossible to exclude them from participating in our subterranean expedition. The unfolding of events, thus far, had created a clear, albeit unspoken, "we're all in this together," kind of bond that intrinsically led us, arm-in-arm, down a "yellow brick road" of discovery toward the answer to a riddle—a riddle that we…or anyone, for that matter, couldn't even clearly articulate.

"C'mon," I yelled waving from the verandah, "let's get started. By the time we make it down to the basement with Mrs. Keating, Livingston should be back."

And so he was.

No sooner had we negotiated the tedious process of escorting Mabel to the basement, than Livingston arrived. Amanda had just pulled open the door to the wine cellar when the steel basement door creaked loudly and Livingston popped in behind us carrying a flashlight. Wasting no time, he hustled across the vast expanse.

"Here, let me get that," he offered as Amanda stretched to reach the light fixture dangling from the wine cellar ceiling. She stood on tiptoe, balanced precariously on the shelf below.

"Here, I'll hold that flashlight for you," Mabel offered, taking it from him.

Livingston reached towards the fixture and with a single yank activated the power-driven mechanisms setting the bank of automated wine shelves in motion.

"Psssssssssssss," the hiss of hydraulic pistons signaled the start of the cycle. "Whirrrrrrrrr," the smooth hum of electric motors jumped in on cue as the broad bank of wine shelves moved effortlessly backward to the beat of a mechanical rhythm. We stood there marveling, once again, as the array of shelving lowered into the floor recess, coming to a halt with a solid "ka-chunk."

Slowly and deliberately, I made my way across the threshold of shelves and approached the heavy vault door. A large, stainless-steel spoked wheel resembling an automobile steering wheel protruded from the face of the heavily armored door. It controlled the locking pistons used to keep the vault's valuable contents in...and intruders out. Only now, we were the intruders, even though we had a key to grant us access. We were on the verge of invading Simon Merriweather's private domain—a domain that for over half a century had been a closely guarded secret that someone had killed to conceal.

With my right hand trembling from excitement, I inserted the long, brass key into the lock. It slid in, but not without some resistance. I paused and glanced over my shoulder towards the others. They were huddled in a group only a few feet away, eyes fixed with anticipation on the heavy steel door.

"Wait a minute! Is that the only key?" Mabel asked abruptly.

I paused for a moment.

"Livingston has one too," I found myself volunteering.

Livingston reached into the side pocket of his jacket and pulled out the backup duplicate the locksmith had made. It gleamed in the dim light.

"The only other one we know about is Aunt Julia's," I said.

"Well, okay. I just wouldn't want to take any risks. Suppose the key broke off in that lock or something. Then what would we do? The door and lock are pretty old you know."

Keeping her warning in mind, I applied force, gradually, in an effort to rotate the key clockwise in the lock. It began to turn. We heard the tumblers click. Haltingly, after taking a deep breath, I gripped the steel-spoked wheel with both hands and tried to turn it. It wouldn't budge.

"Try turning the key in the lock a second time," Mabel suggested.

Gingerly, I rotated the key clockwise a second time. "Click!" The tumblers engaged again.

"Let's try turning it now," Livingston encouraged, placing his hands on the wheel next to mine. With two sets of hands gripping the steel-spoked wheel, we tugged. It moved. It rotated once, twice then four more times until it would turn no farther. I pulled the key out of the lock and put it in my pants pocket. We clustered around the heavy vault door anticipating what lay beyond.

"Okay, give way, please," Livingston said, politely pushing us aside so he could thrust his weight into opening the heavy steel door. The massive door creaked and groaned on corroded hinges, then swung back slowly, stopping with a "thunk" when it hit the wall. Faint light from where we stood spilled through the door but did little to provide visibility into the coal-black darkness beyond. Our eyes fought to adjust to the limited light while Norman unclipped his flashlight from his belt then shined it through the door and Mabel flipped on the flashlight Livingston had brought. We caught glimpses of brilliance as the flashlight beams splashed across rock-ribbed walls.

"See if there's a light switch on the wall near the door inside," Mabel ordered, shining the flashlight around the doorjamb.

"I see one," Amanda said, stepping over the lip of the door to reach it. A muted "gonk" signaled the flow of electric current as

Amanda flipped on the switch. Then, with an intermittent flicker of light, the ancient light bulbs came to life in their turn-of-the-century housings. The mysterious curtain of darkness began to lift. In the background, the trickle of water seeping through cracks in the rock dripped eerily on the rocky floor below. The cave smelled dank and musty, but to the eye it was a different matter.

"Cripes," was all I could say. I wondered if the sight before us could compare to the legendary splendor of King Solomon's Mine. The rocky cavern glittered with a richness and vitality that could be attributed to only one source—*gold*! Light reflecting off the ore-laden rock gave the mineshaft a kind of eerie luminescence.

Standing next to me, I felt Mabel shift her weight on her walking stick as she studied the hidden domain her brother had crafted.

"Help me inside, will you?" she asked Livingston eagerly.

He shrugged. "What are we all waiting for?," he said. Courteously, he offered Mabel his arm. She willingly took it, stepping over the lip of the door. As soon as they both cleared the entrance, the rest of us followed. We found ourselves standing on a reinforced, steel mezzanine bolted to the rock walls of an enormous cavern. The entry point we'd just negotiated was towards the top of the cavern's dome shaped roof. A steel staircase zigzagged its way to the floor about thirty feet below. From our vantage-point, we could see an old mining cart brimming with antique tools, motionless on a rusted section of railway track. A pair of old work-gloves and a miner's helmet sat on a wooden workbench alongside a toolbox where Simon Merriweather must have left them.

With Livingston's help, we were able to maneuver Mabel down the stairs where we paused at the bottom to take in our surroundings. The presence of earlier mining activity was considerable. What looked to be an antiquated, steam-powered boring machine fitted with drilling heads and an earthmoving conveyor filled up a goodly portion of the central cavern. Its corroded and cobweb encrusted carcass gave evidence of decades-worth of nonuse. A large coal bin once used to store massive quantities of steam-generating fuel was completely empty. Livingston explained how it all must have worked.

Catacomb-like tunnels, each with their own track bed, radiated out from the central cavern in varying directions. Each tunnel was separated from the other by a high, rock-formed archway. The arches reminded me of those I'd seen gracing the halls of grand, European cathedrals in my history books. Broad streaks of lustrous gold ore slashed the rock walls in every direction.

I heard Livingston pipe an awe-filled whistle as he soaked up the magnitude of the treasure-laden grotto. His whistle reverberated throughout the cavern for several seconds. While we wandered about the cave, Amanda and Norman gaped in wonderment while Franny simply tagged along, showing no more interest than she might have at the sight of a curbstone.

"Well glory be...!" Mabel wowed. "So *this* is where my brother spent all of his time. He must have been one busy little cuss too, from the looks of things." Her uninhibited candor made me smile.

"A heck of a lot sure went on here," I seconded. "Simon must've been mining this site for years."

"No doubt about it. Explains why I never knew where he was most of the time," she said. "He had to have worked this mine day and night. No wonder that folks thought this house was haunted. Can you imagine all the noise this mining equipment must have made?"

I let my eyes wander, making mental notes of the mine's construction.

"You're right," I said. "This cave had to have acted like a sounding bell or something. The noise must've traveled through the foundation and framework of the whole house. It all had to have sounded pretty spooky. Anyone not knowing this was here could've imagined just about anything. It would be impossible to figure out the real source of the noise."

Mabel nodded.

"Kind of explains why all those people moved in...and then *out* so fast, doesn't it?" she chuckled. In what by now had become a tradition, Mabel punctuated her statement with a rap of her walking stick on the rocky ground. For some reason, the act, for no apparent reason, served as the signal to begin our exploration of the catacombs. I teamed up with Livingston and Franny, while Mabel partnered with Norman and Amanda. Nobody said it, but I knew that Livingston was making sure no one was wandering the mine unaccompanied by an adult.

"It's awfully cold down here," Amanda observed before splitting off to explore the cave with her designated partners. She folded her arms in front of her and rubbed them to generate some warmth. "Do you think we ought to go back and get some coats...and maybe some rope and extra flashlights?," she suggested sensibly.

"No, no," Mabel countered quickly. "There's plenty of light down here, and we've got two flashlights with us," she emphasized, holding the light Livingston had brought with him up for all of us to see, then pointing to Norman's. "And we don't have a lot of time either," she said. "We'd better make the best of the situation while we're here and hop to it."

"Yeah," I said seconding Mabel's opinion. "We don't know how long Father, Elly and Aunt Julia will actually be gone. It's better if we don't waste a second. We'll be all right. Let's just yell out "okay" to each other every few minutes as a signal that everything's all right."

That's a good idea, Eddie," Livingston agreed. "The tunnels are well lit, but we don't know what we might run into, so let's make it a point to do that."

A few seconds later, we were headed down our separate tunnels to see what we might find. After about five minutes and as equally many "okays," Livingston stopped abruptly at the juncture of another tunnel. Just as he did, Norman and Amanda appeared in the adjoining tunnel and it was evident the two routes we'd taken had intersected.

"Dear God!" he said. "Do you know what we've stumbled on?" The implications of the find suddenly dawned on him. It had been evident to me all along. Belle Pierce and Mabel Keating had to be right about their assassination theory.

"It's 'cause of the gold, isn't it, Livingston?," I said. "That's the reason President Kennedy was assassinated last year."

"Yes, Eddie. It's *all* about the gold, I'm afraid. No wonder there's been so much subterfuge. This is *really* serious business."

Livingston didn't have to say it...but I knew what he was thinking: We'll probably be lucky to get out alive.

It was just at this point that suddenly and unannounced, the lights went out...and we realized everyone wasn't present and accounted for. The discovery came as one of those sickening moments when you know you've been betrayed—duped by someone you've trusted. We all heard it—the heavy vault door creaking on its hinges and closing with a resoundingly hollow echo; the equally sickening sound of the key turning in the lock. The mechanism that secured the impervious pistons of the vault door used to keep would-be intruders from entering this private world had become the means of our own imprisonment.

While we had been preoccupied discussing our history-making find, we failed to notice that Norman and Amanda, caught up in the zeal and curiosity of exploration, had significantly widened the gap between themselves and Mabel. In fact, Mabel had intentionally dropped back to allow distance to prevail while Amanda and Norman, at routine intervals, yelled out that all was "okay."

Not only had Mabel managed to distance herself from the team, but as the rest of us were discussing the implications of the gold strike, she had managed to stealthily slip away. Defying all previous signs of age and any evidence of reduced mobility, she caught us completely off guard, stealing up the steep stairs and through the open vault door. She defied our estimation of her physical strength, too. It took no small amount of muscle power to move the vault door on its hinges or initiate the locking pistons so deftly. Turning out the lights was the easiest part of all.

Only a matter of seconds passed before Norman switched on his flashlight—the only one we had now, since Mabel had left with Livingston's. Illuminated by the glow from its beam, I could see looks of panic on Norman's and Amanda's faces. Although Livingston paled a bit, I could tell he was already contemplating our next move. Franny, in keeping with her usual, detached view of life and events, showed no sign of concern whatsoever.

Though stunned by the implications of Mabel's departure, I found myself curiously calm. I wondered how Mabel might have locked the door when I still had the key in my pocket. I recalled the spare key Livingston had.

"Livingston, do you still have that extra key in your pocket?" I asked.

"Why sure, I put it... hey, wait a minute. That's funny. I know I put it right here in this pocket. Now I can't find it."

Norman held the flashlight beam on Livingston while he fished around for the key in his suit pockets—every one of them. He held up his hands, futilely.

"You all saw it a few minutes ago," he pressed. "Remember? I put it in the side pocket of my jacket."

"Mabel saw you put it there, too," I reminded him. His face fell with the realization she'd picked his pocket when he'd helped her through the door.

"Never mind, the key won't do us a bit of good anyway," Norman chimed in. "There's no locking mechanism on this side. I noticed when we came in. It's a one way trip. The lock and rotating wheel for the pistons are all on the other side. There's no way out—at least not the way we came in."

Norman illuminated the way and we followed him to the foot of the stairs. Livingston took the light at that point and scrambled to the top. We could see, as he shined the light on the door that no means of opening it existed from the inside.

"Click, Click, Click." Livingston flipped the light switch next to the doorjamb on and off with no effect.

"She must have cut the power at the main fuse box," he grumbled.

But before any of us could answer, something happened that turned our already tenuous situation into even more of a crisis. Turning to make his way back down the stairs, Livingston stumbled, losing his grip on the flashlight as he grabbed for the railing to catch his balance. We watched in horror as our only source of light somersaulted to the solid-rock surface 30 feet below.

When the flashlight shattered, the panic officially began. Amanda screamed. Franny, who up to that point had been totally detached, decided to join in. The high-pitched screams of both girls reverberated off of the rocky walls. I pressed the palms of my hands over my ears to deaden the sound.

"Now STOP IT!" Livingston called out authoritatively through the din. "That's NOT going to solve anything." The echo of his voice reverberated in the dark, but the forcefulness of his command did its job and both girls stopped.

"It's going to be all right, girls," Livingston assured them. I could feel the confidence in his voice.

"Norman, I saw an old kerosene lantern hanging on a nail above the workbench over there. You were standing closest to it. Do you think you can reach it?"

"I'll try." Norman's voice echoed shakily off the walls from out of the darkness. He was scared, too.

"But we don't have any matches," Amanda fretted.

"I do," Norman answered back. He struck one and it flared beautifully in front of us.

"You been smoking, son?" Livingston asked. There was a pause. In the flicker of match light I saw an I-told-you-so look flash across Amanda's face.

"I know I'm not supposed to..."

"It's okay, Norman," Livingston assured him. "Thank God you have them. Now watch your step and see if you can reach that lantern. If we're lucky, there may still be some kerosene in it."

Reaching for the lantern, Norman stole a private moment and wrinkled up his nose at Amanda.

"It feels pretty empty," Norman said as he lifted the lamp from its hook. "I can feel some kerosene sloshing around in there though. Most of the stuff's probably evaporated over the years."

In less than a minute, Norman had a bright flame kindled that bathed the cavern in soft-hued light. The gold lining the walls and ceiling of the cave shone with a glorious richness. The soft, lustrous tones reminded me of the opulently gilded interior of Marble House— one of the better-known Newport mansions I'd visited with Elly. Norman held the lamp high to maximize the light for Livingston's descent. We watched him make it down the stairs without a hitch.

Although it appeared that Norman's assessment of not getting out the way we came in was correct, I felt sure that another means of escape existed. Recalling the night Aunt Julia disappeared through the wine cellar and then mysteriously reappeared in her room, I reasoned there must be another way out—but where?

"Cripes, there's gotta be another exit somewhere," I said. "I'm sure there is 'cause Aunt Julia *had* to have used it that night I followed her down here. There's no other way she could've gotten back to her room without me seeing her."

"That's right, you mentioned that to me before, Eddie," Livingston remembered. "There isn't much life left in this lantern, so let's make the best use out what we have and try to find another way out...before we're left totally in the dark," he offered sensibly.

With Livingston leading the way, we snaked our way through the tunnels. It proved difficult keeping our bearings and we sometimes wound up retracing ground we'd already covered. Eventually, as bad luck would have it, but not completely to our surprise, the meagerly fueled kerosene lantern finally decided to peter out. The five of us watched the flame slowly die. With darkness encroaching—surrounding us in a kind of dank and foreboding embrace—I have to admit I was scared. But so was everyone else. Only Livingston's steady, unwavering voice gave us reassurance. By now, we were getting cold. The damp, penetrating atmosphere of the cavern couldn't have been more than fifty degrees or so and we were dressed for summer. I could hear Amanda's teeth chattering in the dark. No wonder Mabel nixed Amanda's suggestion to go back for rope and warmer clothing, I remember thinking. She'd already made up her mind to leave us all behind to perish. Norman struck a match.

"You'd better save those, son," Livingston suggested. "We may need them later."

Norman nodded and let the match burn itself out.

"How are we ever going to find our way?" The tremble in Amanda's voice seemed amplified by the dark. "We couldn't even find the way out *with* the kerosene lamp. How can we possibly find it now?" I could hear her struggling not to cry.

"I'm cold," Franny blurted out matter-of-factly. "I want to go to the beach. I don't like it here."

"I know, girls," Livingston answered, his voice infused with a mixture of compassion and resolve. We'll get out of here. Someone will come for us. We just have to sit tight for a while."

How long "a while" turned out to be, I don't really remember. All I can recall is sitting there huddled together for warmth in the dark. At some point I fell asleep and awoke hearing Amanda's voice whispering to me out in the blackness.

"There's something out there. I can hear it."

I strained to listen.

"I hear it too, Norman whispered. "Hear it? It's a silvery sound—almost like the faint sound of sleigh bells...or something."

Indeed I could hear it. The sound was gentle and ever so distant.

"Do you hear it, Livingston?," I asked.

"I do," he answered, anticipating what was coming.

"She's coming now," Franny announced casually out of the pitch-black.

I hesitated before responding.

"Who's coming, Franny?," I finally whispered.

"She is. You know...her."

"Her?"

"Yeah, her. I called her. I told her we needed help getting out of here. I'm cold you know, Eddie. Besides...I want to go to the beach."

If it was the "her" I thought Franny meant, I wasn't quite sure how the others would react. I didn't have long to think about it, though. It started as a warm glow at the end of the tunnel—like embers burning in a fireplace when all the lights are out. Even though I couldn't see either of them, I could feel Norman and Amanda tensing up around me at the sight.

It rose slowly to about mid-height in the tunnel and hovered a good distance away from us. The walls of the cave glowed all yellow and orange. That's when the now familiar sight of metaphysical fireflies began swarming out of the ember-glow—dancing their paranormal dance and gelling into a recognizable form. I saw the horrible marks on the naked and wounded torso manifest, as well. Soon the form was complete—the specter with its sorrowful face and languid green eyes—eyes that peered at us from the far end of the tunnel set against a backdrop of transparent death-pallor.

Amanda gasped.

"It's okay," I said. "I've seen it before. It's not here to hurt us."

It floated there silently—the ghost of Ollie Merriweather; staring at us; glowing at us— a haunting beacon lighting our way. The specter raised its arms motioning us towards it. Not disobediently, I found myself getting to my feet.

"You're not going over to it?" Amanda gasped, pulling me back with a tug on my forearm.

"It wants us to follow, I think. Maybe it's trying to show us the way out. C'mon," I said, grabbing Amanda's hand and pulling her to her feet. Norman and Livingston stood up, too. I looked for Franny but she was already halfway down the tunnel.

"We're coming," she hollered out cheerfully, skipping towards the apparition with its beckoning arms. But as we moved closer, the ghost began pulling away. We followed as it withdrew backward then out into the main cavern where the energy from its bodiless form bathed the surface of the cave in a soft light. But it was no ordinary light—this light that painted the golden-faced walls with the most indescribable spectrum of color...colors that made even the most brilliant of nature's rainbows pale in comparison to its aura of gentle radiance.

Thinking back, I realize now that the beauty we were experiencing extended beyond the physical aspects of the vision around us. It wasn't as much what I saw, but rather more what I felt— a deeper essence filling my senses. It was a feeling that bordered on the edge of immortality; a sudden realization of the power back of the Universe. It was *love*—a feeling of love the likes of which I have never experienced before...or since. Today, I am convinced that at that very moment, I received a glimpse of what awaits all of us when the time comes for transformation from the world of the material to the realm of the spiritual. For whatever reason, this wandering, ghostly soul trapped between worlds had within it the ability to imbue mortals with a foretaste of life in the hereafter. I know I didn't imagine it, because afterwards—many years after the events of that summer had become ancient history—each of my friends sharing that day with me confided that they, too, had felt the presence of love with such indescribable intensity that they knew it was a foretaste of eternity.

It was only moments later that the apparition beckoned us to follow it into a tunnel I knew we'd searched at least once before in our quest to find the way out. The tunnel narrowed to a dead-end leaving no alternative but to turn back.

"There's no way out of here," Amanda insisted as we stared at the wall of unforgiving stone blocking our way.

"She's right you know, Eddie. We've been down this tunnel before," Livingston affirmed. "It's a dead-end."

But the spirit held its ground and motioned us on.

"We never went completely to the end, though," I reminded them. We turned back before the last few feet 'cause our *eyes* told us there wasn't a way out."

The spirit nodded its head.

With that, I began inching my way forward towards the ghost of Ollie Merriweather until I was nose-to-nose with the presence. I could see with great clarity the ulcerated perforations that sliced across its abdomen. Its green eyes stared at me from their hollow sockets urging me forward. Not to my surprise, however, I felt no sense of fear or terror—only love and compassion. Then the vision turned suddenly, pointing a ghostly finger toward the side-wall of the tunnel. That's when I saw it—the opening tucked behind a mass of jutting rock blocking the escape route from our view. I was jubilant. Inside the opening stood a steel, spiral staircase. For those standing directly in front of the jutting mass, it appeared as if the protrusion was actually part of the rear cave wall. An optical illusion created by the grain in the rock made it look as though the two separate areas were actually one.

"CRIPES, there's a staircase here," I hollered, my voice exploding throughout the cavern. "It's a way out!"

"Well, thank God," I heard Livingston say with an *it's-about-time* inflection in his voice. The rest of us cheered. With no more than a nod from Ollie Merriweather's spirit, I began climbing while the others made their way behind me. The ghost hovered at the base of the steps radiating light upward through the stone shaft so we could find our way. The climb wasn't a short one. It took quite a few minutes for me to reach the top where a large rectangular hatch made of thick concrete met me. Crafted into the center of the hatch I could see what looked to be a heavy steel grating with a recessed lever positioned on one side of it. Instinctively, I threw the lever.

"*WHOOSH!*" A huge surge of air roared up the stairwell sucking my loose fitting tee shirt up over my face. The sudden and unexpected updraft did similar things to the others below. Quickly, I threw the lever back to its original position closing the grating and the updraft stopped.

"Good Lord, Eddie, what did you do?" Livingston called up to me.

"Sorry! I flipped a lever up here. It opened up some kind of ventilation system, I guess. The stairwell must double as a ventilating shaft, too."

"Well don't do that again if you can avoid it, will you?," Amanda yelled from below. "If I had a skirt on, Norman would have gotten some free show!"

"I'll try to be more careful, Amanda. There's another gizmo here too," I said. "I'll try that one...but if you get an updraft in your underpants, don't say I didn't warn you."

Mounted on the side of the stairwell just below the hatch, a spoked, stainless steel wheel extended from the rock wall. It resembled the wheel on the vault door.

"Hold on!" I yelled and with that, began rotating the wheel clockwise. I could hear the sound of movement and the rumble of concrete as a heavy slab above me began to ascend. With each turn of the wheel, the slab rose about an inch higher. Eventually, it ascended a total of about twelve inches then began pivoting sideways. Once the seal broke, the updraft from the tunnel started lashing us again. But this time it happened more gradually. I observed in the side of the wall where the hatch had been originally positioned, that a series of steel reinforced notches had been cut to accommodate locking pistons— the same kind of pistons that secured the large, main door to the cavern. Equal care had been taken with this access point to ensure a maximum level of security.

After what seemed like an endless amount of cranks, the hatchway was finally fully opened. But on the other side lay nothing but darkness and silence. I poked my head cautiously through the hole and felt warm, moist air on my face.

"What do you see, Eddie?," Livingston called up the shaft.

"Cripes, it's completely dark. I can't see a thing."

Although I couldn't see or hear anything, my nostrils detected an unmistakable odor.

"Hey, I smell flowers," I called down to the others waiting expectantly on the staircase beneath me.

"Hurry up, will you?" Norman squawked impatiently from the bottom where Ollie Merriweather's apparition still radiated soft, iridescent light upward. I'm getting blown to bits down here by the wind current…and I don't feel real comfortable with this ghost staring me in the face!"

I scrambled up the last few stairs leaving the dank recesses of Simon Merriweather's cave behind. My eyes, now accustomed to the soft, guiding light from Ollie Merriweather's specter, took a few seconds to adjust to the newfound darkness. There wasn't any moon that night, but I could see the stars shining brightly. I could even identify some of the constellations through the panes of glass overhead. I knew where I was. I was standing in the greenhouse.

CHAPTER FIFTEEN

When Livingston checked his watch, the hands read a few minutes past midnight. Although it seemed like an eternity, we had been stranded in the cavern for no more than four hours. I could see that the heavy, cast-iron wood stove in the corner of the greenhouse had been bolted to the concrete hatch cover...and the cover, with stove piggybacked atop, had pivoted a full 90 degrees from its usual resting place on the floor. It was a masterful job of camouflage.

But my focus was quickly diverted as the glow of light that had illuminated our way suddenly started to fade. The five of us had no sooner set foot on the greenhouse floor when the light in the tunnel extinguished...as the beam of a flashlight began moving towards the greenhouse from outside. In the shadows, it was clear that someone was headed our way. Then I heard the unmistakable jingle. The five of us stood staring at each other in a kind of startled paralysis as the flashlight beam drew nearer. The only place to go was back where we'd just come from, which was now in total darkness. And with five of us plus the monumental effort involved in cranking the wood-stove hatch closed, there wasn't the time or means to hide anywhere.

"Livingston, what should we do?" I asked in a pleading whisper.

Before he could even reply, the door to the greenhouse flew open and there stood Aunt Julia, her gold charm bracelets jingling away with the slightest movement of her arms. She was still dressed in the gown that she'd worn to the club earlier. I could see the look of bewilderment on her face as she pondered how to react. It didn't last long. She flipped open her stylish handbag and, to our total amazement, pulled out a revolver. The look on her faced changed from bewilderment to annoyance.

235

While I stood wondering what might happen next, further movement through the windowpanes behind Aunt Julia caught my eye. I saw the outline of a figure slipping quietly towards the greenhouse. Then I could see there were two. As they moved closer, I saw the one silhouetted in the front appeared portly but moved with reasonable dexterity. The shadowy figure behind stood tall and erect. Outside, a twig snapped. But even if it hadn't, I could tell Aunt Julia already sensed their presence.

"Arthur? Is that you?" she asked warily.

Good God, I thought to myself. Father and Aunt Julia *are* in this together. I knew it all along. They're going to kill us and toss our bodies down the mineshaft.

A few seconds later, Aunt Julia shifted her aim in the direction of the door as it creaked open. A familiar face poked around the doorjamb. Then, unaided by the walking stick that had always supported her ailing and ample carriage, a sullen Mabel Keating walked in...effortlessly.

Using her revolver, Aunt Julia motioned Mabel to join us. Astounded, we watched Mabel stride across the greenhouse floor. She had her walking stick with her, but for the first time, carried it under her arm. She took a spot standing next to Franny, avoiding eye contact with any of us. While I dealt with the surprise of seeing Mabel Keating's newly found agility, a second face appeared around the doorjamb. It startled me to such an extent that the memory of seeing it sends shivers up and down my spine even to this day. At first I thought my eyes were playing tricks on me. But then I saw the mane of platinum blonde hair, luminescent under the stars. I recognized the dress from the day I hid in Belle Pierce's room at Newport Hospital only hours before she died. I recognized the shoes too. The sight sent me—and everyone—reeling. Standing there before us stood Aunt Julia...a *second* Aunt Julia. This one, too, with gun in hand.

In the darkness, except for the clothing, it was impossible to tell the two of them apart. The hair, the makeup, the deportment—

everything was identical. Even their voices sounded the same. Father did a perfect impression. As the outlandish surprise sank in, so did the affirmation of my earlier fear. They had to be in this together—Father and Aunt Julia. The fact that Aunt Julia appeared only mildly surprised at Father's physical appearance only confirmed my suspicion.

"Good God, Arthur," Aunt Julia said casually. "I see you're up to your old tricks. I thought you'd given that up *years* ago." A mocking smile blossomed on her lips. "Old habits die hard, I guess," she jibed.

Aunt Julia's response to Father's behavior threw me. But we were thrown even further when Father spontaneously plucked the wig off his head. At this point, I could keep quiet no longer.

"Cripes, Father, what's going on?," I blurted out. "What are you and Aunt Julia doing…and what are you talking about?"

"Shhh, be quiet, Eddie," Father ordered, dropping his impersonation charade. He looked me in the eye for a moment then turned to take in Livingston standing between Franny and Amanda, Livingston's arms draped protectively over their shoulders. Amanda turned and edged closer to Livingston. Franny looked confused and Norman stood next to her, his thoughts no doubt racing. I saw Father's face twitch with anger as he confronted his sister.

"My God, Julia, you've gone insane," he spat at her.

You're a fine one to talk," she shot back. "Look at you!" The brusqueness of her retort caused Father to take pause and his demeanor shifted. It was then I realized we were a captive audience to some bizarre, unscripted melodrama and could do nothing, for the moment, but watch it play out.

"Julia, it looks like you've been overly busy," Father said, his anger coming more under control. I realized he was launching into a game of psychological chess.

"Well, there's gold here, you know—*tons* and *tons* of it," she said getting to the point. It's taken me decades to discover where it was hidden and to plan its recovery. That's why I got you and Elly to buy this house...so we could have the gold."

"But you were planning to keep everything for yourself all along, Julia," Father countered.

Aunt Julia squirmed a bit.

"I had everything figured out—only this blundering idiot got in the way," she hissed, glaring at Mabel Keating. Mabel stared down at her shoes, avoiding eye contact.

Aunt Julia played Father for the pawn, shifting to humiliation tactics.

"So, Arthur, once a transvestite, always a transvestite...although I'm flattered you want to look like me."

Father flushed with embarrassment. I felt humiliated for him. Cripes, I thought, I don't know what a *trans-whatcha-ma-call-it* is, but it must have something to do with a guy wanting to be like a girl. It explained why Father was wearing Elly's pink robe the morning I stumbled on Mr. FitzHugh's body.

"Just one of a number of secrets people would be interested in knowing about, eh Arthur?," Aunt Julia taunted.

What a bitch, I thought. I saw Father look downward as he spoke, but his voice had a surprisingly authoritative tone.

"Regardless of what might have been in the past," he said addressing us all, "I'm going to tell you why I'm dressed like this now."

I was all ears.

"I'm dressed like this to get information," he said. "But I think I've gotten more information than anyone bargained for," he added, eyeing Mabel Keating.

"What are you talking about?" Aunt Julia broke in.

"Well, Mabel, here, gave me an earful a little while ago when she thought I was *you*," Father reveled, looking Mabel squarely in the eye. Mabel grew even more uncomfortable. Aunt Julia glared at her for a moment, no doubt condemning the woman's stupidity.

"Just how *did* you manage to pull *that* off?" she grumbled, sizing up Father's disguise.

"Well, remember when we were back at the club and I excused myself...to go to the *mens'* room?"

Aunt Julia nodded.

"I decided to call the house but there wasn't any answer. That worried me, so I told you and Elly that I wasn't feeling well...and that I was going home."

Aunt Julia nodded again.

"Well, you and Elly naturally assumed Livingston would be coming to get me—which wasn't the case at all. I walked home. Fortunately, Julia, you and Elly both accepted my suggestion to stay at the club and catch a ride home with Janet and Hugh Auchincloss."

Father paused to look his sister in the eye.

"It looks as though you sensed something was going on here, too," he said. "I'm assuming Elly's still at the club with Hugh and Janet Auchincloss?"

Aunt Julia nodded. Father looked relieved.

"When I got to the gate on Ridge Road, I saw Mabel trying to get Dennis Davenport's old delivery truck started. I wondered what she was doing at the house...and if Davenport's delivery truck was here, I knew full well that Norman and Amanda had to be around, too."

"She locked us in the mine and left us there to die," I blurted out, pointing an accusing finger at Mabel Keating.

239

"Shhh, be quiet, Eddie. I know that," Father said, drawing Aunt Julia's focus...and her gun away from me.

"Okay," Aunt Julia countered. "Big deal!"

Father smiled.

"I've known for some time, Julia, what you've been up to. And it isn't anything good. You were making regular trips up to the Annandale Farm when Belle Pierce owned the estate, and you made a number of visits just prior to the Kennedy assassination, too. When George FitzHugh turned up nearly dead in the greenhouse on the day Kennedy was killed last year, I figured old FitzHugh's heart attack probably had something to do with you. Then not long afterwards, when you started pressuring Elly and me into buying this place, I decided to play along. And when FitzHugh got murdered, it confirmed someone had to have a good reason for shutting him up. I tried talking to FitzHugh's sister, Belle Pierce, but she was too petrified to say anything—so petrified, in fact, that she suffered a stroke when she found out her brother had been killed. That's when I decided—like with Mabel Keating over here—that Belle Pierce might be more inclined to talk to me...if she thought she was talking to *you*."

"Not bad, Arthur," Aunt Julia said.

Father frowned. "And poor Belle Pierce; it seems you were blackmailing Belle for a murder she admitted committing."

"Oh? Really?"

"Yes, in fact when I was at the hospital pretending to be you, Belle complained bitterly about how you were bleeding her dry of every penny she had—how even after her brother had accidentally stumbled on the legendary gold while looking for a plumbing leak here in the greenhouse, you were blackmailing both of them for this ancient murder she admitted committing."

"A bit farfetched, I'd say," Aunt Julia downplayed.

"I don't think anything's farfetched at this point," Father shot back. "From what Belle said at the hospital, it sounds like you're the one responsible for killing her brother. And I'd say she was right. Belle figured she'd be next. In fact, she got so panicked at my being there and thinking that I was *you,* that she suffered another stroke shortly after I left...and died."

"HA! I knew it!" Mabel Keating piped in, breaking her lengthy and awkward silence. "I *knew* Belle Pierce was up to no good. And she admitted to committing a murder, you say? She'd known about that hidden gold for *years*...only she just didn't know where my brother Simon had hidden it," Mabel leered.

"And neither did *you,*" Aunt Julia flared back vindictively. "And on top of that, no thanks to *you,* what am I supposed to do with all of *them* now?," Aunt Julia fumed, waving her pistol in our collective direction. "Did it ever occur to you that there might be another way out of the cavern?" she raged at Mabel. Disgusted, Aunt Julia turned on Father.

"A few days before the Kennedy assassination," Aunt Julia reeled off, "I took that idiot FitzHugh down to the gold vault at gunpoint and locked him in...but not without his putting up quite a fuss; in fact that's how the key the children found must have gotten under the wine cellar shelves. George must have dropped it there that day. But even so," she continued, "he somehow found his way out of the gold vault...just like Eddie, Livingston and the others did tonight. I couldn't be certain about George FitzHugh keeping his mouth shut anymore. Whatever it was he experienced down in the gold mine that day kept him off balance for some time after JFK's assassination, but in the end I simply had to get rid of him."

"What went wrong?" Father asked, looking for more insight. "Why did FitzHugh suddenly decide he wouldn't keep quiet any longer?"

"Maybe the heart attack on top of whatever else he experienced that day left his conscience gnawing at him...or he just got

241

tired of playing the game," Aunt Julia conjectured. "It really doesn't matter. The bottom line was that he threatened to spill everything— even if it meant seeing his own sister go to jail for that murder. I tried to reason with him, but George wouldn't hear of it. Well, enough about that idiot FitzHugh," Aunt Julia said making it clear there'd be no more said about him. "And what about you and your secrets, Arthur? There are some rather choice ones to tell...wouldn't you say?," she said, shifting her focus. "And by the way, I'm curious," she added. "How did you manage to change into that getup between the country club and here anyway?"

Father shrugged. "The wig, makeup and clothes were still in the trunk of the Bentley from that day I wore them at the hospital," he said. "While Mabel, here, struggled trying to get that broken down delivery truck started, I changed into this outfit in the bushes. Then, after a quick makeup application, I was you...and Mabel was none the wiser. She told me a lot...at least until you came strolling up the driveway. Once she saw you, though, she realized she'd been duped. "I had to resort to an alternate means of influence." Father raised the gun in *his* hand to illustrate the point. "Oh, and by the way everybody," Father added, "you've probably noticed that old Mabel Keating here is a lot more agile than she's let on."

"So we did, sir," Livingston commented.

Aunt Julia looked at her gun, then at Father's.

"A *Mexican standoff*, Arthur?," she mused.

"Not quite, I'm afraid," a familiar voice replied.

"Now stand clear or little Franny here gets it in the throat."

My stomach took a dip at the sight of Mabel Keating holding Franny by the hair. Franny was terrified. The blade of a twelve-inch poniard glistened at her throat. The sharp-edged steel indented the pale, delicate flesh where Mabel applied pressure. On the ground near her feet I could see the walking stick—or what was left of it. Only the smooth mahogany shaft lay there. The fancy brass handle that had always caught my eye was missing. But I could see Mabel gripping it tightly in her hand—the razor-honed blade of her poniard extending from the ornate brass hand-grip.

Now, curiously, it's just around the time this happened that late-night boaters, and sailors on a passing destroyer, reported seeing the greenhouse aglow with the light of what looked like fifty-million candles. Residents across the bay later said they thought a new lighthouse beacon had been activated by the Navy in keeping with their ongoing military presence at Newport. Others thought it was a great fire in one of the mansions. Someone called the Newport Fire Department.

I didn't notice it right away, myself, but Norman said the illumination started the moment Mabel Keating touched the blade of her knife to Franny's neck. The escape shaft under the wood-stove trapdoor that had faded to darkness sometime before, instantly came aglow. At first, a dozen or so paranormal fireflies radiating preternatural ectoplasm raced out of the opening and swarmed around Mabel's ankles. Seconds later, more of them grafted themselves to her face and neck.

"They're *BURNING* me," Mabel shrieked.

We watched in a kind of detached amazement as Mabel swatted at them. It didn't take long for her to release her grip on Franny and begin thrashing the attackers, pointlessly, with the poniard. Clay flowerpots clattered to the floor as she collided with tables in a desperate attempt to elude the stinging creatures. Soon, the greenhouse was ablaze with legions of the supernatural swarm. The building exploded with light. They were on Aunt Julia too— billowing clouds of them in quantities the likes of which we'd never witnessed before. They swept out in waves from the opening in the ground. Then we had to duck as bullets discharged from Aunt Julia's gun in her frenzy to ward off the attackers.

"Close the trapdoor," she screamed, dropping her revolver to the floor so both hands were free to swat at the swarming menace. It did no good. They were on her like bees on honey. We watched her stumble toward the chimney by the woodstove and pull open a false brick face—a camouflaged section of fake bricks that opened like a door. Behind it was a spoked hand-wheel and slot for a key. She clawed desperately at the mechanism and managed to produce the key from the folds of her dress, but overwhelmed by the intensity of the attack, she gave up.

The cosmic attackers didn't bother anyone but Mabel and Aunt Julia. And the combined light emitted by the ectoplasm eventually proved too dazzling for our eyes. We were forced to shield them from the glare. The intensity was so brilliant it was like trying to look directly into the sun. Through the chaos of shattering crockery and overturned tables, Aunt Julia and Mabel fumbled their way out of the greenhouse and onto the lawn. I lifted my hands from my eyes long enough to see them sprint across the grass towards the driveway. As they fled, the cloak of cosmic fireflies engulfing them made the women's bodies look like flaming human torches. In the distance, the sound of sirens responding to the misplaced fire alert began wailing. Then, as quickly as they came, the remainder of the supernatural swarm still ablaze in the greenhouse began retreating in waves to the depths of Simon Merriweather's mine. Impervious to the counter-force of the updraft, they swirled down the stairwell like water down a drain.

It was then that I noticed Father lying face down on the ground unconscious—a bullet wound in his back. The platinum blonde wig that he'd worn lay beside him smeared with blood.

"*FATHER*," I screamed, running to his side. He was still breathing, but the growing stain of scarlet seeping from the bullet hole darkened the clothing he wore by the second.

"Livingston, it's Father," I yelled. "He's been shot."

Livingston raced over, pulling his jacket off along the way. He pressed it to the wound in an effort to stop the flow of blood.

"Eddie, run to the house and call an ambulance and Captain

Karl immediately. I'll stay here with the Master."

As I leapt to my feet, I saw Amanda looking scared and confused.

"Norman," I yelled, "stay here with Franny and Amanda while I call for help, okay?"

"O-O-Okay," Norman stammered, shocked by the unfolding drama. He fumbled through his pockets for a cigarette.

Bolting out the greenhouse door, I saw Mabel and Aunt Julia scrambling into the Duesenberg with a throng of lingering fireflies buzzing angrily around them. Moments later, the Duesenberg's powerful engine roared to life. Aunt Julia threw the car into gear and made a mad dash for the main gate. Gravel spouted like fountains from the rear tires as she pressed the sticky accelerator pedal to the floor in an effort to escape the psychic tormentors. The car traveled about half the distance of the drive when oncoming headlights announced the arrival of a fire brigade as it surged through the main gate. Frantically, Aunt Julia whipped the steering wheel around and headed back in the direction of the house. Great clumps of turf and pulverized flowers were tossed through the air as the huge tires of the Duesenberg sliced up the lawn and demolished the flowerbeds. The car skidded wildly then lurched forward again.

I couldn't have been more than halfway across the lawn in my heart-pounding race to the phone when the remaining swarm of paranormal fireflies badgering Mabel and Aunt Julia so mercilessly all at once began to lift. At first I thought the cloud of cosmic ectoplasm would retreat back to the greenhouse and the inner sanctum of the mine with the rest of them. But then the unanticipated metamorphoses began. The hovering cloud in front of the windshield transformed into the ghostly manifestation I'd grown accustomed to recognizing—the ghost of Ollie Merriweather. I could see Mabel and Aunt Julia recoil with terror at its appearance.

Although in itself a disconcerting sight to any unsuspecting first time observer, the vision with its wounded, gnome-like body and languid green eyes had never shown evidence of malice towards any of *us*. But there, with dozens of firefighters looking on, the specter of Ollie Merriweather all at once morphed into the likeness of a raging demon. The soft, green eyes became orange and glowering with ferocity. The facial structure of the apparition's head—its jaw line, nose, and mouth shifted violently as it assumed the form of some wild, raging beast. Part human and part monster in appearance, the prehistoric looking wraith, for the first time, emitted a devastating roar through evil looking, fang-infested teeth. That's when the Duesenberg hit the single concrete step marking the beginning of the broad front walk. The car went airborne. Seated in the car, Aunt Julia and Mabel soared past the great sculptured lions guarding either side of the brick walkway.

Now this is the point at which I insist I saw something that nobody else admits to having seen—although in deference to others, I have to confess that no one else had the benefit of being so close to the action. Just as the evil specter hounding Aunt Julia reared its demonic head, I swear I saw the sculpted lions move. The action was very subtle—little more than a cursory deference with their heads and bodies as the speeding Duesenberg charged between them on its pell-mell flight. To this day I'll swear that I witnessed it...although I'm careful about insisting on it too much.

Imprisoned in the wildly pitching car, Aunt Julia fought frantically to gain control as the Duesenberg touched down directly in front of the front portico. Accompanied by the sound of screaming rubber, the car plowed, full throttle, into the giant pillars. I saw the windshield shatter with the impact of Mabel's and Aunt Julia's heads simultaneously hitting the glass. Moments later, the demolished automobile settled to rest amidst the architectural destruction. As quickly as the monstrous vision had materialized, the demonic apparition dissolved into firefly fragments and dispersed among the ruins.

Looking back in the direction of the fire trucks and an arriving ambulance, I could see the intimidated men making a halfhearted dash for the crash scene. I also realized that a call to Captain Karl was no longer necessary since he was stepping out of his patrol car nearby.

By now, one would think there wasn't much more that could happen on this clear and moonless night on Narragansett Bay. But chance—or some would call it destiny—stepped in yet another time to move events forward in a most unusual way.

When the Duesenberg smashed into the pillars supporting the front portico, the impact dislocated the columns on their footings. Three of the four load-bearing structures now leaned precariously inward on each other at the top. Their misarranged configuration could barely support the dangerously balanced weight of the pediment overhead. Meanwhile, the fourth column—the one just outside the porthole window whose list had always bothered Father to no end—had broken loose completely from the pediment and teetered ominously over the car. Firemen scurried in the mayhem stringing ropes to stabilize the architectural damage, barking warnings and instructions to each other.

Meanwhile, Livingston had managed to get Captain Karl's attention and together they had conscripted the ambulance crew to tend to Father. I could see them rushing towards the greenhouse with a gurney and some oxygen cylinders. Franny and Norman stumbled out as the men went in.

"I hope your father's gonna to be okay," Norman yelled from across the lawn.

"How's Amanda?" I hollered back.

"Pretty scared," came his reply.

A moment later, Captain Karl walked back towards his patrol car. I heard his request for a second ambulance crackle over the amplifier of his police radio. "It's Arthur Sutton...up at Annandale Farm. He's been shot...and there's just been a bad automobile wreck up here," I heard him tell the dispatcher.

"We've already sent a second ambulance unit...just in case," the dispatcher's voice crackled back. "It should be there any minute."

Everything was happening so fast. A black Cadillac limousine pulled through the front gate and stopped behind the line of emergency equipment. Before the chauffeur could even take his hands off the steering wheel, the back door burst open and Elly jumped out in her evening gown. Mr. and Mrs. Auchincloss stepped out after her. They, too, were dressed in formal evening attire. Elly hiked up her long dress and made a beeline across the lawn towards Captain Karl. I saw her exchange a few words with him then hurry into the greenhouse to be with Father. Mr. and Mrs. Auchincloss stayed by their car, away from the commotion.

Just then, the second ambulance burst through the front gate. It dodged the Auchincloss limousine, missing it by inches and cut across the lawn to the wreck. The men jumped out and ran over towards Aunt Julia and Mabel Keating where the Duesenberg sat motionless in a settling cloud of dust. By now, several ropes had been looped around the rogue support column and the firemen were tying it off to stakes they'd driven into the ground. Just as some of the turmoil seemed to be coming under control, I heard one of the men yell.

"Get away from that car! She's going to fall!"

With a "creek" and a "crack" then a "snap" of breaking rope, the towering pillar teetered forward on its base. The men scattered. We watched powerlessly as the column groaned menacingly then toppled forward towards the crippled Duesenberg. Just at that moment, Aunt Julia suddenly came to—as if her sensory powers were warning her of the impending danger. But it was too late. She regained consciousness only long enough to see the bone-crushing column bearing down on her. The air pulsed and the ground trembled as what was left of the Duesenberg flattened like a pancake under the weight of the giant monolith. I could see Aunt Julia's left hand and charm bracelet-laden wrist sticking out from under the wreckage—her pink manicured fingers still amply adorned with expensive jewelry. Surprisingly, the violent contact spared Mabel Keating whose badly bruised body had already flopped halfway out the door on the passenger side of the car. Ambulance attendants rushed to her aid. They quickly extracted her from the smashed remnants on the chance the rest of the portico might suddenly come tumbling down. Then I heard the voice of someone from the emergency crew speaking to Captain Karl through the commotion.

"Captain," he said in a low and solemn voice. "There's something here you need to see."

I watched the captain follow the fellow over to the base of the toppled pillar where the two men stood looking down into a newly formed opening in the ground—an opening that revealed the disintegrated concrete footing beneath the listing pillar.

"Those are human bones down there, Captain," the man said, pointing into the newly opened hole.

CHAPTER SIXTEEN

Dawn had long since broken by the time the emergency crew managed to separate Aunt Julia's squashed remains from the pulverized Duesenberg. More than one brawny rescue worker lost the contents of his stomach at the sight of her obliterated corpse.

The coroner carried away the remnants of two ended lives that day: Aunt Julia's and the newly discovered skeleton from beneath the front portico. Miraculously, Mabel Keating had been extracted from the wreckage without incident, although she, along with Father, remained in critical condition at Newport Hospital. The newfound skeleton was carefully extracted and placed in plastic after a team of detectives combed and photographed every inch of the site. A crane had been called in to raise the fallen column plus secure the teetering pediment and severely skewed pillars now barely supporting its unevenly distributed weight. Unfortunately, time ran out when it came to the latter and the badly damaged portico soon collapsed, without warning. Fortunately, nobody was injured when it fell.

After everyone had cleared out of the greenhouse, Livingston managed to steal back unnoticed and access the closing mechanism behind the chimney face. Using the key I'd handed over to him, he cranked the wood-stove back to its closed position and locked it. Elly accompanied Father in the ambulance to the hospital, and Norman and Amanda were taken home to their respective families in a patrol car by Captain Karl.

Franny and I stayed behind at Annandale Farm with Livingston, and after making a quick trip to the basement to verify that Mabel had closed the movable shelves in the wine cellar when she'd left, we restored power to the interior vault lighting. Tired and hungry, we buttoned up the basement and went up to the kitchen where the three of us each managed to force down a bowl of *Cheerios*. We were so stunned and exhausted we scarcely spoke two words among us. I spent the brief time we had together reading the back of the cereal box—something about a sweepstakes, the winner of which would receive an all-expense paid trip to Disneyland in California.

After that, Franny went up to bed and dozed off almost immediately. Livingston and I couldn't sleep though, and soon we got word from Elly that Father's condition wasn't good. The bullet had damaged his spine and he had slipped into a coma. At that point, Livingston put in a call to Captain Karl and asked if he would come back out to the house—alone.

When Captain Karl arrived, Livingston ushered him into the drawing room where we filled him in on *everything* that had happened since our early summer arrival—up to and including the previous night's adventure and the discovery of the legendary hidden gold. Then we escorted him down to the basement where I demonstrated the amazing wine cellar shelves and we opened the secret vault door. To say the least, Captain Karl was dumbfounded.

"So you see, Captain," Livingston summed up, "It would be *most* inappropriate if word got out to the general public about the story behind what happened last night. Do you agree?"

Any signs of Captain Karl's being tired had vanished. "There'll have to be an investigation," he insisted, "even though Julia Sutton confessed to killing George FitzHugh before she died. And there's the matter of that skeleton we just discovered...to say nothing of this Kennedy conspiracy you say has been going on. It's hard to predict what's going to happen. All I can say is don't leave Newport, and certainly don't touch anything either above or below ground for the time being—anything that might be related to the crime scene, that is. I'll be back to you once I've found out more about what's been going on here, myself."

With that, we walked Captain Karl out to his police cruiser and watched him drive off. So much had happened in just a few short hours. I wondered if the skeleton belonged to Ollie Merriweather—and if its discovery would put an end to the presence of her spirit at Annandale Farm. And although I felt strangely relieved, I found it difficult to accept the fact that Aunt Julia was dead. Despite the fact that Father's condition bothered me a great deal, I found myself thinking mostly about the earlier incident with Mabel Keating in the basement and how she'd deceived us. From what information we could get about her from the hospital, we were able to piece together that she, too, was unconscious.

In an effort to collect myself, I took time to walk around the yard a bit and absorb some of my Newport surroundings. My psyche had been subjected to so many distressful situations that day that I felt a need to clear my head. The bay, with its blue water and pristine shoreline, helped soothe my nerves. But the sight of the greenhouse and the jarring testimony of the collapsed front portico with the carcass of the Duesenberg still languishing beneath the rubble, were vivid reminders of the chaos and horrors that preceded the dawn.

As I began regaining my composure, the gnawing pangs of hunger reminded me that other than some *Cheerios*, I had scarcely eaten for a day. I headed back toward the house—its dramatically wounded façade staring at me from across the wide expanse of lawn. In the distance I could see a tow-truck and a flatbed with emergency lights flashing, pulling through the front gate to claim the shattered remains of the Duesenberg. While Franny still slept, Livingston and I watched from the verandah as the crane operator maneuvered the heavy pieces of collapsed portico away from the car then hauled the bloodied wreck out of the rubble, hoisting it onto the nearby flatbed. A police photographer was there, too, taking pictures of the destruction and related crime scene from every possible angle.

"It's somewhat ironic, Eddie, isn't it?" Livingston said philosophically, looking at the annihilated automobile. "The very car your grandparents died in so many years ago became the vehicle of your Aunt Julia's demise. Thinking about it kind of gives me the willies…and makes me wonder if there might have been something more to your grandparents' deaths than met the eye at the time."

We stood there together on the verandah, each of us silently contemplating the gravity of the inference he'd made. Could Aunt Julia have played a part in that disaster, as well?

"Oh well," he said breaking the silence and dismissing the thought before either of us had time to acknowledge it, "This is all history now; best that we move forward with our lives and try to forget about what's happened."

"But how can we, Livingston," I found myself saying. "Cripes, how could Aunt Julia have been so rotten?" I couldn't let it go.

"Greed has a lot to do with it, son," he offered. "You know that old saying, *'The love of money is the root of all evil.'*"

"I guess Aunt Julia discovered a lot of stuff during that visit back in 1944," I said. "When they held that first séance here at the house she must have found out more than she let on. And what did she mean in the greenhouse—you know—when she told us that Father had secrets?"

"I'm not quite sure myself, Eddie, but it's evident your Aunt Julia knew a great deal about other people—about things they were willing to go to extremes to *keep* secret."

"Well, she knew that a bunch of gold existed on the property. But that really wasn't a secret. Plenty of people knew about the legend," I suggested. The idea of the gold legend made me think of Simon Merriweather and how it might have all started. I thought about Ollie Merriweather's sudden disappearance back in 1900 and the newly found bones exhumed from under the front portico.

"No, the legend wasn't a secret, Eddie, but the gold's actual existence certainly was," Livingston offered with conviction. "Simon Merriweather knew about the gold. It's evident from the design of the house and placement of the vault that he had to have been aware of its existence during the initial stages of construction. The big question is who *else* knew about it? Simon went to great lengths to keep it all a secret. Evidently he alone held the key."

Livingston's comment about "the key" triggered my memory

of something Myra Davenport shared about the 1944 séance. *"Oswald holds the key"* were words Myra said had been spoken by the spirit during that early-on encounter. Now, it made me wonder if past psychic inferences made about *Oswald* applied to Oswald Keating...or Lee Harvey Oswald. Another missing piece in the still-to-be-assembled puzzle, I reasoned.

"I'm guessing that Ollie Merriweather knew about the gold too, son," Livingston concluded. "Perhaps *that's* why someone may have murdered her...of course, nobody knows for sure yet if Ollie Merriweather actually was murdered—although I must confess it appears likely."

"Well I'm as eager as you are to hear about the lab findings on that skeleton. Meanwhile, I just want Father to get better. I can't wait to talk to him and find out what else he learned about Belle Pierce and Mabel Keating. I'll bet Father knows something about Ollie Merriweather's disappearance, too."

"I'm sure Captain Karl will get to the bottom of it all in good time, son. Meanwhile, we'd best make sure these workmen here get off the property without making any more of a mess."

With that, Livingston and I descended the steps from the verandah and he began directing the trucks around so as to avoid any further damage to the already badly massacred yard. Aunt Julia's Duesenberg—or what was left of it—departed unceremoniously on the back of the flatbed destined for the police impound and eventually the junkyard.

Franny woke up shortly afterwards quite refreshed from her sleep. She sat out on the verandah with Livingston and me while we waited for further news from Elly who was still at the hospital with Father. We sat in a row of comfortable old rocking chairs looking out over the water.

"Are you okay, Franny?" I probed. "Are you upset or scared?"

"A little bit. I didn't like what that Mabel did to me. She was really mean—like when I dropped that ice cream on her foot."

Livingston and I both nodded our heads, remembering the day. The sound of the nearby surf and the rhythmically hollow creak of the floorboards under the runners of our rockers provided a reassuring kind of reality, reminding us we weren't dreaming.

"That was a really bad thing," Franny expounded further.

"I know, Franny," I comforted. "None of it'll ever happen again. Aunt Julia's gone forever...and Mabel Keating's in the hospital. The police are watching her. You don't have to worry about them anymore."

Franny rocked to and fro with the rhythm of the waves while staring blankly at the ocean.

"Where's Daddy?" she asked.

Livingston and I looked at each other.

"He's in the hospital for a while," I said. "He's not feeling real well."

Rock! Rock! Rock! Franny didn't respond right away.

"Will he be all right?" she pursued. I looked at Livingston for a second.

"We hope so. It'll probably take a while though," I said to her with a lump in my throat.

"Aunt Julia shot him, didn't she?" Franny said angrily. "She was really mean."

I looked at Livingston again.

"Yeah, she was. They were both really mean—Aunt Julia and Mabel."

255

Rock! Rock! Rock! Franny's rocking got more vigorous.

"Mabel killed people too, you know," she announced matter-of-factly.

Livingston and I abruptly stopped rocking. It wasn't as much the idea of Mabel's killing that came as a surprise to either of us—it was more the fact that Franny spoke about it with such unwavering conviction. Livingston leaned forward in his chair closer to her.

"How do you know that, Franny dear?" he asked gently.

Franny rocked solo and silently for a bit more before answering.

"Because Ollie told me," she finally answered. I leaned in closer to Franny too.

"When did you see Ollie?" I asked bluntly.

"While I was sleeping—just a little while ago. She came to my room."

"How long has she been coming to your room?" I queried.

"For a while now—she came to that room on the third floor too. But she always frightened me there. I know her now so I'm not frightened anymore. Now that I'm not scared of her she's started coming to my room."

"Did she tell you anything?" I persisted.

"Yes."

"What did she tell you?"

"About things that other people don't know."

"Like what?"

"She told me that someone tried to kill her—and that the person who did was really mean."

"Did she say *who* tried to kill her, Franny?" Livingston injected. "Did she mention anybody's name?"

"Uh-huh."

Franny just sat there rocking.

"She told me that the person was really bad and killed other people too," she added simply.

"Cripes, *who?* What name did Ollie tell you?" I pressed her, sounding a little too annoyed, even by my own standards.

Franny stopped rocking and leaned forward to look me directly in the eye.

"Ollie said it was Mabel," she announced matter-of-factly.

"Livingston, did you hear that?"

"I heard."

Then it struck me.

"Franny, did Ollie say *which* Mabel.'

Franny paused reflectively for a moment.

"What do you mean?"

"Belle Pierce's real name is Mabel, too. Did Ollie happen to tell you Mabel's last name?"

"Nope!"

Just what I'd feared—it could be either one of them—the late Mabel *"Belle"* Pierce or the deceitfully greedy and now unconscious

Mabel Keating.

"Oh," was all I could reply.

"Sounds like the puzzle has fewer and fewer missing pieces—but the missing ones get bigger and bigger all the time," Livingston noted.

"Livingston, back in the greenhouse Father said that Aunt Julia had been blackmailing Belle Pierce for a murder Belle said she committed. Right now there are two people I can think of that Belle might have killed. Ollie Merriweather's one of them and Oswald Keating's the other. 'Course the papers labeled Oswald's death accidental. The only two people alive who could possibly know anything about either one of them right now are Father and Mabel Keating."

"True, son, and with both of them so badly injured—and comatose to boot—I doubt they'll be able to say anything all too soon."

"Livingston? You know what I'm thinkin'? What if we held another one of Franny's special séances? We'd have to get a new antenna for the roof...and a TV of course..."

"Wait a minute, Eddie. We've had an awful lot of excitement since yesterday. I don't know if I can even handle *thinking* about an idea like that, let alone acting on it."

"But it would be different this time. We wouldn't have to sneak around like we did before. We could have Captain Karl come...and whoever else he thought should. It would be a controlled situation this time. We'd have to wait for the right weather and all—but we're bound to have another thunderstorm sooner or later."

"Well...let's talk about it *later* rather than *sooner*. Right now I just want to catch my breath and try to get beyond yesterday and last night. I'll tell you what, though; what if we mention it to Captain Karl later?"

When Livingston did approach Captain Karl about the possibility of conducting a structured séance, Captain Karl agreed, albeit apprehensively.

Following that, the days went by rather slowly. Mabel Keating came out of her coma three days following what the town's people called, "the haunted fire mystery." Meanwhile, she refused to talk to anybody about anything and claimed, either genuinely or otherwise, that she couldn't remember one iota about the night's drama or the circumstances leading up to it. She had been badly injured in the crash, but her doctors were quite astounded by her rate of recovery and remarkable resiliency. They monitored her steady progress and allowed increasingly more frequent periods of interrogation by the authorities—despite the consistently unfruitful outcome.

With each day that Mabel Keating's health improved, however, Father's grew progressively worse. The coma persisted. Eventually he had to be moved onto life support equipment. They put a feeding tube into his stomach and hooked him up to breathing apparatus. Elly spent nearly every waking hour at his side, and slept on a cot in his hospital room at night. Franny and I visited him along with Livingston, regularly. We would sit in somber silence at his side listening to the steady blip of the cardiac machine monitoring his vital signs. Nurses would come in at periodic intervals rotating his position in bed like a rotisserie chicken to prevent the formation of bedsores. Despite this disheartening scene and a discouraging prognosis from the doctors, we proceeded as planned with the upcoming séance. Newport Electric was contacted and a new, even more powerful antenna soon occupied the same spot on the chimney where its unfortunate predecessor had been. The *Zenith* console television set reappeared in the drawing room in all its glory. Newport Electric custom wired it by attaching special, copper handgrip-like ends on the antenna leads, incorporating special fuses to ensure Franny's safety. We opted to bring back the *Zenith* rather than use the little TV set I'd bought. All told, it took nearly a week before we had the broadcast infrastructure in place and the appropriate weather brewing from the Northeast.

On the day of the séance, Captain Karl made arrangements for Mabel Keating to be transported to Annandale Farm. Much to her objection, some brawny orderlies hoisted her overweight carriage onto a gurney and loaded her into an ambulance. She squawked and blustered when they hauled her into the drawing room at Annandale Farm and deposited her there—bedclothes and all.

The only people present besides Mabel Keating and Captain Karl were Livingston, Franny and me. Elly said she'd have nothing to do with it and refused to go.

During the days leading up to this last séance, Ollie Merriweather's specter never did pay another visit to Franny or anybody else for that matter—at least that we knew of. It seemed as if her earthbound spirit sensed the final moment of its reckoning drawing near, and chose to wait for an appropriate forum when all would be revealed.

When we gathered in the drawing room a little after 4:00 PM on a Saturday, thunder and lightning had been moving in from the Northeast. It arrived right on cue as predicted by the weather service. Additionally, the mercury that day hung at a misery-producing 98 degrees with a humidity reading of nearly 100%.

Livingston and I placed a comfortable armchair next to the *Zenith* for Franny, and as rain began to plop on the windowsills, lightning lit the sky. I switched on the television while Livingston handed the special, copper-gripped ends of the antenna cables to Franny. She sat in the armchair and seemed unflustered, as usual. The typical prelude of TV snow drifted across the screen and it took about 10 minutes before the first images began forming on the tube. In conjunction with the window-rattling thunder now booming down on us from overhead, a good deal of lightning blazed across the sky. The reception began coming in clear as crystal—including the audio.

The first scenes were aerials of Annandale Farm as Amanda, Norman, and I had seen it before on TV—circa 1900. Antique excavating equipment surrounded the raised prominence of property accommodating the foundation of Annandale Farm's soon to be built, forty-room mansion. Captain Karl watched, wide-eyed, as a cloud of ectoplasmic fireflies appeared out of nowhere, swarming above the TV console. Then the swarm melded into the familiar hologram of Ollie Merriweather's head—its green eyes peering out from a form of undulating psychic clay.

Mabel Keating sat propped up on her gurney, an unwilling captive of the melodrama playing out. A nearby strike of lightning on the beach outside instantly shifted the picture to a close-up of the man we thought, in an earlier séance, to be Oswald Keating. Seeing Mabel's reaction left no question that the man was Mabel's late husband. The video turned out to be a rerun of the horrifying electrocution scene. Once again we heard Oswald scream his final words, *"MY GOD, MABEL, NO!"*

Sitting upright on her gurney with handkerchief in hand, Mabel shed some tears.

The next scene turned out to be a rerun of the infamous 1944 séance. I held my breath when it got to the point of the lightning strike that last time wiped out the powerful antenna on the roof. Fortunately this time, nothing like that happened and in full view of us all, a psychically transmitted Belle Pierce confessed to her brother that she'd killed Ollie Merriweather. We listened as she spoke openly to her brother, George.

"Several days after Simon discovered gold on the excavation site," Belle said, "I went to the site at sunset in an effort to rendezvous with Oswald Keating."

Mabel Keating's face frosted over, hearing Belle Pierce talk about the rendezvous with her husband.

"Oswald had the contract to do all the electrical work there," Belle continued. "I'd heard the men were working around the clock to complete the foundation and pour the concrete footings. General Greene's wife wanted the house finished in time for the summer social season and the pressure was on to make the deadline. Anyway,

George, I'd baked a batch of Oswald's favorite cookies and thought they'd be a good excuse for me to go over and see him. He and I were lovers, you see. You did know that didn't you, George?"

George nodded. Mabel Keating sat upright on her gurney.

"That home-wrecking harlot," she raged.

We tried to concentrate on the television while Mabel seethed with jealousy over long past indiscretions. Belle Pierce continued.

"When I got to the construction site," she said, "everyone had already gone and Ollie was the only one there. She sat alone next to the newly dug foundation trench laid out for the front portico. I asked her where everybody had gone. She told me they'd left for the day. She answered me in that stammering retarded voice of hers."

"Papa forgot I was here again and left me," we heard Belle say, mimicking Ollie's voice, with a kind of cruel delight.

"You see, George," she continued. "That's when Ollie accidentally spilled it all about the gold and how her father had told her to keep the secret between them. I asked Ollie if she'd told anybody else about it. She said she hadn't."

We saw Belle mimic Ollie again.

"No, I haven't," she mocked. *"Daddy told me not to...but now I'll have to tell him that I told you about it and he's going to be mad."*

"I just wanted to find out where the gold was, George—I certainly didn't plan to kill her," Belle lamented. "I offered her some of the cookies I'd made for Oswald. Then I sat down on the edge of that trench with her and popped open the lid of the tin." Belle shuddered visibly.

"Then what happened?," George asked.

"Well, Ollie reached in one of those dirty little hands of hers and grabbed a fistful of Oswald's cookies then squashed them into her mouth. I asked her again nicely to tell me where the gold was, but she wouldn't."

"I can't. Papa would be mad at me. I have to tell him I told you about it now," Belle mimicked.

"Then she tried to grab the tin of cookies from me, so I pushed her away. She lost her balance and fell into the foundation trench on the rocks at the bottom...and it killed her—and that's how it happened, George," Belle told her brother. "I swear! I just panicked and left her there. Then, when the concrete got poured for the portico footings the next day, they mustn't have noticed the child's body. Ollie Merriweather has been buried under the front portico of this house since the turn of the century."

"There you have it," Mabel Keating piped up all at once from her gurney, a trail of tears cascading down her cheeks. "That society harlot, Belle Pierce, was nothing but a no good child-killer!"

"Quite telling!" Captain Karl commented. "No doubt she murdered the electrician in the midst of a jealous fit too! You know—electrocuted her lover as he worked on the wiring in her house."

From her perch on the hospital gurney, Mabel Keating fussed, blowing her nose and wiping tears from her eyes. Outside, the thunder crashed even more violently above us. The rain poured down in torrents and lightning slashed the sky like a machete. Franny sat in her chair next to the *Zenith* oblivious to the atmospheric holocaust exploding around her. The apparition over the television set undulated next to her silently.

"Well, I guess that confirms who those bones belong to that we found under the portico," Captain Karl concluded.

"I dare say it does," Mabel affirmed.

I sat quietly in my chair studying her. Mabel didn't realize I was watching. I saw her tap Captain Karl on the shoulder and speak to him softly.

"Now you'd better get that little girl unhooked from all that television paraphernalia before she gets struck by lightning," I heard Mabel encourage him.

With that, Captain Karl nodded and began heading in Franny's direction.

Why would this greedy woman who earlier had no qualms about putting a dagger to Franny's throat or locking us all in her brother's mine to die, suddenly care if Franny got struck by lightning? I looked at the bodiless head of the apparition still undulating noiselessly above the console of the *Zenith*. Its eyes were glowering with anger. I wondered about the terrible puncture wounds on the apparition's body—the metaphysical body that wasn't visible above the TV right now. How could the deep and no doubt fatally inflicted injuries have occurred? Certainly not by falling on some rocks in a trench. There had to be more!

"Wait!" I found myself hollering to Captain Karl as he reached to disconnect Franny from the antenna. "There's got to be more!"

I jumped to my feet. "Cripes, I know there's more; I'm sure of it—just wait and see." I pointed to the *Zenith*. The expression of anger on the face of the wraith hovering above the TV softened a bit. We watched quietly for about a minute and nothing happened.

"What are you talking about, son?" Mabel interjected in an intimidating tone. "It's all over. Didn't you see? Your sister and that cosmic contraption she's hooked up to over there proved all of that. There's nothing more to tell. That no-good Belle Pierce murdered my Ollie and got away with it all these years."

Now what? I thought to myself. Without paranormal proof, my accusations were meaningless.

"I think not," Livingston spoke up suddenly with confidence.

264

"Take a look at *that*."

There on the screen, dazed and dirt-covered but still alive stood Ollie Merriweather. She emerged from the open foundation trench, wobbling on her feet. Nearby, an enormous power-shovel stood idle—its large, earthmoving bucket dangling on a steel cable from the derrick supporting it. Then, from behind the shadows of the power-shovel, a young, somewhat portly woman appeared and ran over to the injured girl. She knelt down next to Ollie examining the wound on her head.

The woman, with her stoutly muscular figure was easily recognizable. There, significantly less rotund and with a face more than half a century younger, stood Mabel Keating. She had been watching and listening in the shadows all the while Belle Pierce had been there. Now, some 60 years later, propped up on the gurney in the drawing room of Annandale Farm, Mabel Keating's jaw dropped as the scene she'd hoped to short-circuit played out on the *Zenith*.

An argument ensued between a badly injured Ollie and her aunt. Mabel demanded that Ollie show her where the hidden gold was located, but Ollie refused. She slapped Ollie angrily across the face. Battered and terrified, Ollie ran as fast as she could. She headed towards the giant power-shovel nearby, and managed to climb up into the cab. Mabel followed with no sense of urgency, confident there would be no escape. Making her way to the cab, she cornered her niece there where the two of them struggled. Surprisingly, Ollie fought valiantly and eventually broke free. She dashed out of the cab, jumping onto the earthmover's tread then leapt to the ground directly in front of the machine. Mabel started after her but tripped. Losing her balance, she reached out and grabbed an operating lever protruding from the floor of the cab to regain her balance. With that, the lever ratcheted backward releasing the heavy, steel-toothed bucket suspended above the ground. And just at that moment, innocent Ollie stepped directly underneath. We watched, horrified, on the sidelines while the *Zenith* broadcast Ollie Merriweather's violent death. The jaws of the plummeting apparatus tore into her small, helpless body.

"It was an accident," Mabel screamed from her gurney. "Damn that Ollie! She ran right underneath the bucket of that earthmover. All I wanted her to do was to tell me where that gold was hidden. It was all a bunch of bad luck."

But the show wasn't over. Moments later we saw Mabel start the engine of the earthmoving monster and raise the bucket back to its original position. Then, wiping tears of remorse from her eyes, the youthful Mabel climbed down from the machine and dragged the mangled remnants of her niece to the edge of the foundation trench. Grabbing hold of a nearby ladder left by workmen, she lowered it into the excavation site and descended—but not before plucking a shovel from a barrel of tools by the edge of the pit. Once at the bottom, she dug a hole big enough to hold the tiny corpse, and after climbing back out, rolled the girl's mutilated remains over the lip of the trench. Then, she climbed back down the ladder and put the broken body into the grave. It took a few more minutes for Mabel to bury Ollie's remains. Smoothing over the burial area neatly with the shovel, she finished her work then left.

"It had to have killed her instantly, don't you think?" Mabel said trying to rationalize the death of her niece as she broke down into a flood of tears.

Studying the specter hovering above the *Zenith,* I detected for a second time since its initial appearance in our world, the shadow of that Cheshire smile blooming on its preternatural lips. The first time had been at the previous séance just prior to the destruction of the roof antenna—moments before all would have been psychically revealed had lightning not chosen that very moment to take out the antenna.

We watched, now, in the drawing room, as the apparition took on a look of serenity, savoring the moment of Mabel Keating's defeat and the victory of truth finally brought to light. Then, with a look of deference and gratitude the green and languid eyes—the eyes that shone with the life and soul embodied on earth in the being known as Ollie Merriweather—gently closed. In a blink, the specter was gone and the screen on the *Zenith* turned to snow. Just as instantly, the pounding thunder and pouring rain ceased and Franny came out of the trance-like state she'd been in. Through the windows, a brilliant rainbow appeared over the bay in front of Annandale Farm, while the room flooded with the scent of fragrant, rain-washed air. I looked over at Livingston and caught a glimpse of him wiping a tear from the corner of his eye. I would have cried myself, at that moment, had I not been overtaken with such a feeling of joy at the victory and freedom that Ollie had finally won.

Needless to say, Mabel made a full confession—not just to the murder of Ollie Merriweather, but also to the murder of Oswald Keating...and Captain Karl was more than happy to label both cases closed.

Word also came back from the crime lab shortly afterwards that the skeleton found under Annandale Farm's colonnade proved to be the remains of a female child judged to be about 12 years of age. The victim had died from a string of bone-crushing wounds to the torso—so deep and forceful that they had cut clear through the front ribcage and in some places penetrated to the backbone. The torso had been nearly severed in two. A fracture on the skull had also been discovered, but was judged not to be a contributing factor to the cause of death. Dating of the bones put the year of death to be about 1900. The forensic report fit neatly with what we had witnessed during the séance.

Curiously, Father chose the exact time of that final séance to emerge from his coma at Newport Hospital. He had a period of extreme lucidity that lasted for slightly less than two days enabling him to share a number of important, corroborating facts with Captain Karl. Most of his information came from the two Oscar-winning performances he delivered for Belle Pierce and Mabel Keating while decked out in full, Aunt Julia drag. Shortly after sharing this vital information, however, Father slipped back into a coma and died. The ever-loyal Elly was with him at his bedside when he left us.

Thanks to Father's clues, Mabel Keating's confession, and

Franny's television séances—seasoned with some amount of conjecture—we were able to piece together a reasonably accurate picture of what had happened at Annandale Farm over the years. I remember assembling the patchwork-quilt of findings with Livingston and Elly a day or two after Father's burial in Newport. We were sitting on the verandah looking out onto Narragansett Bay.

"Cripes, it's all so complicated," I said to Livingston and Elly. "So, Aunt Julia was blackmailing both Mabel Keating *and* Belle Pierce for Ollie Merriweather's murder?"

"Yes, Eddie, apparently so—as sad as that truth might be," Livingston lamented. "One can only surmise that somehow during the course of that infamous 1944 séance, Ollie Merriweather's haunting presence must have revealed to your aunt the circumstances surrounding her own disappearance and slaying back in 1900...while at the same time revealing that the legend of hidden gold was more than just a legend."

"Why would Ollie do that?," I wanted to know.

"Because," Elly interjected, "the specter no doubt hoped your Aunt Julia would be an instrument of aid in exposing the long-hidden crime that took her life. But instead, Julia used that information for personal gain. Greed outweighed morality in this case, and Julia opted to blackmail Mabel Keating *and* Belle Pierce—even though Belle was actually innocent of the crime."

"OK, but how come Ollie didn't tell Aunt Julia where the gold was hidden?," I persisted.

"Well," Livingston said, "with your Aunt Julia's evil intentions exposed, the estate-bound spirit no doubt ceased communicating with her, sensing her insincerity. Although Ollie was mentally challenged, it's evident the child wasn't without moral standards or the ability to apply them. To Ollie's credit, she was able to withhold vital information that pinpointed the actual location of her father's gold and keep it off your aunt's psychic radar—a situation that no doubt must have tormented and frustrated your aunt for the nearly two decades following."

"Cripes, but when it came to Oswald Keating," I said all excited, "he *held the key* for sure!"

"Yes," Livingston agreed. "Apparently Oswald Keating *and* Simon Merriweather each held one. When he snapped out of his coma, the Master told Captain Karl that before Belle Pierce passed away, she shared that Oswald and Simon were lifelong friends. No doubt they gained access to the mine through the greenhouse tunnel—slipping in after dark and leaving before dawn."

"Whaddya 'spose they did with all the money they got for that gold?" I wanted to know. "There had to have been an awful lot of it."

"Funny you should ask," Elly said. "Arthur wasn't simply sitting on the verandah idly reading the newspaper and monitoring his stock portfolio all summer long. I was there at the hospital with him at the end when he told Captain Karl what he'd discovered. Evidently, Simon Merriweather used the bulk of his fortune to build hospitals and facilities dedicated to Down syndrome research. Apparently, Simon did this anonymously through a philanthropic California foundation he established called the Olivia Marston Charitable Trust."

"Well, how did he know that?" I pressed Elly.

"Lord knows, Arthur had a lot of secrets...but he had a greater number of connections. He said he discovered it from a trustee of one of the Sutton Trusts who also happened to also be a trustee on the Olivia Marston Charitable Trust. You might be happy to know, Eddie," Elly said warmly to me, "that the charitable trust Simon Merriweather created bears the first name of his daughter, Ollie, and the maiden name of his late wife, Felicity Marston."

Hearing Elly share this news made me remember the pictures in Mabel's locket—the photos of Ollie and her parents. Somehow, I knew they were safe and surrounded by that same, golden hue...the aura of indescribable love I'd felt that day Ollie led us out of the cavern and up to ultimate safety above ground.

In fact, the more I learned about the mysteries Father helped unravel, the more proud I felt that he'd been working on the side of right. Yet, at the same time, I felt guilty because of the things I'd imagined about him—mentally casting him as an accessory to evil with my diabolical Aunt Julia. As these truths manifested, I realized how Elly's numerous chastisements about my overactive imagination—the verbal warnings I'd grown to resent—were not unfounded.

"When Simon eventually died of natural causes back in 1932," Livingston further expounded, "he had no idea that Ollie's body was so close to the subterranean world where he spent so much of his time. And as near as anyone can tell, he made no provision in his will for his sister, leaving everything to the foundations and institutions he'd founded in his wife's and daughter's names. Then when that miserly, philandering husband of Mabel's inherited Simon's legacy, Mabel never saw any of the bounty. In fact, she spent the bulk of her days living in relative poverty and isolation—even feigning that physical handicap of hers, supported by falsified medical records, to obtain badly needed disability payments from the government."

"Cripes, she was really a good actress," I said. "You couldn't even tell that she was faking that limp."

"Yes, she had us all fooled, Eddie," Elly said wistfully. "Living a lie always catches up with you at some point."

"Hmm, that's what Belle Pierce told me the day I visited her at Newport Hospital just before she died," I recollected. 'Here's what happens when you try to be someone you're not'—or somethin' like that is what she told me."

"She was right, Eddie," Livingston said with conviction. I saw him look long and hard at Elly, who flushed a bit then turned away. Given her Brooklyn roots and social pursuits, I guessed Livingston's comment pulled her own conscience into a game of tug-of-war.

"Yeah, I guess so," I agreed. "If Belle Pierce hadn't been such a greedy social climber, Aunt Julia would never have been able to get her blackmailing hooks into her."

"Yes," Elly said stoically. "There's no question Belle was greedy. She invested everything in trying to find that hidden gold...and who's to say that long-ago affair she had with Mabel Keating's husband wasn't for that sole purpose. Until the time she finally leased the place to the Kennedys, she let the mansion deteriorate with neglect, burning up what little money she had on upkeep and making blackmail payments to Julia."

"One could rationalize just about anything," Livingston conceded. "And it must be that the Master's sister, aware of the fact that Belle Pierce's lease agreement and the federal government's option to buy would be cancelled upon President Kennedy's death, somehow played a part in JFK's assassination...although it all sounds so inconceivable. But regardless of whether that happens to be true or not, one can see that Belle and her brother certainly had little choice but to remain silent or face the consequences associated with the Master's sister's blackmail scheme."

Today, looking back on that conversation and the complex trail of treachery that it helped to explain, I'm still astounded by the outcome of social and legal justice that prevailed. But to take an opposite position—one of denying truth's ever-presence and its ability to prevail—would mean dismissing any positive outcome as pure chance and accepting a belief that evil triumphs and happenstance is the ruling order of the day.

While some might say that *chance* is the only plausible explanation for the way things turned out, Livingston, Elly and I hold a differing opinion. To us, it's proof of a higher purpose and order—an overarching, divine intelligence that comprehends a greater good and structures events for the achievement of that purpose. If I didn't believe that was right, it would mean ruling out all the Frannys and Ollie Merriweathers of the world and discounting their presence or worth here on earth—labeling them mishaps of nature with no specific role or influence. Well, that's what we think, anyway.

EPILOGUE

So now you know the whole story—or nearly the whole story—about the mysterious mansion that used to stand on the empty prominence of land just off Ridge Road. The long and high brick wall that used to protect our privacy still borders the perimeter of the empty grounds today—guarding the dormant treasure lying beneath its carefully maintained surface. Everything else is gone too—the house, the garage, and even the elegant greenhouse. Boaters on the bay can still see the flat plateau where the house once stood, when they navigate the waters off Brenton Point between Castle Hill Cove and Fort Adams State Park.

You're probably wondering why the 40-room house and surrounding outbuildings were razed back in 1969. I can tell you, for certain, it didn't have anything to do with the gold.

When Father died that summer of '64, he left the bulk of his substantial estate to Franny and me. Based on the terms of a prenuptial agreement, Elly received a generous trust fund that provided nicely for her for the remainder of her life. Livingston did too. Under the terms of Father's will, Elly and Livingston also became trustees of his estate until I reached the age of thirty. And suffice it to say, they executed their jobs faithfully in the best interests of both Franny and me until I finally came of age. Once that happened, I assumed full responsibility of Father's fortune, including management of an irrevocable trust established for Franny—an instrument Father drew up on her behalf before his death.

Not to be excluded completely from affairs of "estate," too, Franny sometimes had ideas regarding her own investments, and occasionally interjected an opinion. Thus at one point I directed our broker to make a sizable purchase of stock in the manufacturer of *Chiclets Chewing Gum*—an isolated act of empowerment that for some years following would bring Franny considerable pleasure.

We had moved out of Annandale Farm in August of '64 some

weeks after Father's funeral. Elly bought a plot at St. Mary's church in Newport where we laid him to rest after a simple and very private closed-casket service.

Aunt Julia's personal possessions along with her largely ill-gotten assets were quickly seized by the Federal Government and impounded. We never did see them again—not that we really cared. Curiously, the enormous diamond ring missing from Belle Pierce's finger the day I visited her at Newport Hospital, showed up in the IRS accounting of Aunt Julia's possessions. The diamond, it turned out, was a fake.

The bulk of our own belongings were shipped back to New York City by boat. When it came time for us to leave, Livingston loaded up the Bentley and drove us home to our Manhattan duplex on Central Park West. Shortly thereafter, an arrangement was made with the Federal Government by Father's attorneys, and President Johnson had Congress declare Annandale Farm an emergency gold reserve. Nearby Fort Adams provided an appropriate measure of security, and a lucrative contract was drawn up between Father's estate and the United Sates Government. With the signing of that contract, the already sizable Sutton fortune that Father had left us transformed into billions.

After that, not one of us ever set foot in the Newport house again—that is until the summer of 1969, five years later. The house had been restored following Aunt Julia's infamous 1964 "accident." Part of the renovation included the demolition of the greenhouse—an act which Elly ordered as a symbolic gesture in light of the association the structure had with Father's death.

Because of the even more jaded reputation the mansion house now enjoyed, few people could be found to rent it. Those who did were mostly old-time acquaintances of Elly's from Brooklyn who relished the idea of living a storybook summer among the cream of America's industrial royalty. Curiously though, none of the renters ever returned for a second season, always offering some excuse or another that got them off the hook without a lengthy or detailed explanation.

So, when that summer of 1969 rolled around, we couldn't get anyone to rent the property. And during a weak moment that bordered on the threshold of insanity and nostalgia, Elly decided to try spending another season there. We returned to Annandale Farm for a second time in the early part of June. I was 19 by then and would soon graduate from Duke University (my late grandparents' friendship with Doris Duke helped with admission considerably). Franny was blossoming into womanhood, and as an adult no longer experienced visits from Ollie Merriweather or any other apparitions—at least to our knowledge.

Those first days back at the house were uneventful enough, however, and we experienced no disruptions. While we lived there, Livingston went about his usual business preparing delicious meals and taking care of the mansion's interior. A local property management firm handled the maintenance of the estate's exterior, including the 15 acres of landscaped property.

It was on the anniversary of George FitzHugh's murder that the first signs of trouble began. It started late one night as I lay in my bed staring out the open window at the moon reflecting on the bay. I had long since abandoned the practice of hanging my tambourine on the doorknob, but having become an enthusiast of the instrument, I made it a point to generally have one around. That second season at Annandale Farm proved no exception, and I had left my tambourine lying flat on the top of my dresser. Elly, Livingston and Franny had already turned in for the night, and to my knowledge were fast asleep.

The incident began with the gentle sound of footfall just outside my bedroom door. I could hear the creak of the floorboards from beneath the thick layer of Persian carpet. Initially, I thought nothing of it, but the more I realized everyone else had retired, the more edgy I became. I lay there, naked, on top of my sheets, afraid to move—the bed linen growing damp from anxiety-generated perspiration. I had no sooner found the courage to sit up when the faint jingle of tambourine bells could be heard coming from the top of my bureau. With no visible stimulus present, the sound grew louder. Aided by moonlight shining in on the doorknob of my room, I could suddenly see the doorknob turning. I remember the wave of panic that hit me. But I was 19 by then, and the adolescent giraffe-like build of my earlier years had evolved into a muscled physique that mirrored Livingston's well-proportioned anatomy.

With all my courage and tightly coiled strength, I leapt naked out of my bed and pounced on the floor in front of my door. Grabbing the doorknob tightly, I twisted it hard and flung the door open wide, instinctively raising my fists to protect myself from whoever might be there.

To my surprise, nobody was—at least nobody I could see. As I stood, muscles flexed—naked and alone in the light of the brilliant full moon—I felt something caress, ever so lightly, my exposed masculinity. Had it been any time other than this adrenaline-packed moment, I would have been aroused by the erotically invisible touch. But it was then that I noticed for the first time a potent and familiar scent that for years announced the presence of someone I had grown to detest with all my heart. I was surrounded by the overwhelming fragrance of lilacs. All at once, the touch that had been so tantalizing slipped tightly around my scrotum, squeezing it in an unforgiving grip.

While I stood there startled and naked in the grasp of this intimidating presence, I saw the bedroom door open down the hall. A second later, Franny stepped out. And the moment she appeared, the excruciating pressure stopped.

"Are you okay, Eddie?" Franny asked groggily as I ducked back into the doorway to hide my nakedness and grab my robe. "I had a really bad dream that you were in trouble so I got up to see if you were all right," she reported. "Should I call Livingston?"

I was just about to tell her "yes" when the door to the master bedroom opened and Livingston walked out in his night clothes. He flipped on the hall light, and moments later, Elly appeared in the doorway behind him, tying the sash of her robe around her narrow waist. She hesitated by the door, anxiously twisting the wedding ring on her left hand. She and Livingston had been married for about two years by then—a union that delighted both Franny and me. Only now my mind raced with thoughts of dread. Both of them realized something was wrong too. I could see them inhaling the all too familiar fragrance that filled the corridor.

"Good God," Elly gasped, "is that what I think it is?"

"There's more too, I'm afraid," I added, telling them about the tambourine, the turning doorknob and the fiendishly invisible touch. By then, I'd donned my robe and the four of us were standing out in the hall a few feet from my room. We went into a family huddle for a few minutes before arriving at a unanimous decision. The four of us stacked our hands palms down, one on top of the other, in sandwich format, and yelled at the top of our voices:

"Keep a secret, save a life. Tell what happened—pay the price!"

Then we lowered our hands to knee level, sweeping them upward high above our heads.

"It's settled then?," I asked.

"Without question," Livingston affirmed. "We're checking in at the Hotel Viking this very minute and we'll be gone for good by first thing tomorrow morning. Pack an overnight bag," he told us authoritatively. "We'll not spend another night in this God-forsaken house."

As we turned to go back to our rooms, the overpowering odor of lilacs pervading the corridor suddenly diminished. We had only taken a few steps when each of us paused dead in our tracks. In the distance on the stairs we could hear it quite plainly. It started at the top and made its way slowly but purposefully down the risers. We hurried over to the balustrade at the landing and peered down into the darkened foyer below. Livingston ran to the light switch and flipped on the lights. While we watched in spine-chilling silence, the great front door creaked slowly open on its hinges, and the spooky sound of jingling charms faded away, eerily, into the night.

Elly and Livingston spent the following morning at the Hotel Viking on the telephone where they put the wheels in motion to auction off the furnishings and tear down the mansion. Thus it was in the fall of that very year Newport Landscapes razed the forty-room landmark, ending a reign of mystery that lasted for nearly seven decades. None of us was present at the time the wrecking ball dealt its fatal blow to the enigmatic house. But folks from the Newport Historical Society who witnessed the demolition swore they heard the bellowing shriek of a spiteful woman at the very moment the wrecking-ball sliced its destructive path through the middle of the grand Newport lady.

We were told that an angry and bitter Mabel Keating heard the news at the nursing facility that had become her permanent home ever since her 1965 conviction. She received a double life sentence for the murders of Ollie Merriweather and her husband, Oswald. Five counts of attempted murder directly related to our collective but temporary internment in Simon Merriweather's mine, earned her an additional fifty years. Mabel would have lived out the rest of her days in the state penitentiary, but fate stepped in on the day of her sentencing. While leaving the courthouse, she tripped on her lawyer's cane and fell headlong down the granite steps. As a result, she spent the remainder of her life as paraplegic in—The Annandale Nursing Home.

As for Livingston and Elly, they celebrated their 33rd wedding anniversary with the arrival of the new millennium...and my 50th birthday.

The "secrets" that Aunt Julia used to cement her hold on Father surfaced over time during the course of Livingston's and Elly's courtship and marriage. Elly eventually shared that Father indeed had a penchant for dressing up in women's clothing, although she never knew it until after they were already wed. His habits as a long-tenured transvestite included absolutely zero interest in the sexual trappings of matrimony. In fact, Elly once commented in later years that she thought Father married her more for her extensive wardrobe than for her womanly charms. Although suspect of his unorthodox habits at the time she married him, Elly confessed that Father's kindly demeanor, coupled with his wealth and social standing, far outshone any of his oddball shortcomings...at least in her mind. Thus it would be with astonished trepidation that Livingston and I would learn that the closed-casket service she chose, provided the means for discretely burying Father in her strapless, emerald-green Oscar De La Renta evening gown—his absolute favorite.

Now, one might wonder if this demented secret alone could have been enough to control a man as wealthy and strategically connected as Father. But as I would find out in later years, there remained a secret so important to him that he sacrificed everything to keep it hidden from society's judgmental and unforgiving eye...to say nothing of avoiding the legal implications its discovery would pose.

I would share that secret with you now but for the pact that's been made between Elly, Livingston and me in Father's memory—an oath of silence to keep the secret among those who know the enormous implications it wields. Although if *you* were to guess, I might, by a subtle nod of my head or wink of the eye, indicate that you've figured it out. Perhaps I'd even flash an understated grin, knowing full well it couldn't compare with the famous Sutton smile that graced the face of Father and illuminated the lovely but evil countenance of my notorious Aunt Julia. There are those, I suspect, who've put the pieces together by now. But should anyone ask or even openly challenge me on the matter, I can honestly say I'd angrily dispute it. That applies not only to my lovely wife, Margie—Amanda Davenport's older sister—but to our two children, Arthur and Olivia as well. The same holds true for dear Amanda and Norman Tate...who became husband and wife back in the mid-1970s.

You might be interested to know that Norman finally gave up smoking shortly after he and Amanda were married. The newlyweds ran Davenport's grocery store, along with Myra and Dennis, until the upscale shop accidentally burned to the ground one night—the result of an unattended cigarette left smoldering on the check-out counter. Now, years later and the incident behind them, Norman, Amanda and her parents are frequent and welcome visitors to our oceanfront summer home on lovely...and gold-free Cape Cod.

Well, I guess that's pretty much everything I can think of to share with you. I'll let you fill in any blanks on your own. Soon Livingston, Elly and I will be going out for one of our afternoon rides in the Cape Cod sunshine. It's become a special little tradition that just the three of us do together. You might be interested to know we still have Father's black Bentley convertible. I keep it meticulously preserved, and polished like a jewel, although the red leather upholstery is faded, creased and cracked a bit from nearly four decades of loyal service. We only take it out on special summer days when the New England sky is a vivid blue and the seagulls are gliding and swooping over the sea. That's when we lower the convertible top so Elly and Livingston can climb into the backseat and be driven in grand style along the ocean.

Elly's shining auburn hair that used to waft so alluringly in the breeze of the open-topped car is an aristocratic blend of silver and white now...and Livingston doesn't have to worry about any wind in his hair.

Occasionally, just for fun, I'll put on Livingston's old uniform—the one he wore in the early 1960s—and I'll don a chauffeur's cap when we drive around town on the Cape. His uniform fits me perfectly, by the way. In fact, at age 50, I now share the same broad-shouldered, muscular build that Livingston did when he was my age...to the exact size and measurements.

It's the little touches of tradition that I've come to appreciate most as I grow steadily older—like when we swing the big old Bentley into the parking lot at Four Seas Ice Cream to pick up waffle cones on the way back from our drive. When I hear the crunch of gravel under the enormous tires and smell the sea air, I'm instantly transported back to that unforgettable summer at Annandale Farm with its haunting memories...and the long departed but benevolent specter of

Ollie Merriweather.

Livingston and Elly have their little traditions, too. He likes to sit in the parked Bentley enjoying his ice cream to the sound of music on the radio, hoping that on an off-chance he might just catch the Boston Pops playing at the Hatch Memorial Shell. In contrast, Elly, still slim, loyal and lovely, always makes it a point to find a last minute excuse for holding off on the calories. And when she chastises Livingston about his weight, it's one of those rare occasions when she calls him by his given name.

"I'm not about to start getting one of these extra bonuses, *Edward*," she'll say, pinching the skin of his double chin that's blossomed over the years. Then she'll plant a kiss on his cheek just to let him know it really doesn't matter.

I've got my own little ice cream tradition, too. I order a double-dip cone of vanilla fudge twirl and stand out front on the sidewalk when I eat it. I take great care not to spill any on Dad's carefully preserved chauffeur's regalia...and I'm *extra* careful not to let any accidentally drop on the foot of some plump, elderly lady who just might happen to be lumbering by.

THE END

HISTORICAL BACKGROUND AND PHOTOS

Although the characters and plot of this mystery are fictional, Annandale Farm enjoys intriguing real-world history. In 1963, President Kennedy and First Lady Jacqueline Kennedy signed a lease on the 15 acre, oceanfront estate whose perimeter once adjoined Hammersmith Farm – home of the First Lady's mother and stepfather. The lease, along with plans for turning the house and grounds over to the Department of Interior for use as a permanent Summer White House were scrapped following JFK's assassination. Several years later, the mansion was demolished. No new structure has ever been built on the original site of the historic Newport cottage, and the reasons behind its untimely demolition remain a riddle.

Built in 1900 and designed by architect Francis Vinton Hoppin (the designer of author Edith Wharton's historic mansion, The Mount), Annandale Farm stood as a familiar landmark to boaters frequenting Narragansett Bay until its 1969 demolition. Originally dubbed Armsea Hall, the house holds the number-one spot on the Preservation Society of Newport County's website, *The Lost Houses of Newport*

(http://www.newportmansions.org/learn/history-highlights/lost-newport/1896-1910).

Additional information pertaining to Annandale Farm (a.k.a. Armsea Hall) and its intended use as a permanent summer White House is also available through the John F. Kennedy Presidential Library and Museum website (www.jfklibrary.org – key "Annandale Farm" into the search window).

Front of postcard referring to President Kennedy's lease of Annandale Farm for the 1964 summer season – circa 1963 (Postcard from author's private collection – Published by H.B. Settle, Co., Newport, R.I.; Aerial photo by Jerry Taylor, Newport, R.I.)

Back of postcard referring to President Kennedy's lease of Annandale Farm for the 1964 summer season – circa 1963 (Postcard from author's private collection – Published by H.B. Settle, Co., Newport, R.I.; Aerial photo by Jerry Taylor, Newport, R.I.)

<u>Text reads:</u> **Annandale Farm Newport, R.I.** – This estate overlooking the narrows at the entrance to Narragansett Bay is owned by Barclay Douglas. Mrs. Jacqueline Kennedy who grew up in Newport will spend the summer months at Annandale Farm along with her children Caroline and John, Jr.

View of house from Narragansett Bay – circa 1950
(Photo from author's private collection)

View of brick walkway and sculpted lions overlooking
Narragansett Bay from portico – circa 1950
(Photo from author's private collection)

Driveway and approach to house from main gate – circa 1950
(Photo from author's private collection)

Rose Garden – circa 1950
(Photo from author's private collection)

PROPOSED SUMMER WHITE HOUSE — This is aerial view of "Annandale Farm." Ridge Road estate of Barclay Douglas, which is under consideration as a permanent summer White House to be owned by the federal government. The 14-acre estate ad- | joins "Hammersmith Farm," the Hugh D. Auchincloss estate and "Broad Lawns," Mrs. Mansfield Ferry's estate (the tree-covered property in background.) Ridge Road runs across top of photo.
Daily News : Hopf Photo

Dec. 3, 1962.

Text reads: PROPOSED SUMMER WHITE HOUSE – This is aerial view of "Annandale Farm." Ridge Road estate of Barclay Douglas which is under consideration as a permanent summer White House to be owned by the federal government. The 14-acre estate adjoins "Hammersmith Farm," the Hugh D. Auchincloss estate and "Broad Lawns," Mrs. Mansfield Ferry's estate (the tree-covered property in background). Ridge Road runs across top of photo. – Daily News: Hopf Photo (circa 1963)

WRITING "FATHER'S SECRET"

Significant research was conducted by the author during the writing of *Father's Secret*. The Newport Historical Society and members of its staff played an important part in obtaining insights into Annandale Farm's history, as well as in obtaining names of 1960s-era Newport business establishments and locales used throughout the story. An early copy of the manuscript (originally titled *Whatever Happened at Annandale Farm?*) was sent to the Newport Historical Society to glean feedback on content accuracy, including the interior of the Society building itself which is used as a physical setting in several chapters of the book.

The Preservation Society of Newport County was a source of information about Newport mansions referenced and described in the manuscript. The author felt it was important to incorporate "educational moments" by unobtrusively embedding background information about certain Newport landmarks and locales used as character/plot settings throughout. The accuracy of city architectural and historical attributes was considered to be of importance in creating readership awareness of Newport and the distinctly unique attractions the town has to offer.

That said, given the fact that the mansion and its outbuildings were demolished in 1969 and have been out of existence for over 40 years, the author chose to take some liberties regarding a few physical aspects of the estate. This was done in order to facilitate development of the storyline and enhance the entertainment value to the reader. In light of the obvious, fictional nature of the supernatural plot, the author deemed this an acceptable tradeoff – a compromise with which you may or may not agree.

For instance, the swimming pool, added some years after the author's wife's family owned the estate (1945-1952), isn't acknowledged or referenced in the book. Also, the elaborate, Victorian greenhouse, which is an integral fixture in the storytelling, never existed; nor did Davenport's Grocery Store – the only fictional business establishment utilized in the book.

Additionally, there was never any evidence of a TV antenna affixed to the mansion's chimneys, nor were any of the basement windows (if there were any – no one could remember) cemented up. There were never "numerous owners" of the property (only a select few)...and there was never any known intention on the part of the United States Government to build a connecting tunnel between Annandale Farm and Hammersmith Farm. Most assuredly, there was never any hidden gold mine on the grounds, nor even the legend of one. And so the story goes...

Hopefully, those readers who can recall Annandale Farm/Armsea Hall and surrounding Newport during the 1960s-era will accept these fictional modifications made purely for entertainment purposes...and experience some twinges of nostalgia that might spawn a sigh or a smile when more accurate representations of the town they once knew are employed in the storytelling.

ABOUT THE AUTHOR

Shirley & Peter Markwith

Peter Markwith is an international management consultant, author and educator whose professional career spans more than 30 years. He has held business leadership positions in the US, Canada and Europe and has worked in more than 35 different clients/corporations.

Prior to founding Unified Business Technologies in 1999, an information technology and operations improvement consulting firm, he held the position of Director/Advisor in H. Ross Perot's majority owned Perot Systems Corporation.

Mr. Markwith has authored seven books, and was an Adjunct Professor of Business Management at Bentley University in Waltham, Massachusetts (2001-2007). He has also taught English as a second language to MIT Sloane business professionals through the Boston Language Institute, and has served on the University of New Hampshire's Executives-in-Residence Program at the former Whittemore School of Business and Economics.

A graduate of New York's Pratt Institute, the author and his wife live in New Hampshire.

ACKNOWLEDGEMENTS

This story, although short in its initial writing time, has been long in its editing, rewrites and years to press. Its debut in the literary marketplace, now, would not have been possible without these wonderful people – literary professionals, subject matter experts, business colleagues, family members and friends who provided professional services, validated content...or simply took time out of their own busy lives to read various versions of the manuscript and share constructive feedback:

- Dennis Adler (Author of The Nethercutt collection – The Cars of San Sylmar)
- Don Alusic
- Anne Markwith Archambault (my favorite youngest daughter)
- Carol Bambrick
- Mary Molloy Brown (Author of The Buck Starts Here and Design Your Own Destiny)
- Robin Caffrey
- Debbie Mawer Campbell (my sister-in-law)
- Katie Campbell (my niece)
- David B. Clark
- B.J. Elliott (editor and friend)
- Steve Fjestad (Publisher of The Nethercutt collection – The Cars of San Sylmar)
- Arthur Fleming
- Mary Gagliardo
- Don Jacobs
- Juliet Jacobs
- Diane Mawer James & Ray James (my sister-in-law and brother-in-law)
- Dick & Ginny Jones
- Karen Galley
- Ellen Greten
- Emily Markwith Greten (my favorite eldest daughter)

- Aliza Hedges
- Michael C. Kathrens (Author of Newport Villas – The Revival Styles, 1885-1935)
- Jerry Krattiger
- Bertram Lippincott III–The Newport Historical Society
- Lucy Lovrien
- Bruce MacLeish–Curator Emeritus, Newport Restoration Foundation: Rough Point, The Doris Duke Estate
- Helen & Roy Markwith (my giving and gifted parents whose creativity and command of the English language, hopefully, didn't miss the next generation completely)
- Shirley Mawer Markwith (my wife of 39 years – the love-of-my-life who puts up with all my crazy nonsense and loves me in spite of it)
- Steven F. Markwith (my brother)
- Steven R. Markwith (my nephew)
- Audrey Oliver Mawer (my mother-in-law whose memory and photo album brought added color to both the story and printed page)
- Anne McAnulty
- Paul Miller–Curator, The Preservation Society of Newport County
- Jennifer Naughton
- Jane Vance Nickerson
- Faviana Olivier (editor and friend – special thanks!)
- Papergraphics–Toni McGranaghan and Frank Lagana (book cover design)
- Tony Paradiso (Author of The Management Mind Field)
- Janice Pieroni (literary manager, editor and friend – special thanks!)
- Andrea Pokladowski
- William P. Robinson III
- Betty & Doug Russell
- Peggy Silva
- Cheryl Sonk
- Gregory Michael Teicher
- Heinz & Lea Von Däniken
- Betty Wight
- Joan Youngken–The Newport Historical Society

Thank you all! (continued)

Betty Jean Mawer
July 21, 1932 – October 10, 1988

Last, singly, and most importantly, I acknowledge the person to whom this book is dedicated – Betty Jean Mawer (last name rhymes with "power"), my sister-in-law.

Betty used to "ride the lions" at Annandale Farm during childhood visits to her paternal grandparents' summer estate known then as Armsea Hall. It was she who inspired the characters of Franny Sutton and Ollie Merriweather – my own creations of fiction fashioned to serve, in some small measure, as worthy memorials to her life. Hopefully, that's how you, the reader, perceive them.

Despite the affluence and social prestige associated with the surroundings of her early years, Betty's was not an easy life – not only for the handicap she endured (she was fourth-grade-level, Down syndrome), but because of later-to-come deteriorating family circumstances that ultimately led to her institutionalization – events that resulted in an adult life spent living as a ward of the State of New Jersey.

My wife, Shirley (half-sister to Betty through her father's first marriage), and I made it a point, over the course of our own married lives, to include Betty in family celebrations at Thanksgiving and Christmas. Our daughters came to know her simply as "Aunt Betty" – Mom's sister who came to spend the holidays with us.

Our girls accepted Betty through their own adolescent years, their eyes and their ears as an adult no different than any other, save for the added measures of warmth, innocence and honesty that were "gifts" attributed to her condition. It was a privilege having her in our lives.

When she died in October of 1988, Betty's remains were cremated and the ashes disposed of by the State of New Jersey. We held a family memorial service at our home in Berkeley Heights, NJ and we planted an evergreen tree on the front lawn in her memory. Some years later, after our house had been sold and we'd moved to New England, we were back visiting relatives and drove by the property. The tree wasn't there anymore. The humble memorial to the humble soul who'd been part of our family was gone without a trace...and with it any physical trace of Betty's 56 years on earth.

Now, looking back a good many years later, I'm not sure if it's the fact there wasn't a marker of any kind left to identify Betty's time here, that ultimately spawned the first draft of this story in 1999 (originally titled: Whatever Happened at Annandale Farm?), or if the idea of the story came first...and the dedication to her memory emerged in the natural course of writing it.

Regardless, the only thing that really matters (at least to me), is that the publication of this book, with its dedication to Betty's memory, serves as a marker – a tablet with a date that tells the world Betty Jean Mawer lived. It's a right (and a rite) that each of us expects when we leave Planet Earth; one that belongs to everyone...regardless of how different, insignificant, limited or powerless one might appear to be in the eyes of science, the powers of politics or the minds of the multitudes.

"But God hath chosen the foolish things of the world to confound the wise; and God hath chosen the weak things of the world to confound the things which are mighty; and base things of the world, and things which are despised, hath God chosen, yea, and things which are not, to bring to nought things that are." – 1 Corinthians, 1, 27:28

Other Books by Peter George Markwith

The Consultancy

Take a wild ride in this fast-paced, fun, mystery-suspense thriller, and satirical exposé on the consulting industry. New consulting recruit, Marla Vaughn, gets caught in a web of 1970s hi-tech espionage, trying to foil a group of Third Reich, Nazi loyalists bent on seizing control of the free world.

Taking a Healthy Byte Out of the Tech-Knowledgy Pie

In this clarifying little book with a bent on holistic business wellness, purpose and work provide the context for information technology in recently widowed Priscilla BarnSwallow's booming new pie business. The story applies proven, commonsense concepts to the enigmas associated with complex, I.T. system implementations.

A Quick Guide to Publishing

If you've researched how to publish your book, you've seen the sophisticated websites, and expensive books that offer publishing advice and contract services. This easy-to-follow, quick-guide gives you the information you need, before signing up for a web-publisher's service offerings.

Unified Business Technologies
PRESS

www.UnifiedBizTech.com